Ice Cream Man

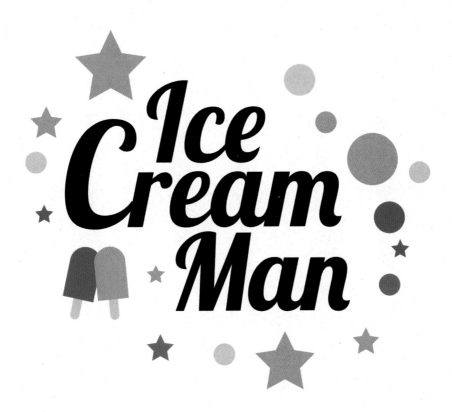

VOLUME FOUR

• TINY LIVES •

WRITTEN BY **W. MAXWELL PRINCE**

ART BY **MARTÍN MORAZZO**

COLORS BY **CHRIS O'HALLORAN**

LETTERING BY **GOOD OLD NEON**

COVER DESIGN BY **SHANNA MATUSZAK & DREW GILL**

INTERIOR DESIGN BY **GOOD OLD NEON**

image

IMAGE COMICS, INC.
Robert Kirkman – Chief Operating Officer; Erik Larsen – Chief Financial Officer
Todd McFarlane – President; Marc Silvestri – Chief Executive Officer
Jim Valentino – Vice President; Eric Stephenson – Publisher
Corey Hart – Director of Sales; Jeremy Sullivan – Director of Digital Sales
Jeff Boison – Director of Publishing Planning & Book Trade Sales
Kat Salazar – Director of PR & Marketing; Branwyn Bigglestone – Controller
Drew Gill – Art Director; Jonathan Chan – Production Manager
Meredith Wallace – Print Manager; Briah Skelly – Publicist
Sasha Head – Sales & Marketing Production Designer
Randy Okamura – Digital Production Designer
David Brothers – Branding Manager
Olivia Ngai – Content Manager
Addison Duke – Production Artist
Vincent Kukua – Production Artist
Tricia Ramos – Production Artist
Jeff Stang – Direct Market Sales Representative
Emilio Bautista – Digital Sales Associate
Leanna Caunter – Accounting Assistant
Chloe Ramos-Peterson – Library Market Sales Representative
IMAGECOMICS.COM

IMAGE COMICS, INC.
Robert Kirkman: Chief Operating Officer
Erik Larsen: Chief Financial Officer
Todd McFarlane: President
Marc Silvestri: Chief Executive Officer
Jim Valentino: Vice President
Eric Stephenson: Publisher / Chief Creative Officer
Jeff Boison: Director of Publishing Planning & Book Trade Sales
Chris Ross: Director of Digital Sales
Jeff Stang: Director of Direct Market Sales
Kat Salazar: Director of PR & Marketing
Drew Gill: Cover Editor
Heather Doornink: Production Director
Nicole Lapalme: Controller
IMAGECOMICS.COM

"It has to be admitted that the clouds can descend, take you up, carry you to all kind of places, some of them terrible, and you don't get back where you came from for years and years."
–Denis Johnson, *Triumph Over the Grave*

What did your parents pass down to you?
Email wmaxwellprince@gmail.com

ICE CREAM MAN, VOL. 4: TINY LIVES. First printing. December 2019. Published by Image Comics, Inc. Office of publication: 2701 NW Vaughn St., Suite 780, Portland, OR 97210. Copyright © 2019 W. Maxwell Prince, Martin Morazzo & Chris O'Halloran. All rights reserved. Contains material originally published in single magazine form as ICE CREAM MAN #13-16. "Ice Cream Man," its logos, and the likenesses of all characters herein are trademarks of W. Maxwell Prince, Martin Morazzo & Chris O'Halloran unless otherwise noted. "Image" and the Image Comics logos are registered trademarks of Image Comics, Inc. No part of this publication may be reproduced or transmitted, in any form or by any means (except for short excerpts for journalistic or review purposes), without the express written permission of W. Maxwell Prince, Martin Morazzo & Chris O'Halloran, or Image Comics, Inc. All names, characters, events, and locales in this publication are entirely fictional. Any resemblance to actual persons (living or dead), events, or places, without satiric intent, is coincidental. Printed in the USA. For information regarding the CPSIA on this printed material call: 203-595-3636. For international rights, contact: foreignlicensing@imagecomics.com. ISBN: 978-1-5343-1376-7

Palindromes

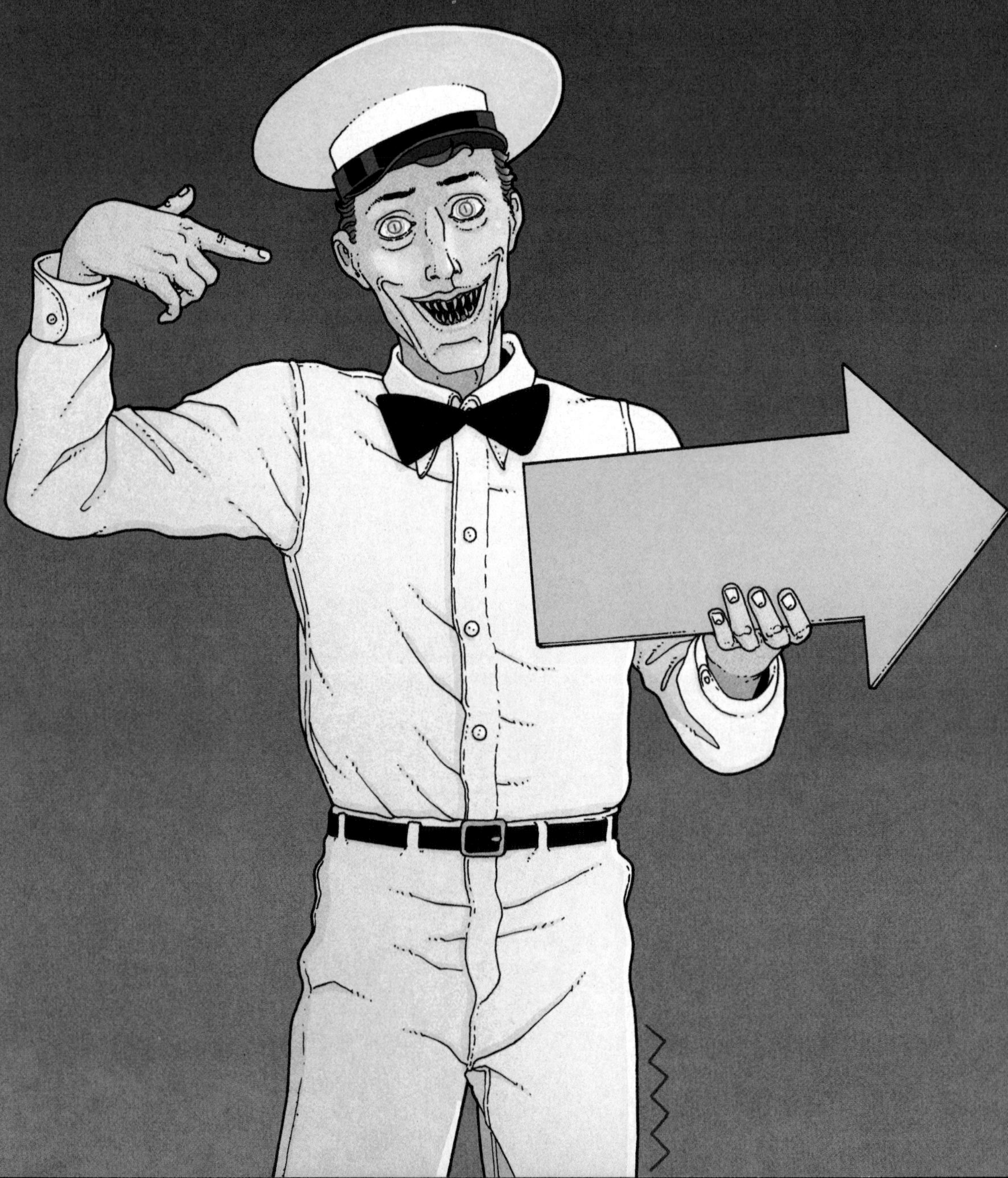

THIS COMIC IS A
PALINDROME

IT CAN BE READ
FORWARDS
(from first to last panel)
OR
BACKWARDS
(from last to first panel)

IT'S UP TO YOU

Author's note: if you
choose to enjoy the story backwards,
read panels from bottom to top
and right to left.

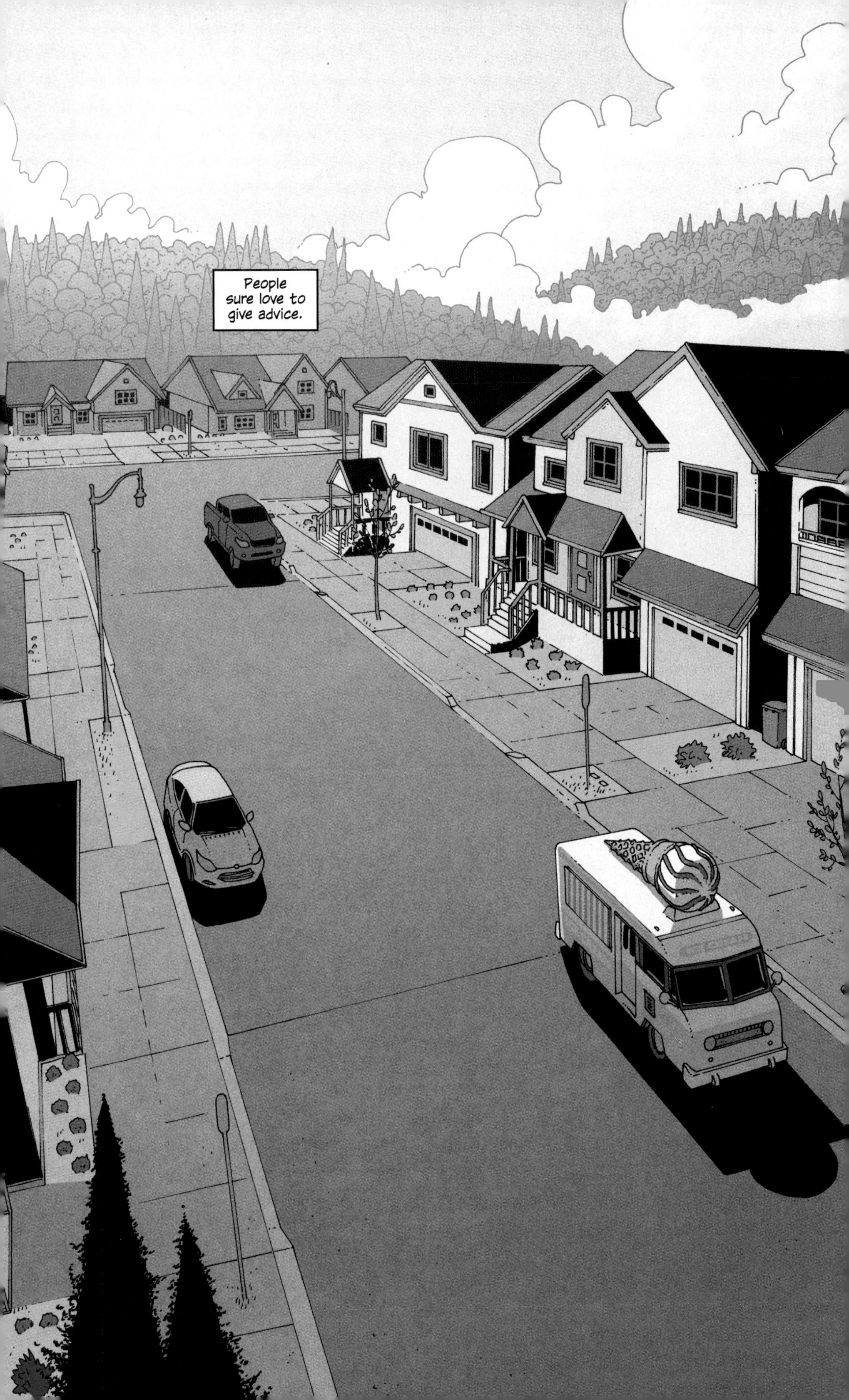
People sure love to give advice.

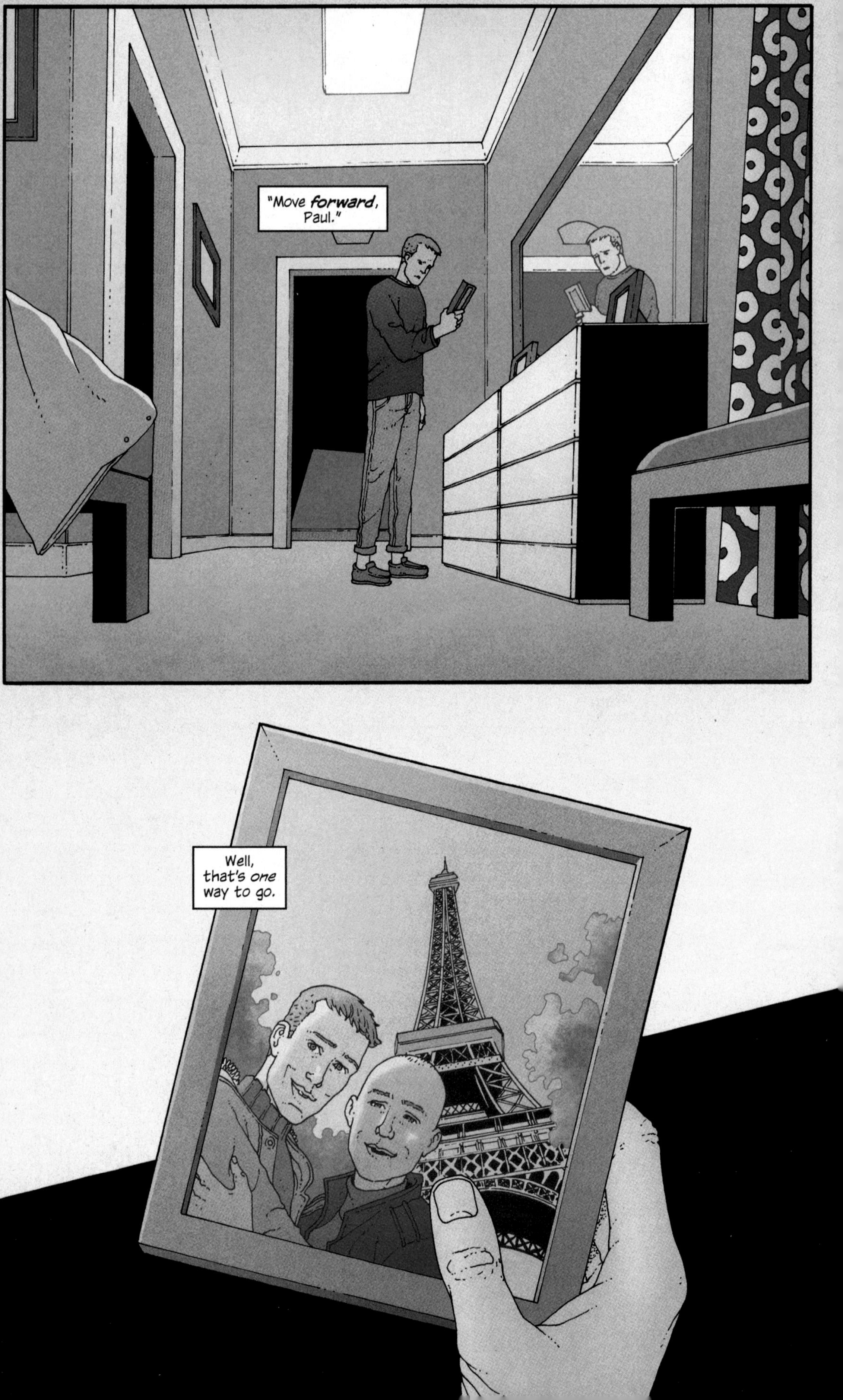
"Move forward, Paul."
Well, that's one way to go.

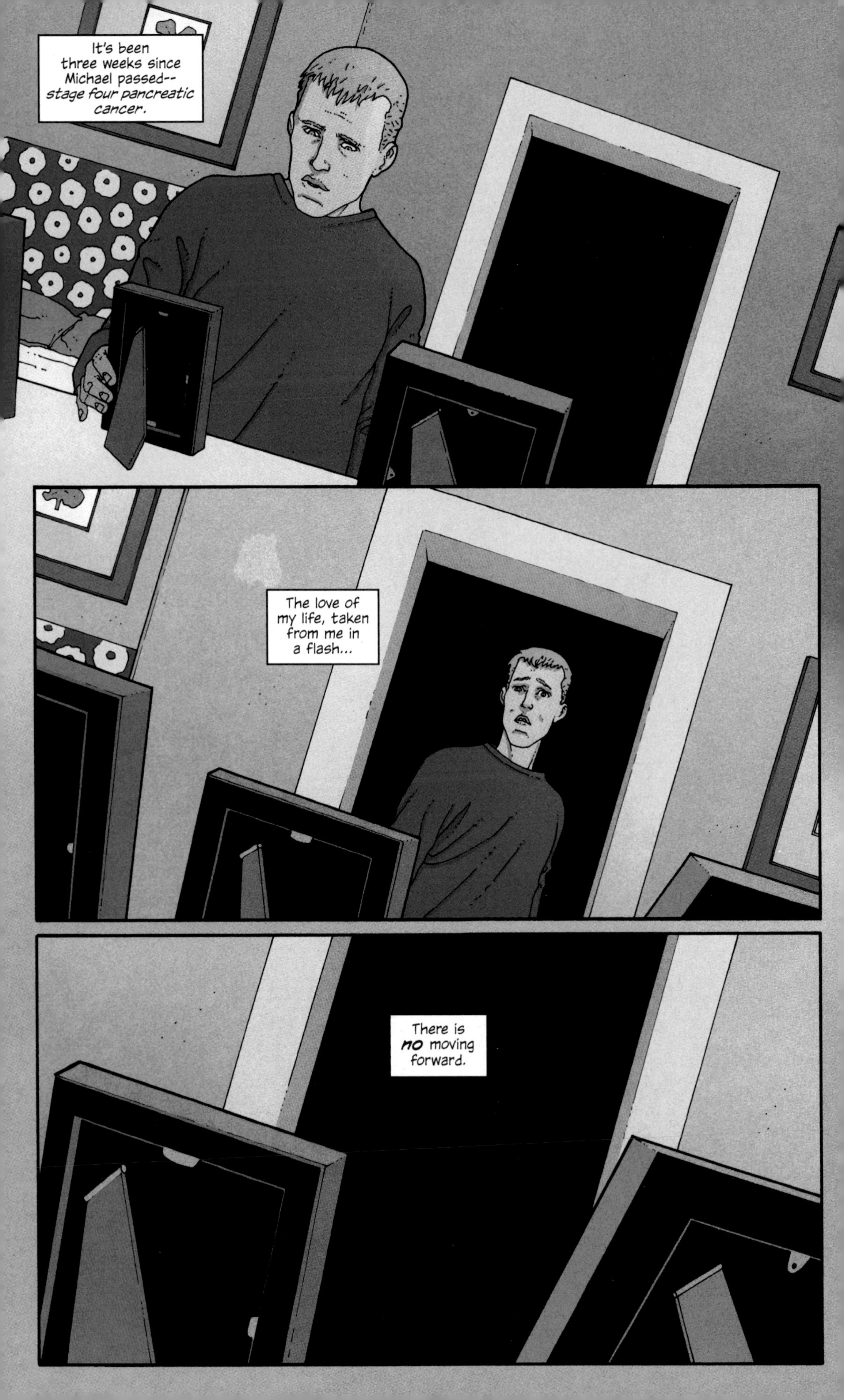
It's been three weeks since Michael passed-- *stage four pancreatic cancer.*
The love of my life, taken from me in a flash...
There is ***NO*** moving forward.

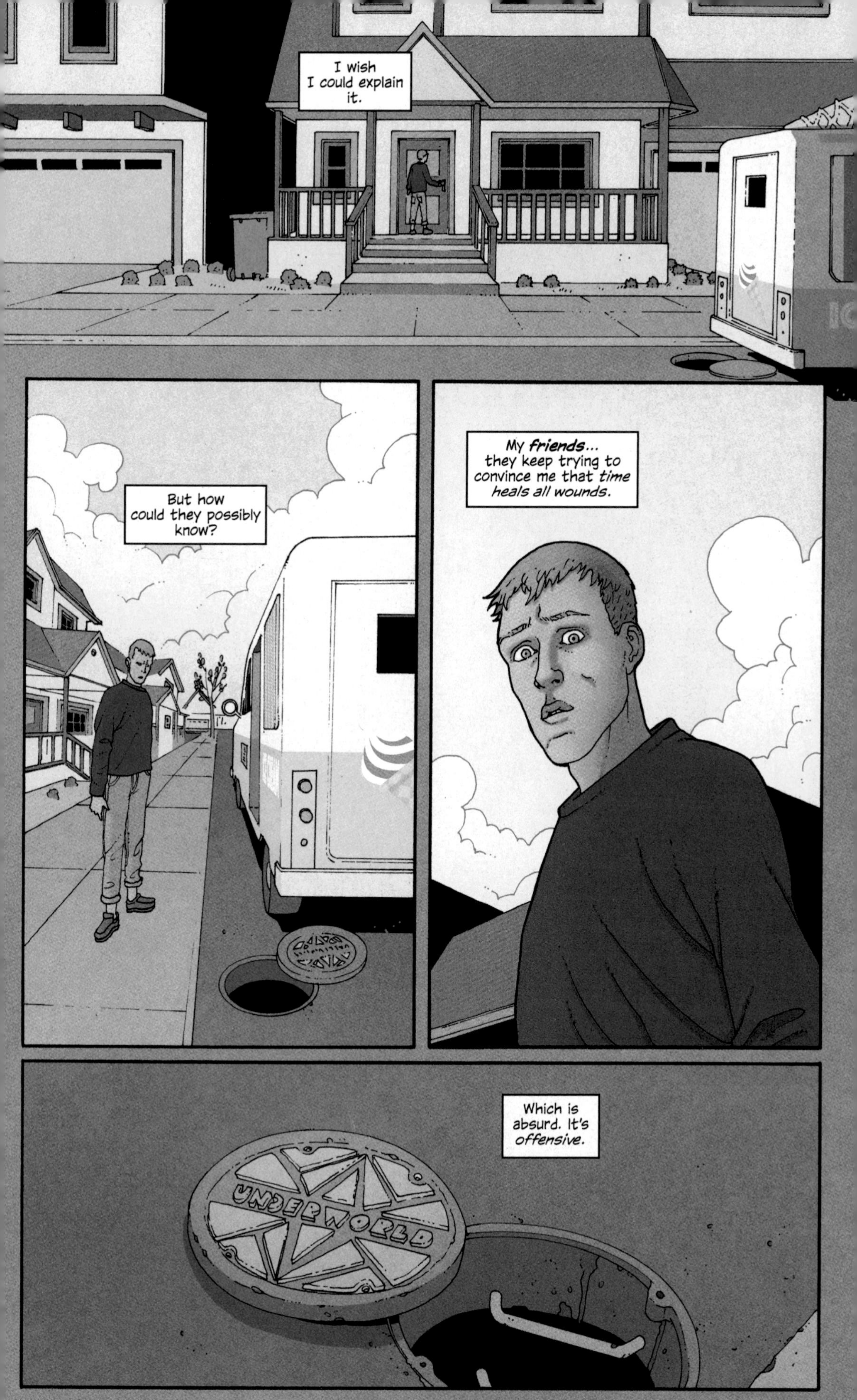
I wish I could explain it.
But how could they possibly know?
My ***friends***... they keep trying to convince me that *time heals all wounds.*
Which is absurd. It's *offensive.*
UNDERWORLD

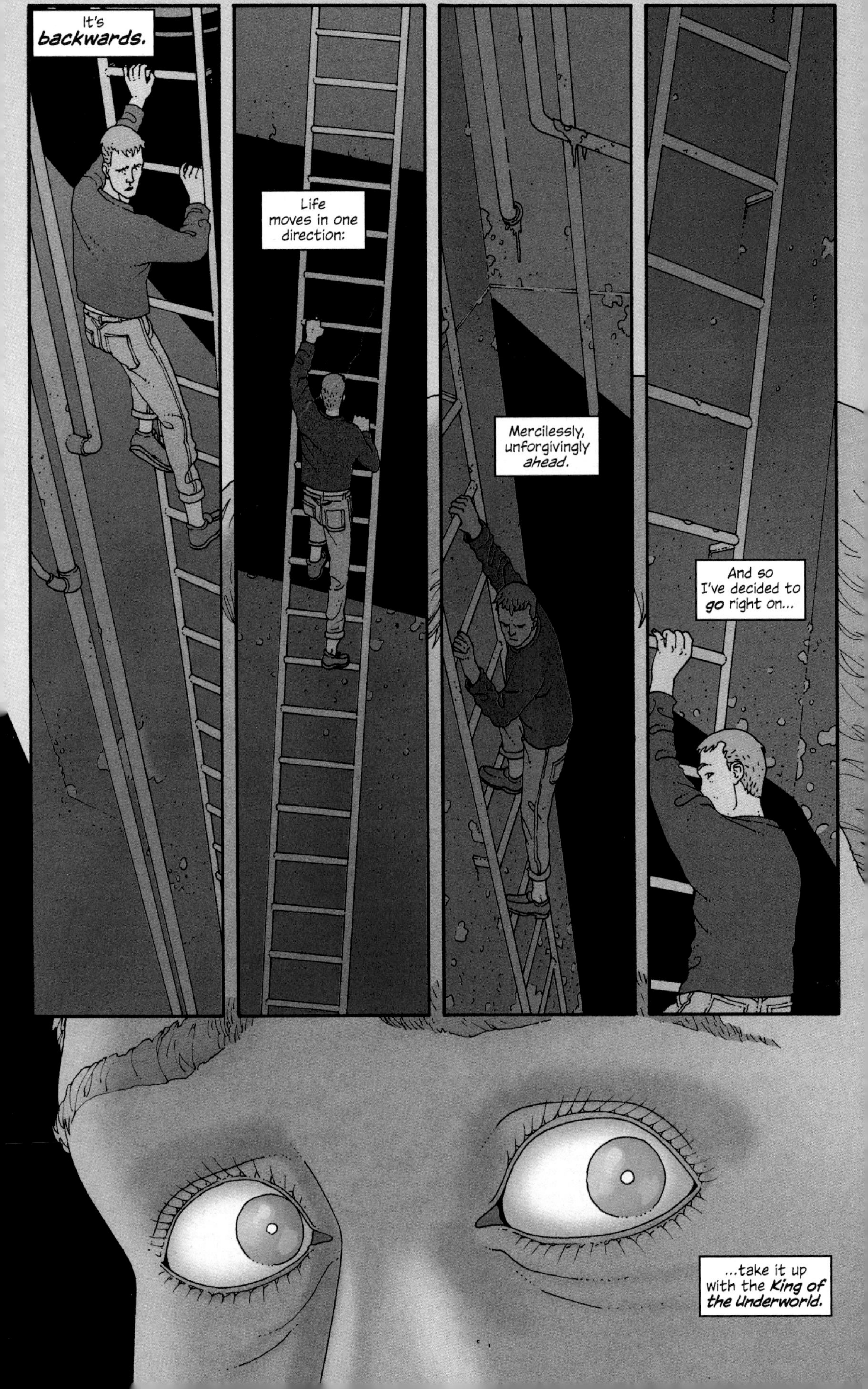

It's *backwards.*
Life moves in one direction:
Mercilessly, unforgivingly *ahead.*
And so I've decided to ***go*** right on...
...take it up with the ***King of the Underworld.***

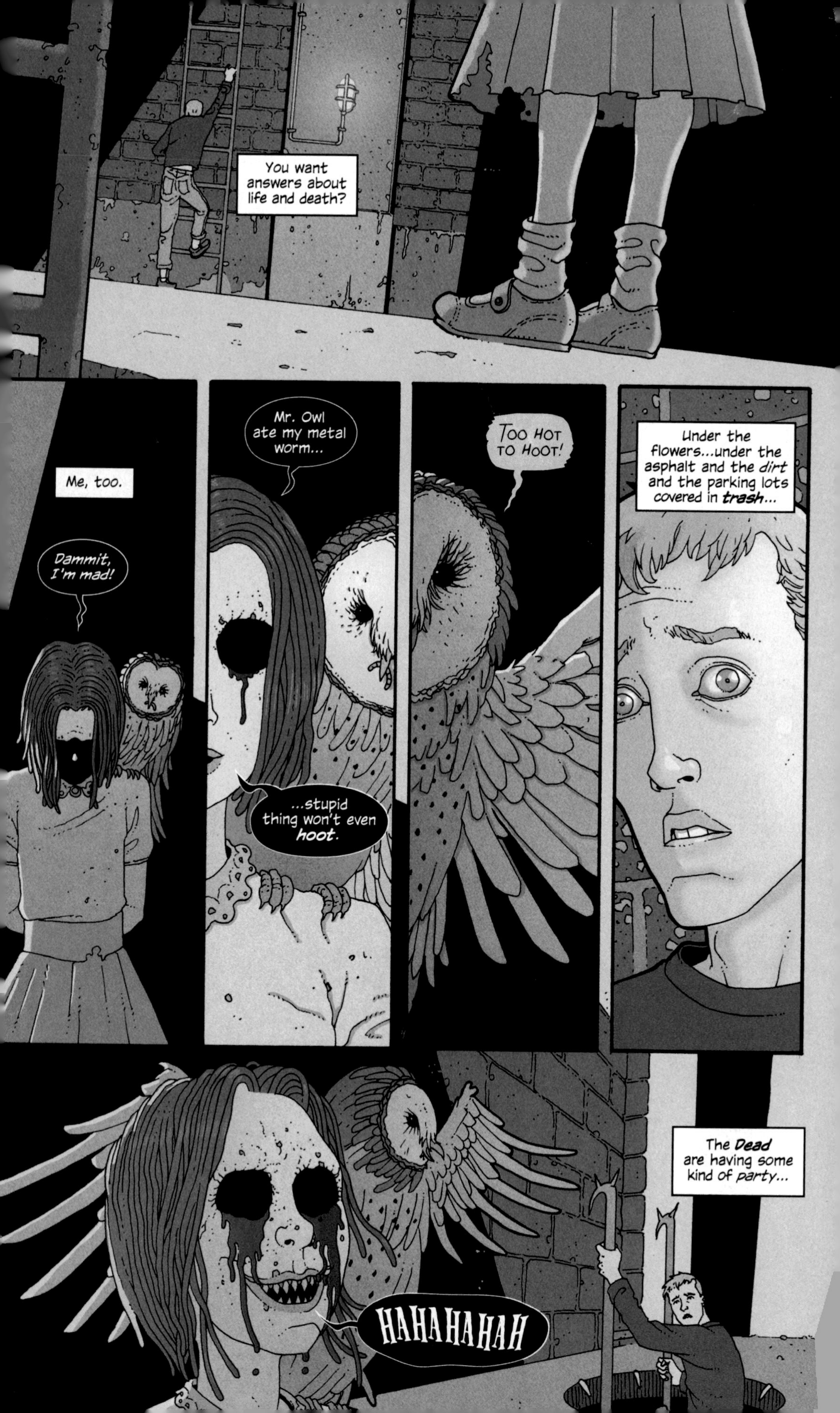
You want answers about life and death?
Me, too.
Dammit, I'm mad!
Mr. Owl ate my metal worm...
...stupid thing won't even **hoot**.
TOO HOT TO HOOT!
Under the flowers...under the asphalt and the *dirt* and the parking lots covered in ***trash***...
HAHAHAHAH
The **Dead** are having some kind of *party*...

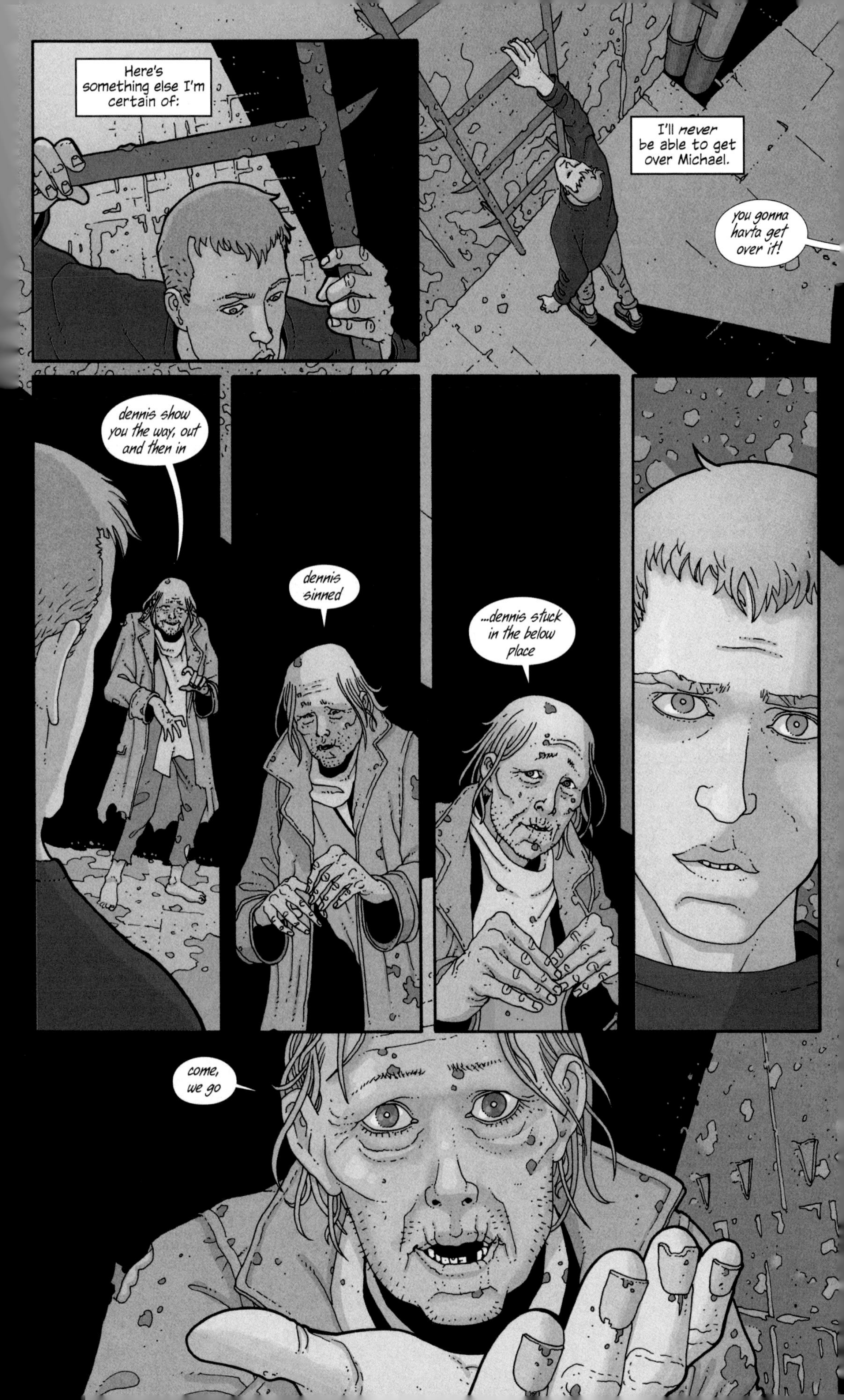
Here's something else I'm certain of:
I'll *never* be able to get over Michael.
you gonna havta get over it!
dennis show you the way, out and then in
dennis sinned
...dennis stuck in the below place
come, we go

these are my friends

senile felines

was it a rat i saw?

was it a bat i saw?

goddam mad dog

Dog, as a devil deified, lived as a God!

bird rib

PEEP!

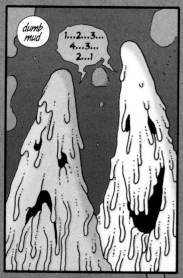

dumb mud

1...2...3... 4...3... 2...1

NEVER ODD OR EVEN

you see my friends, yes?

come...

It's all so familiar...

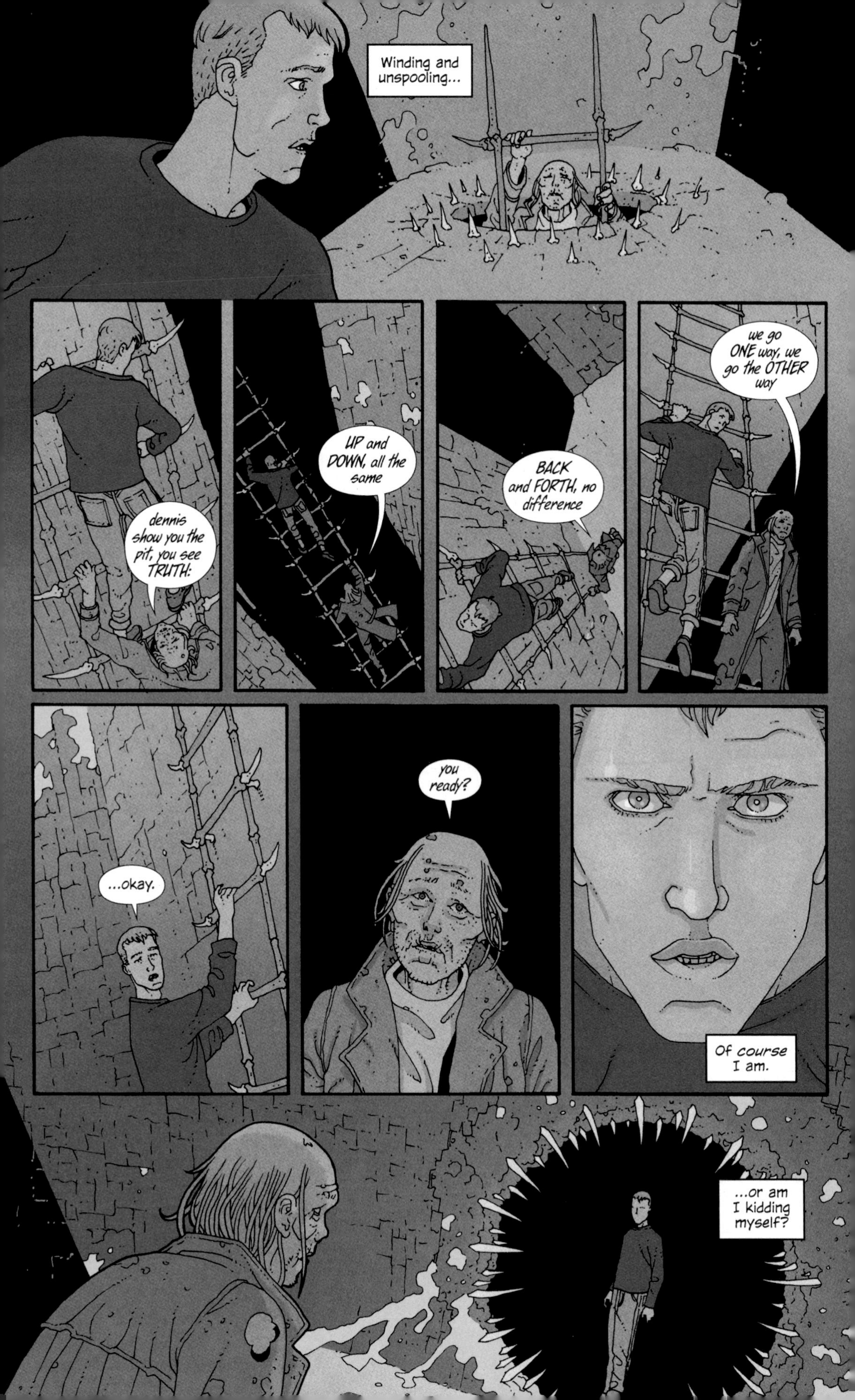

Winding and unspooling...
dennis show you the pit, you see TRUTH:
UP and DOWN, all the same
BACK and FORTH, no difference
we go ONE way, we go the OTHER way
...okay.
you ready?
Of course I am.
...or am I kidding myself?

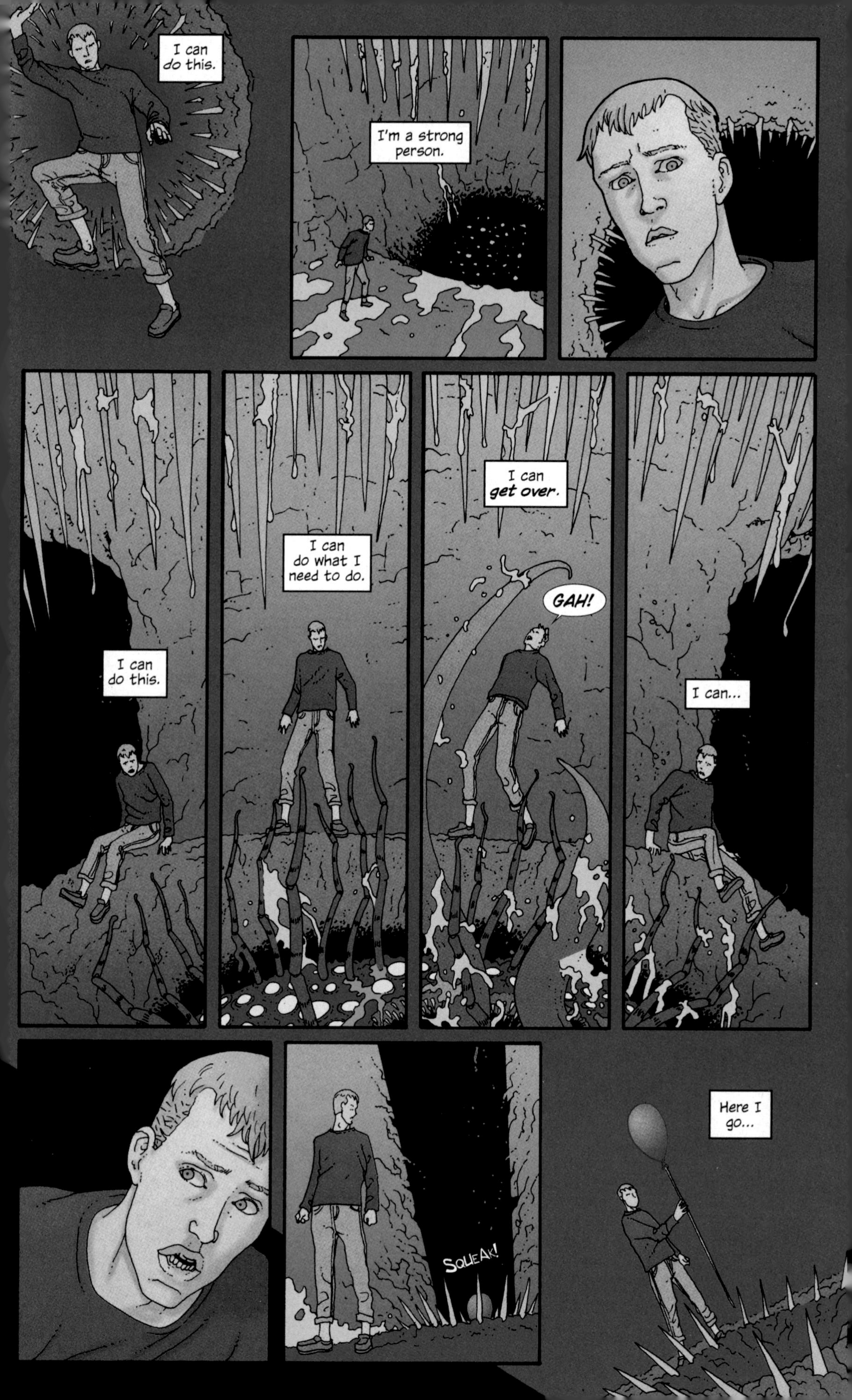
I can do this.
I'm a strong person.
I can do this.
I can do what I need to do.
I can get over.
GAH!
I can...
SQUEAK!
Here I go...

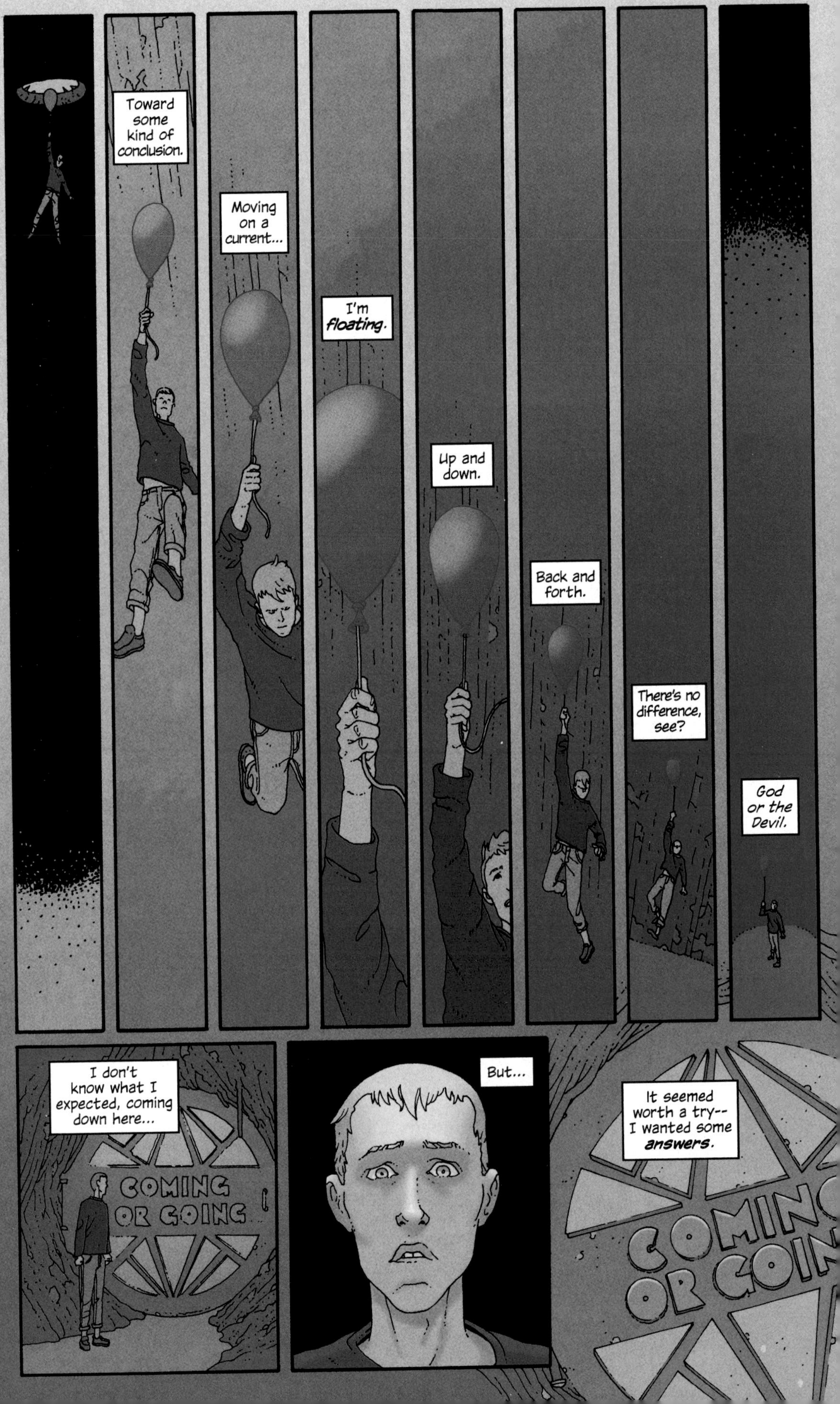
Toward some kind of conclusion.
Moving on a current...
I'm *floating*.
Up and down.
Back and forth.
There's no difference, see?
God or the Devil.
I don't know what I expected, coming down here...
COMING OR GOING
But...
It seemed worth a try--I wanted some *answers*.

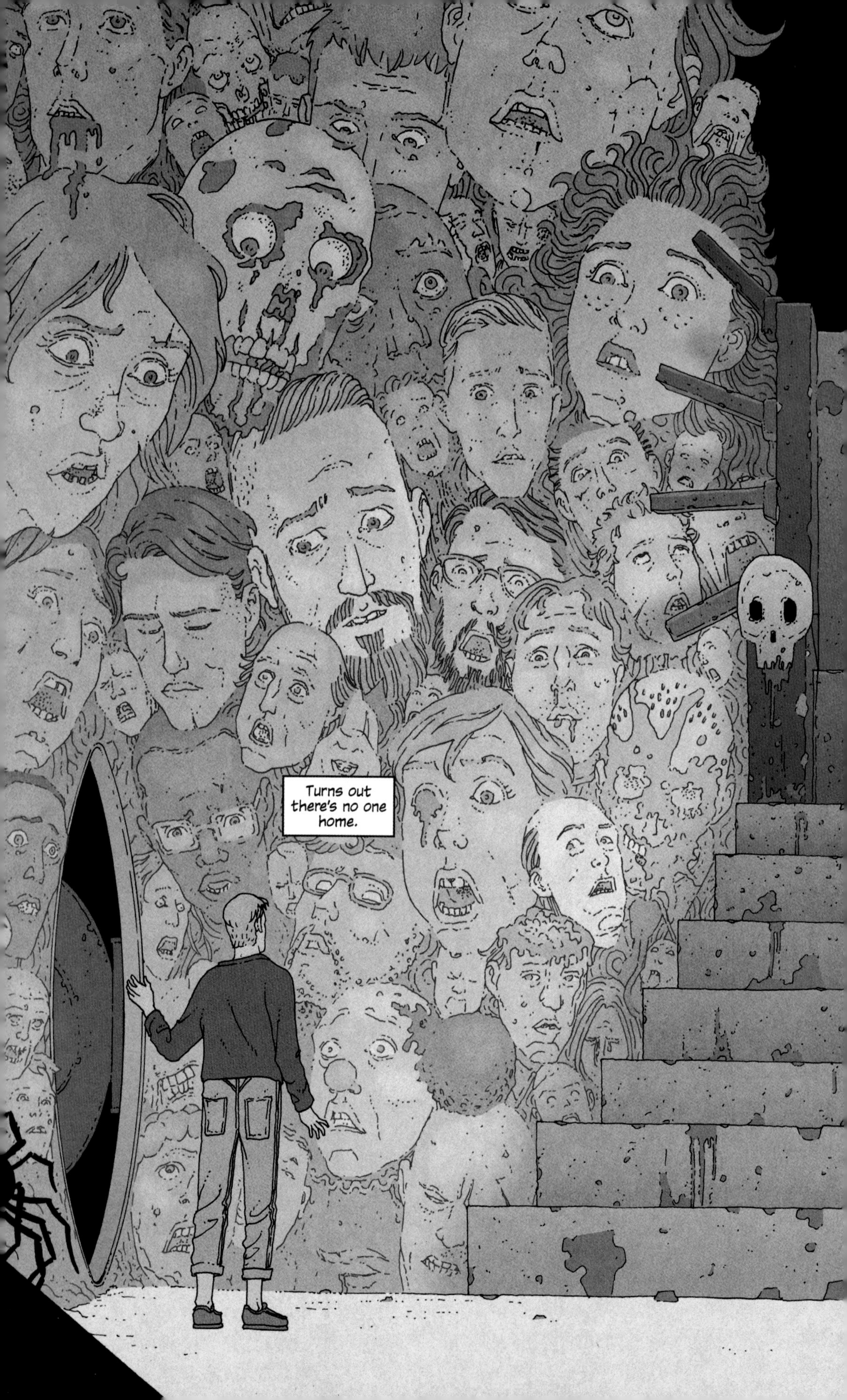
Turns out there's no one home.

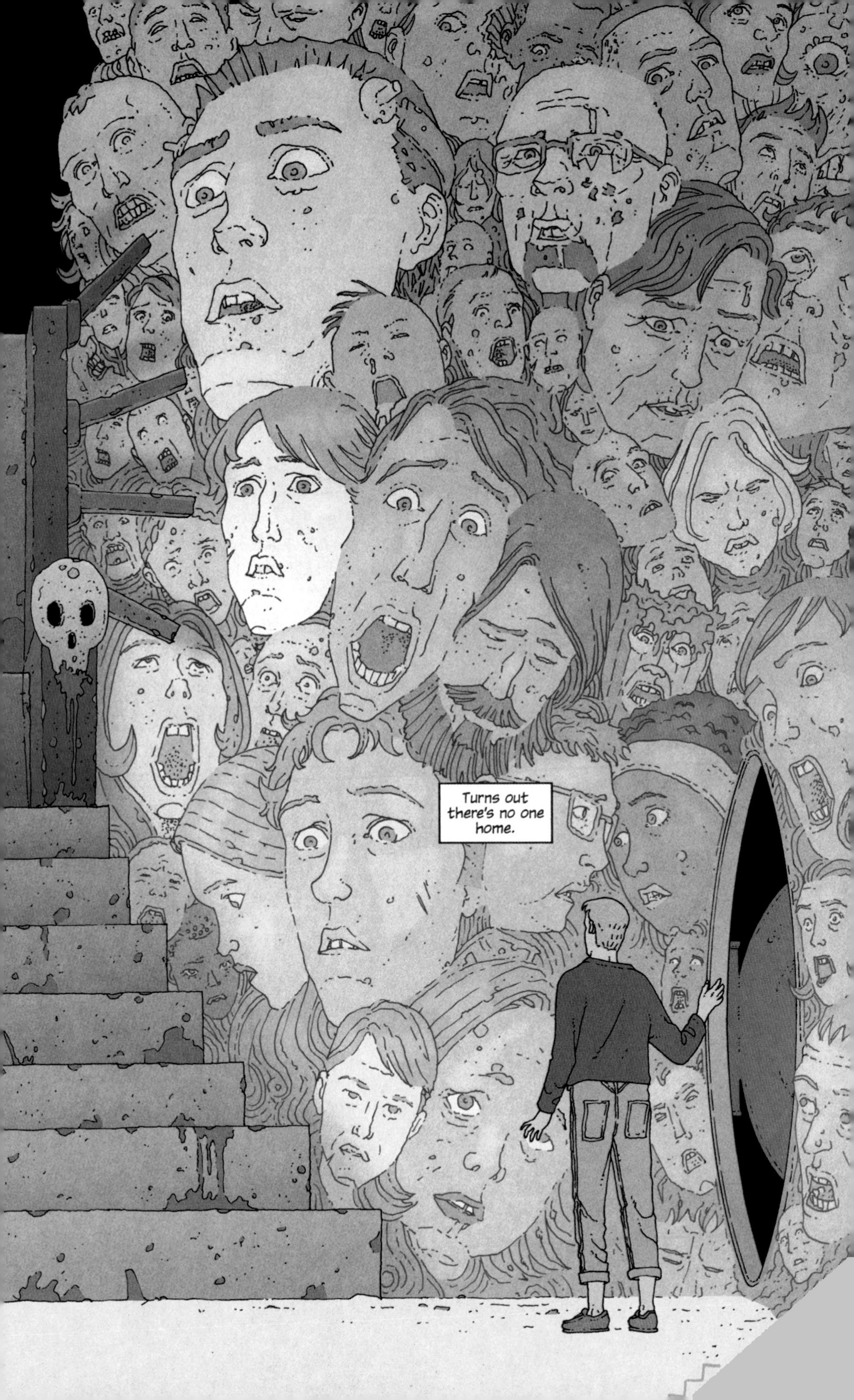
Turns out there's no one home.

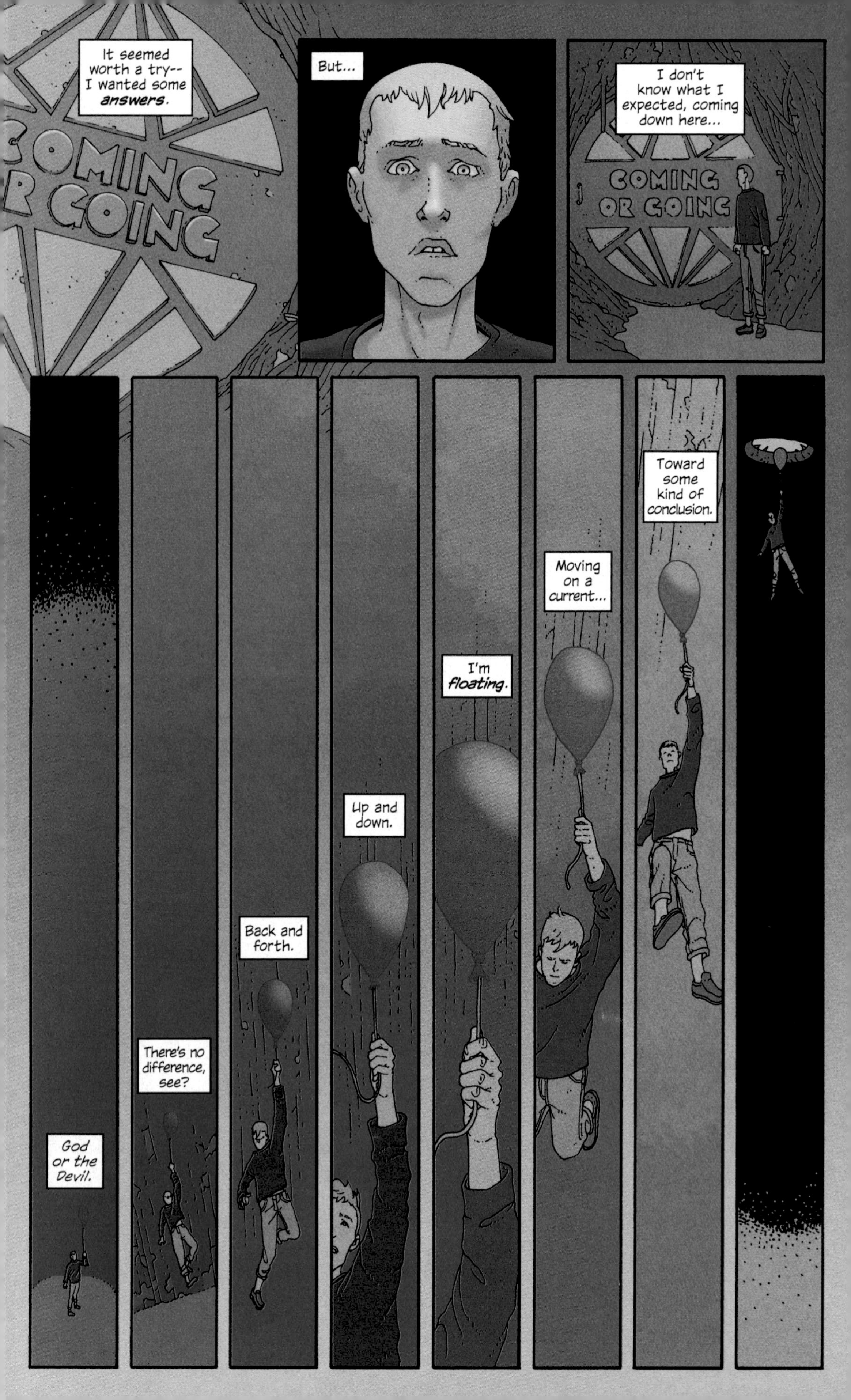
It seemed worth a try-- I wanted some **answers**.
COMING OR GOING
But...
I don't know what I expected, coming down here...
COMING OR GOING
God or the Devil.
There's no difference, see?
Back and forth.
Up and down.
I'm **floating**.
Moving on a current...
Toward some kind of conclusion.

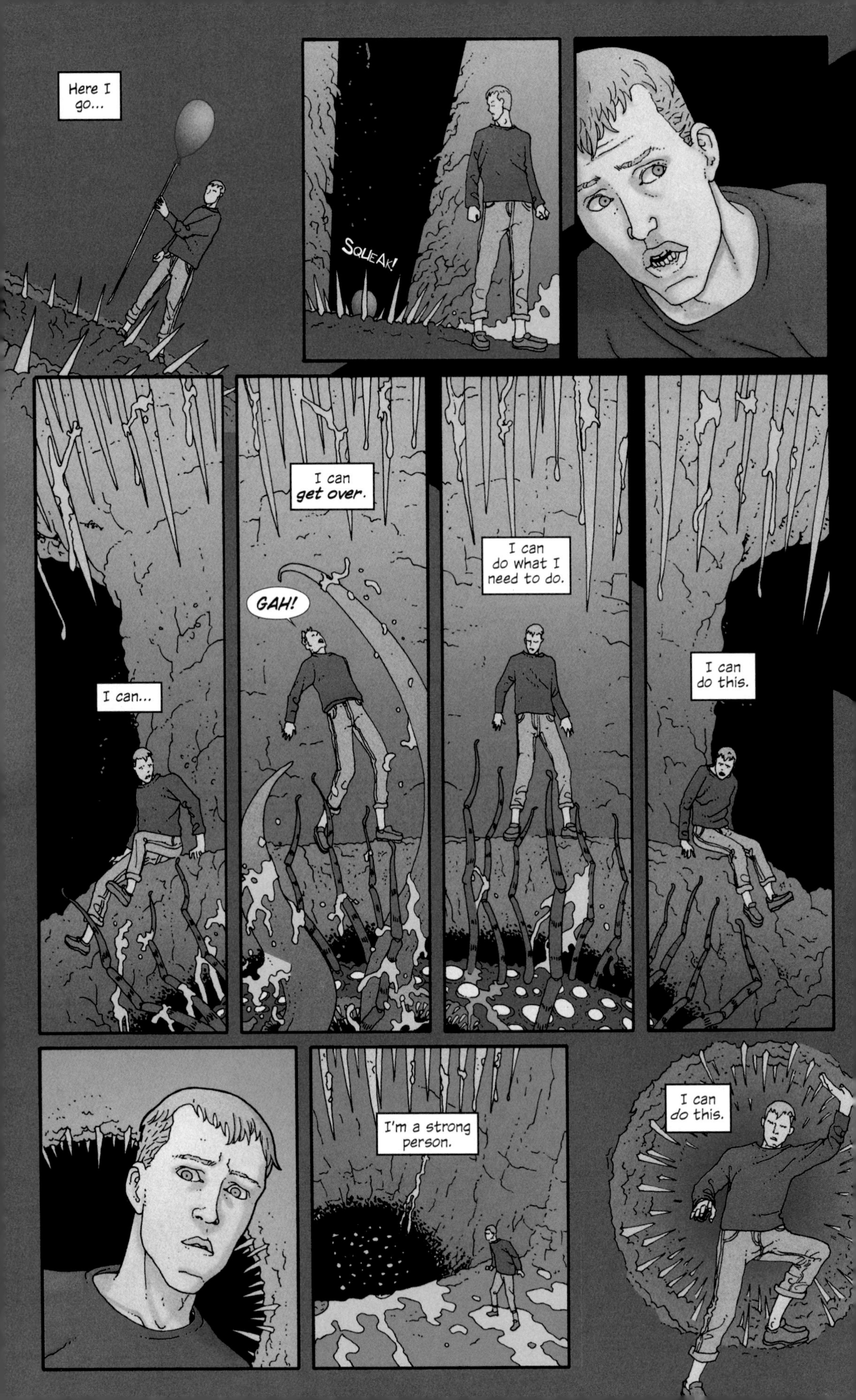
Here I go...
SQUEAK!
I can...
I can **get over**.
GAH!
I can do what I need to do.
I can do this.
I'm a strong person.
I can do this.

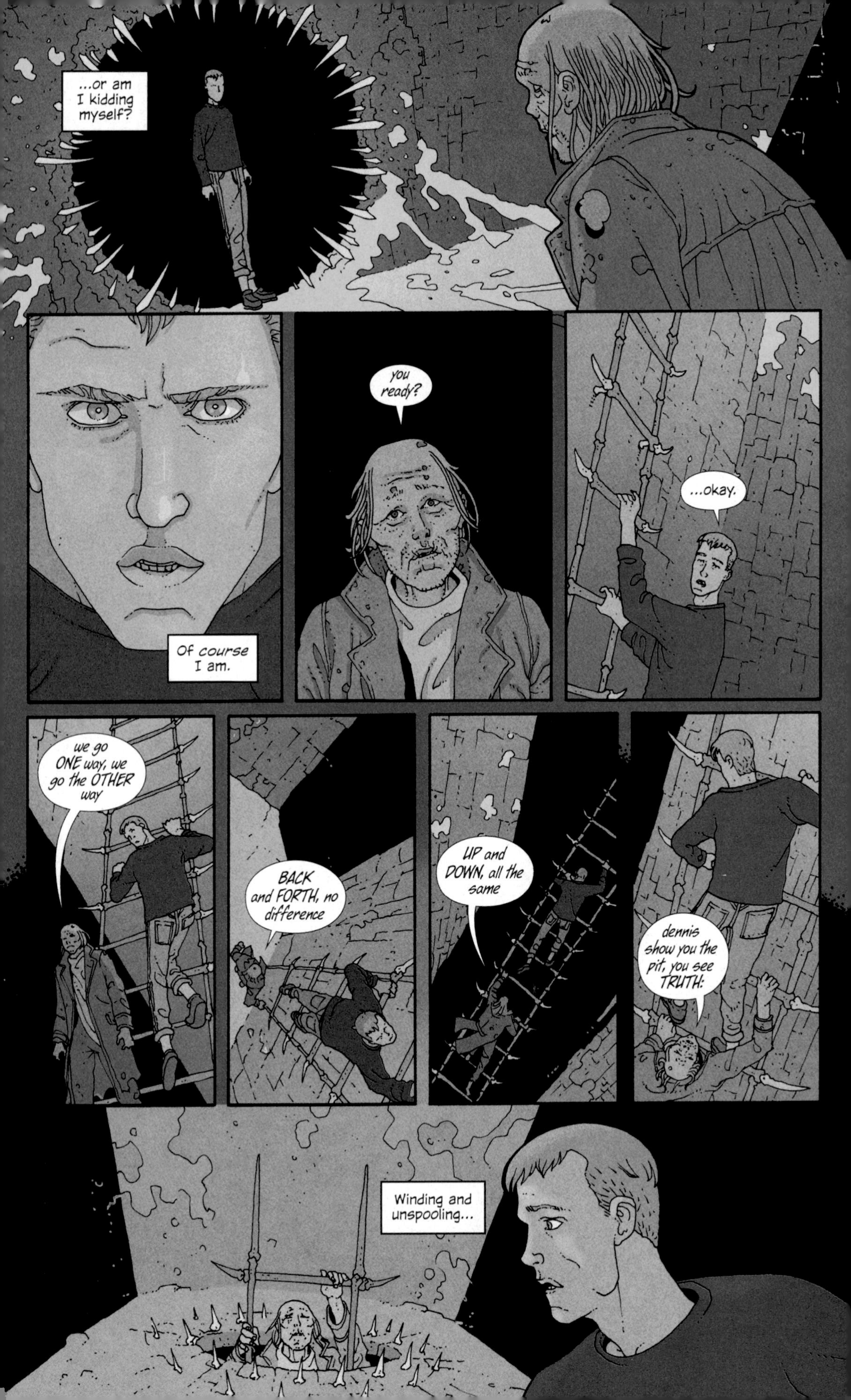
...or am I kidding myself?
Of course I am.
you ready?
...okay.
we go ONE way, we go the OTHER way
BACK and FORTH, no difference
UP and DOWN, all the same
dennis show you the pit, you see TRUTH:
Winding and unspooling...

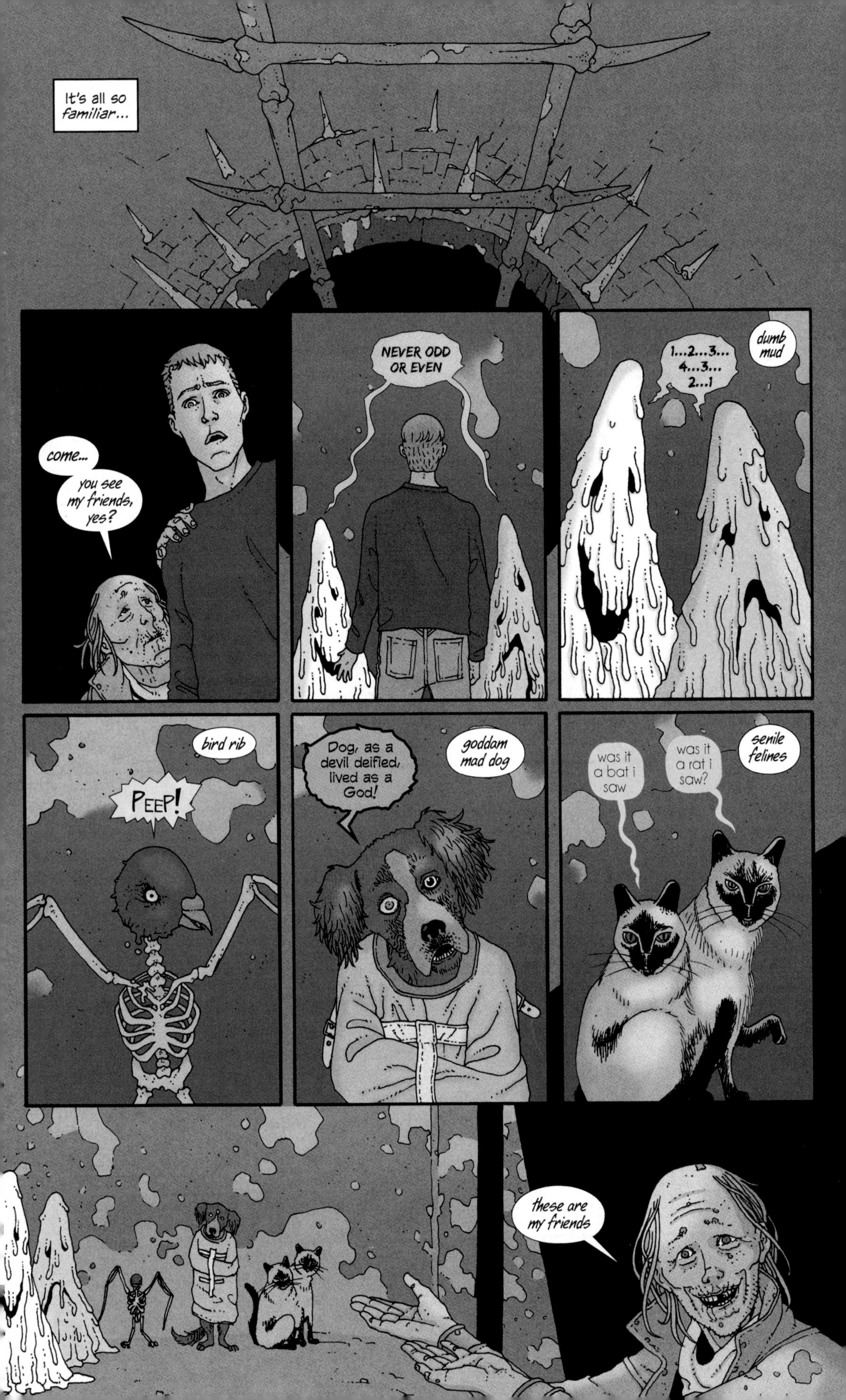
It's all so familiar...
come...
you see my friends, yes?
NEVER ODD OR EVEN
1...2...3... 4...3... 2...1
dumb mud
bird rib
PEEP!
Dog, as a devil deified, lived as a God!
goddam mad dog
was it a bat i saw
was it a rat i saw?
senile felines
these are my friends

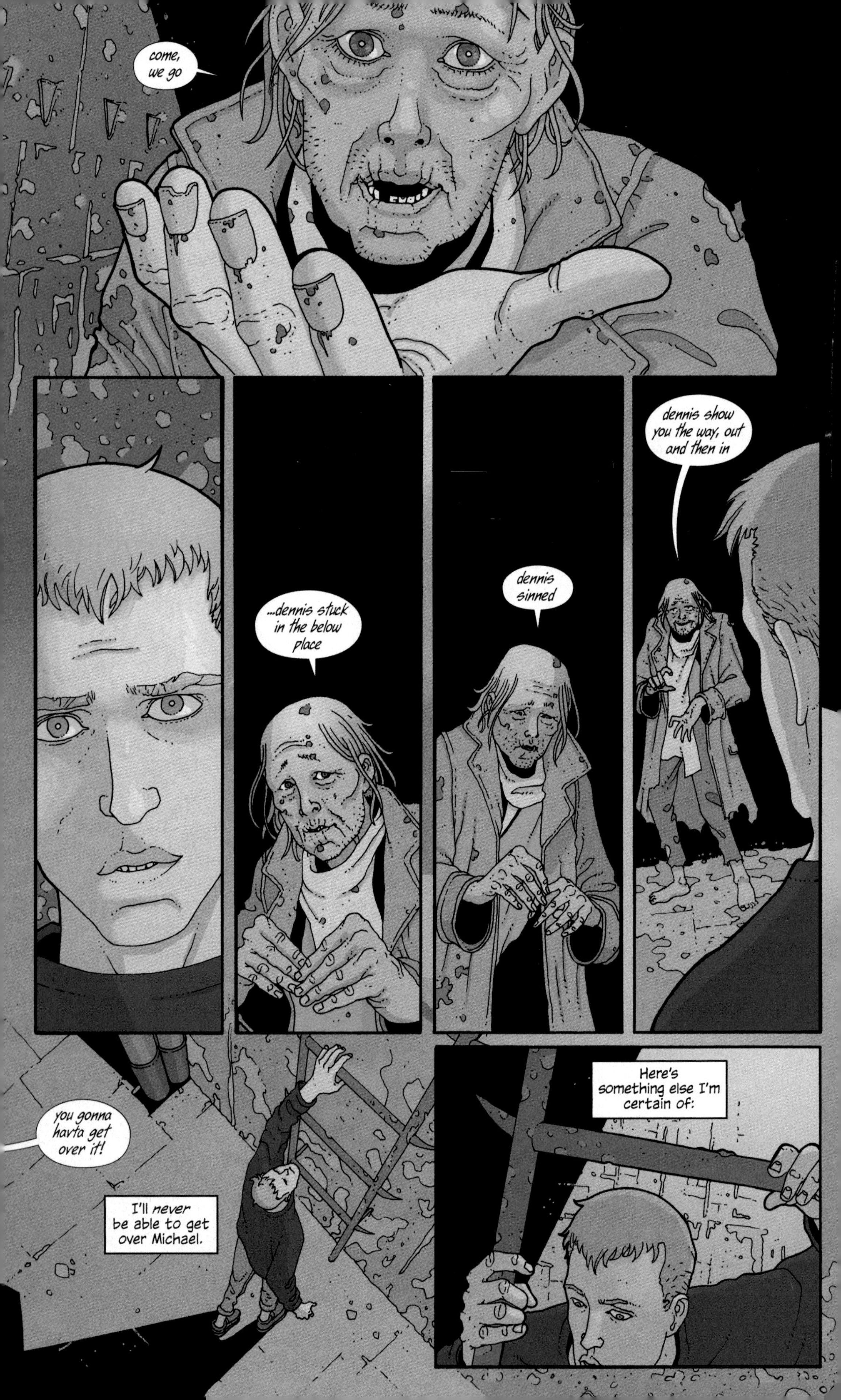
come, we go
...dennis stuck in the below place
dennis sinned
dennis show you the way, out and then in
you gonna havta get over it!
I'll *never* be able to get over Michael.
Here's something else I'm certain of:

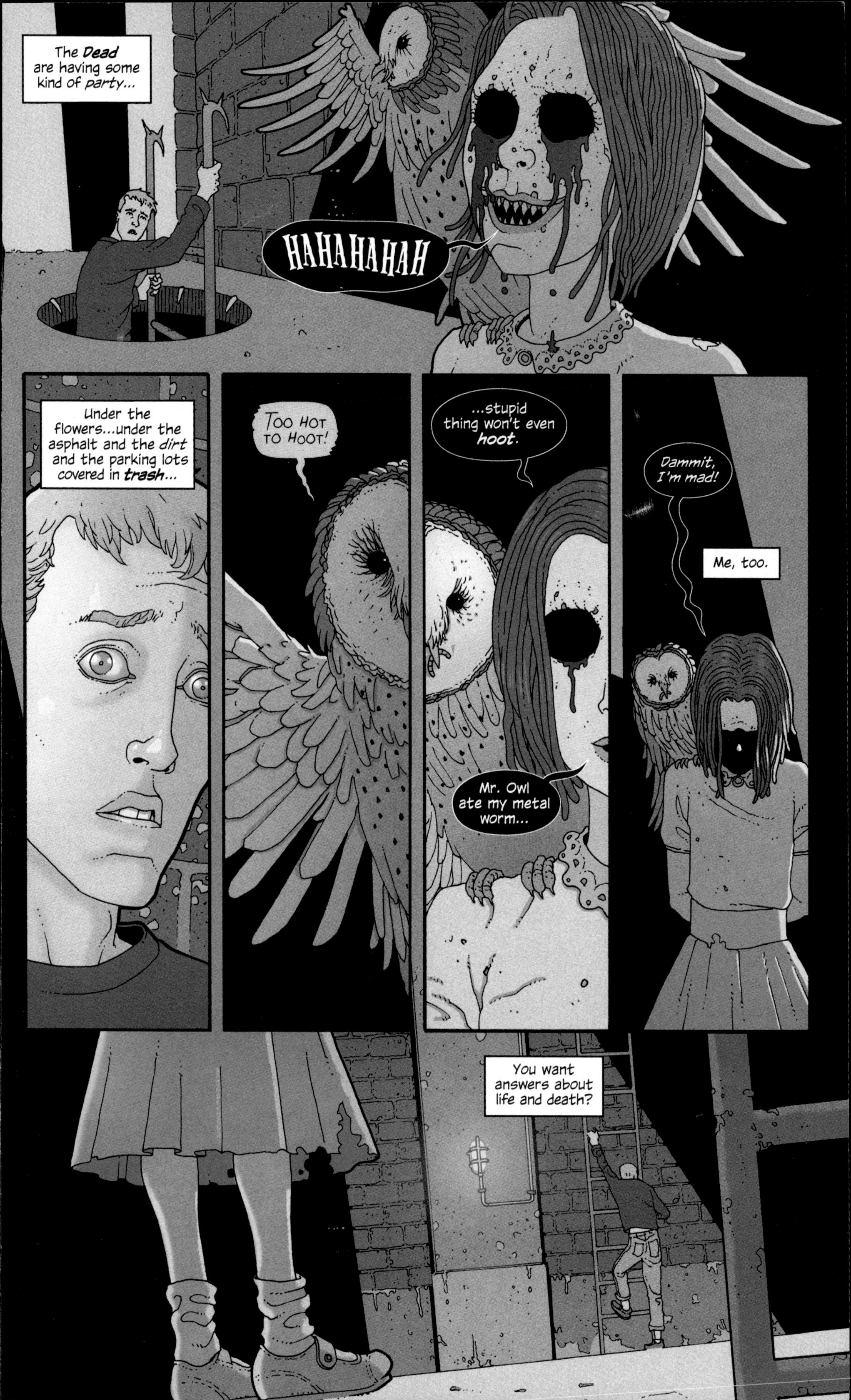
The *Dead* are having some kind of *party*...
HAHAHAHAH
Under the flowers...under the asphalt and the *dirt* and the parking lots covered in ***trash***...
Too hot to hoot!
...stupid thing won't even ***hoot***.
Mr. Owl ate my metal worm...
Dammit, I'm mad!
Me, too.
You want answers about life and death?

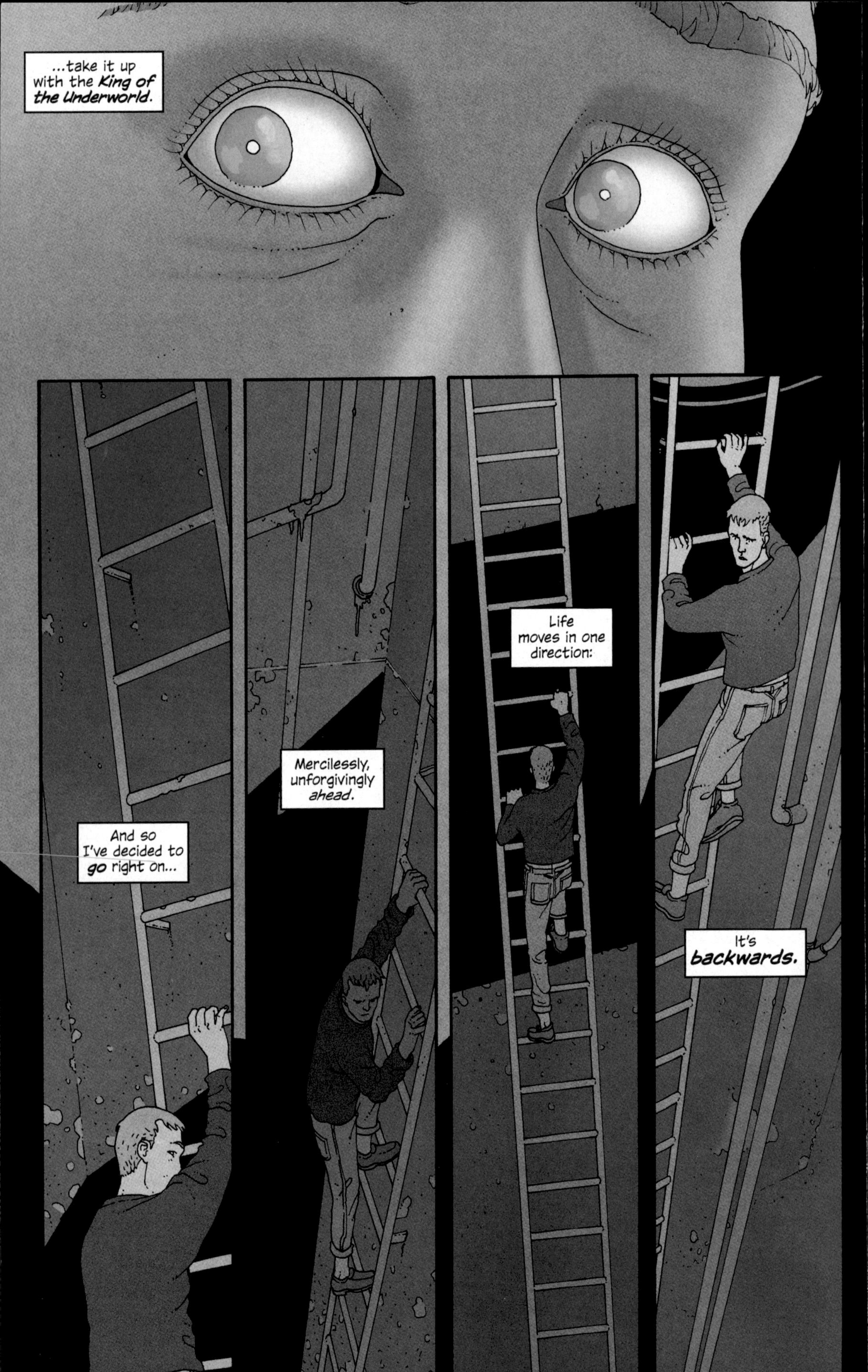
...take it up with the *King of the Underworld*.
And so I've decided to *go* right on...
Mercilessly, unforgivingly *ahead*.
Life moves in one direction:
It's ***backwards.***

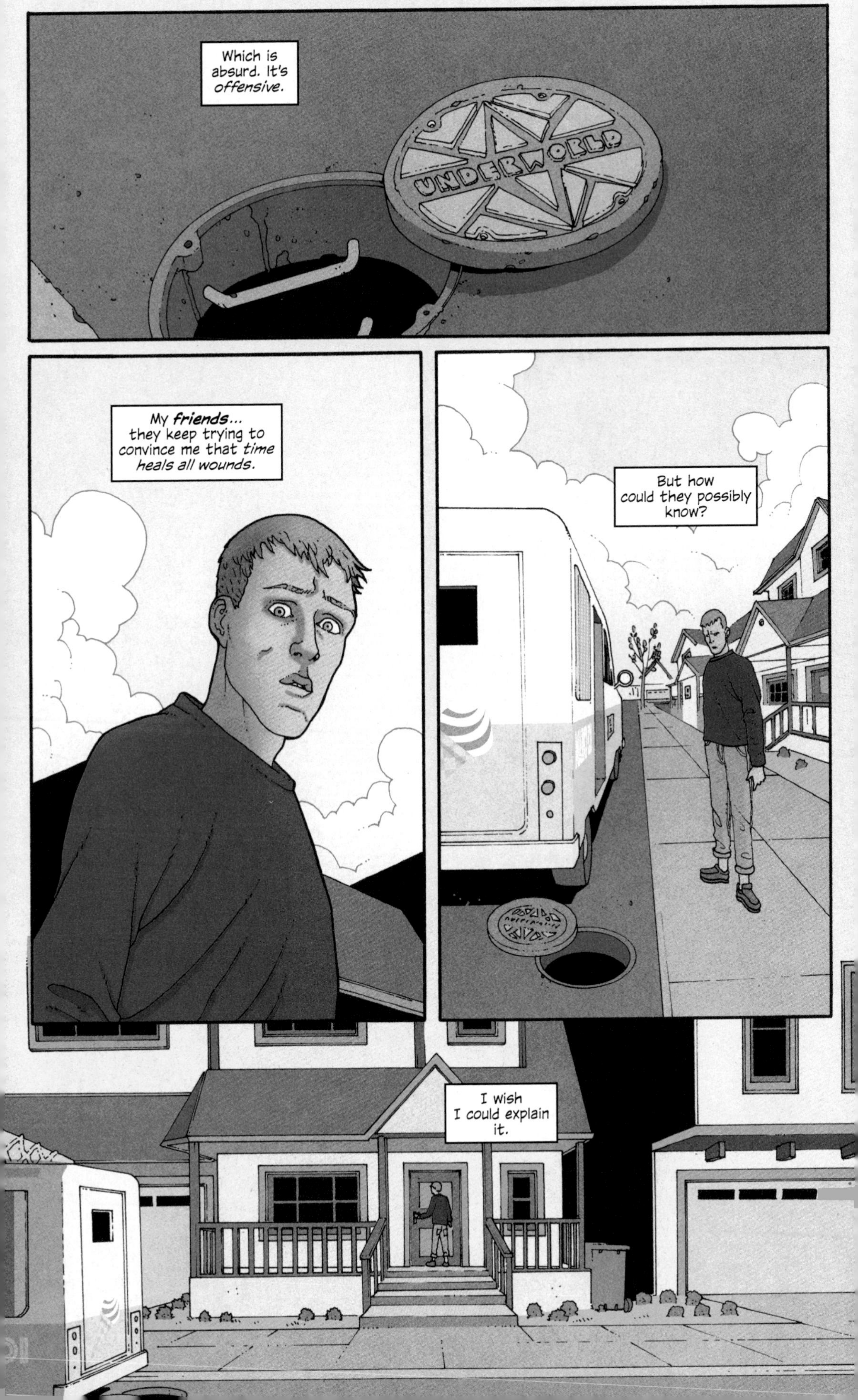
Which is absurd. It's *offensive*.
UNDERWORLD
My ***friends***... they keep trying to convince me that *time heals all wounds.*
But how could they possibly know?
I wish I could explain it.

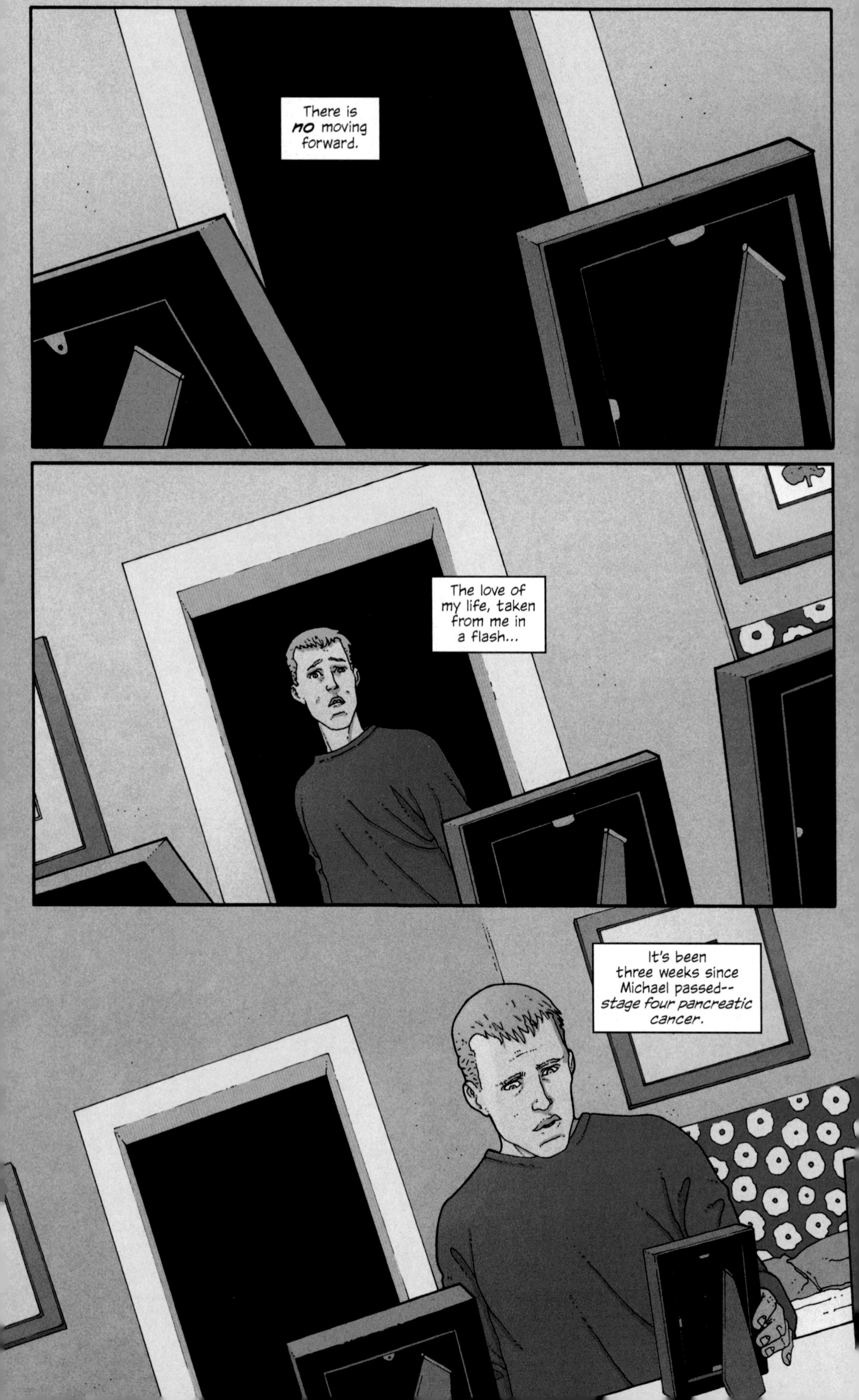
There is *no* moving forward.
The love of my life, taken from me in a flash...
It's been three weeks since Michael passed-- *stage four pancreatic cancer.*

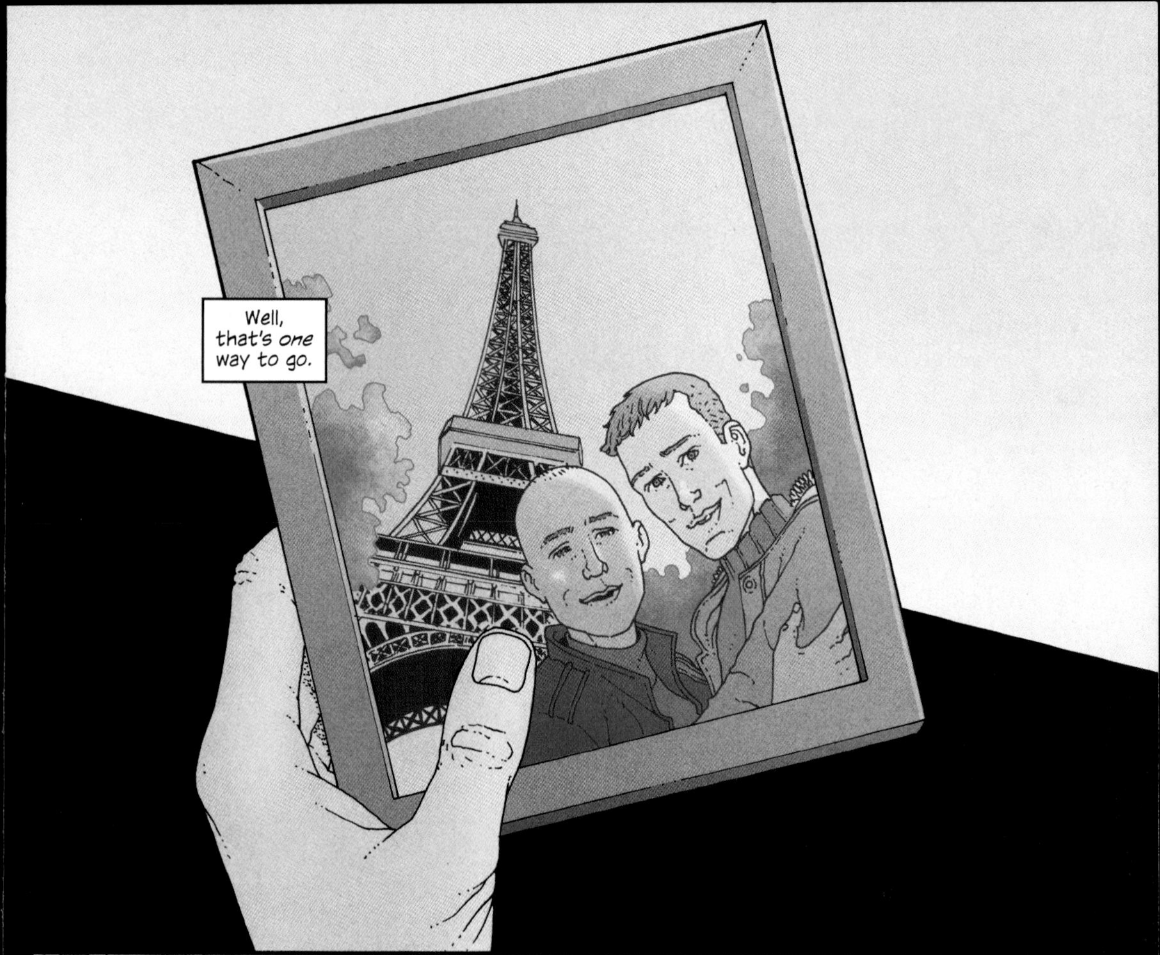
Well, that's *one* way to go.

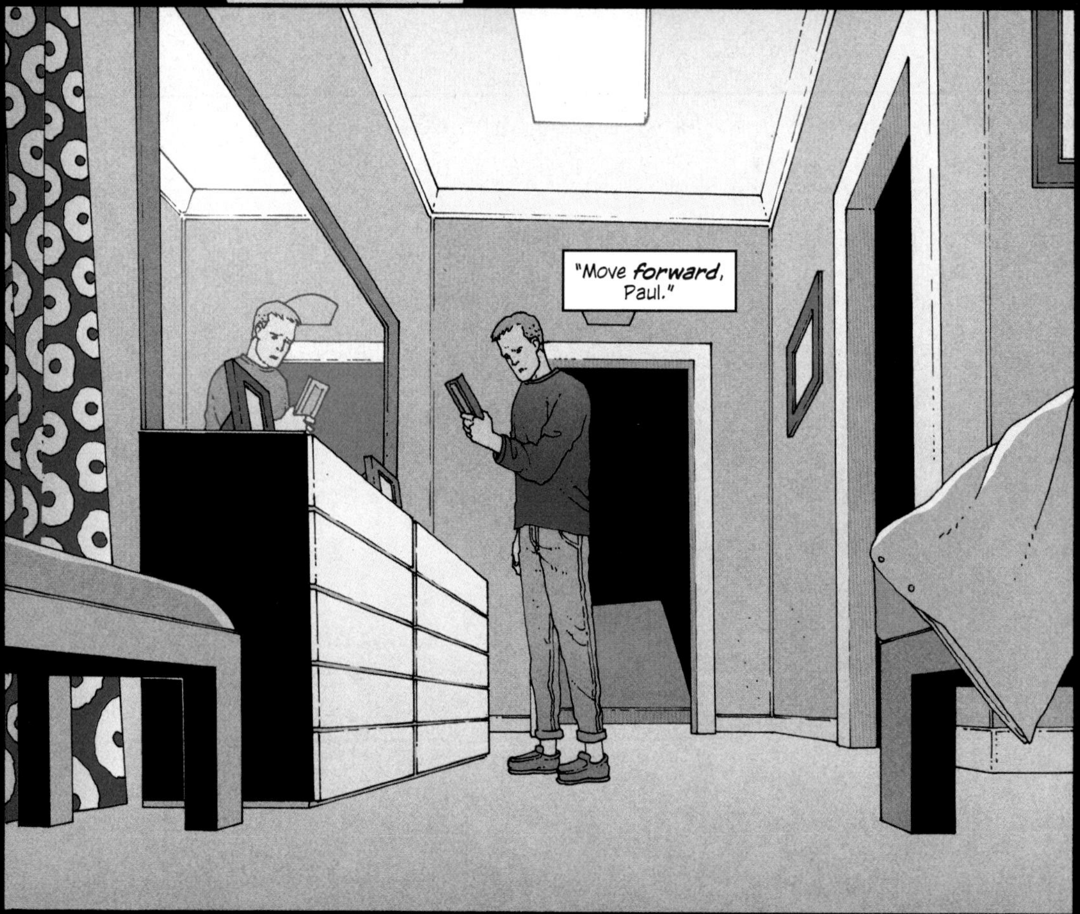
"Move **forward**, Paul."

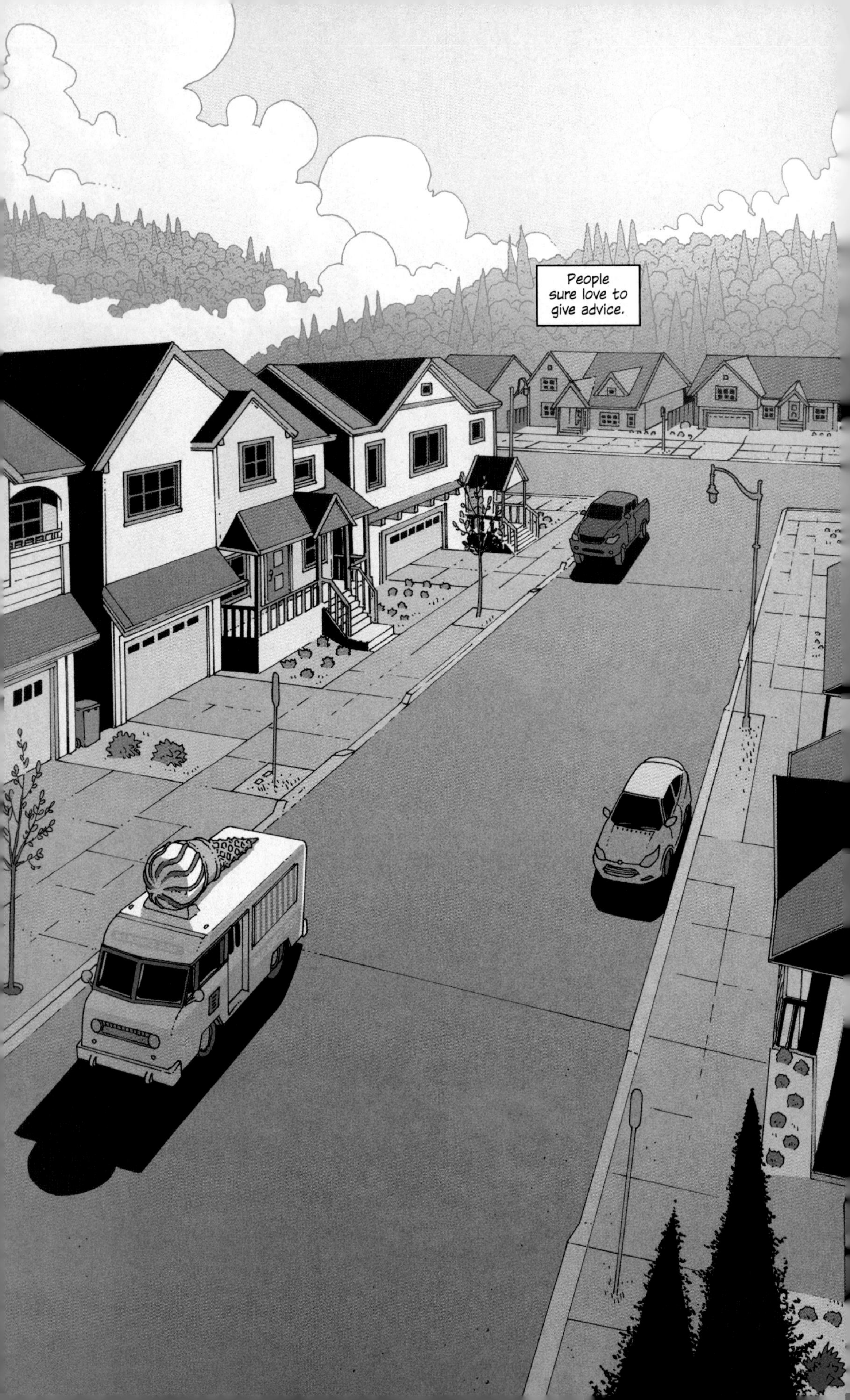
People sure love to give advice.

Author's note: if you
choose to enjoy the story backwards,
read panels from bottom to top
and right to left.

THIS COMIC IS A
PALINDROME

IT CAN BE READ
FORWARDS
(from first to last panel)
OR
BACKWARDS
(from last to first panel)

IT'S UP TO YOU

Chapter Thirteen

Palindromes

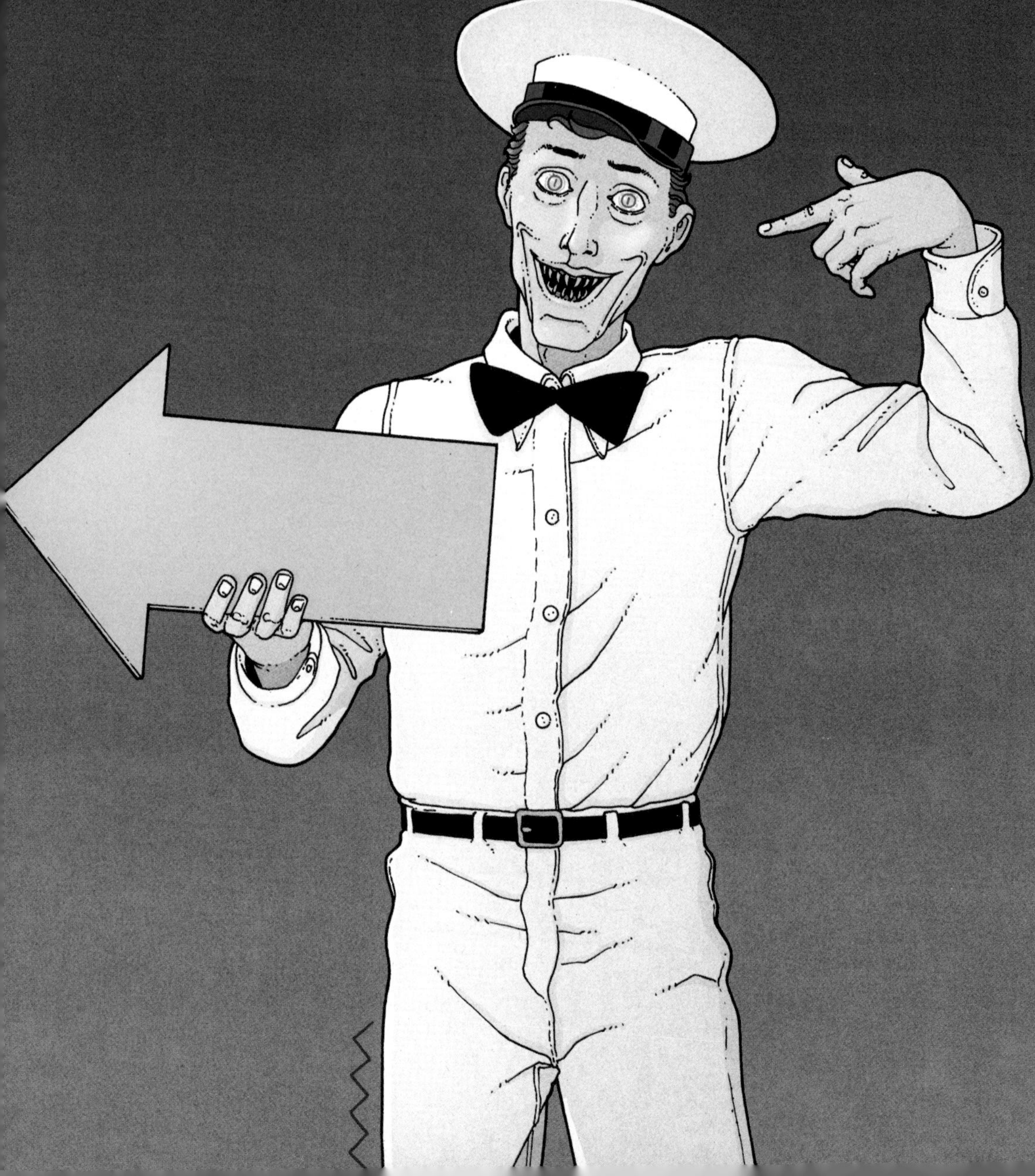

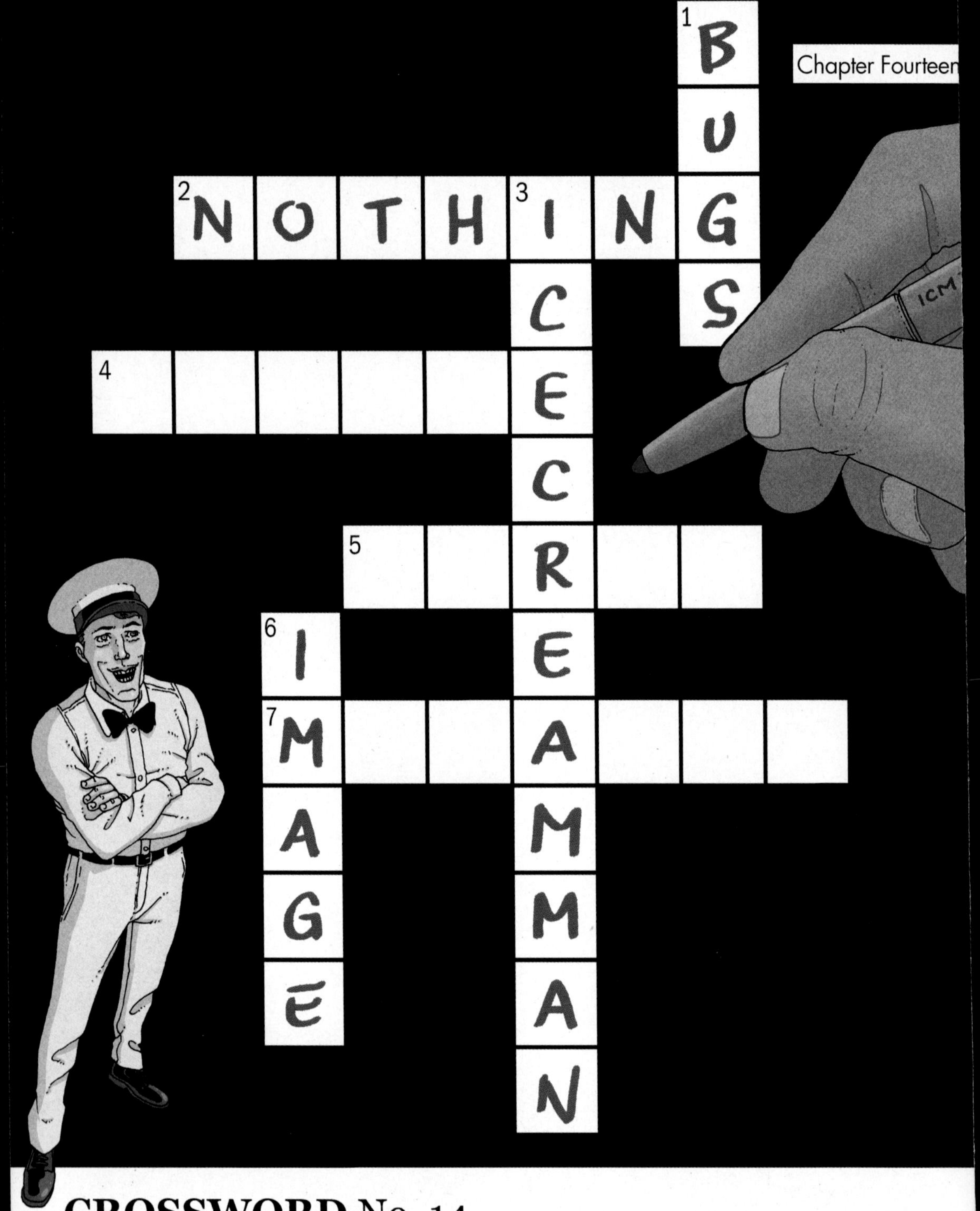
Chapter Fourteen
1 BUGS
2 NOTHING
3 ICECREAMMAN
4
5
6 IMAGE
7 M

CROSSWORD No. 14

DOWN

1 The things that will eat you (slowly, at first)

3 The title of this here comic book series periodical

6 The name of our esteemed publisher, or a representation of a thing

ACROSS

2 What everything means

4 W. Maxwell _______, a writer tolerated by some

5 _____ O'Halloran, colorist and expert of mood lighting

7 Martín ________, artist and illustrator extraordinaire

Down and Across

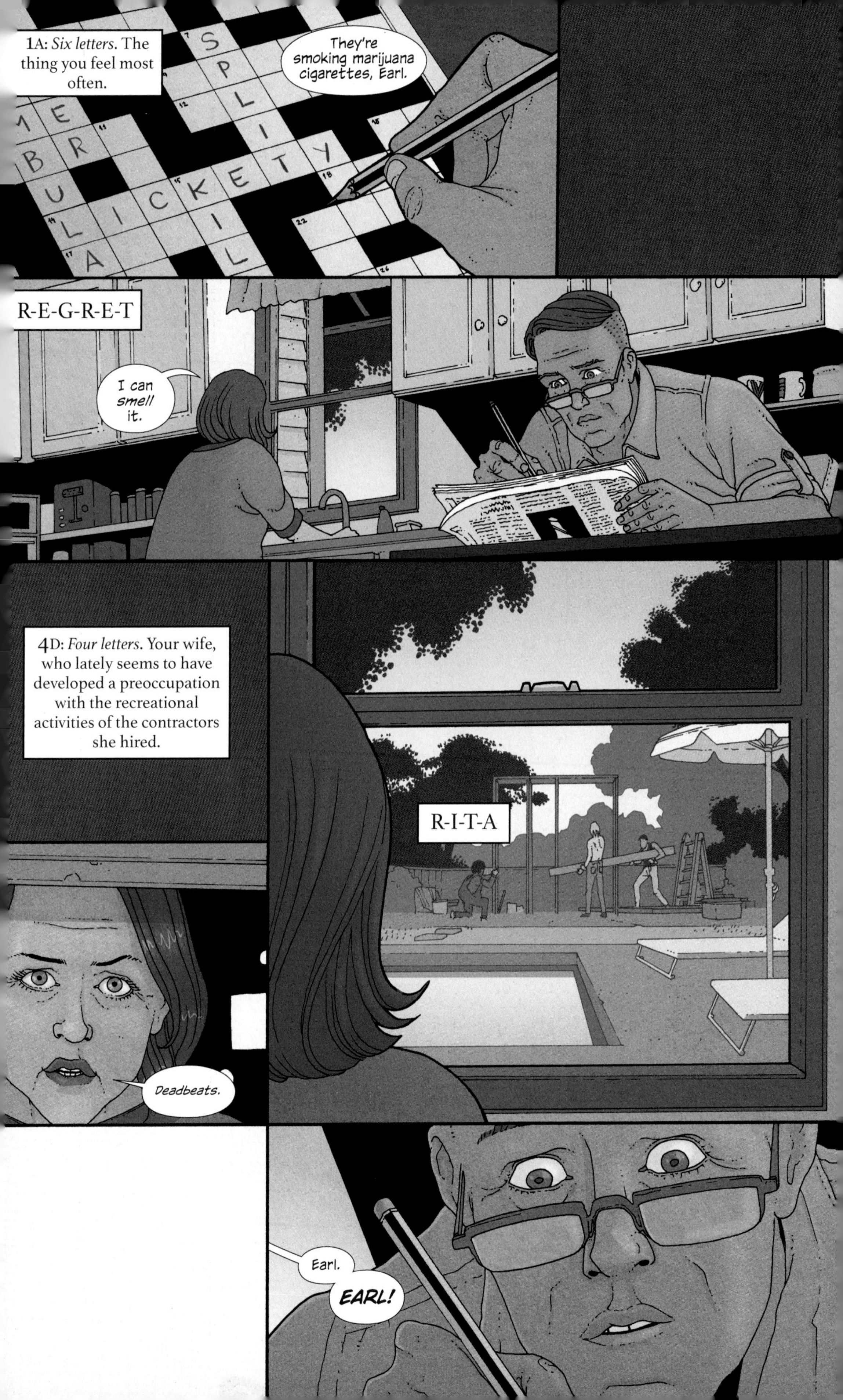

1A: *Six letters*. The thing you feel most often.
They're smoking marijuana cigarettes, Earl.
R-E-G-R-E-T
I can *smell* it.
4D: *Four letters*. Your wife, who lately seems to have developed a preoccupation with the recreational activities of the contractors she hired.
R-I-T-A
Deadbeats.
Earl.
EARL!

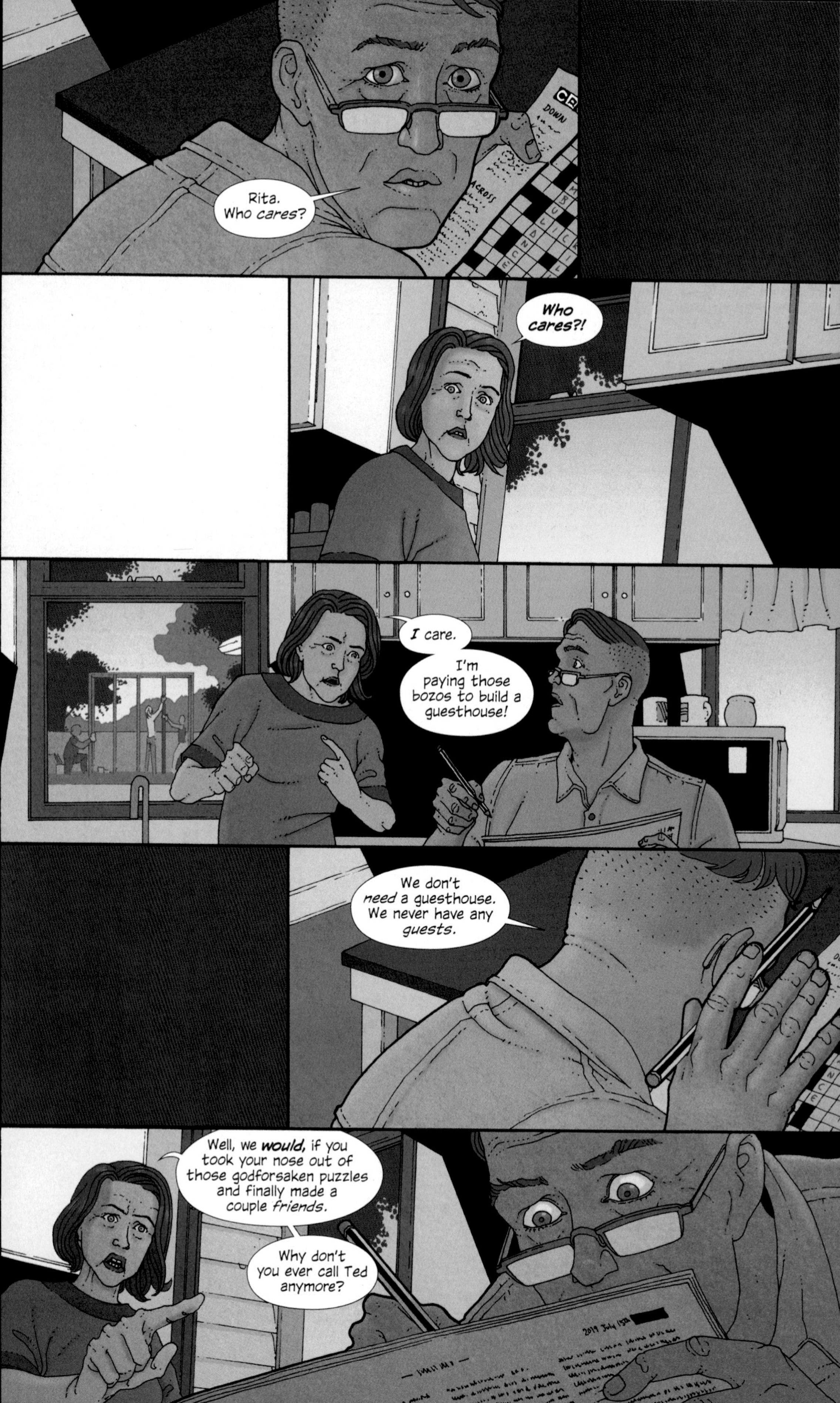
Rita.
Who *cares?*
Who cares?!
I care.
I'm paying those bozos to build a guesthouse!
We don't *need* a guesthouse. We never have any *guests*.
Well, we ***would,*** if you took your nose out of those godforsaken puzzles and finally made a couple *friends*.
Why don't you ever call Ted anymore?

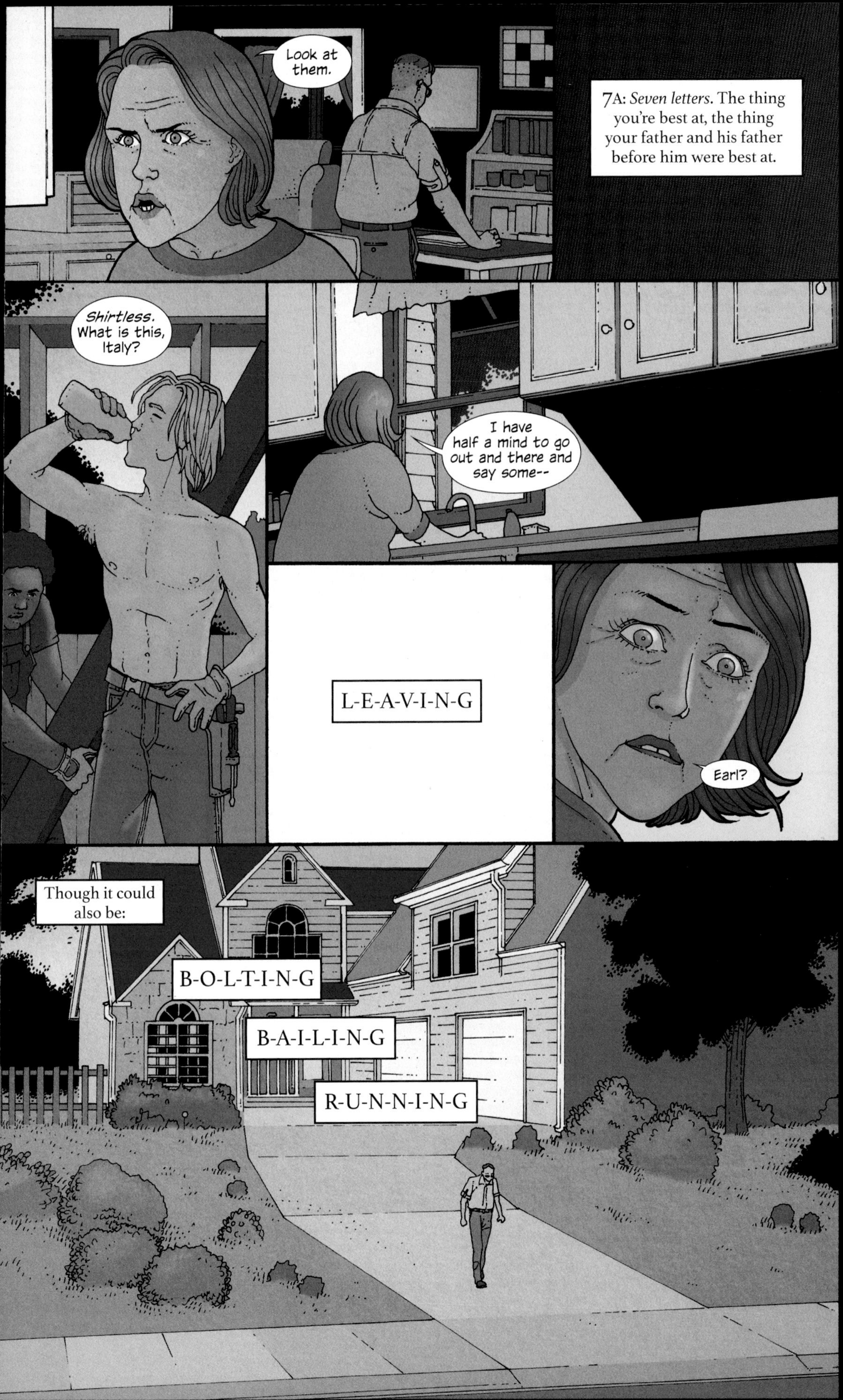
Look at them.
7A: *Seven letters*. The thing you're best at, the thing your father and his father before him were best at.
Shirtless. What is this, Italy?
I have half a mind to go out and there and say some--
L-E-A-V-I-N-G
Earl?
Though it could also be:
B-O-L-T-I-N-G
B-A-I-L-I-N-G
R-U-N-N-I-N-G

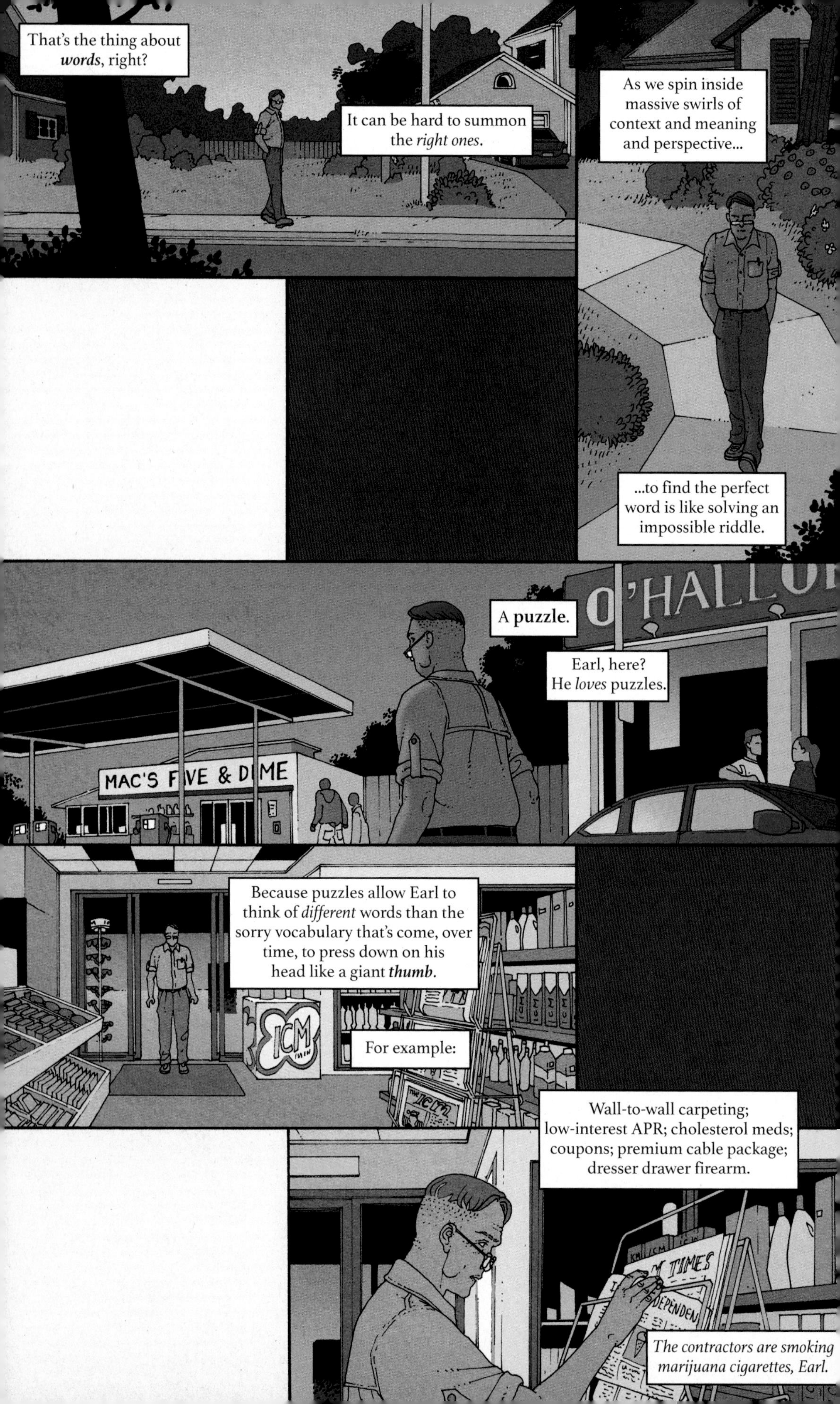

That's the thing about ***words***, right?
It can be hard to summon the *right ones*.
As we spin inside massive swirls of context and meaning and perspective...
...to find the perfect word is like solving an impossible riddle.
MAC'S F VE & D ME
A **puzzle**.
O'HALL
Earl, here? He *loves* puzzles.
Because puzzles allow Earl to think of *different* words than the sorry vocabulary that's come, over time, to press down on his head like a giant ***thumb***.
For example:
Wall-to-wall carpeting; low-interest APR; cholesterol meds; coupons; premium cable package; dresser drawer firearm.
The contractors are smoking marijuana cigarettes, Earl.

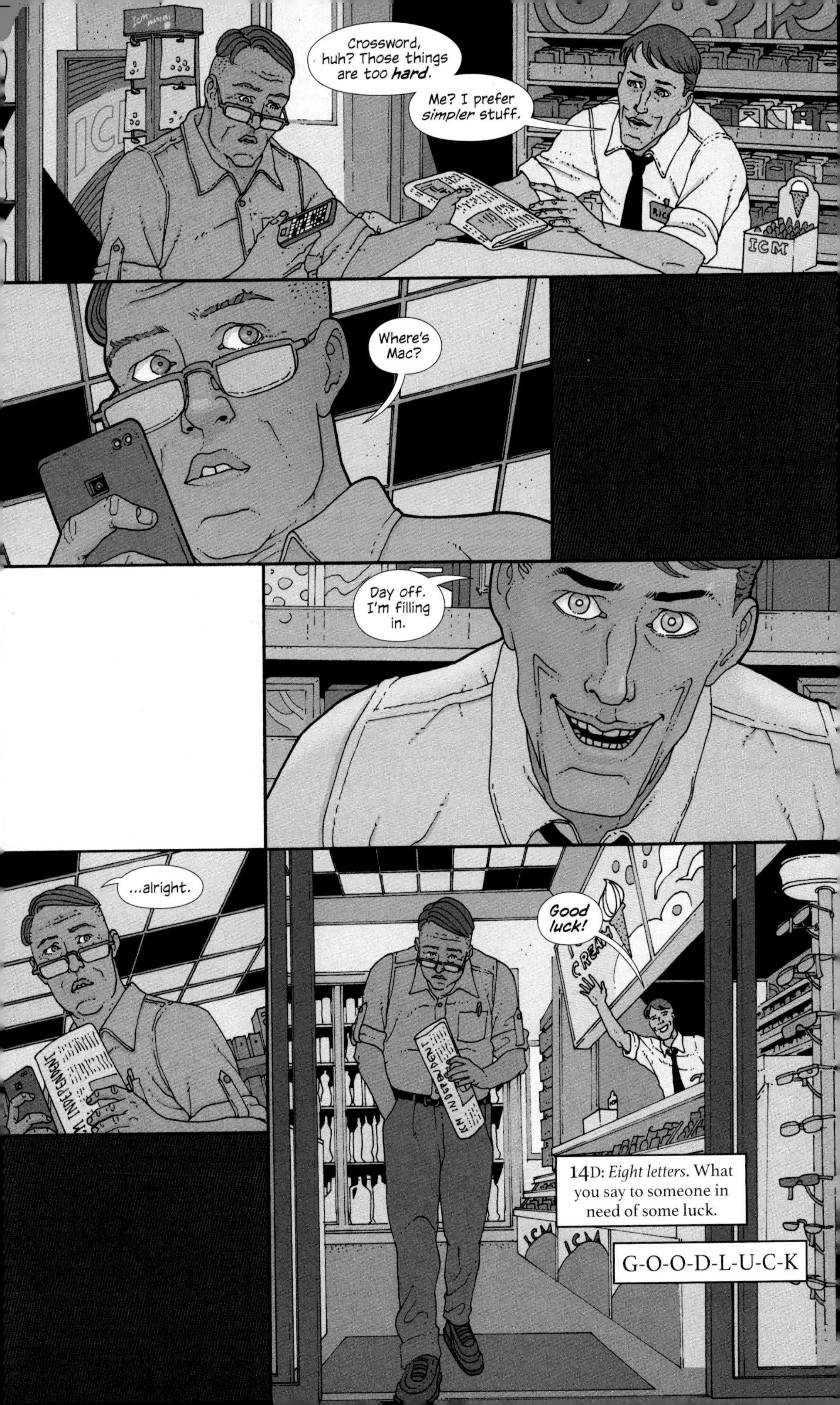
Crossword, huh? Those things are too **hard**.
Me? I prefer *simpler* stuff.
Where's Mac?
Day off. I'm filling in.
...alright.
Good luck!
14D: *Eight letters.* What you say to someone in need of some luck.
G-O-O-D-L-U-C-K

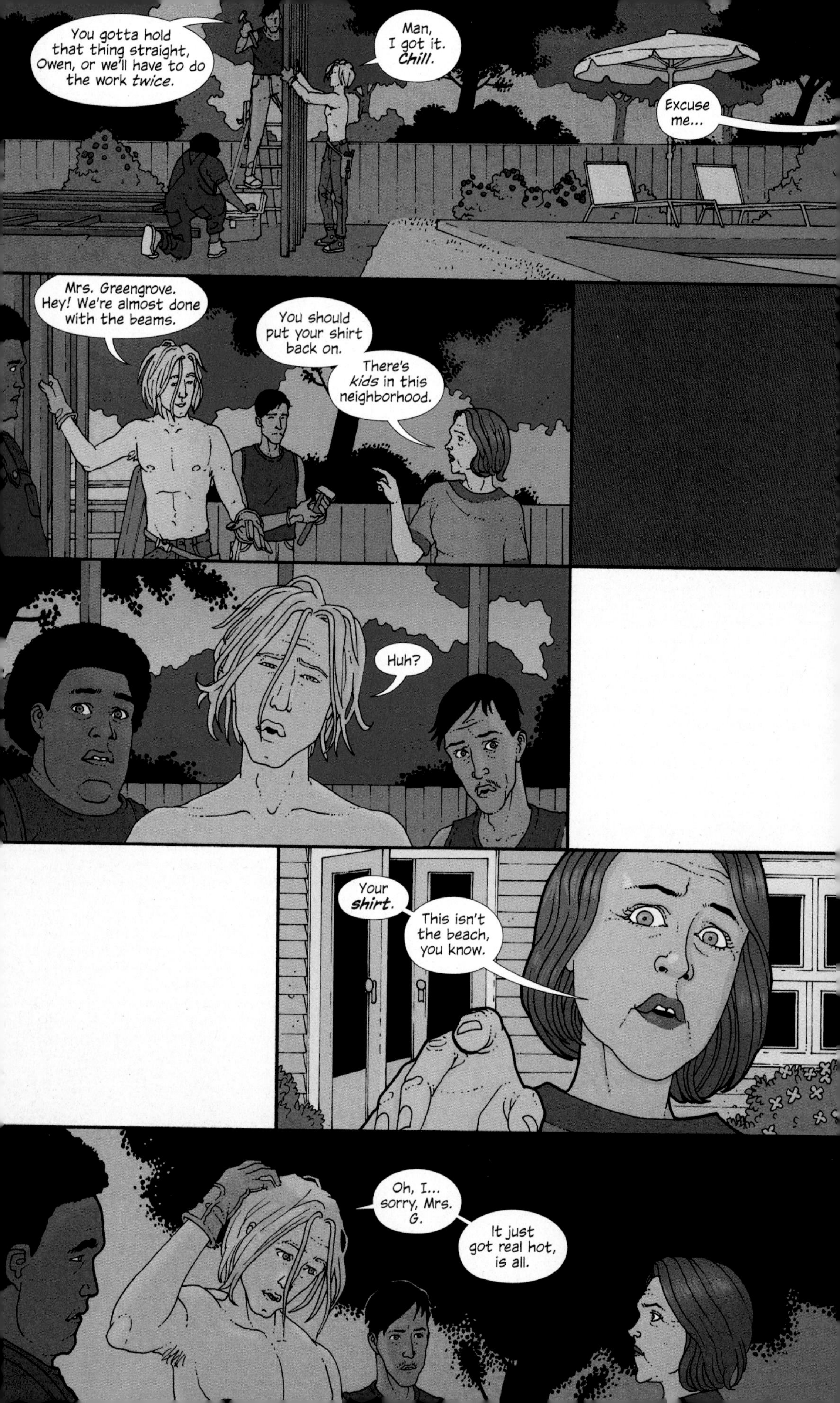
You gotta hold that thing straight, Owen, or we'll have to do the work *twice*.
Man, I got it. ***Chill***.
Excuse me...
Mrs. Greengrove. Hey! We're almost done with the beams.
You should put your shirt back on.
There's *kids* in this neighborhood.
Huh?
Your ***shirt***.
This isn't the beach, you know.
Oh, I... sorry, Mrs. G.
It just got real hot, is all.

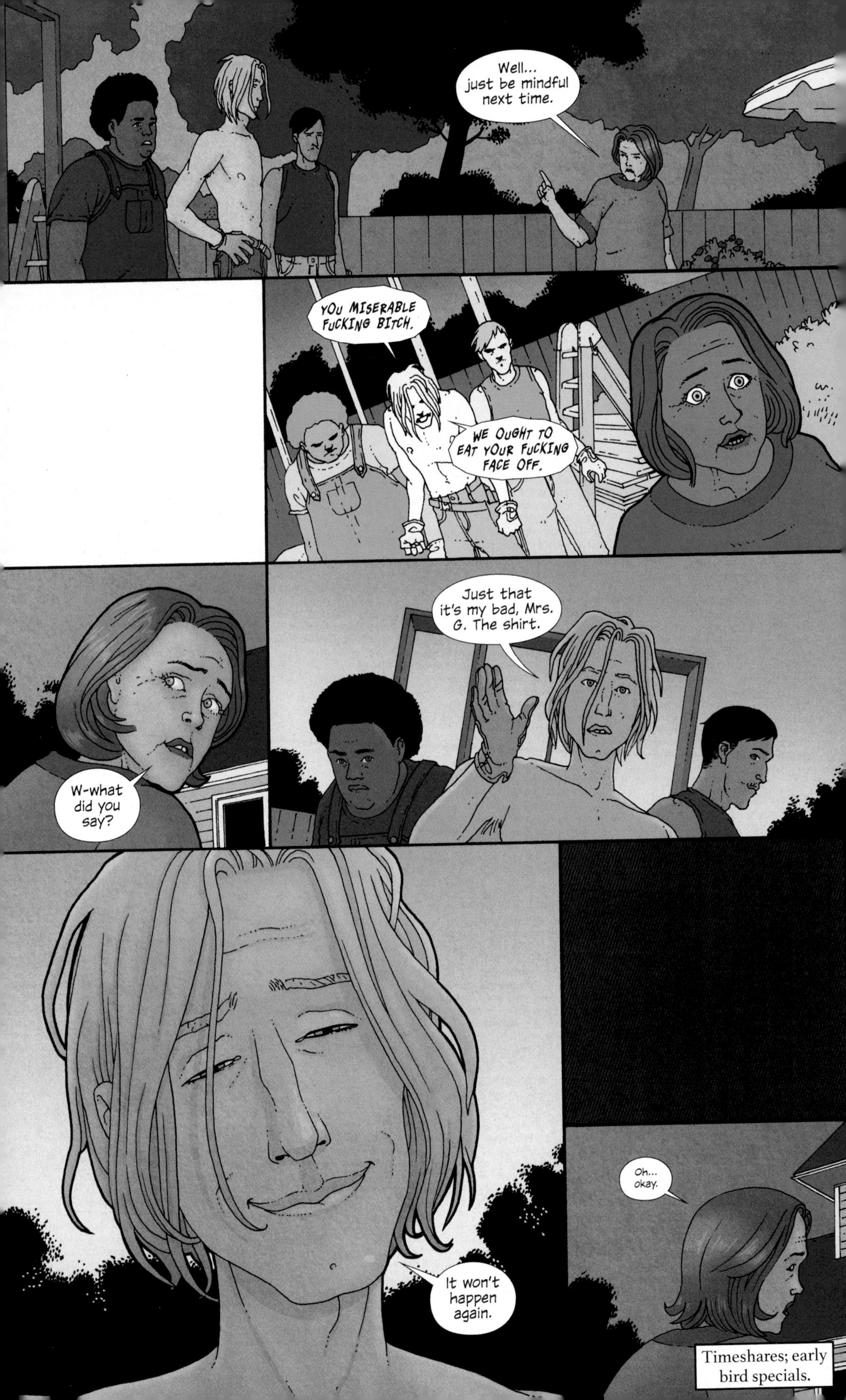
Well... just be mindful next time.
YOU MISERABLE FUCKING BITCH.
WE OUGHT TO EAT YOUR FUCKING FACE OFF.
W-what did you say?
Just that it's my bad, Mrs. G. The shirt.
It won't happen again.
Oh... okay.
Timeshares; early bird specials.

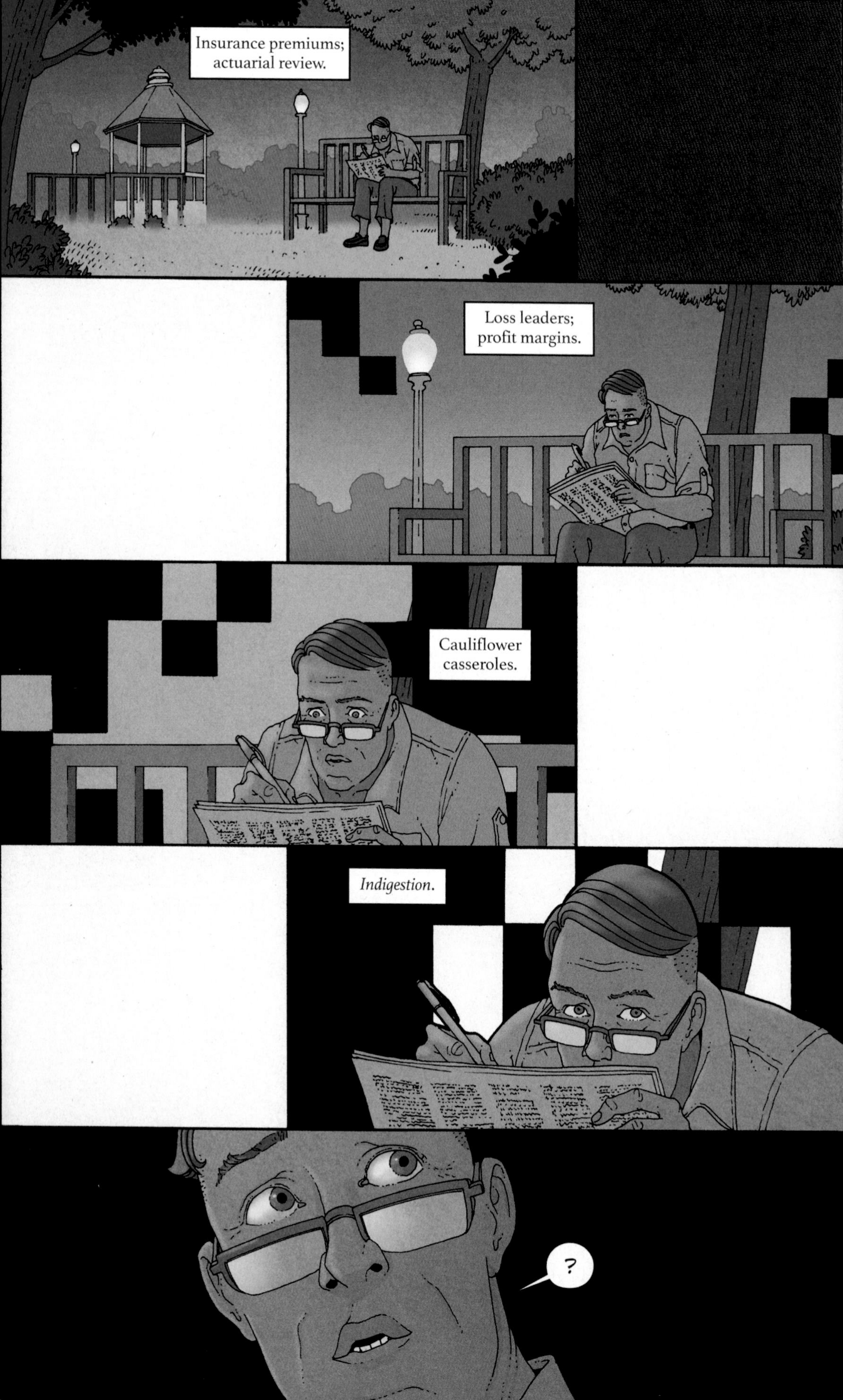
Insurance premiums; actuarial review.
Loss leaders; profit margins.
Cauliflower casseroles.
Indigestion.
?

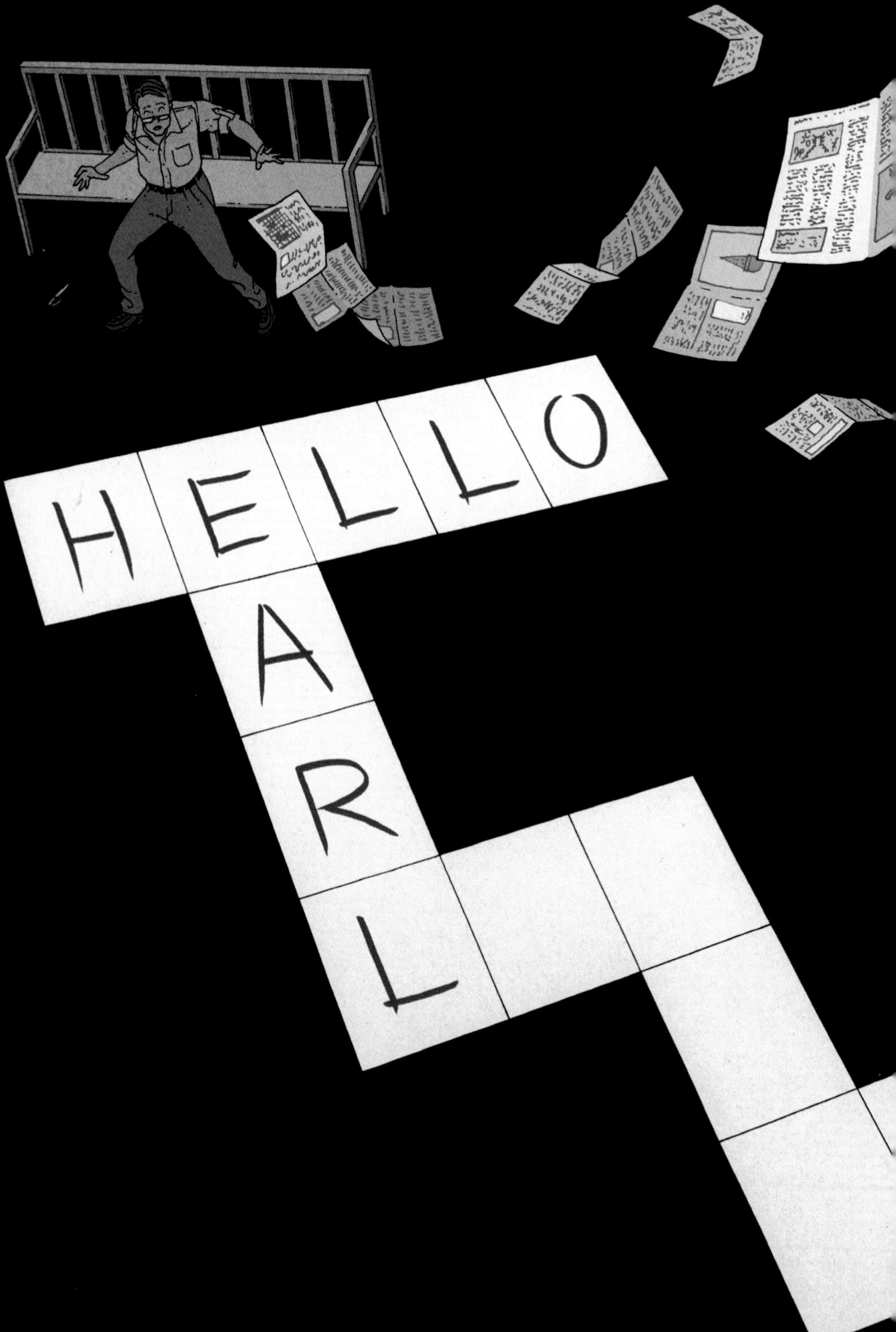
HELLO
EARL

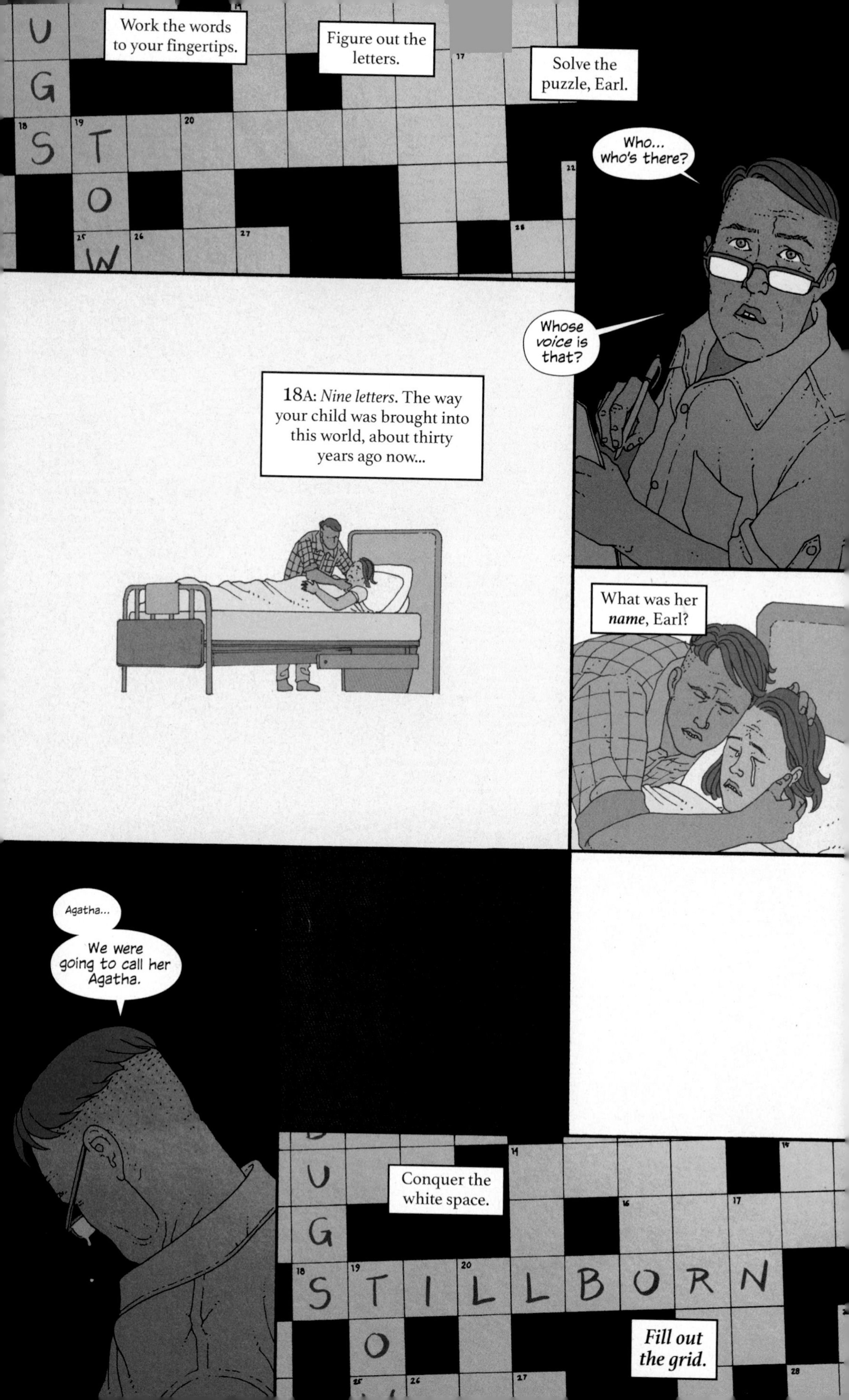
Work the words to your fingertips.
Figure out the letters.
Solve the puzzle, Earl.
Who... who's there?
Whose *voice* is that?
18A: *Nine letters*. The way your child was brought into this world, about thirty years ago now...
What was her *name*, Earl?
Agatha...
We were going to call her Agatha.
Conquer the white space.
STILLBORN
Fill out the grid.

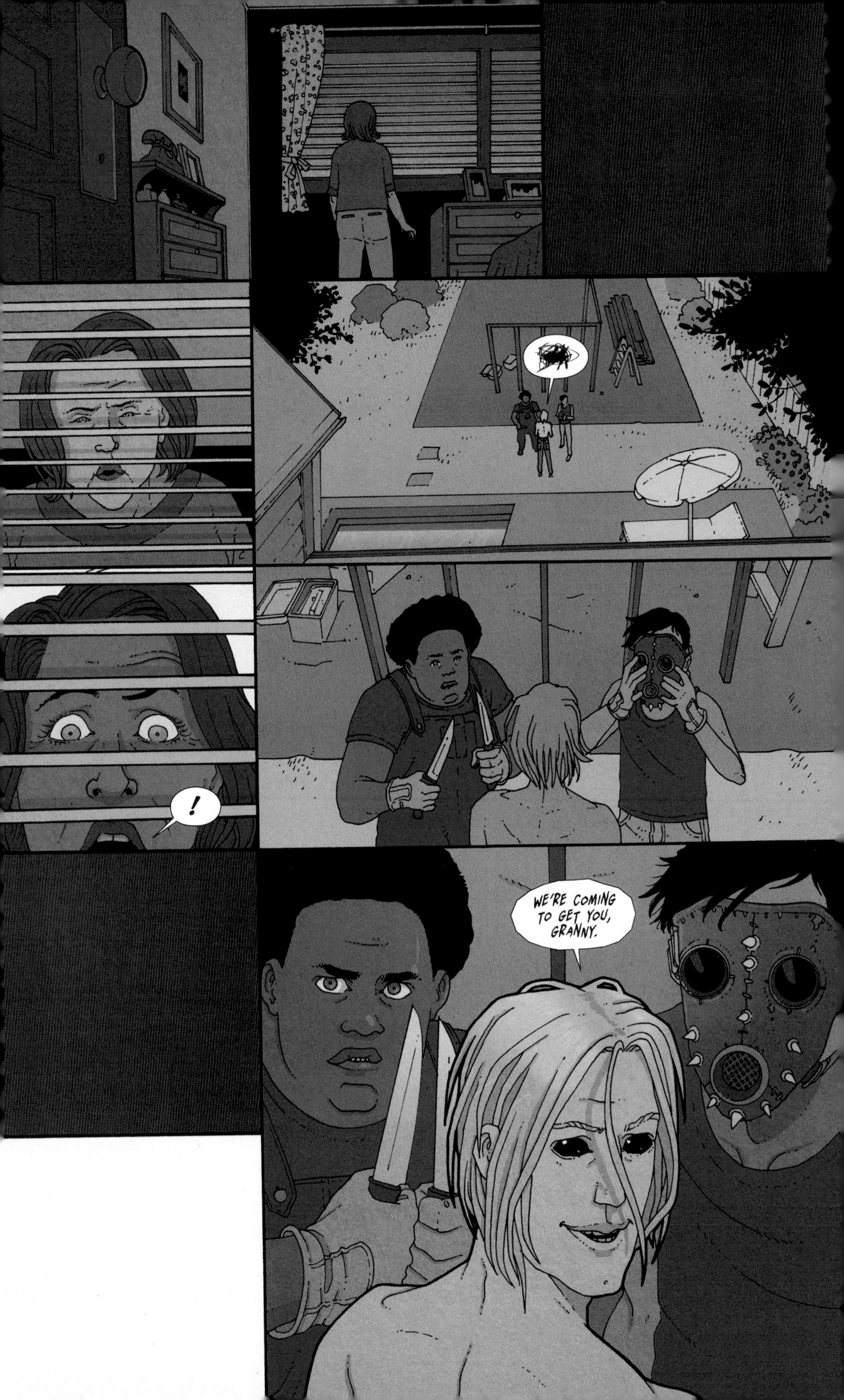
!
WE'RE COMING TO GET YOU, GRANNY.

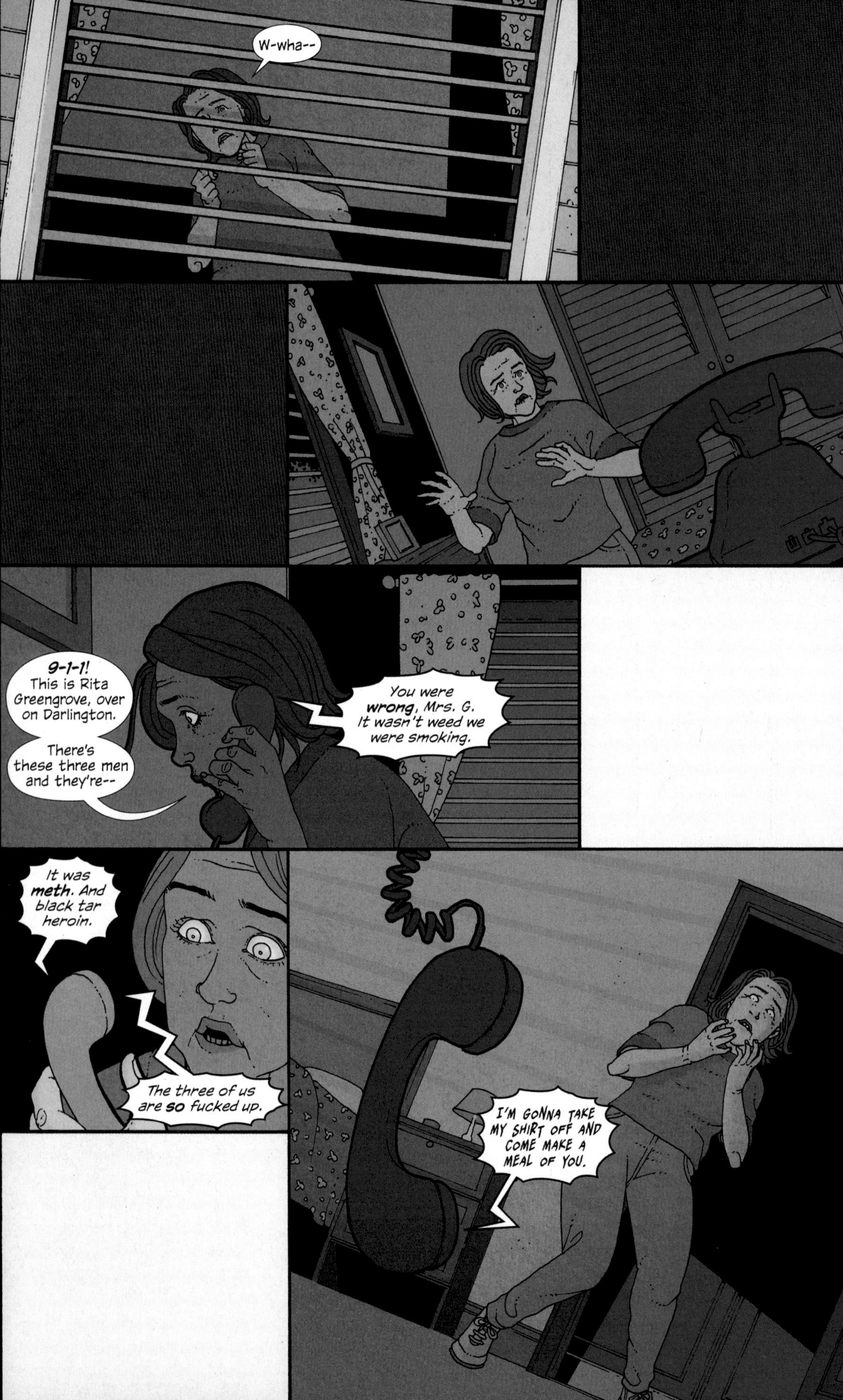
W-wha--
9-1-1! This is Rita Greengrove, over on Darlington.
There's these three men and they're--
You were wrong, Mrs. G. It wasn't weed we were smoking.
It was meth. And black tar heroin.
The three of us are so fucked up.
I'M GONNA TAKE MY SHIRT OFF AND COME MAKE A MEAL OF YOU.

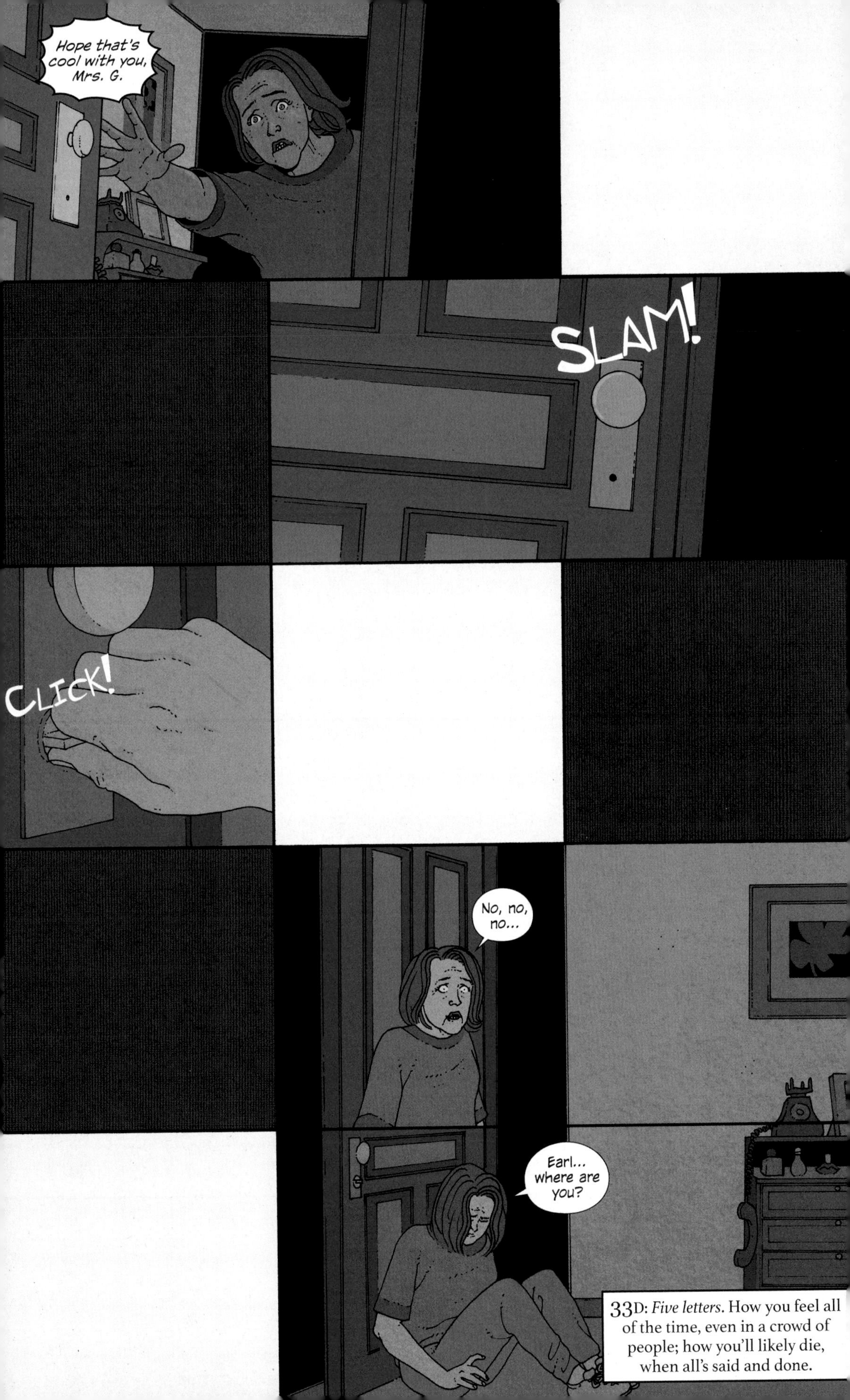
Hope that's cool with you, Mrs. G.
SLAM!
CLICK!
No, no, no...
Earl... where are you?
33D: *Five letters.* How you feel all of the time, even in a crowd of people; how you'll likely die, when all's said and done.

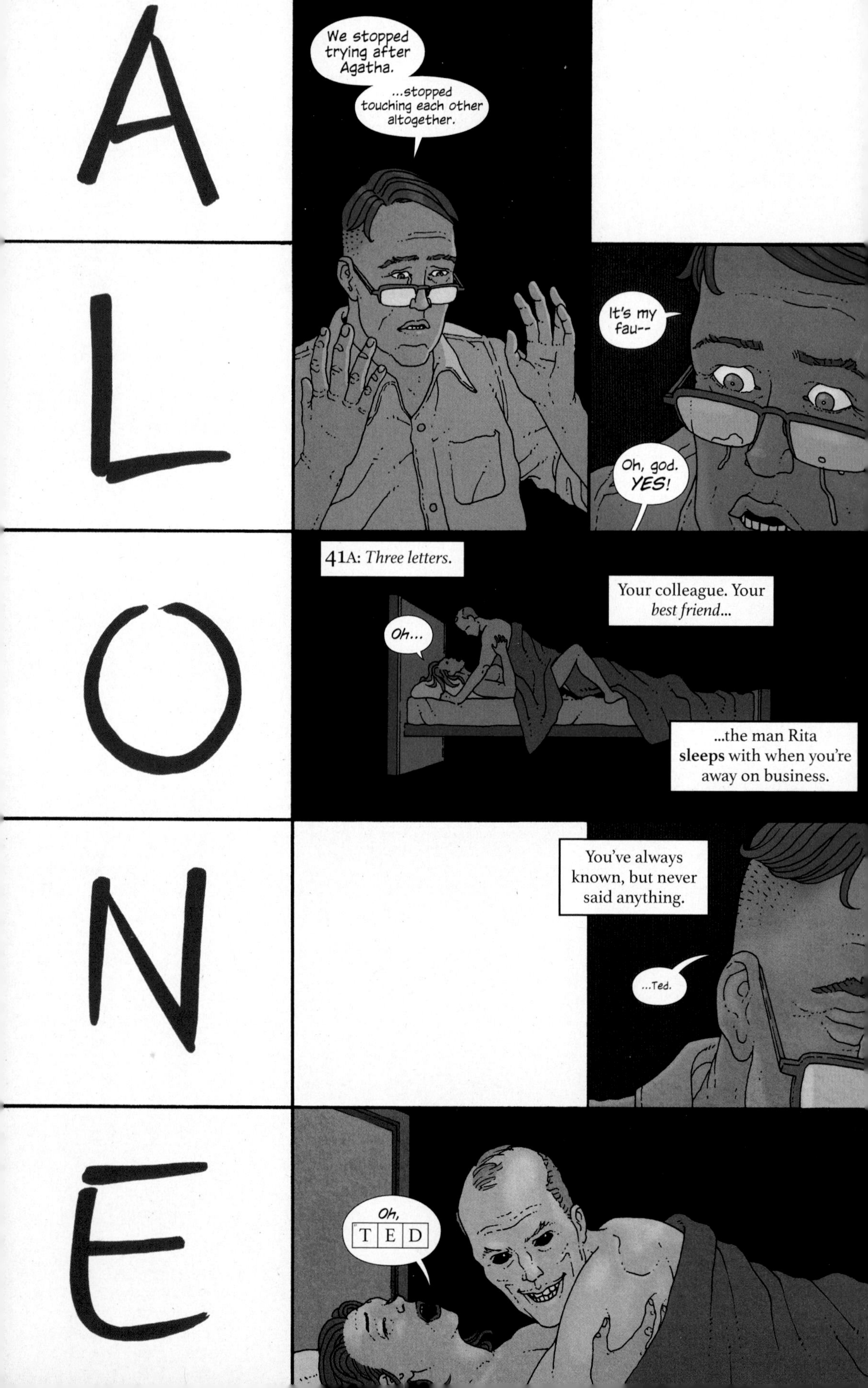
A
We stopped trying after Agatha.
...stopped touching each other altogether.
L
It's my fau--
Oh, god. YES!
O
41A: Three letters.
Oh...
Your colleague. Your best friend...
...the man Rita sleeps with when you're away on business.
N
You've always known, but never said anything.
...Ted.
E
Oh, TED

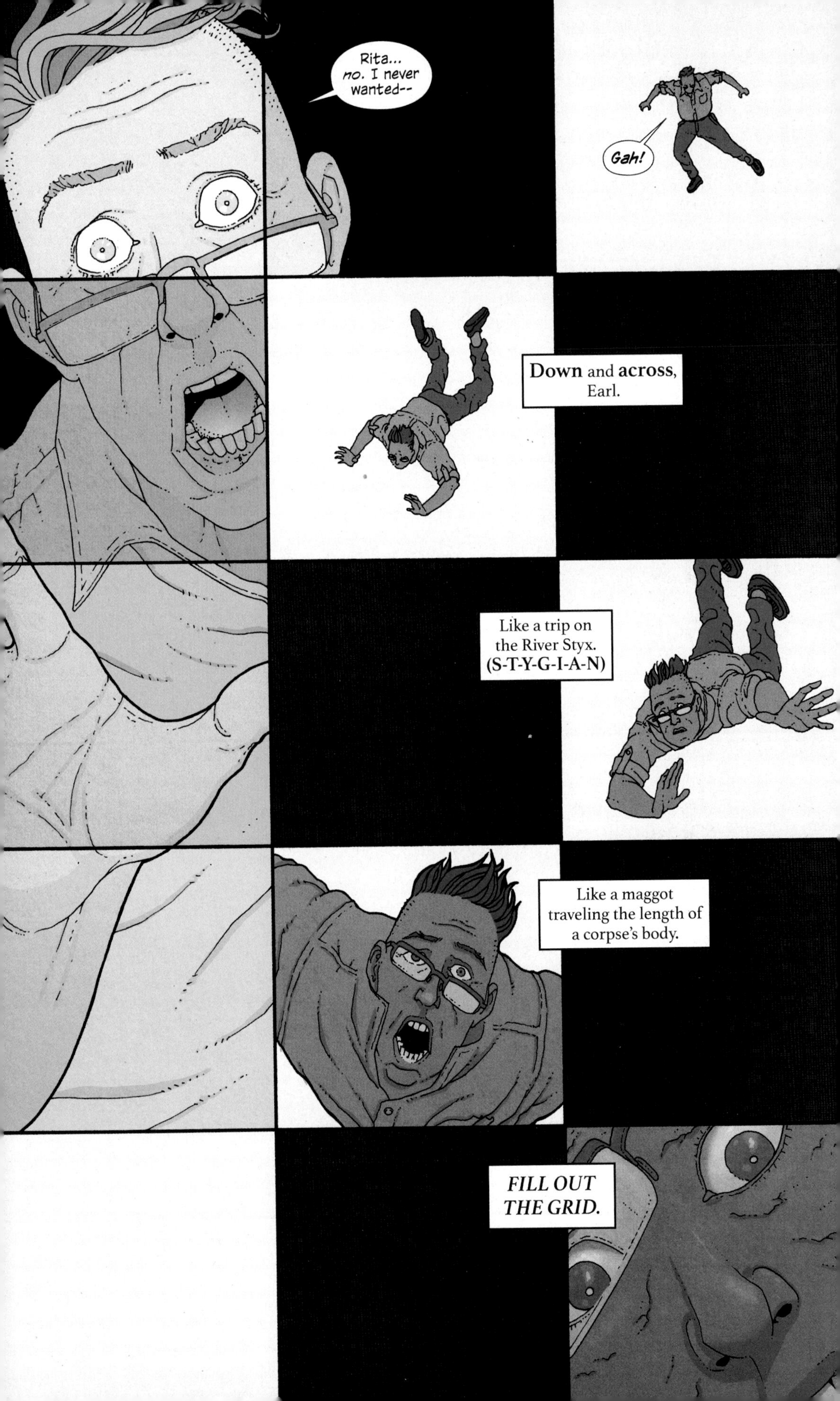
Rita... no. I never wanted--
Gah!
Down and across, Earl.
Like a trip on the River Styx. (S-T-Y-G-I-A-N)
Like a maggot traveling the length of a corpse's body.
FILL OUT THE GRID.

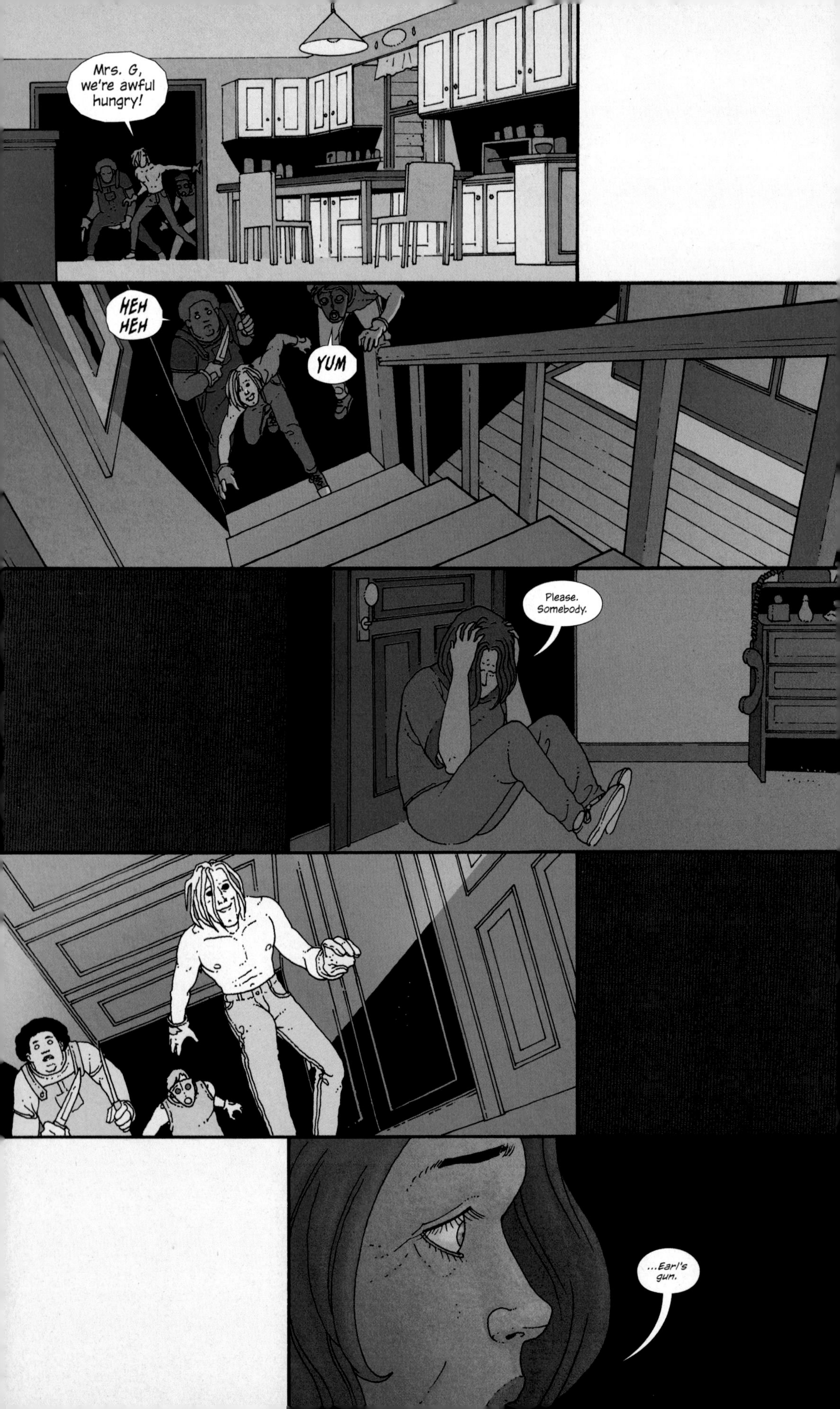
Mrs. G, we're awful hungry!
HEH HEH
YUM
Please. Somebody.
...Earl's gun.

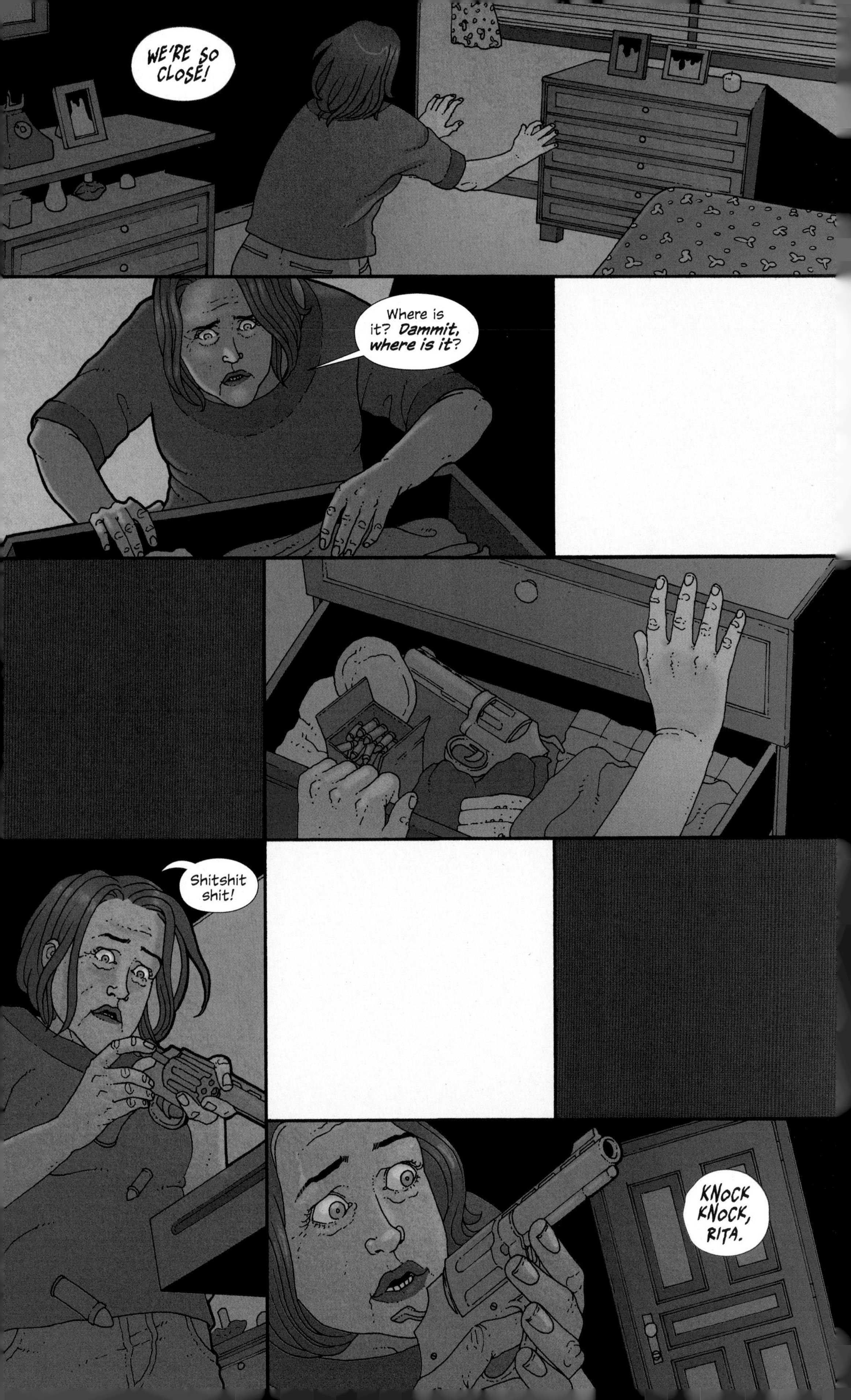
WE'RE SO CLOSE!
Where is it? Dammit, where is it?
Shitshit shit!
KNOCK KNOCK, RITA.

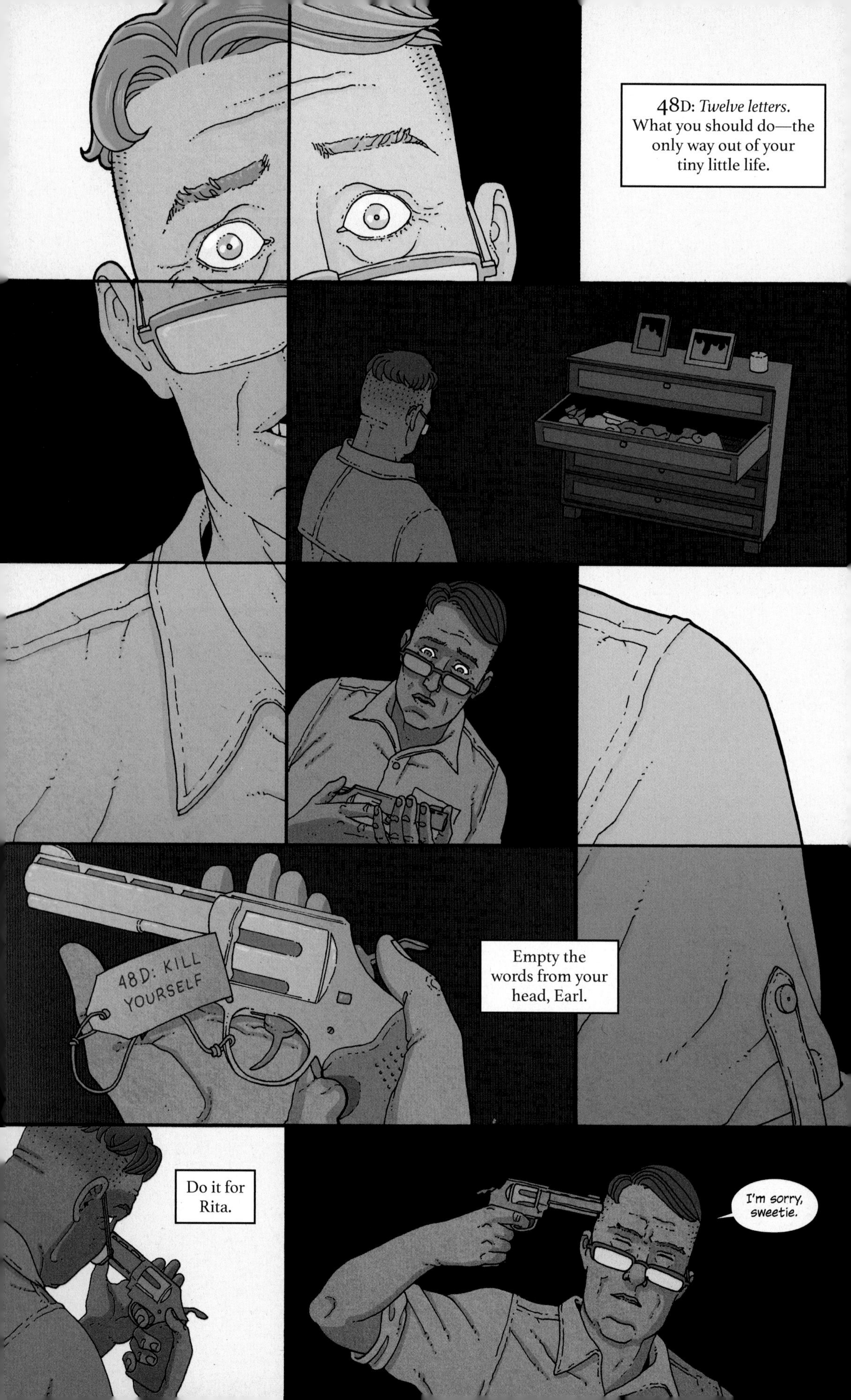
48D: *Twelve letters.* What you should do—the only way out of your tiny little life.
48D: KILL YOURSELF
Empty the words from your head, Earl.
Do it for Rita.
I'm sorry, sweetie.

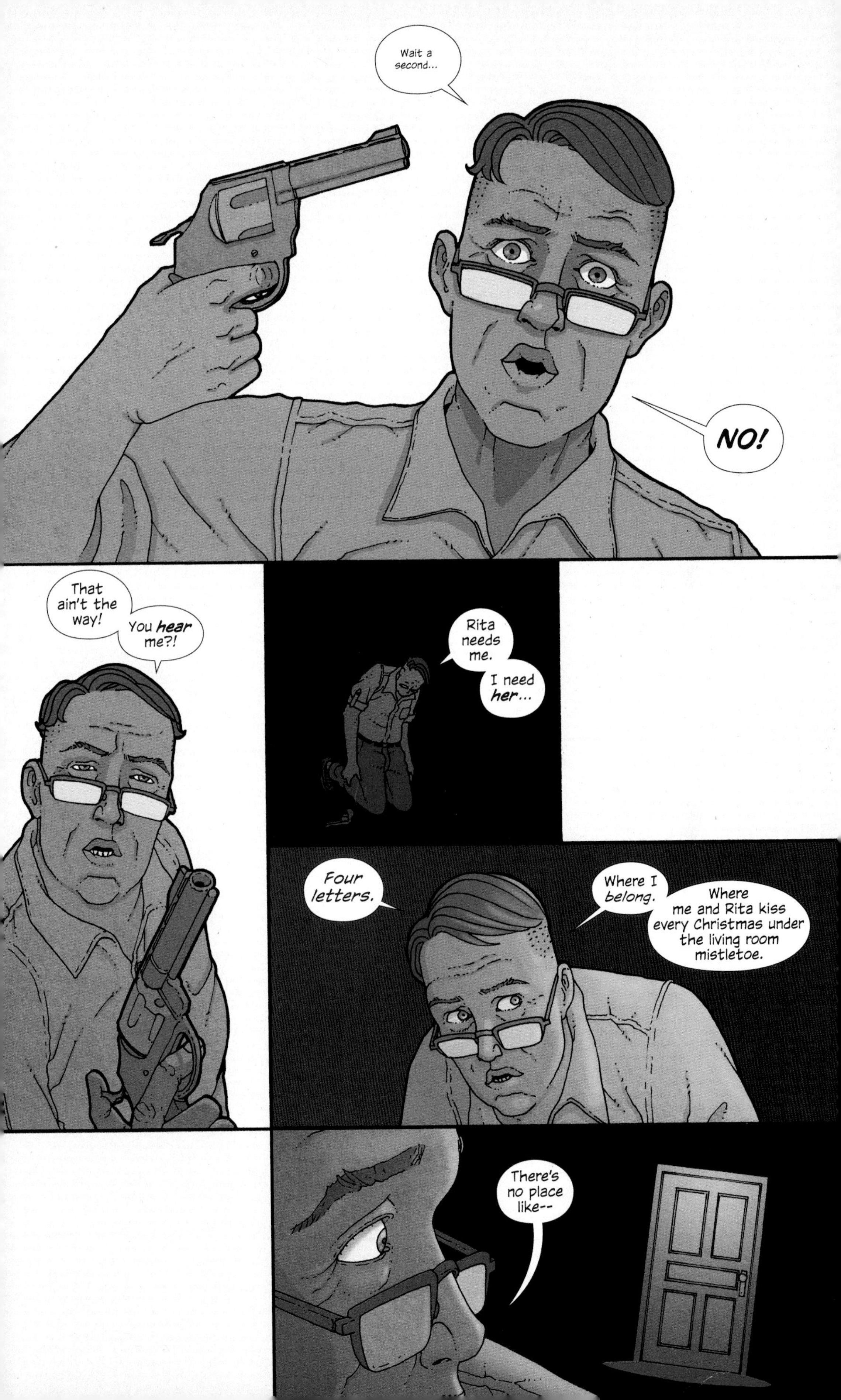
Wait a second...
NO!
That ain't the way!
You **hear** me?!
Rita needs me.
I need **her**...
Four letters.
Where I *belong.*
Where me and Rita kiss every Christmas under the living room mistletoe.
There's no place like--

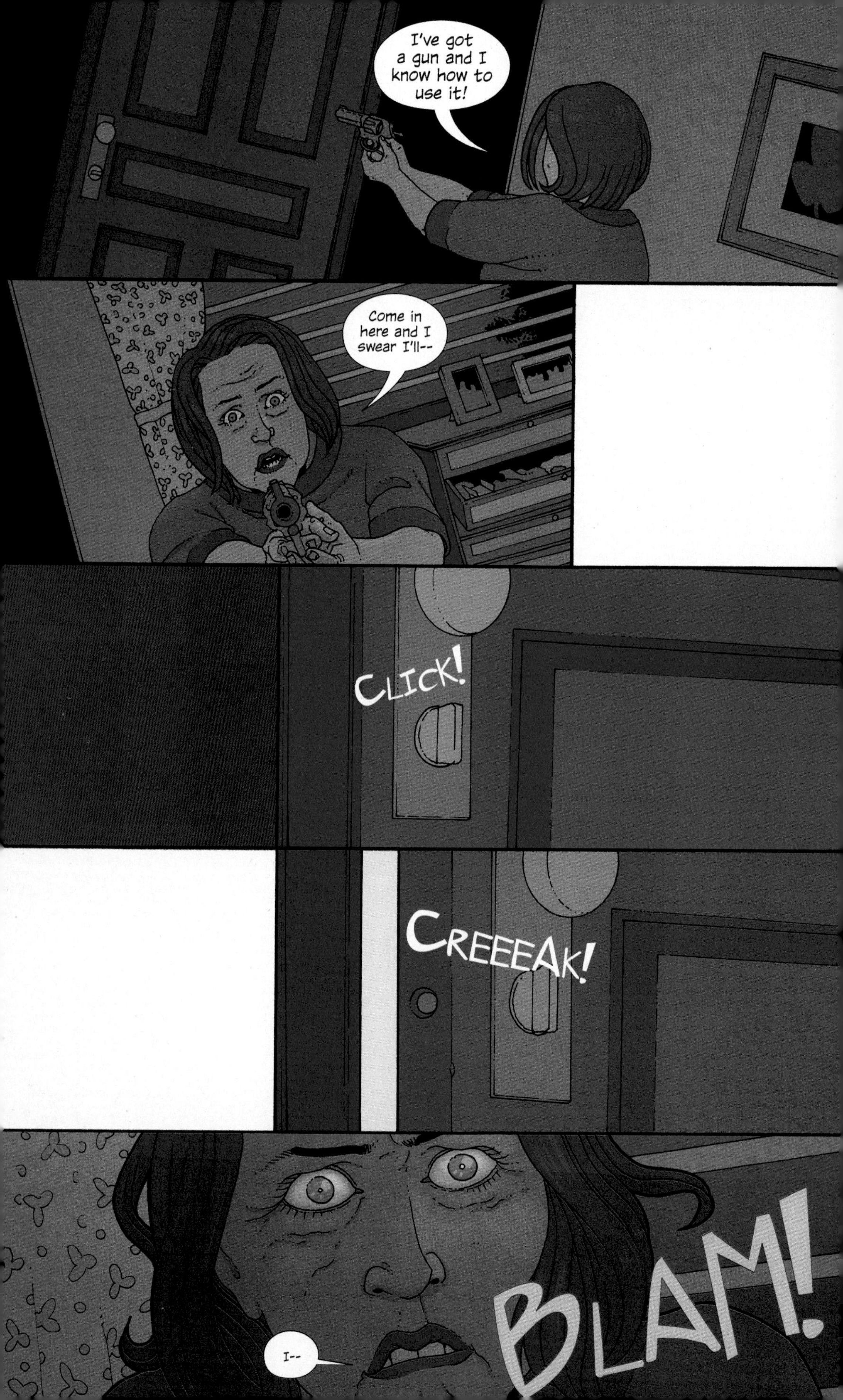
I've got a gun and I know how to use it!
Come in here and I swear I'll--
CLICK!
CREEEAK!
I--
BLAM!

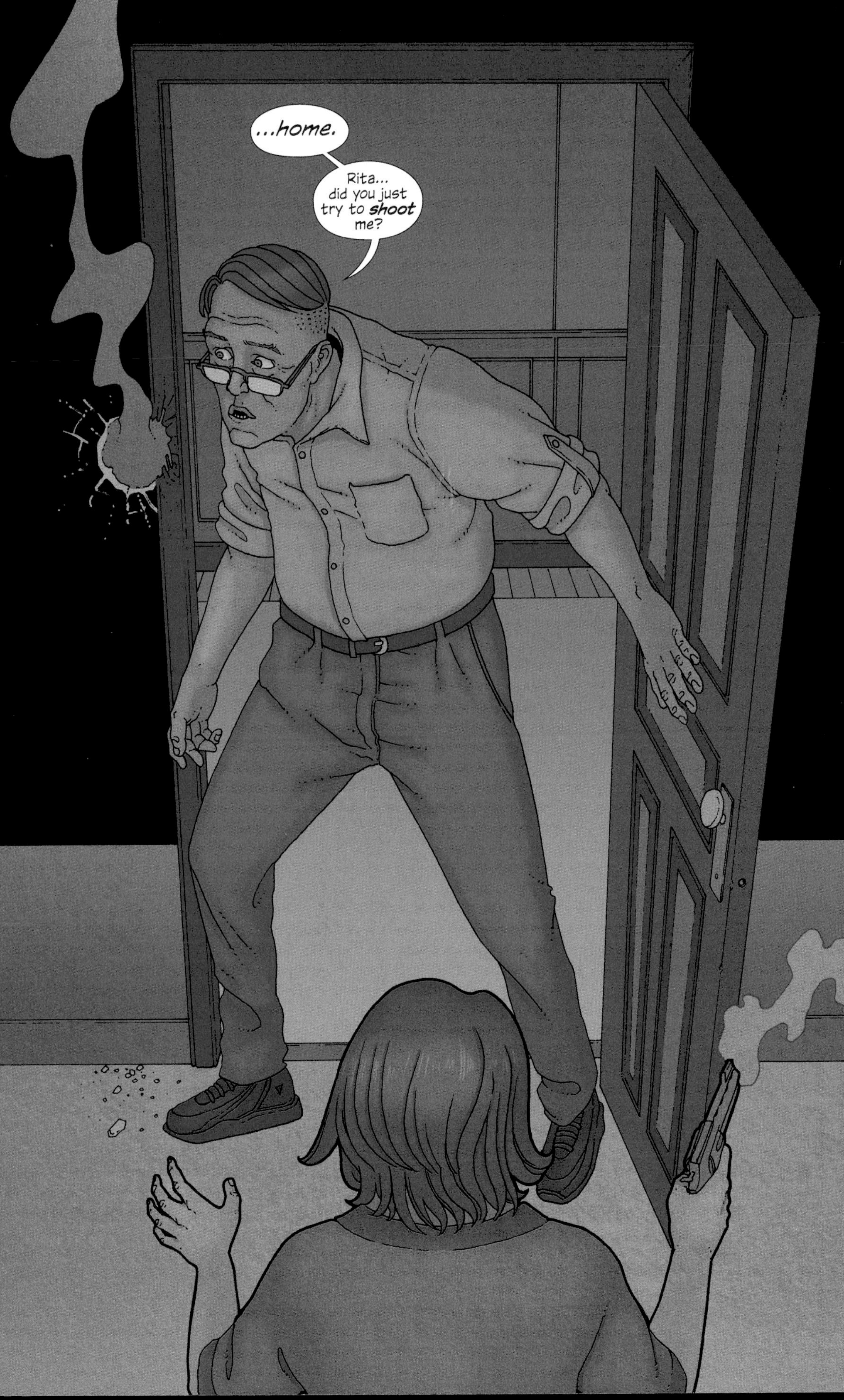
...home.
Rita... did you just try to shoot me?

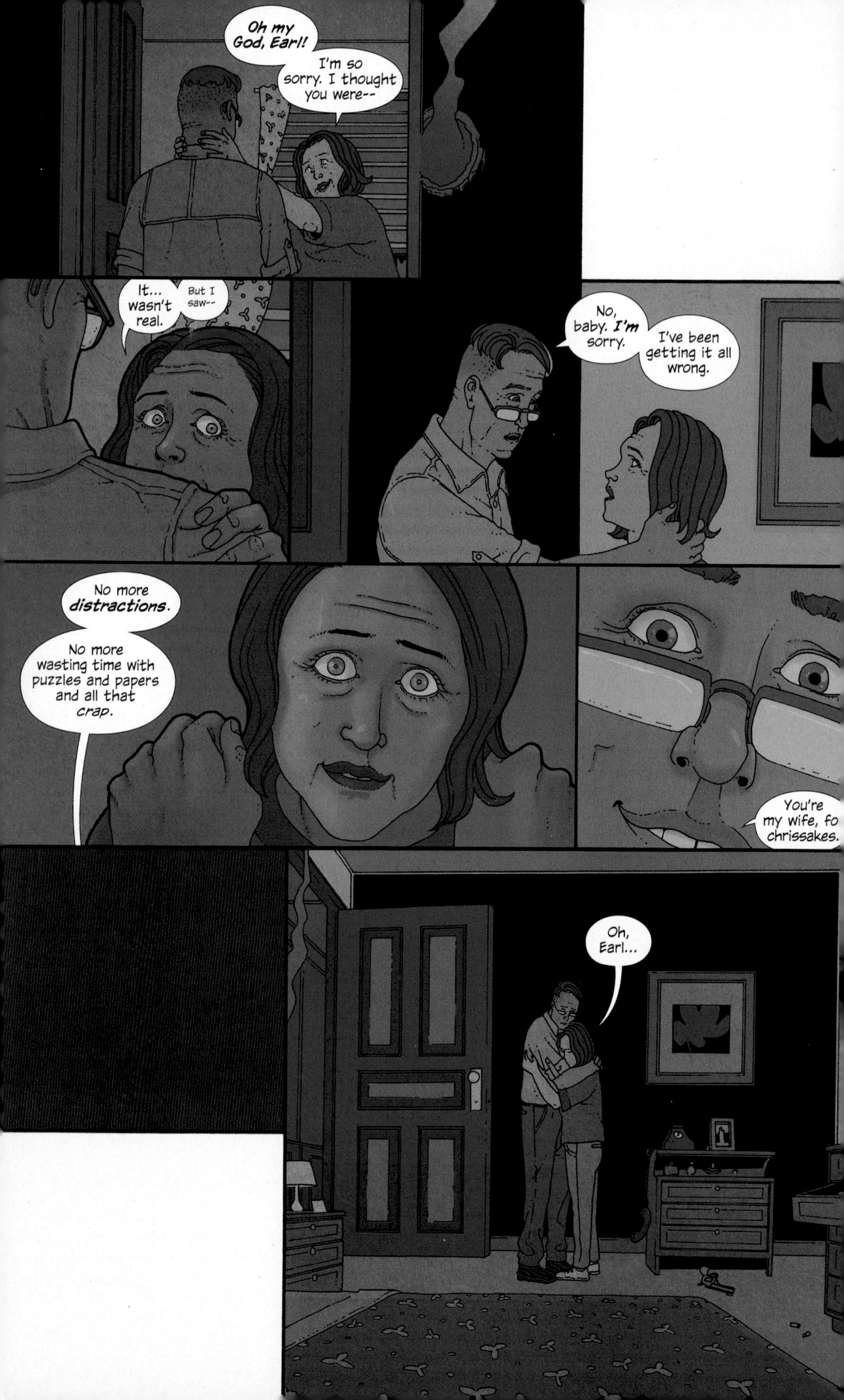
Oh my God, Earl!
I'm so sorry. I thought you were--
It... wasn't real.
But I saw--
No, baby. I'm sorry.
I've been getting it all wrong.
No more distractions.
No more wasting time with puzzles and papers and all that crap.
You're my wife, fo chrissakes.
Oh, Earl...

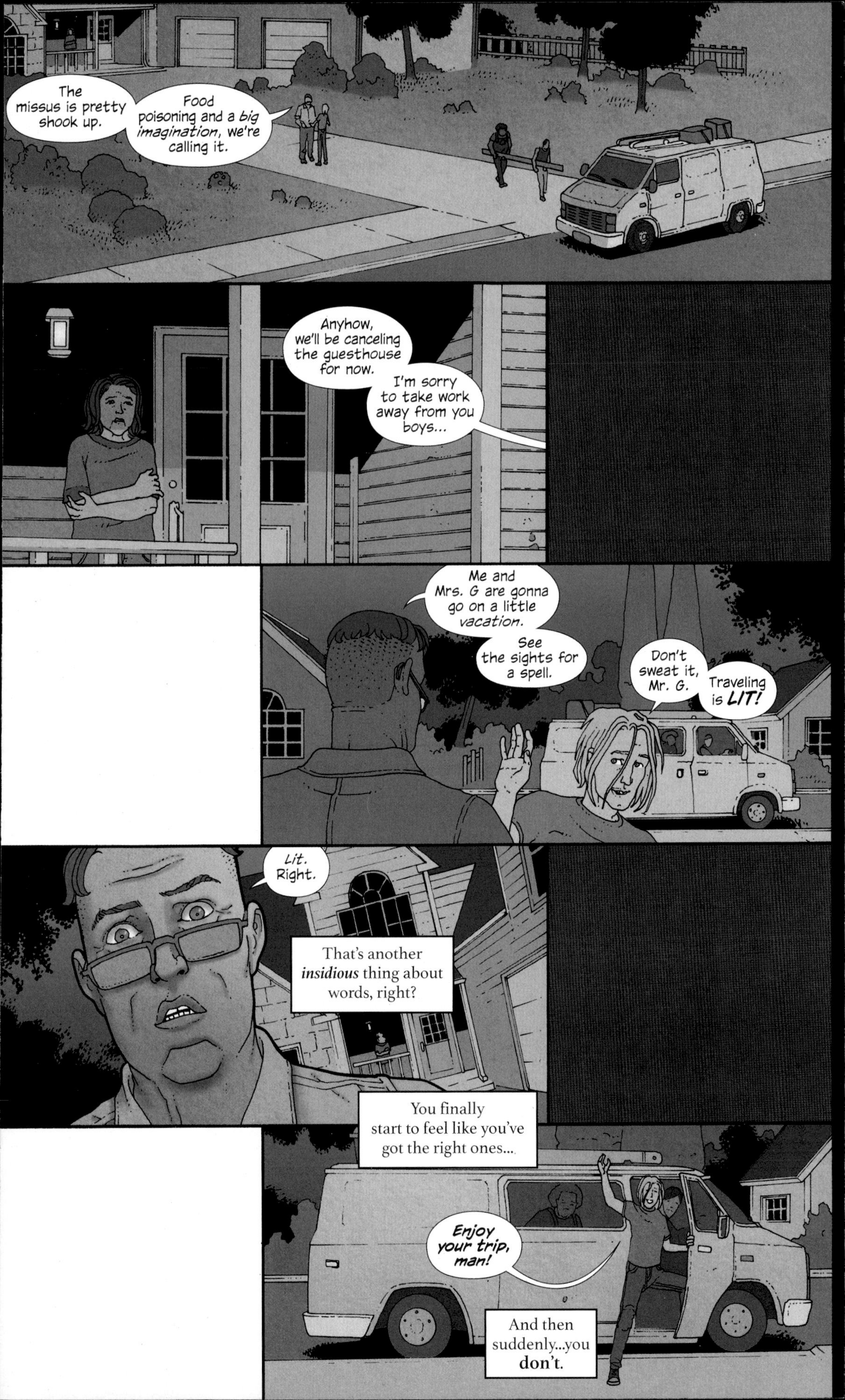

The missus is pretty shook up.
Food poisoning and a *big imagination*, we're calling it.
Anyhow, we'll be canceling the guesthouse for now.
I'm sorry to take work away from you boys...
Me and Mrs. G are gonna go on a little *vacation*.
See the sights for a spell.
Don't sweat it, Mr. G.
Traveling is ***LIT!***
Lit. Right.
That's another *insidious* thing about words, right?
You finally start to feel like you've got the right ones...
Enjoy your trip, man!
And then suddenly...you **don't**.

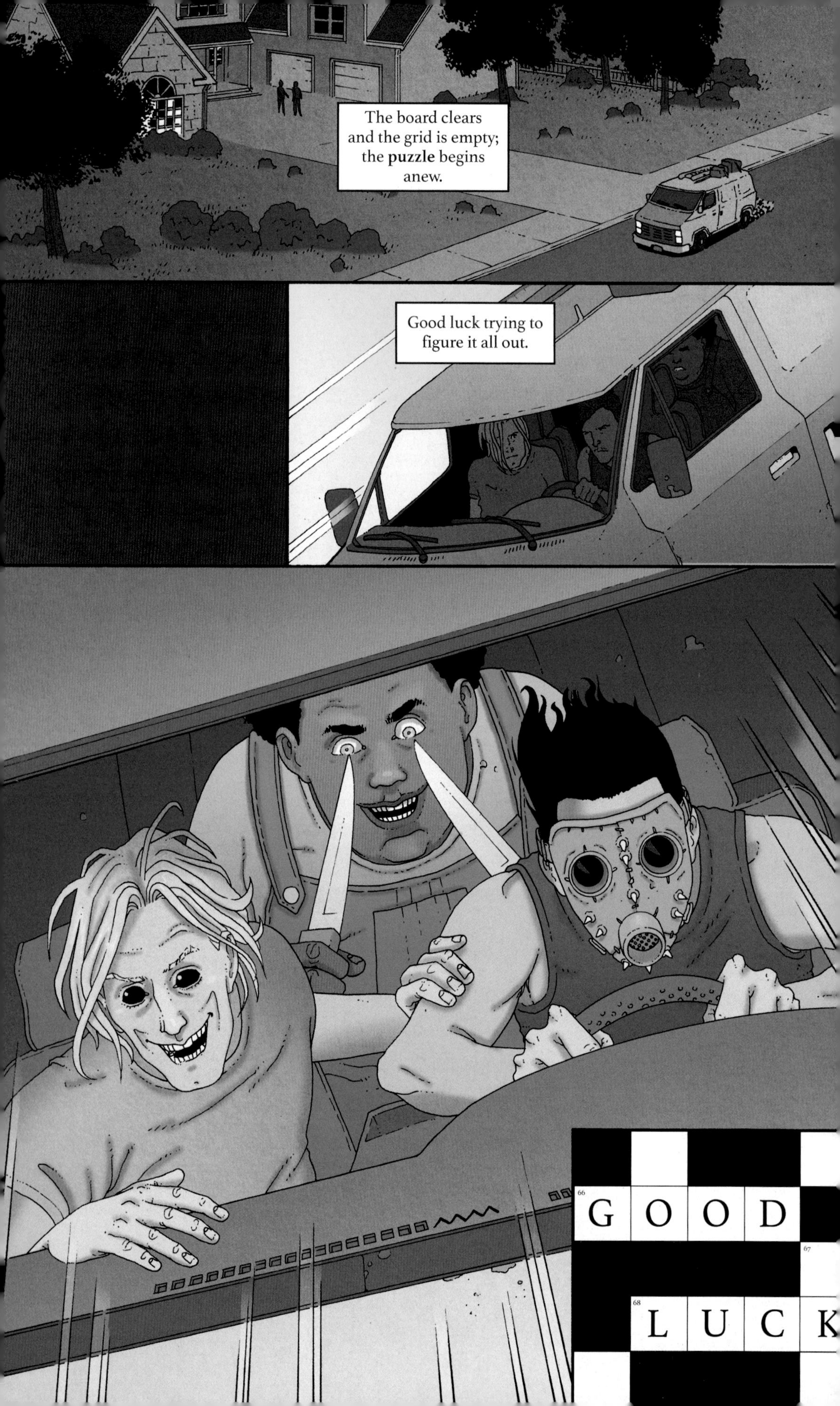
The board clears and the grid is empty; the **puzzle** begins anew.
Good luck trying to figure it all out.
66
GOOD
67
68
LUCK

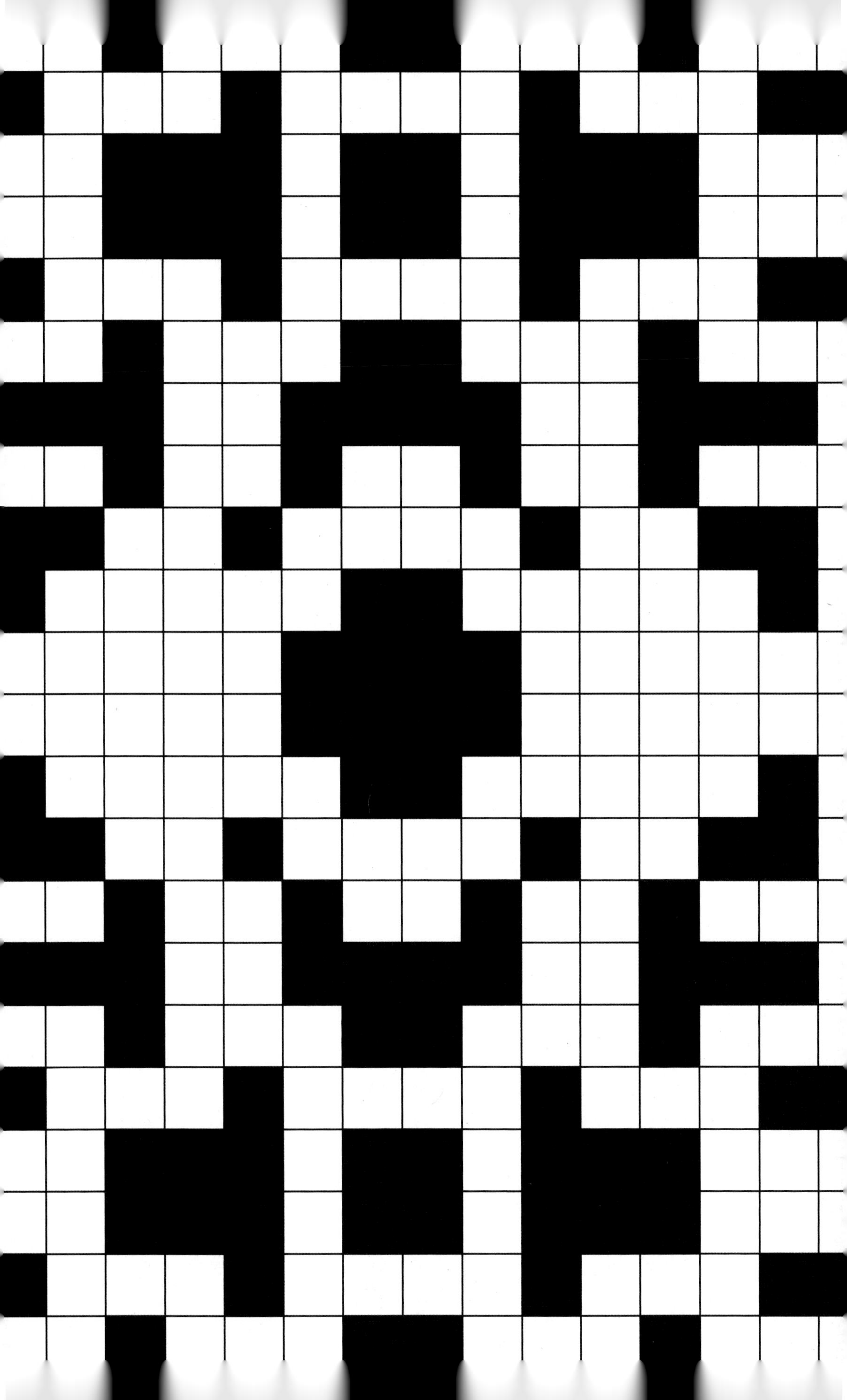

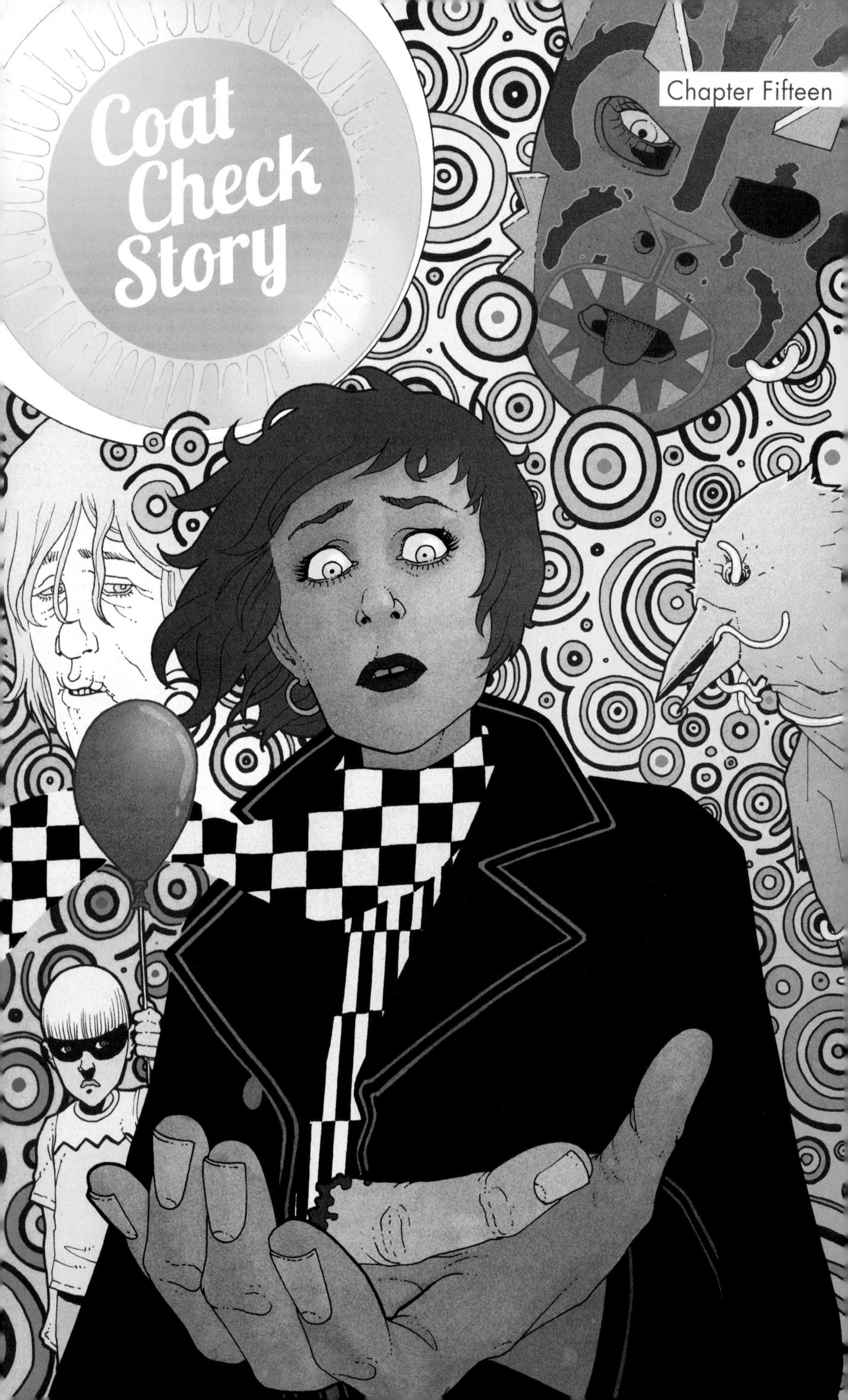
Chapter Fifteen
Coat Check Story

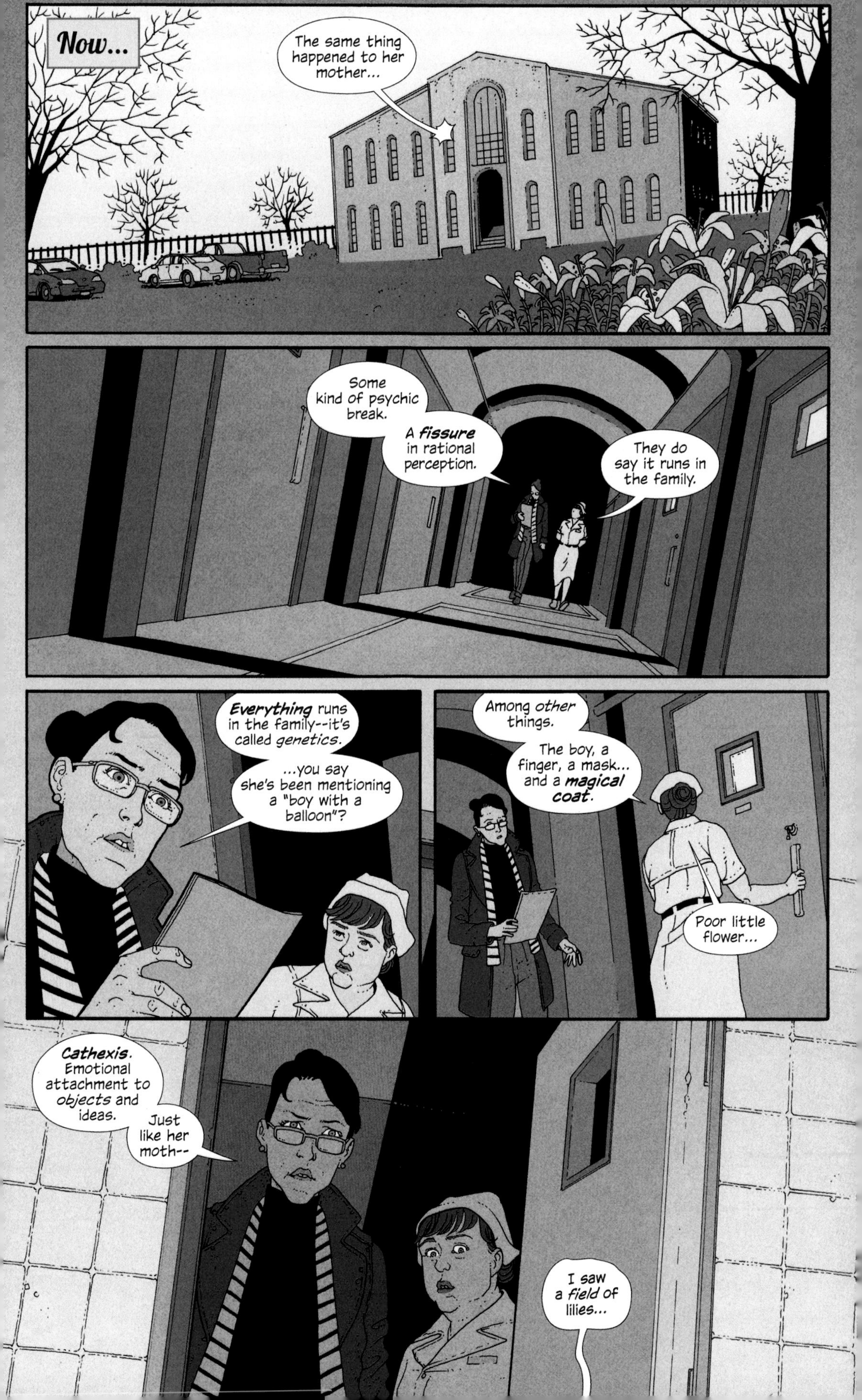

Now...
The same thing happened to her mother...
Some kind of psychic break.
A *fissure* in rational perception.
They do say it runs in the family.
Everything runs in the family--it's called *genetics*.
...you say she's been mentioning a "boy with a balloon"?
Among *other* things.
The boy, a finger, a mask... and a *magical coat*.
Poor little flower...
Cathexis. Emotional attachment to *objects* and ideas.
Just like her moth--
I saw a *field* of lilies...

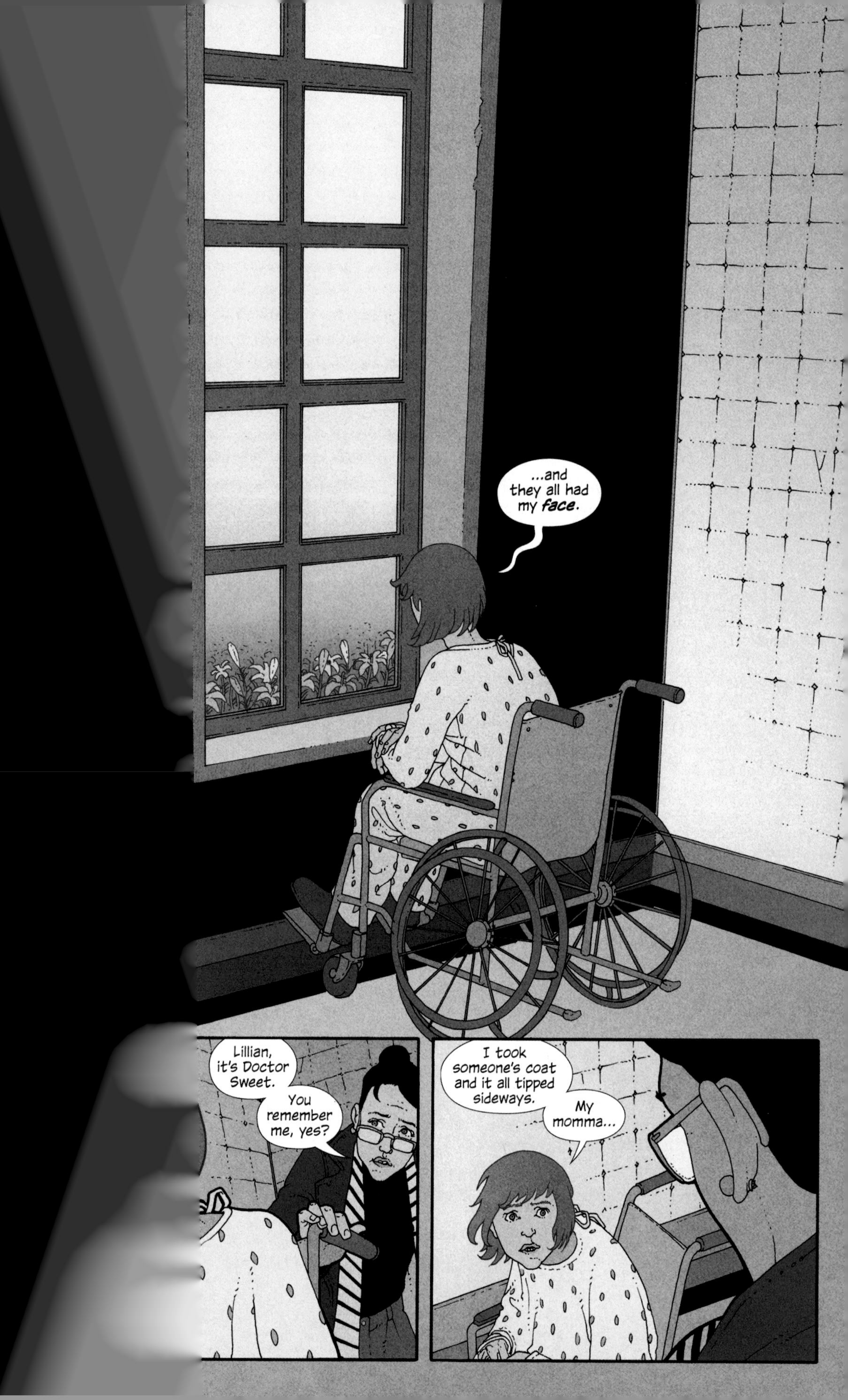
...and they all had my *face*.
Lillian, it's Doctor Sweet.
You remember me, yes?
I took someone's coat and it all tipped sideways.
My momma...

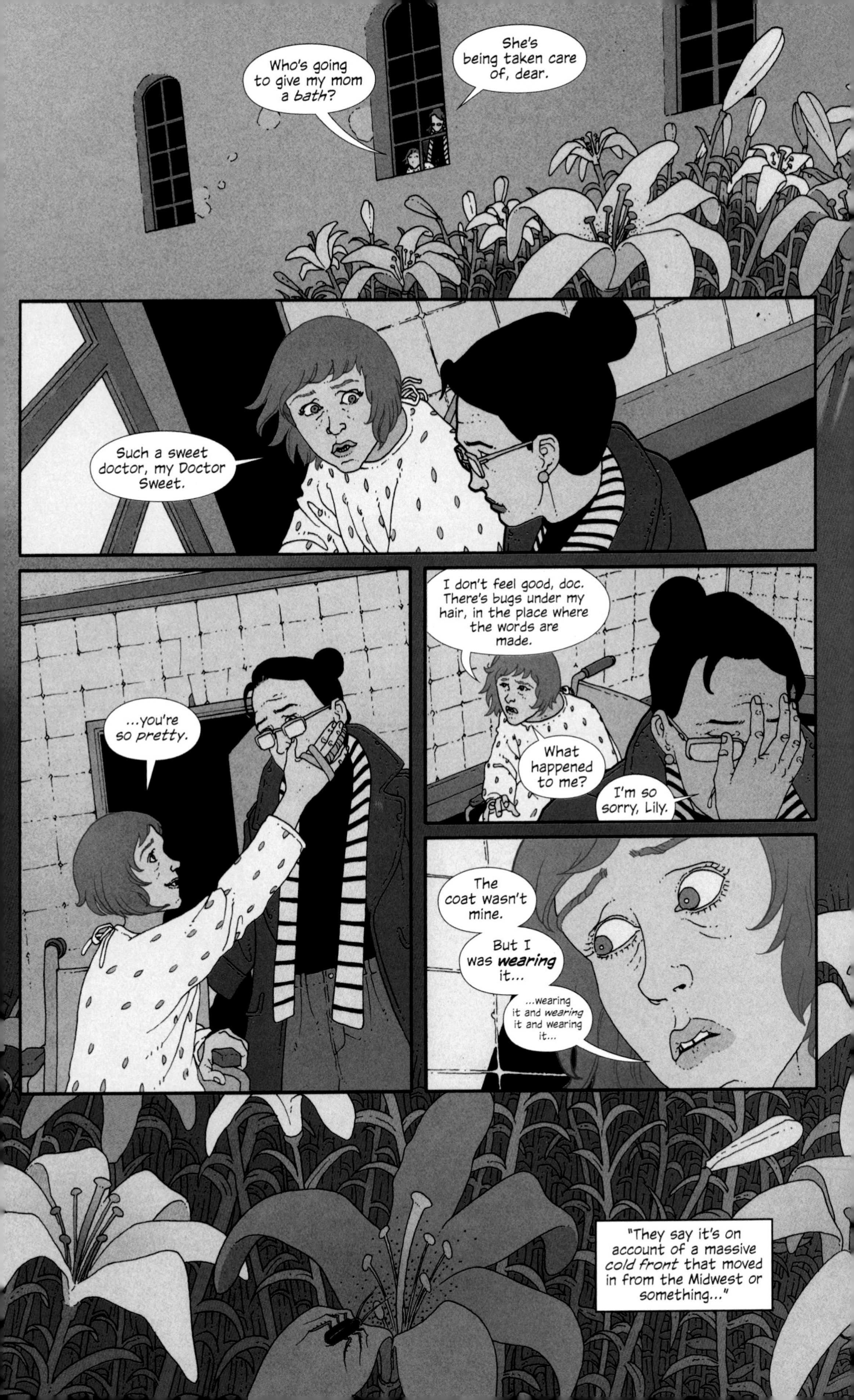
Who's going to give my mom a *bath*?
She's being taken care of, dear.
Such a sweet doctor, my Doctor Sweet.
...you're so *pretty*.
I don't feel good, doc. There's bugs under my hair, in the place where the words are made.
What happened to me?
I'm so sorry, Lily.
The coat wasn't mine.
But I was ***wearing*** it...
...wearing it and *wearing* it and wearing it...
"They say it's on account of a massive *cold front* that moved in from the Midwest or something..."

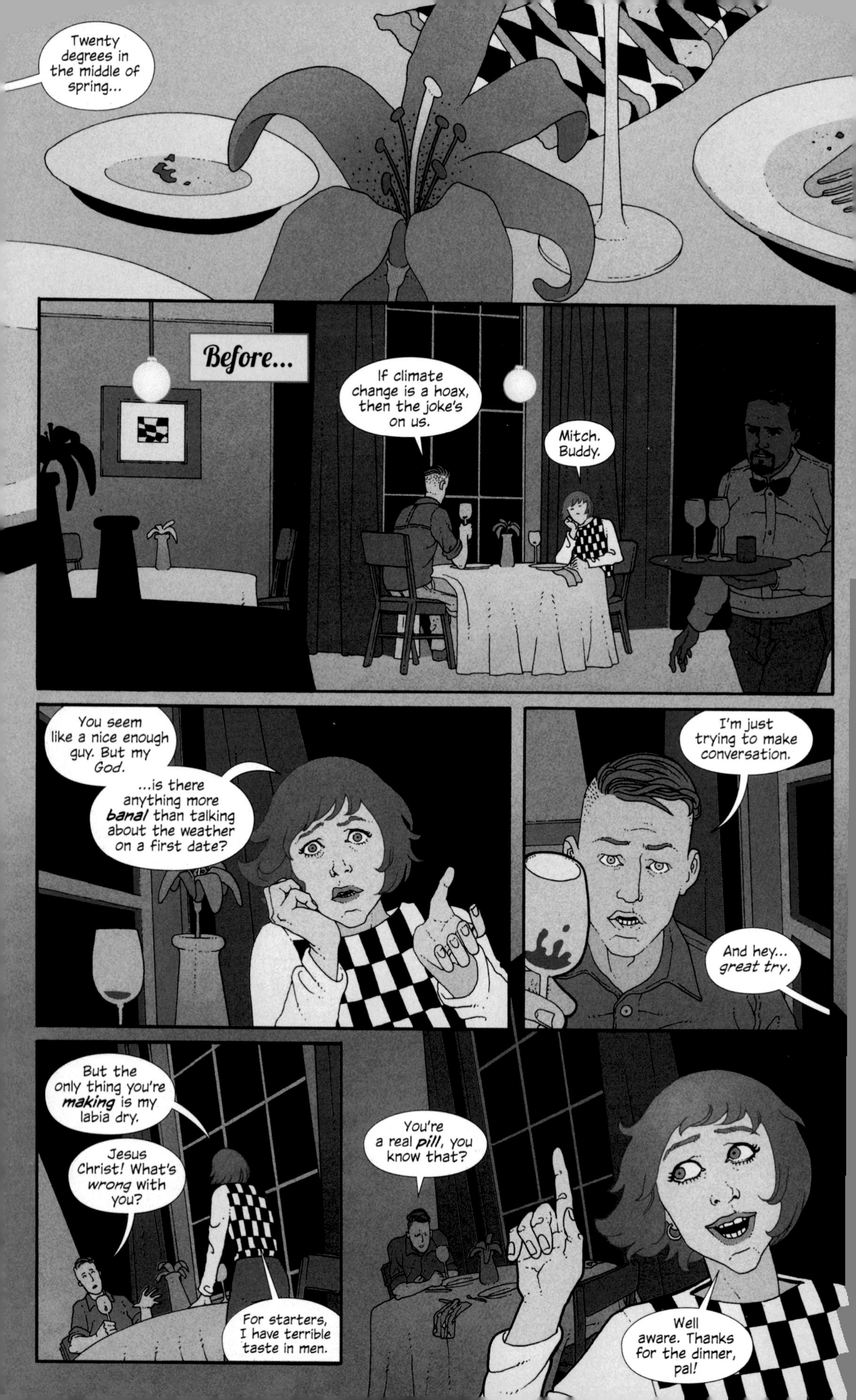
Twenty degrees in the middle of spring...
Before...
If climate change is a hoax, then the joke's on us.
Mitch. Buddy.
You seem like a nice enough guy. But my *God.*
...is there anything more ***banal*** than talking about the weather on a first date?
I'm just trying to make conversation.
And hey... *great try.*
But the only thing you're ***making*** is my labia dry.
Jesus Christ! What's *wrong* with you?
For starters, I have terrible taste in men.
You're a real ***pill***, you know that?
Well aware. Thanks for the dinner, pal!

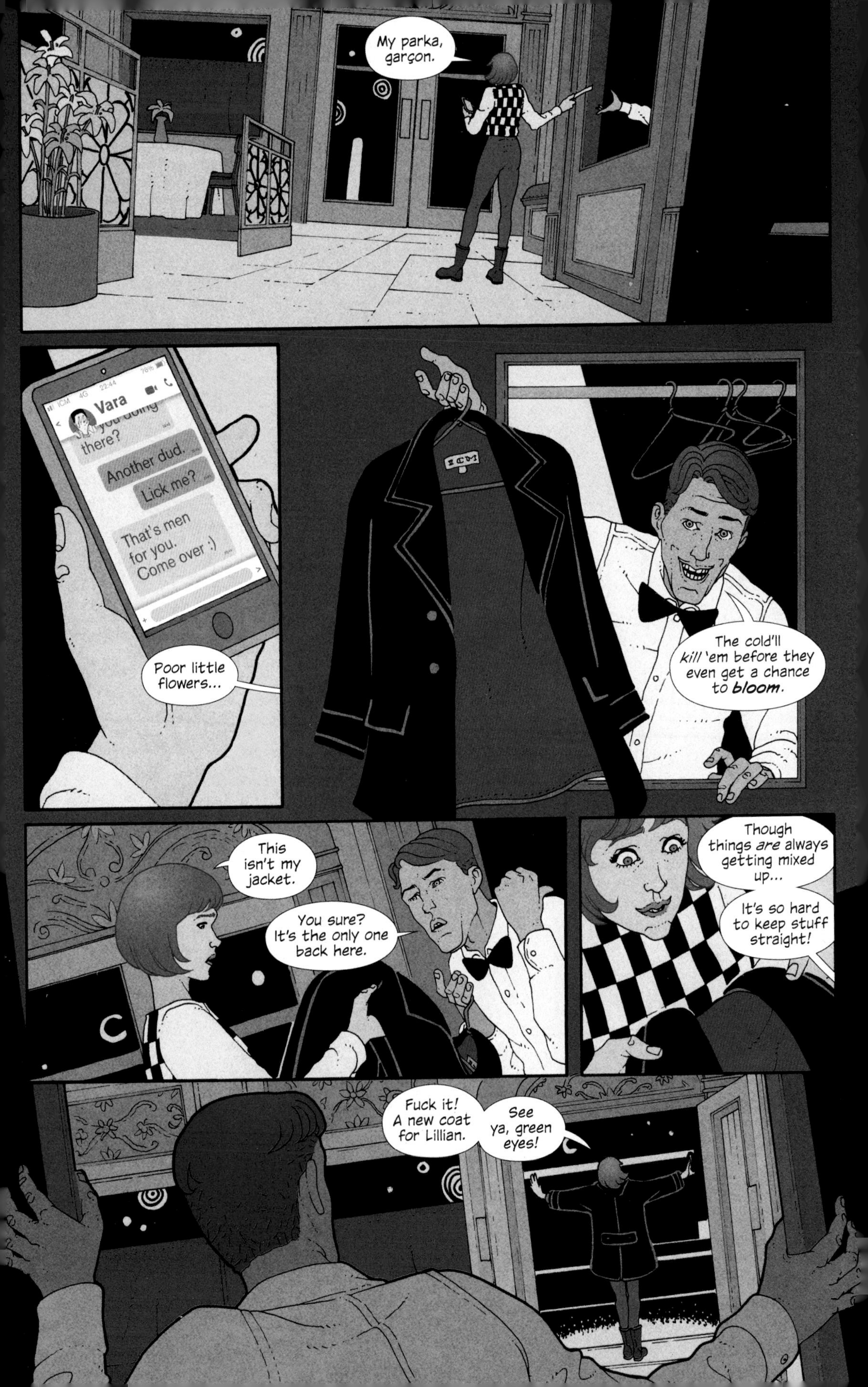
My parka, garçon.
Vara
there?
Another dud.
Lick me?
That's men for you. Come over :)
Poor little flowers...
The cold'll *kill* 'em before they even get a chance to ***bloom***.
This isn't my jacket.
You sure? It's the only one back here.
Though things *are* always getting mixed up...
It's so hard to keep stuff straight!
Fuck it! A new coat for Lillian.
See ya, green eyes!

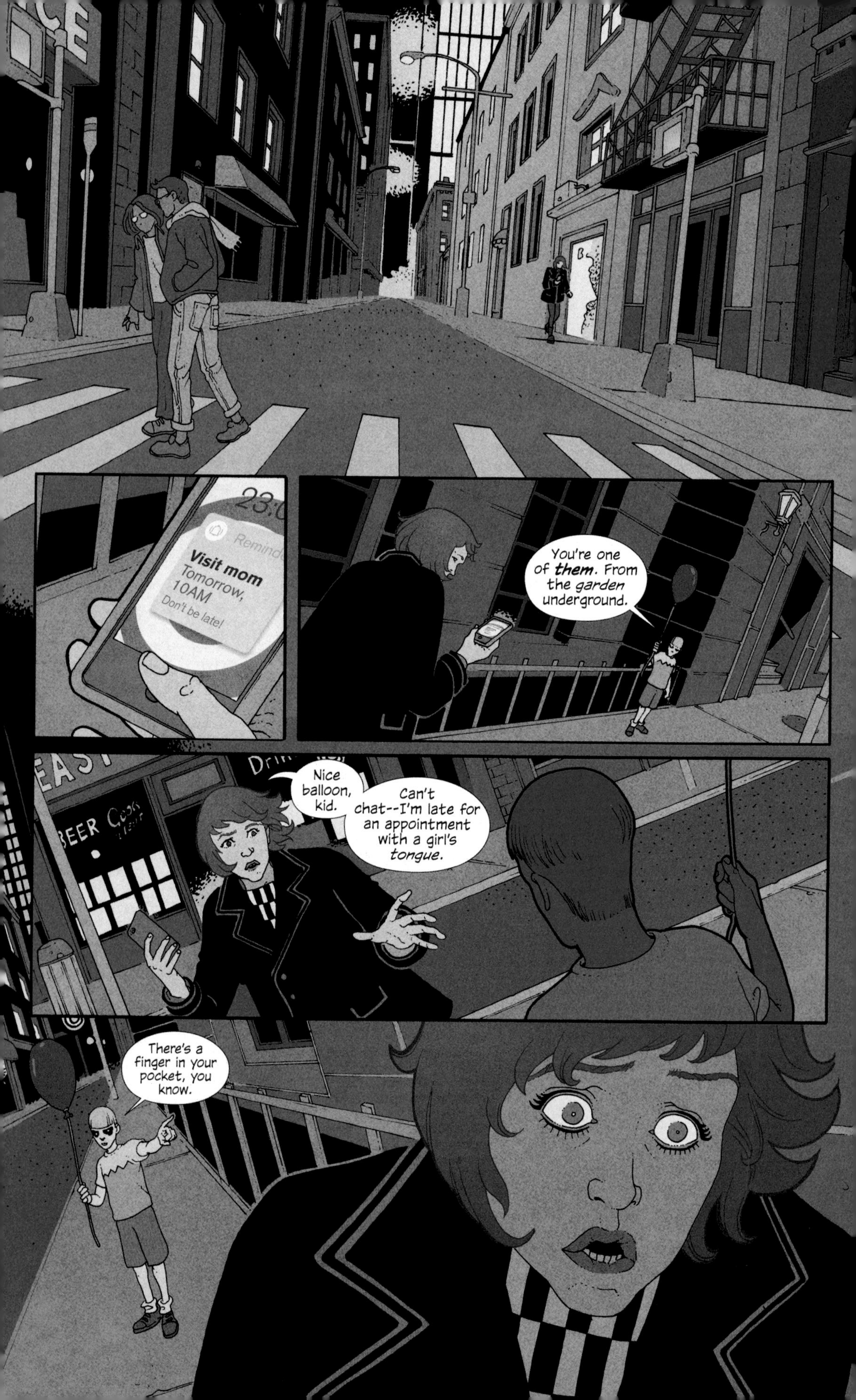
Visit mom
Tomorrow, 10AM
Don't be late!
You're one of **them**. From the *garden* underground.
Nice balloon, kid.
Can't chat--I'm late for an appointment with a girl's *tongue*.
There's a finger in your pocket, you know.

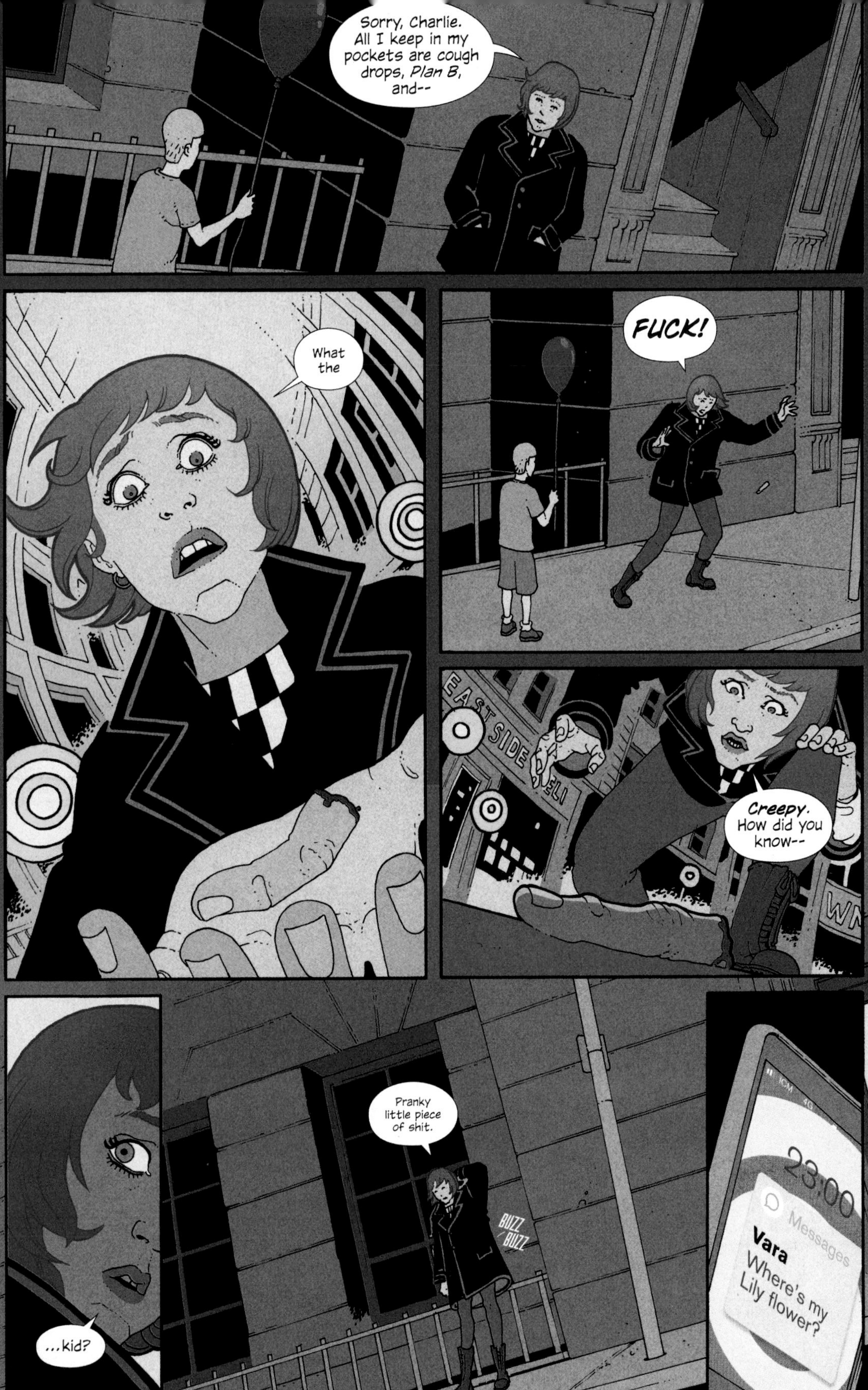
Sorry, Charlie. All I keep in my pockets are cough drops, *Plan B*, and--
What the
FUCK!
Creepy. How did you know--
EAST SIDE DELI
...kid?
Pranky little piece of shit.
BUZZ BUZZ
23:00
Messages
Vara
Where's my Lily flower?

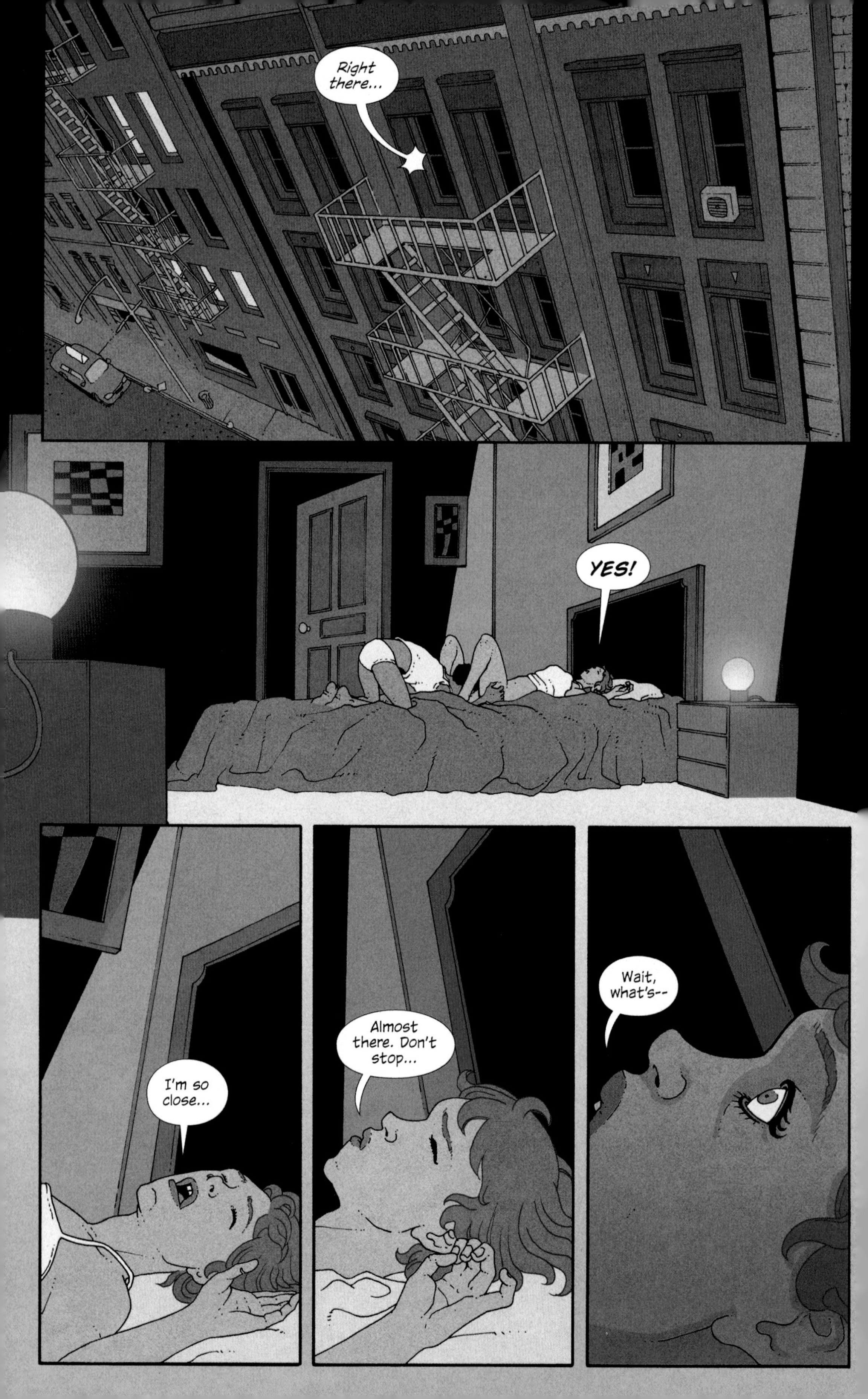
Right there...
YES!
I'm so close...
Almost there. Don't stop...
Wait, what's--

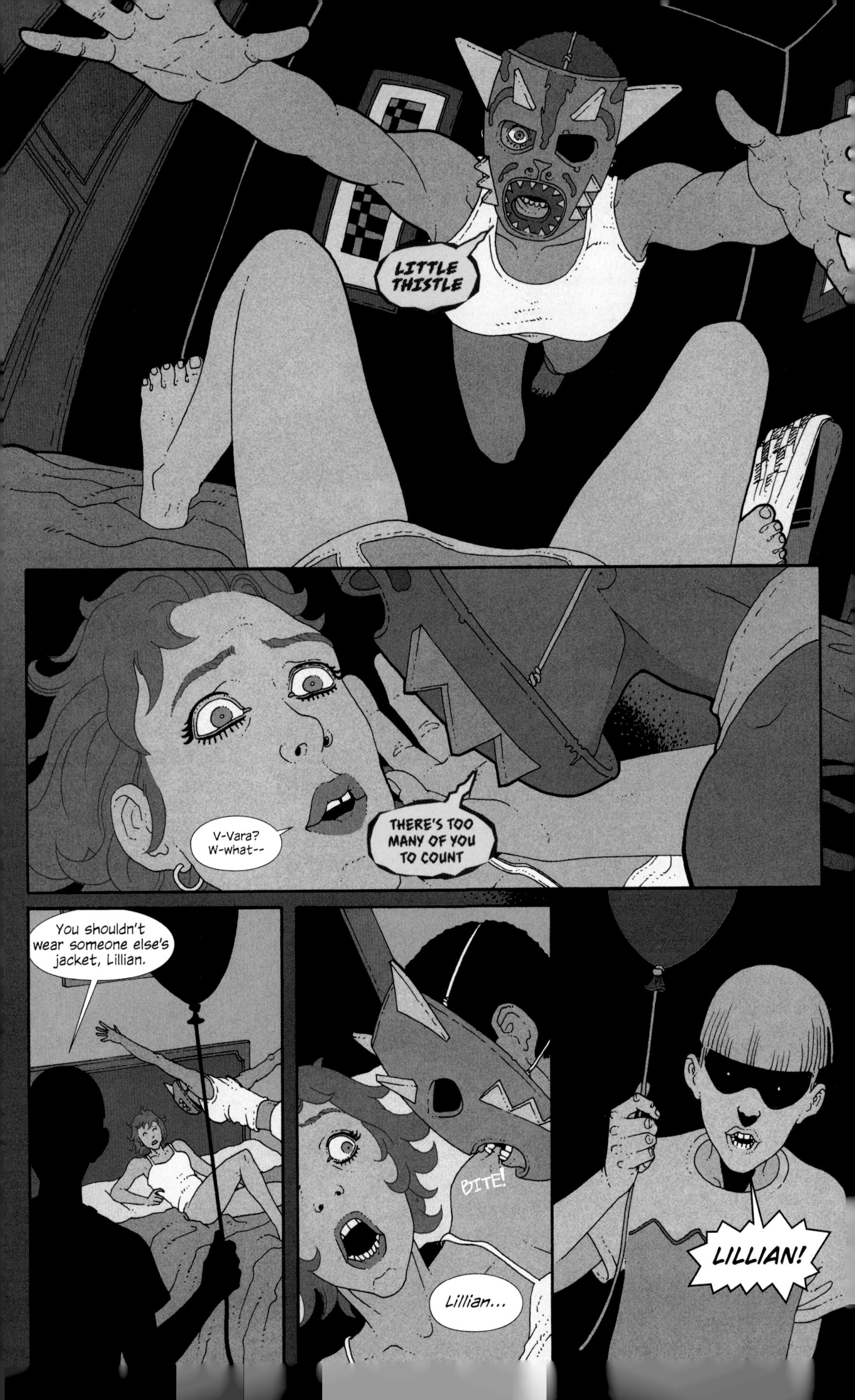
LITTLE THISTLE
V-Vara? W-what--
THERE'S TOO MANY OF YOU TO COUNT
You shouldn't wear someone else's jacket, Lillian.
BITE!
Lillian...
LILLIAN!

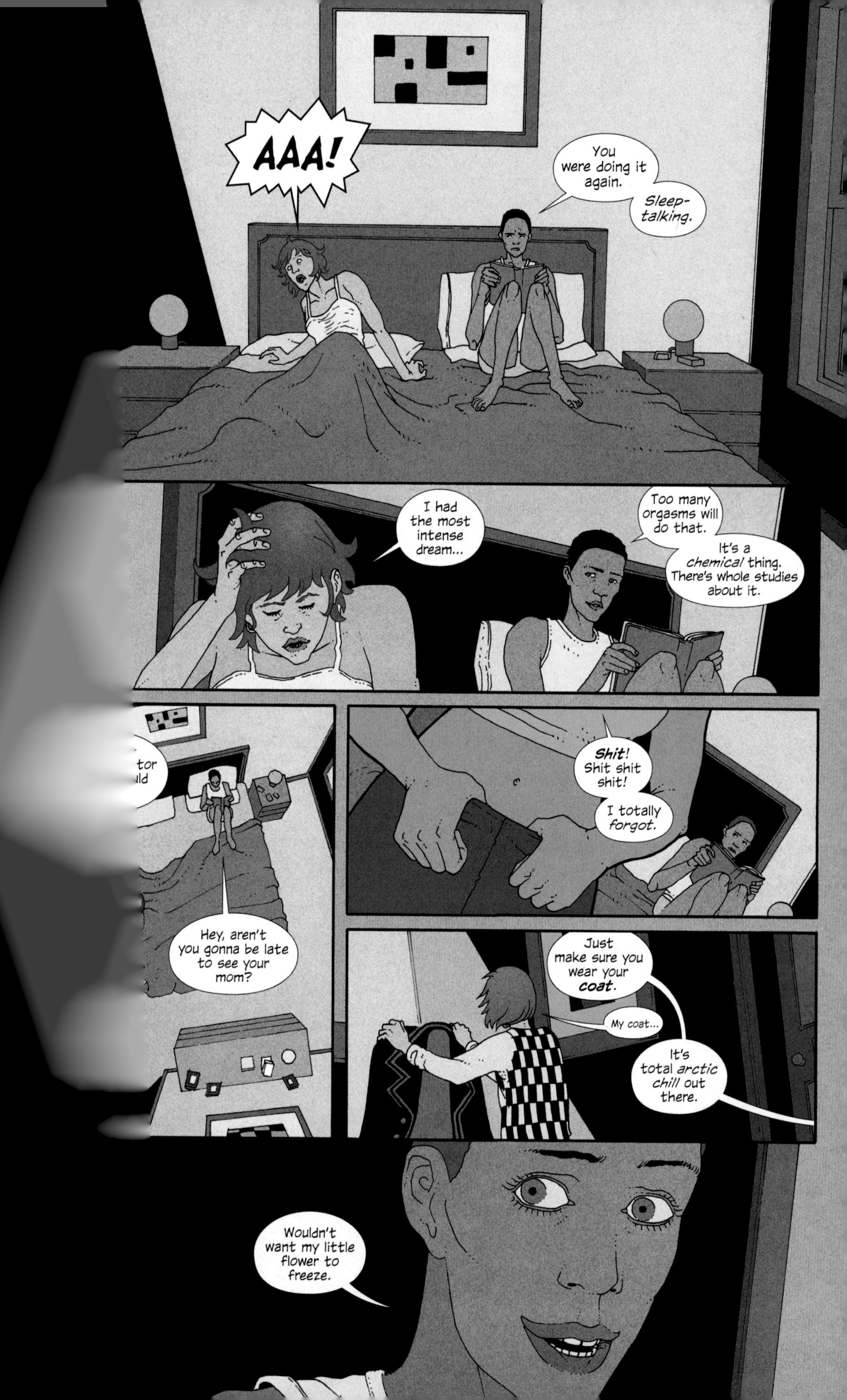
AAA!
You were doing it again.
Sleep-talking.
I had the most intense dream...
Too many orgasms will do that.
It's a *chemical* thing. There's whole studies about it.
Hey, aren't you gonna be late to see your mom?
Shit! Shit shit *shit!*
I totally *forgot.*
Just make sure you wear your ***coat***.
My coat...
It's total *arctic chill* out there.
Wouldn't want my little flower to freeze.

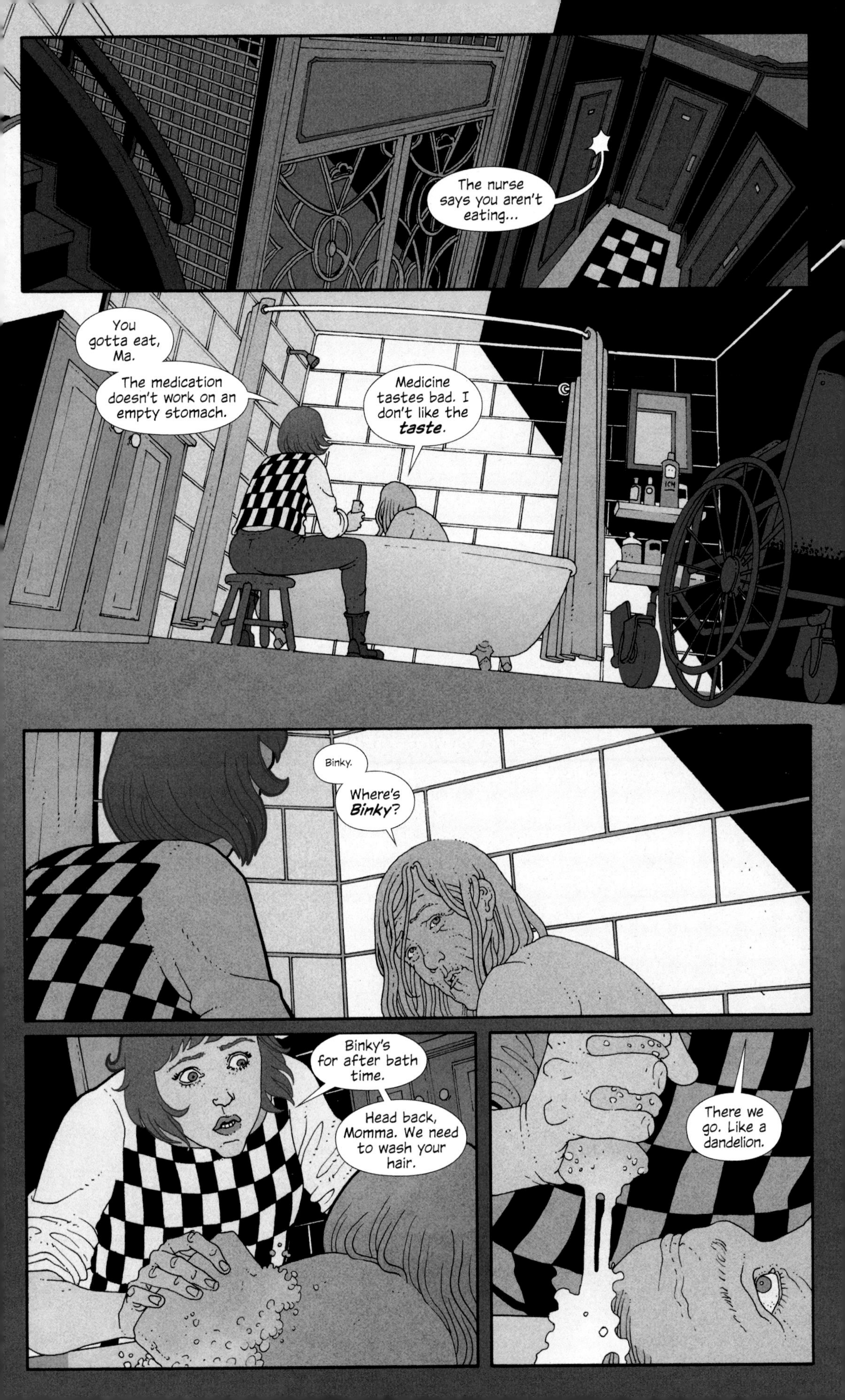
The nurse says you aren't eating...
You gotta eat, Ma.
The medication doesn't work on an empty stomach.
Medicine tastes bad. I don't like the *taste*.
Binky.
Where's *Binky*?
Binky's for after bath time.
Head back, Momma. We need to wash your hair.
There we go. Like a dandelion.

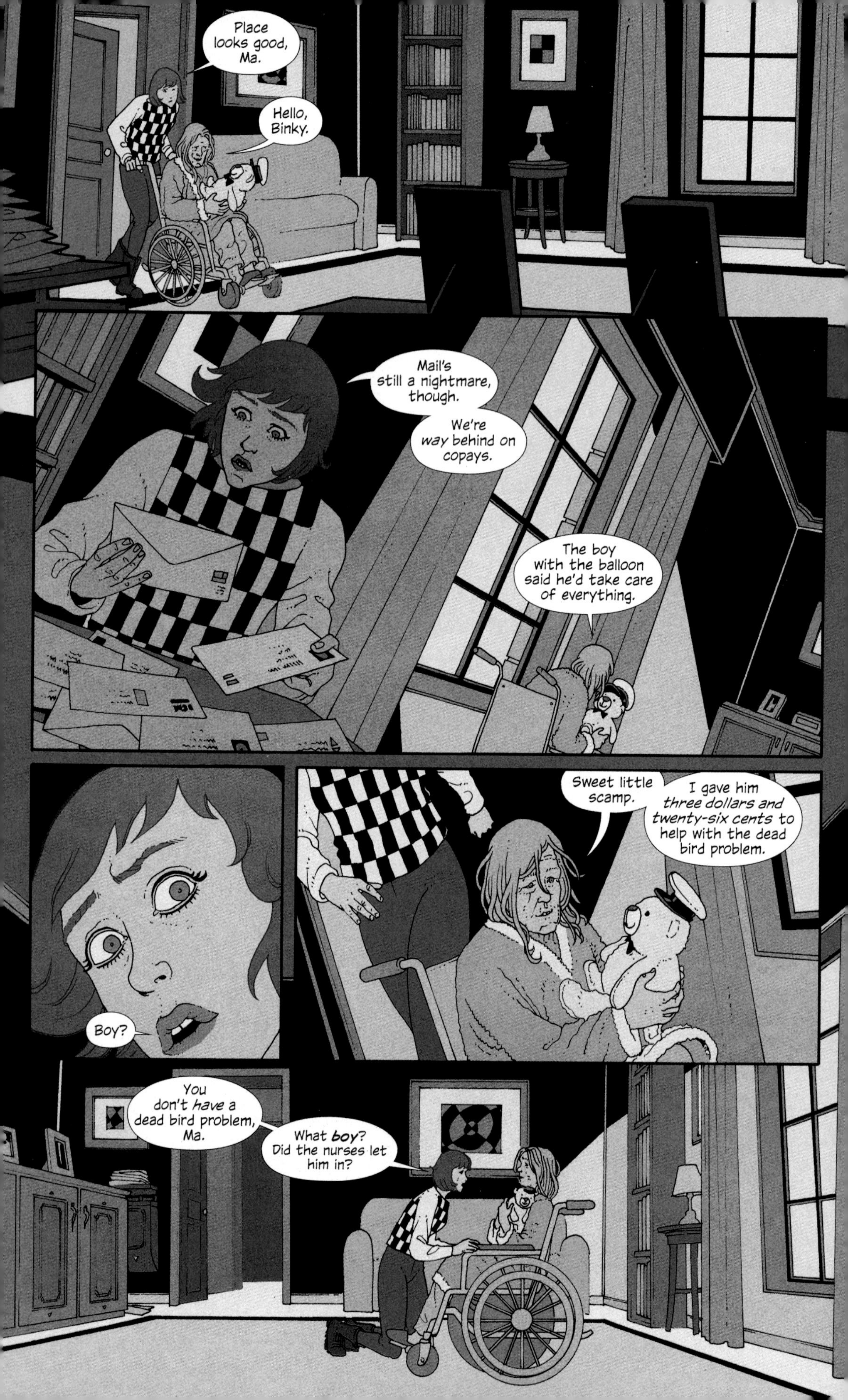
Place looks good, Ma.
Hello, Binky.
Mail's still a nightmare, though.
We're *way* behind on copays.
The boy with the balloon said he'd take care of everything.
Boy?
Sweet little scamp.
I gave him *three dollars and twenty-six cents* to help with the dead bird problem.
You don't *have* a dead bird problem, Ma.
What *boy*? Did the nurses let him in?

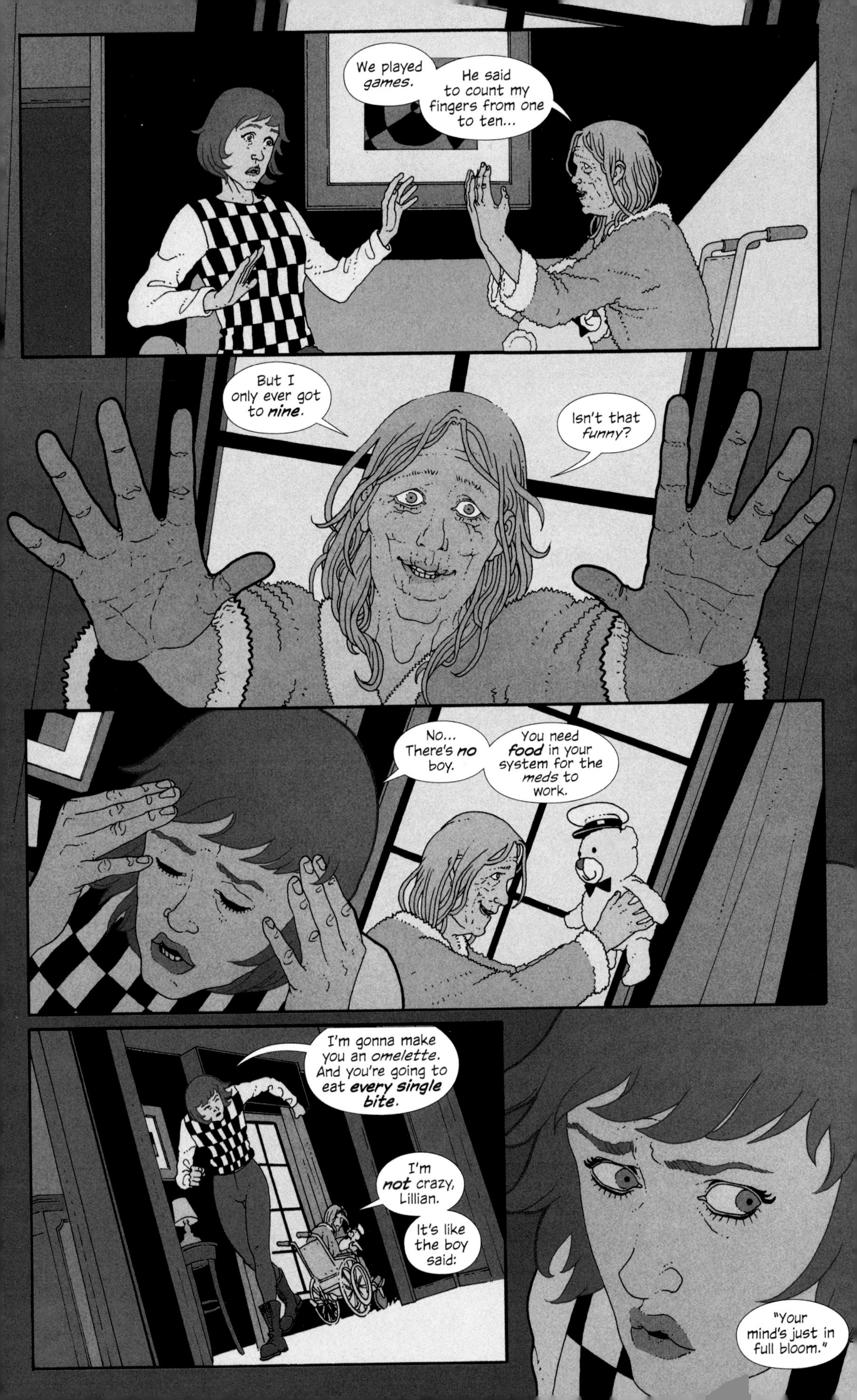
We played *games.*
He said to count my fingers from one to ten...
But I only ever got to ***nine.***
Isn't that *funny?*
No... There's ***no*** boy.
You need ***food*** in your system for the *meds* to work.
I'm gonna make you an *omelette.* And you're going to eat ***every single bite.***
I'm ***not*** crazy, Lillian.
It's like the boy said:
"Your mind's just in full bloom."

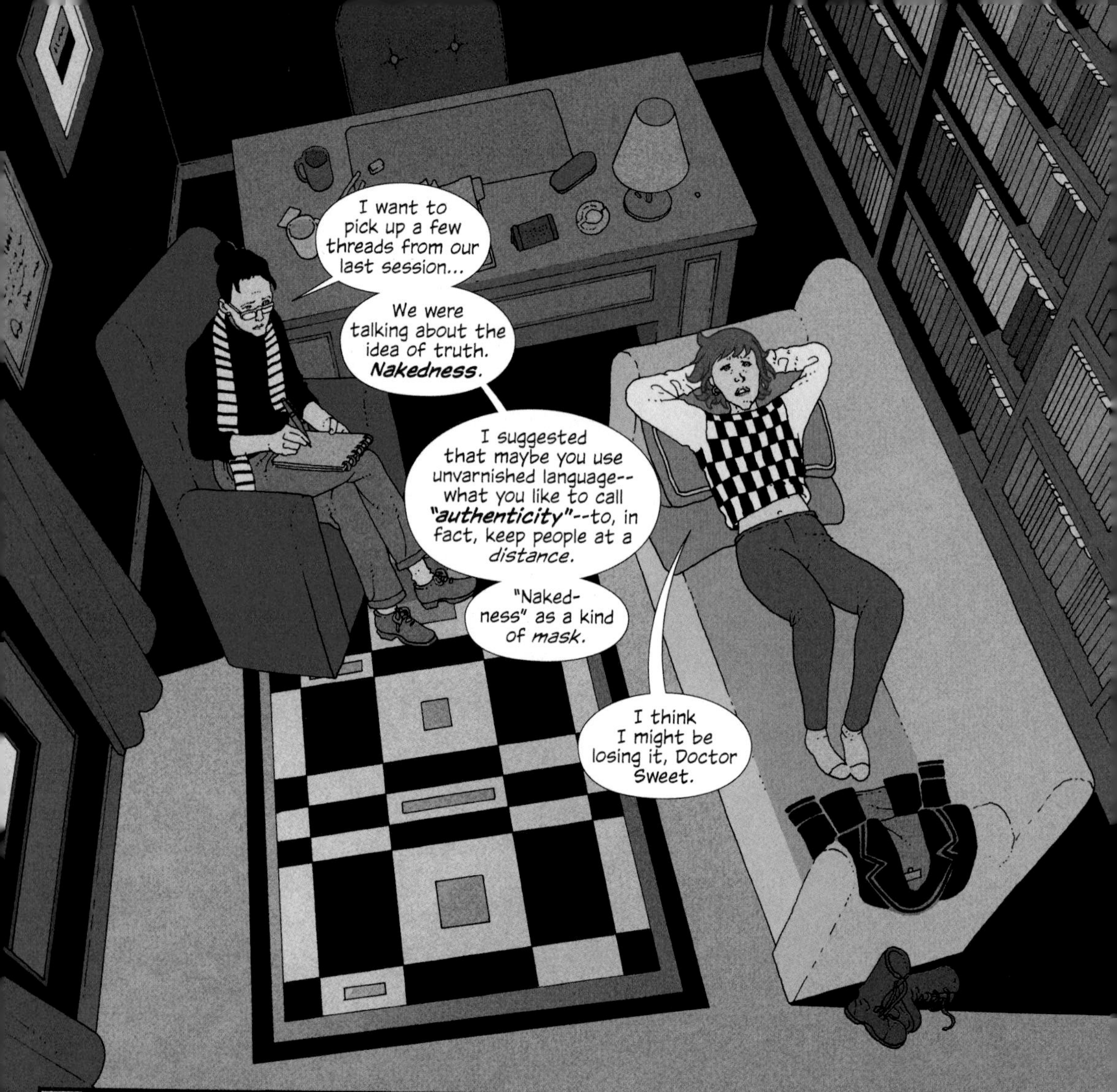
I want to pick up a few threads from our last session...
We were talking about the idea of truth. ***Nakedness***.
I suggested that maybe you use unvarnished language--what you like to call ***"authenticity"***--to, in fact, keep people at a *distance*.
"Nakedness" as a kind of *mask*.
I think I might be losing it, Doctor Sweet.
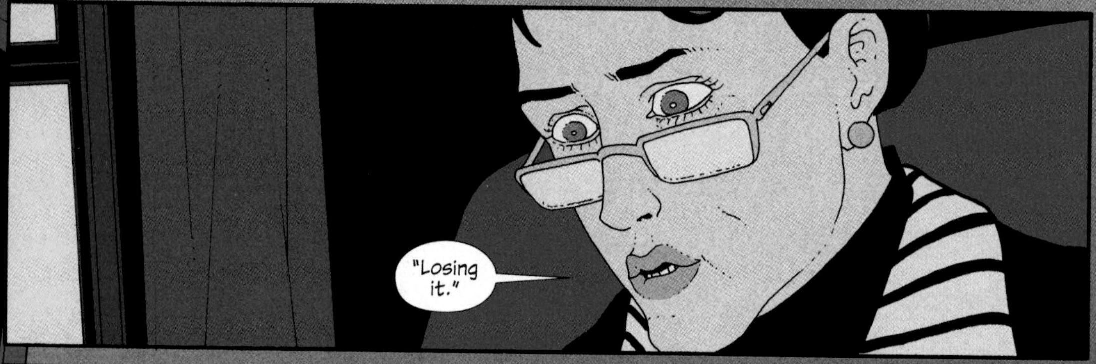
"Losing it."
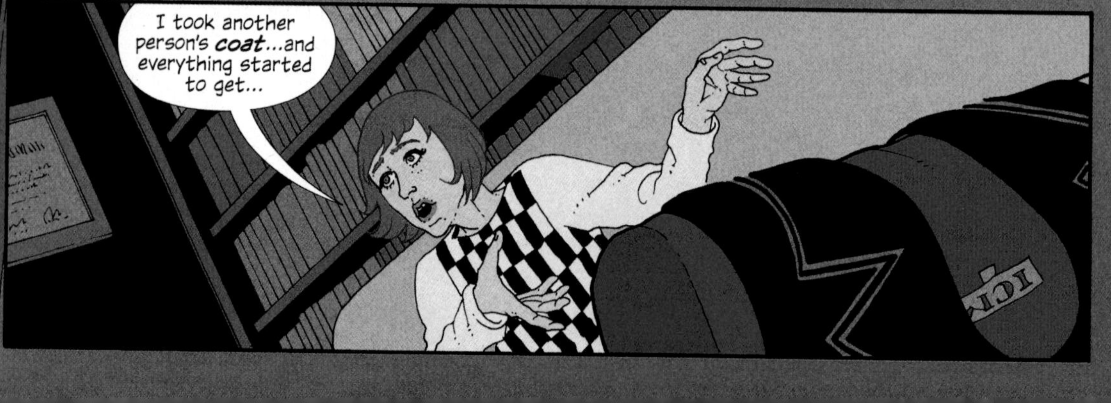
I took another person's ***coat***...and everything started to get...

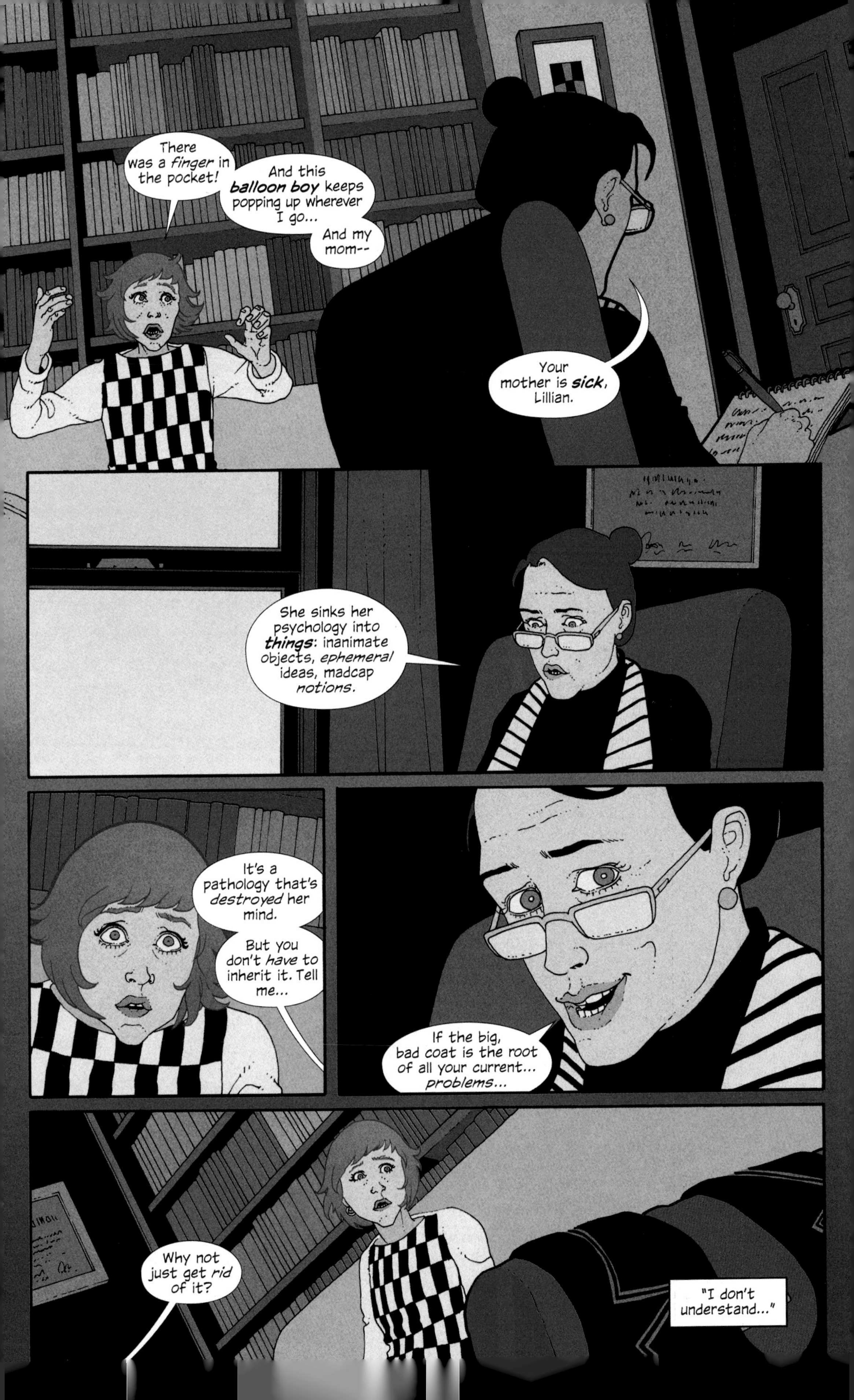

There was a *finger* in the pocket!
And this **balloon boy** keeps popping up wherever I go...
And my mom--
Your mother is **sick**, Lillian.
She sinks her psychology into ***things***: inanimate objects, *ephemeral* ideas, madcap *notions.*
It's a pathology that's *destroyed* her mind.
But you don't *have* to inherit it. Tell me...
If the big, bad coat is the root of all your current... *problems*...
Why not just get *rid* of it?
"I don't understand..."

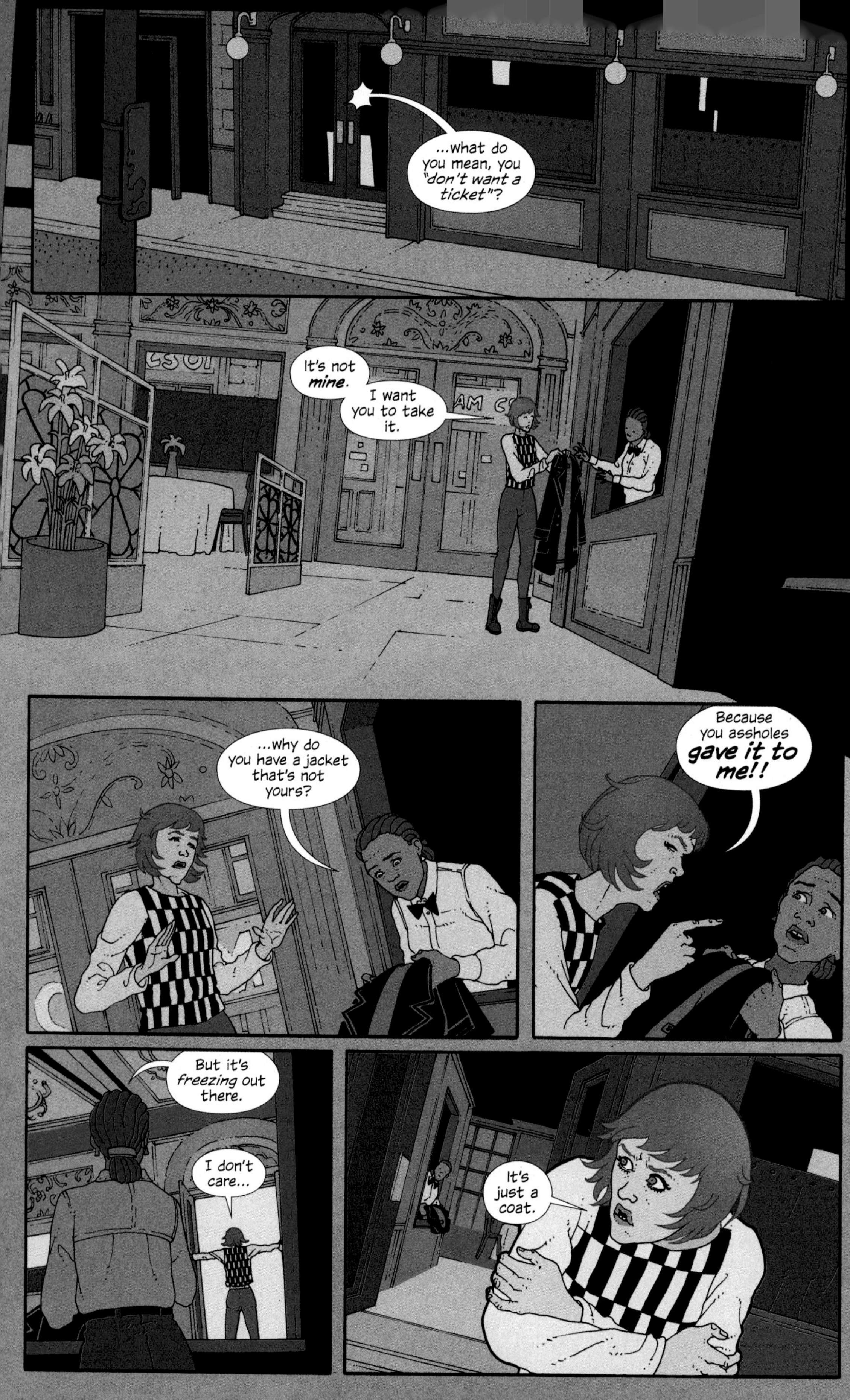
...what do you mean, you *"don't want a ticket"*?
It's not ***mine.***
I want you to take it.
...why do you have a jacket that's not yours?
Because you assholes ***gave it to me!!***
But it's *freezing* out there.
I don't care...
It's just a coat.

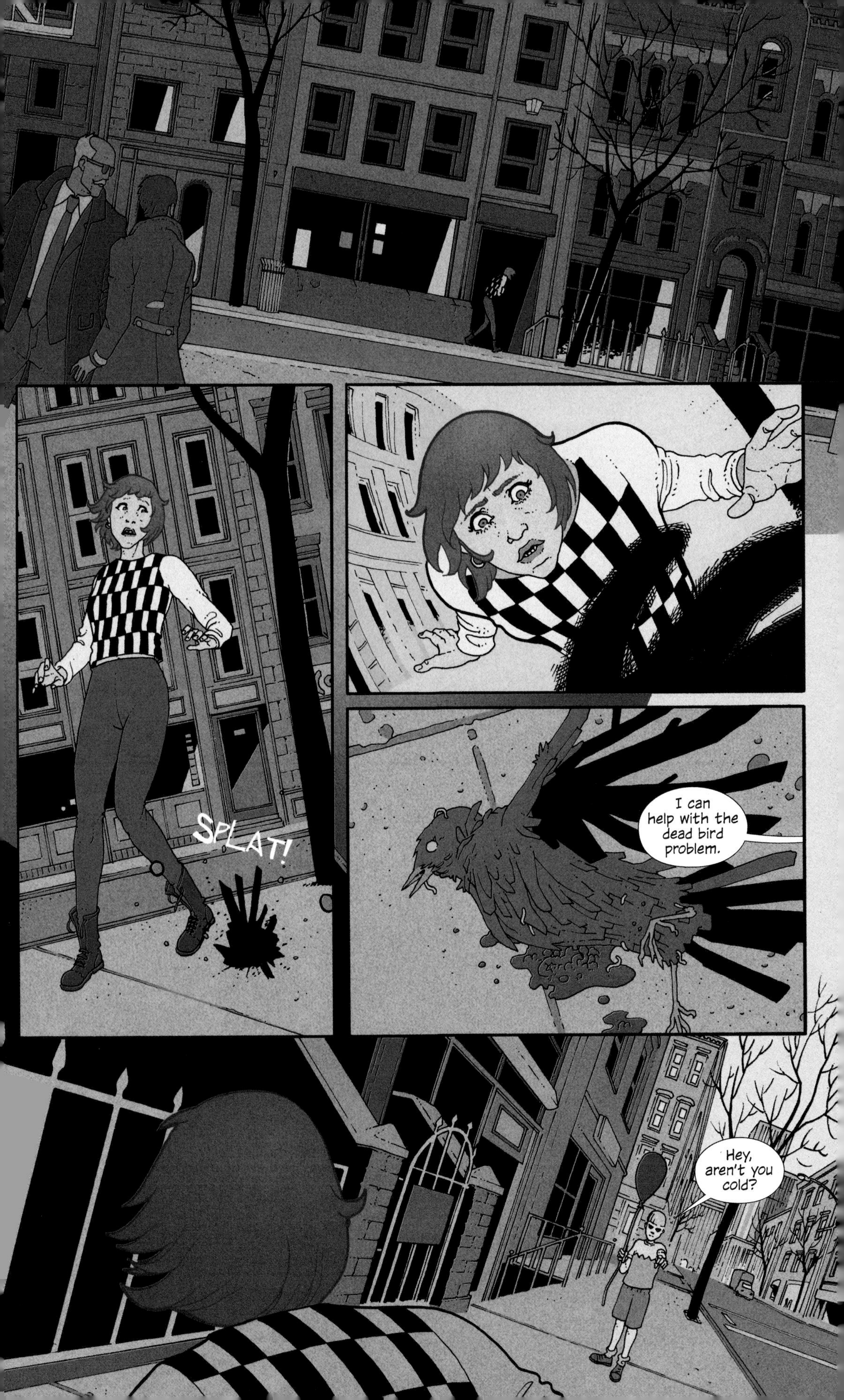
SPLAT!
I can help with the dead bird problem.
Hey, aren't you cold?

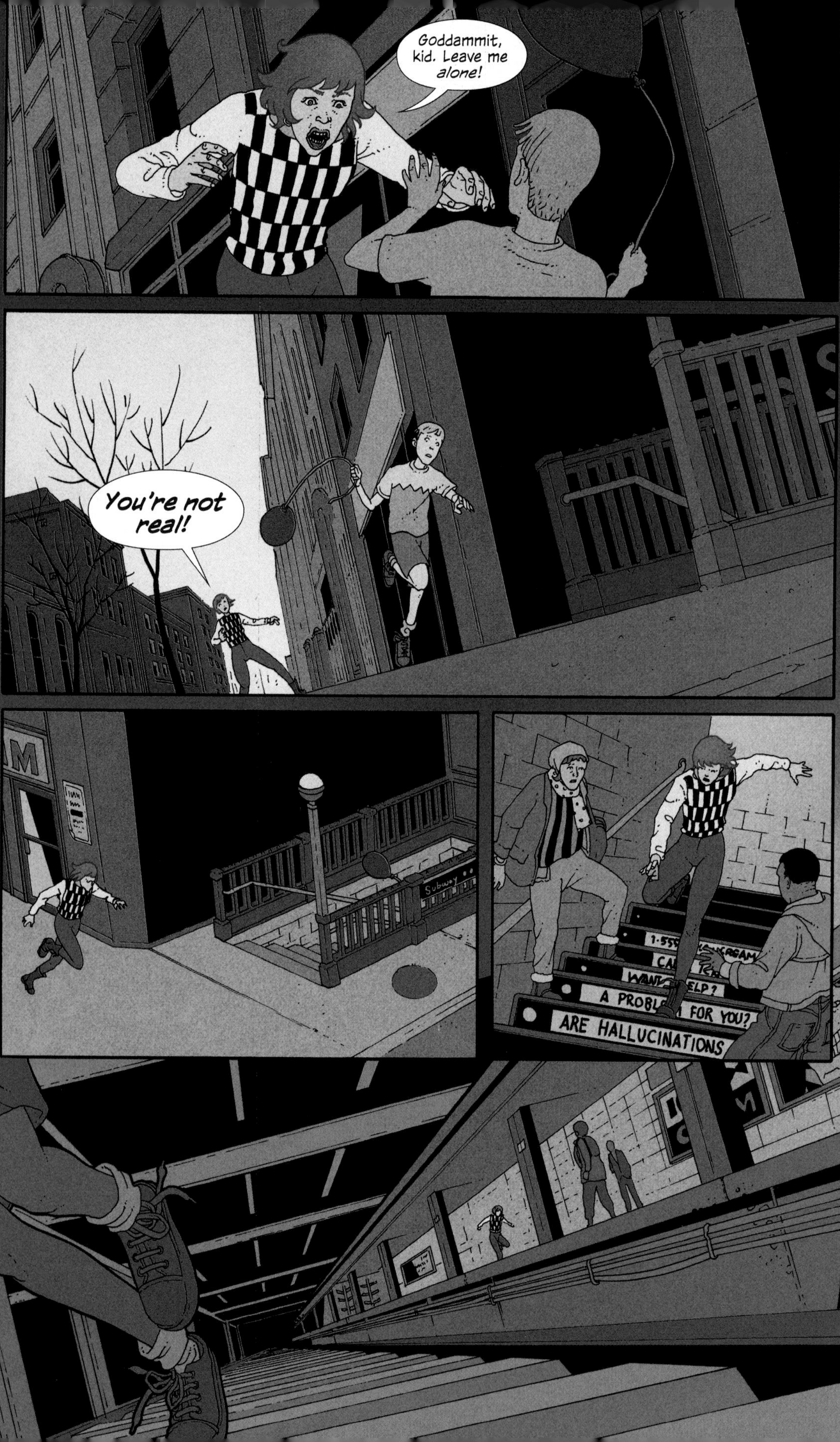
Goddammit, kid. Leave me *alone!*
You're not real!
Subway
ARE HALLUCINATIONS
A PROBL
FOR YOU?
ELP?
1-555

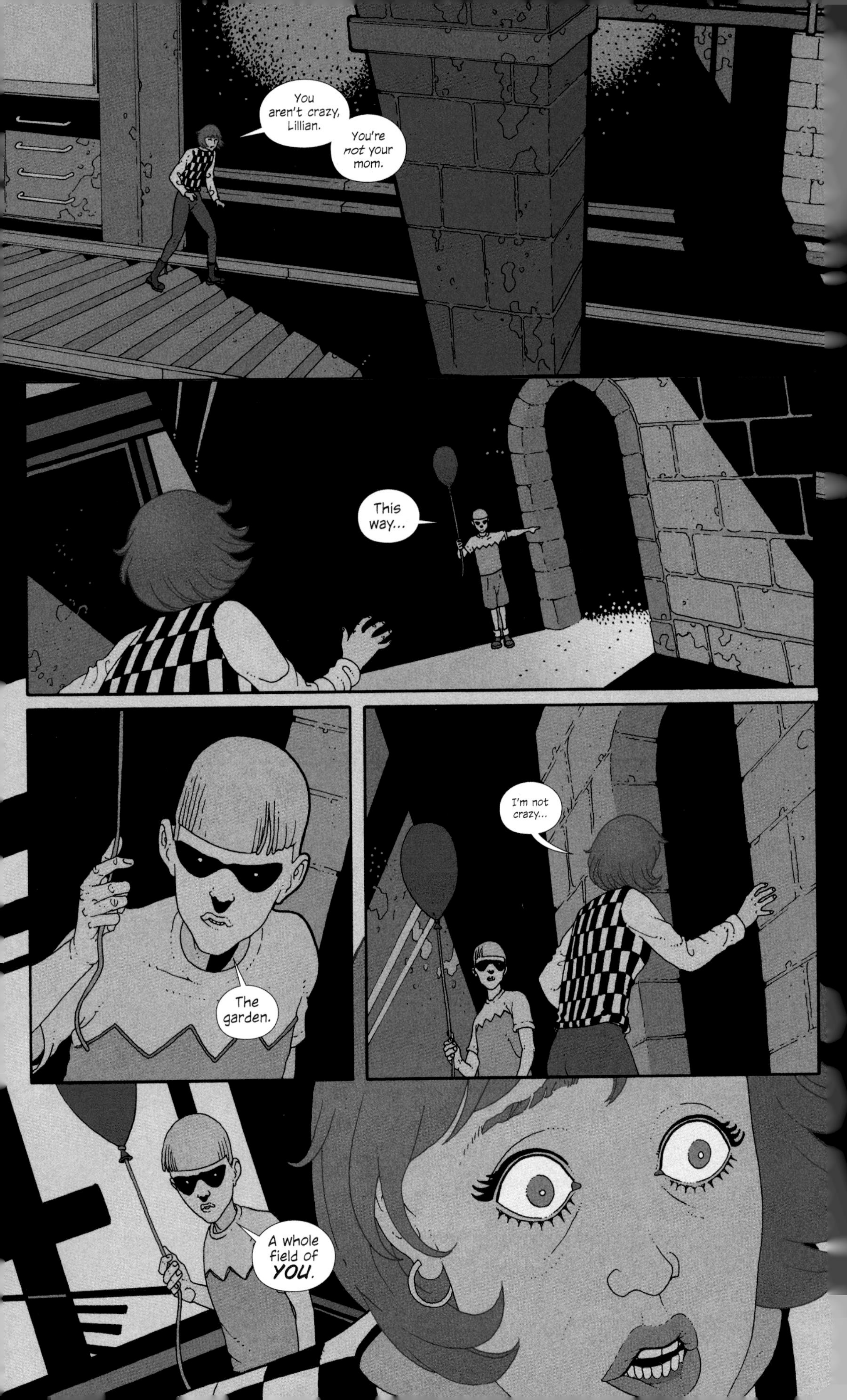
You aren't crazy, Lillian.
You're *not* your mom.
This way...
The garden.
I'm not crazy...
A whole field of ***YOU***.

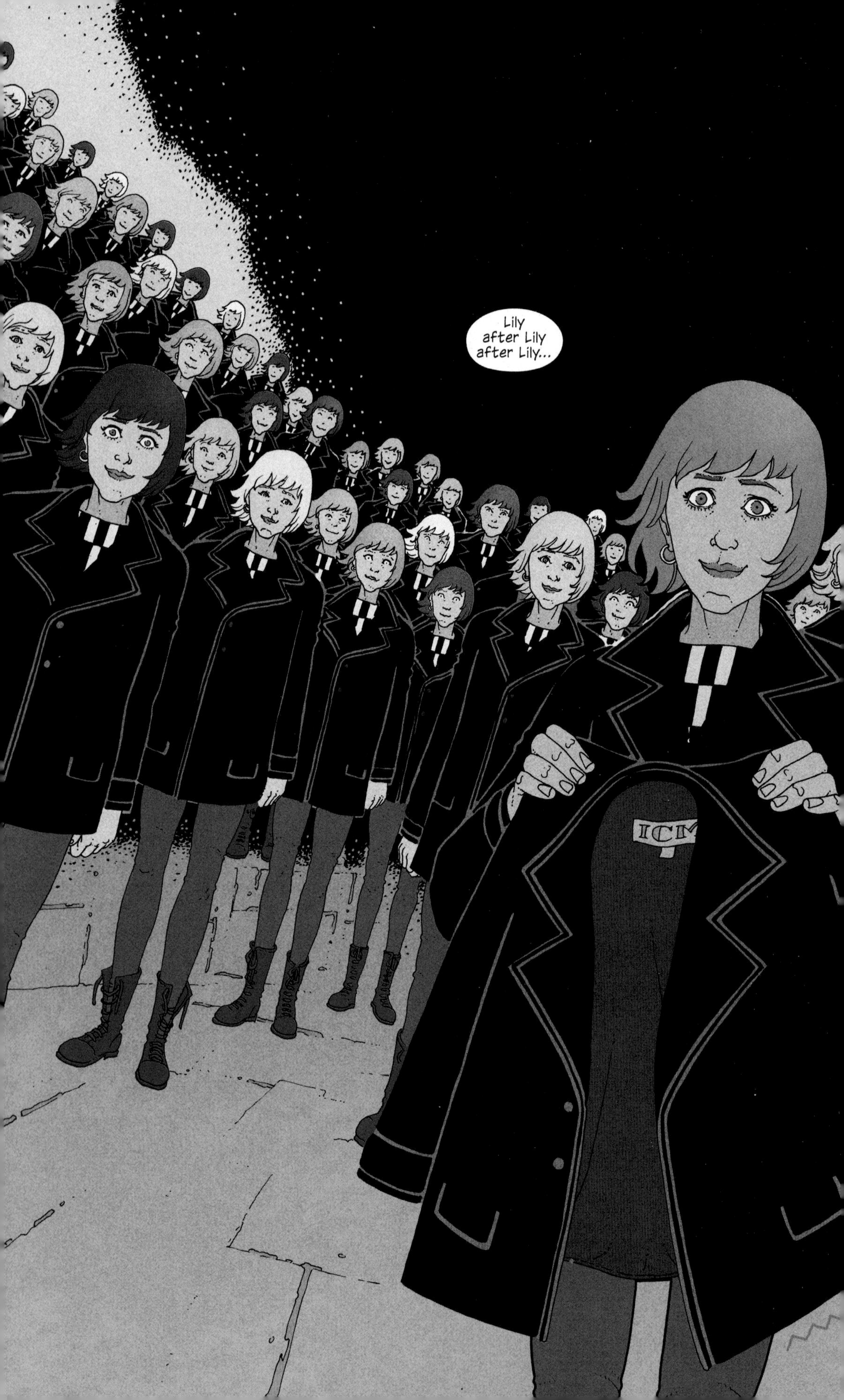
Lily after Lily after Lily...
ICM

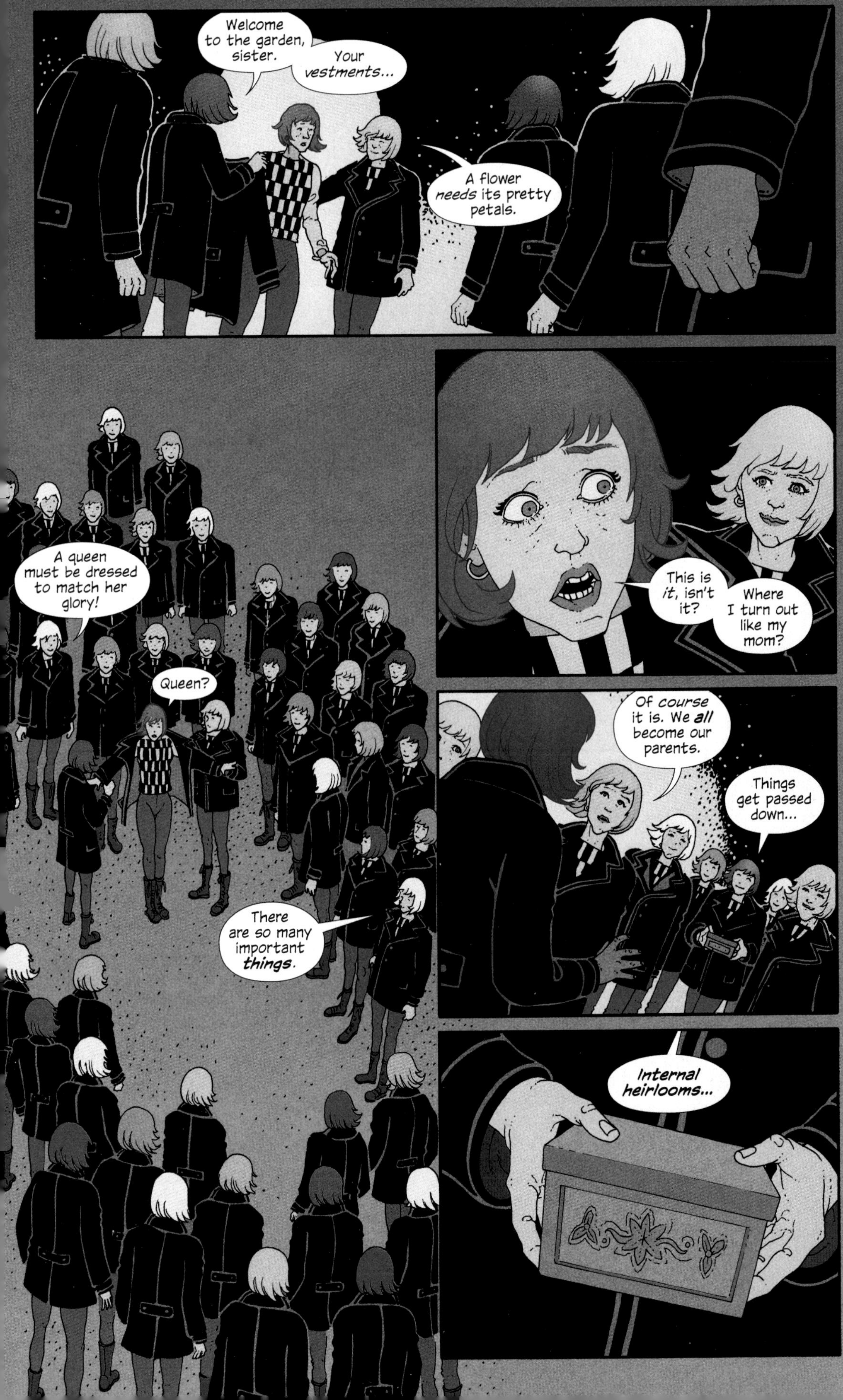
Welcome to the garden, sister.
Your *vestments...*
A flower *needs* its pretty petals.
A queen must be dressed to match her glory!
Queen?
There are so many important ***things***.
This is *it*, isn't it?
Where I turn out like my mom?
Of *course* it is. We ***all*** become our parents.
Things get passed down...
Internal heirlooms...

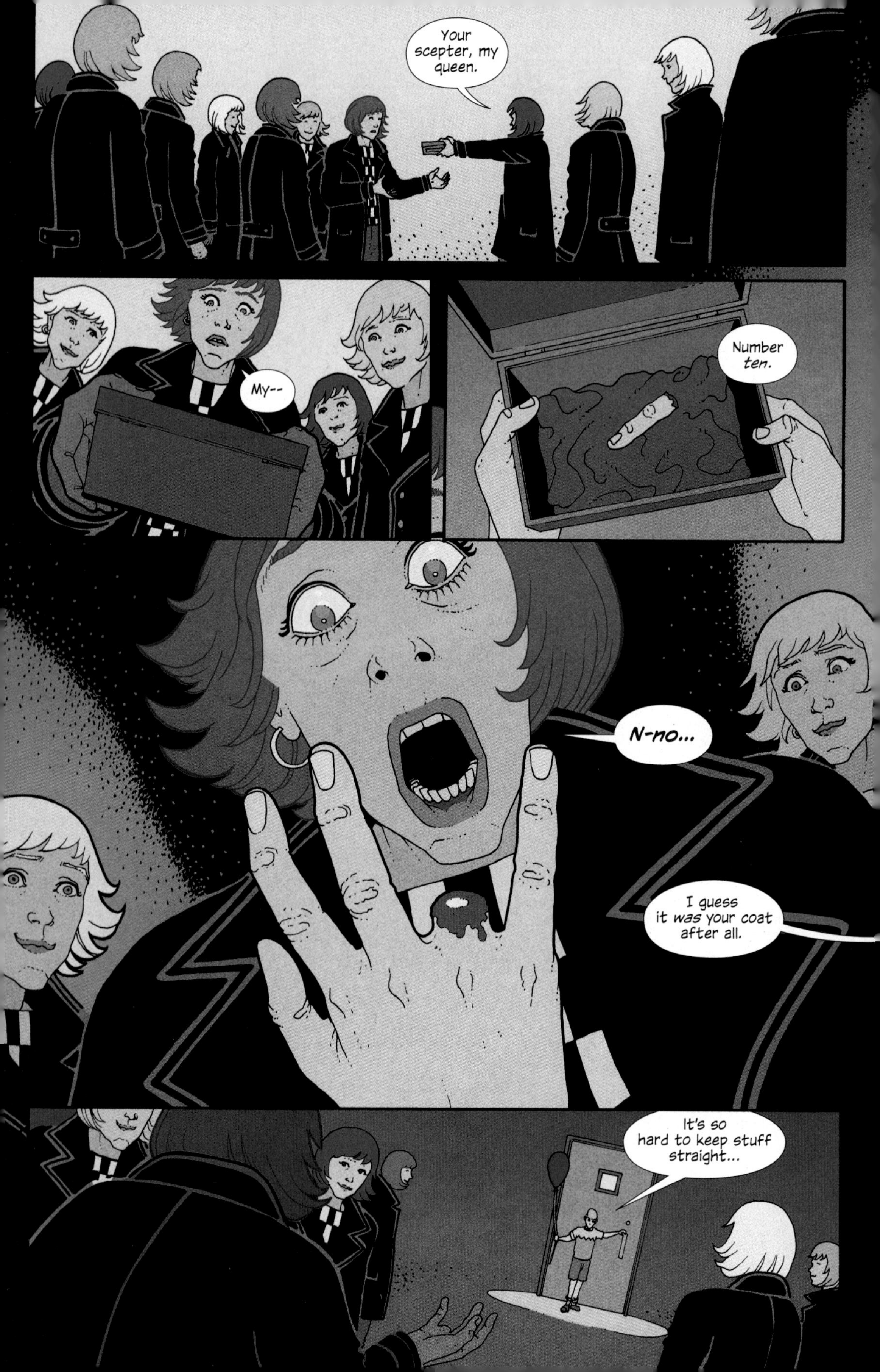

Your scepter, my queen.
My--
Number *ten.*
N-no...
I guess it *was* your coat after all.
It's so hard to keep stuff straight...

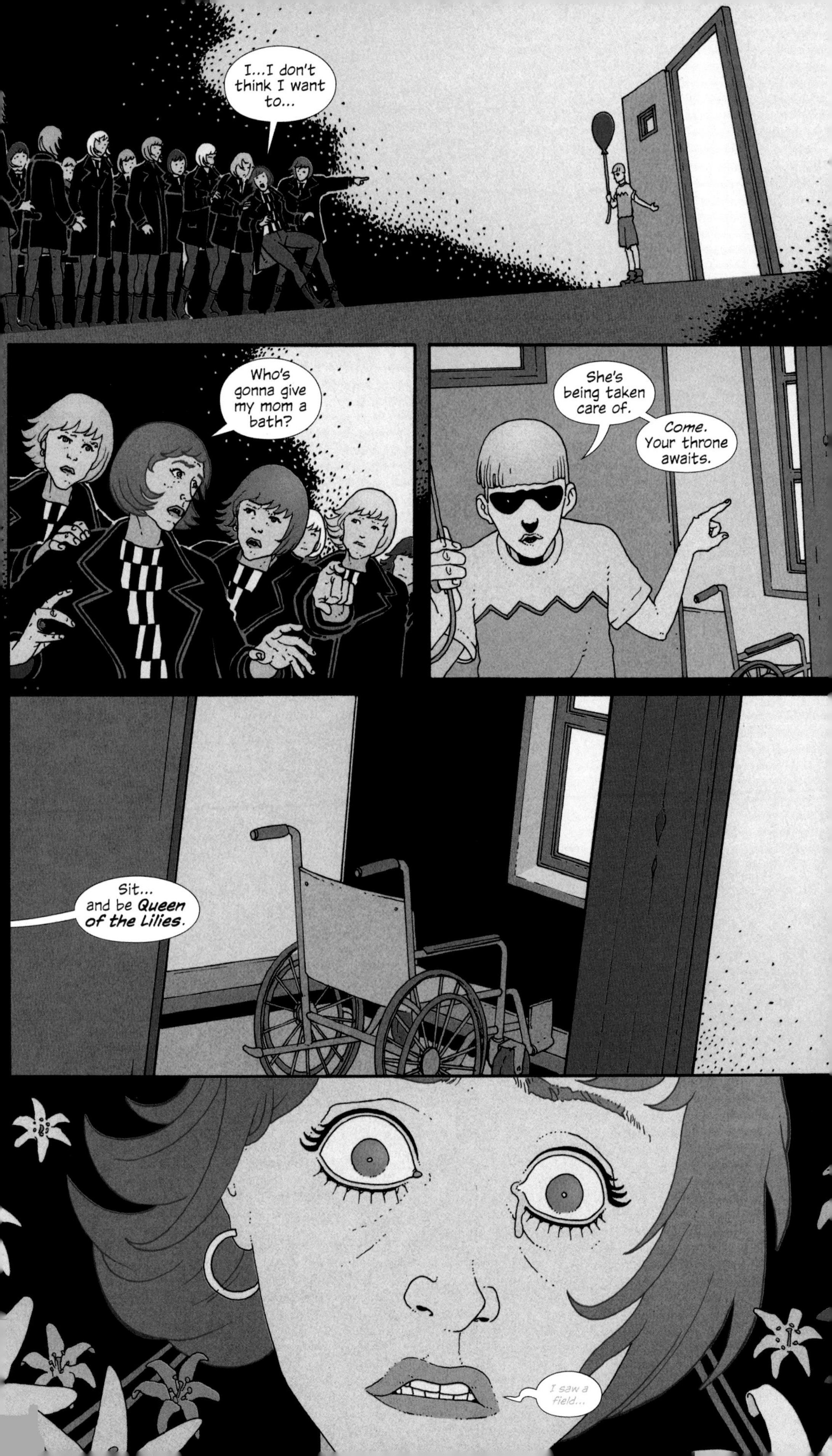
I...I don't think I want to...
Who's gonna give my mom a bath?
She's being taken care of.
Come. Your throne awaits.
Sit... and be Queen of the Lilies.
I saw a field...

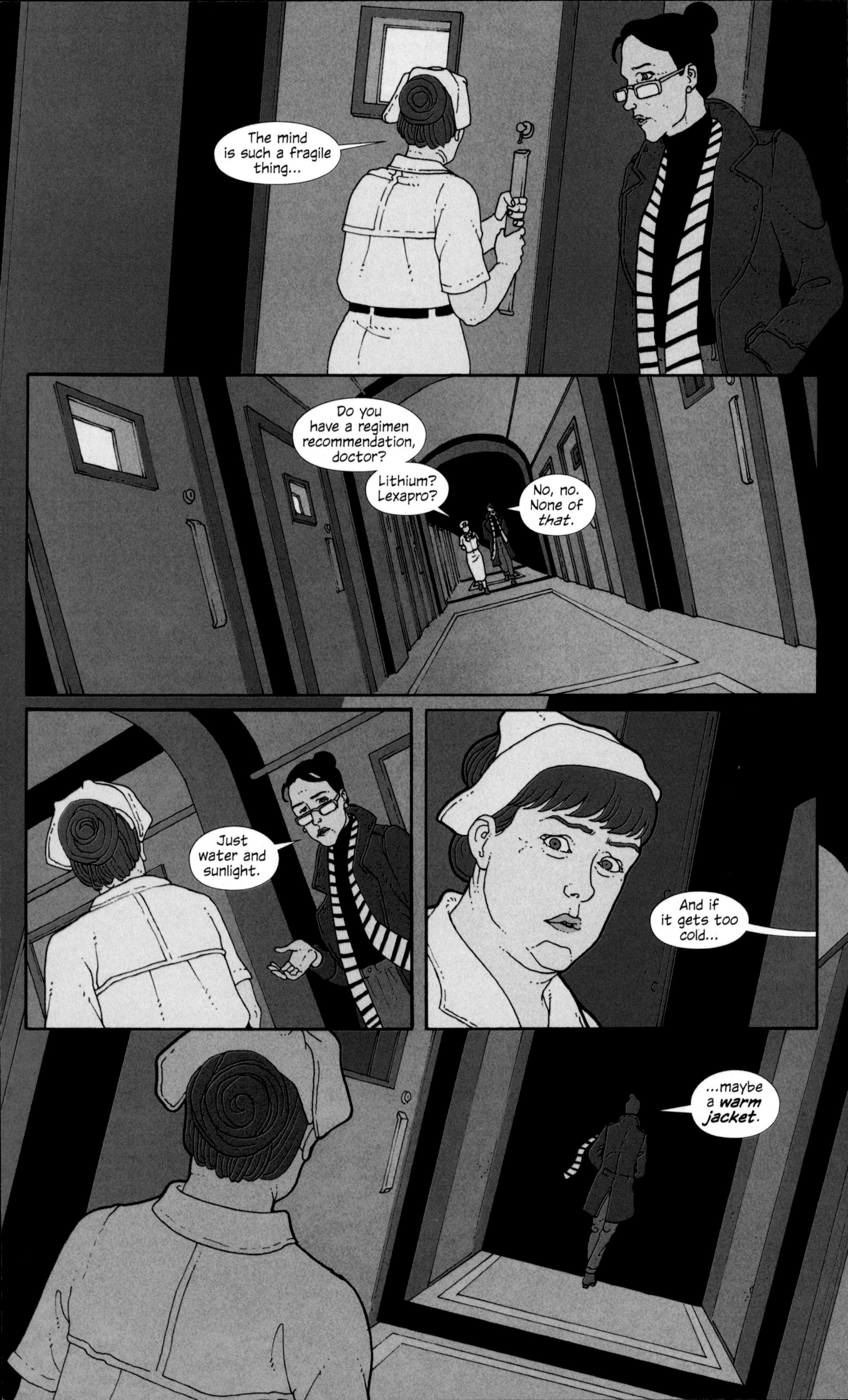
The mind is such a fragile thing...
Do you have a regimen recommendation, doctor?
Lithium? Lexapro?
No, no. None of *that*.
Just water and sunlight.
And if it gets too cold...
...maybe a ***warm jacket***.

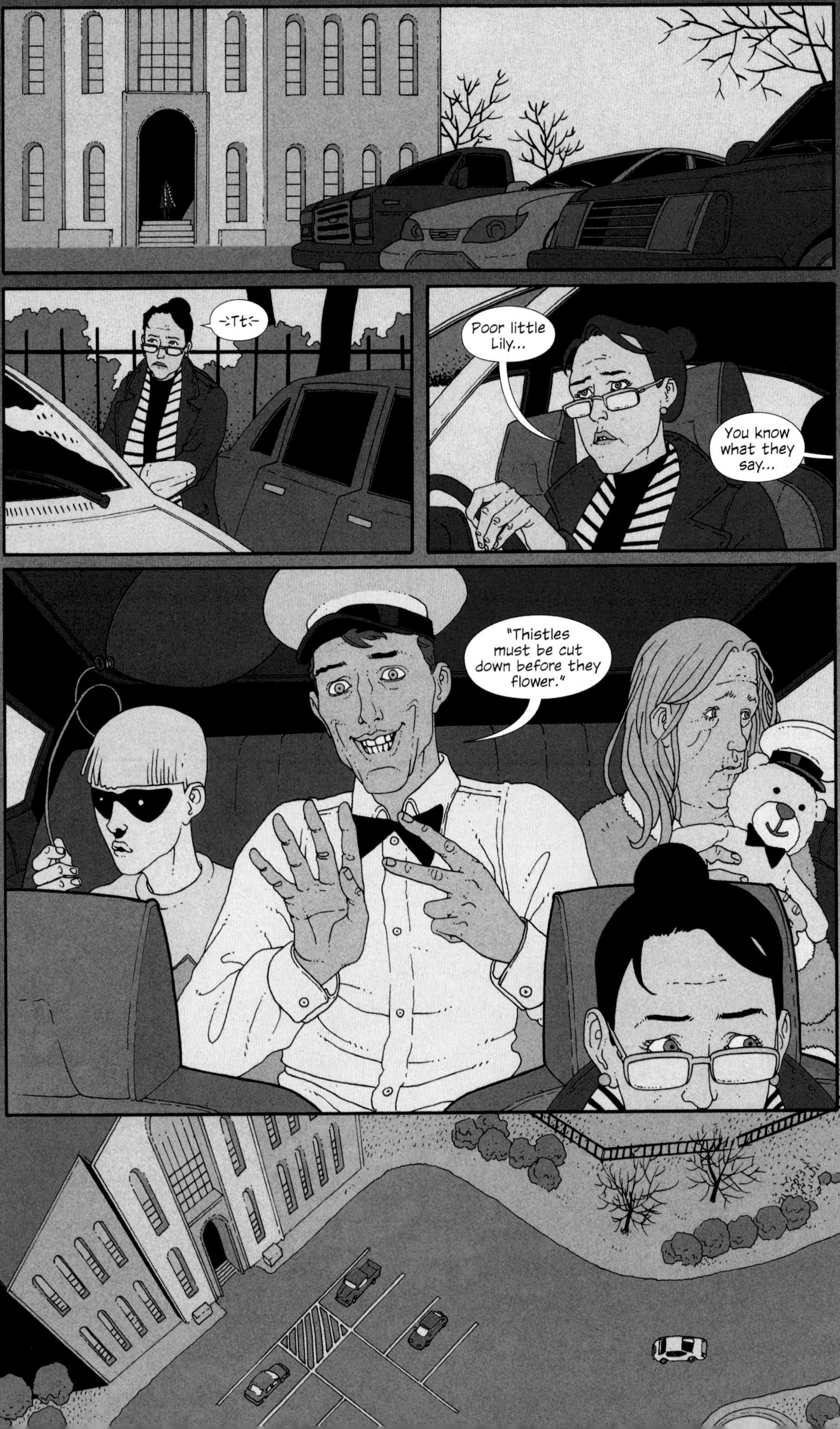
-Tt-
Poor little Lily...
You know what they say...
"Thistles must be cut down before they flower."

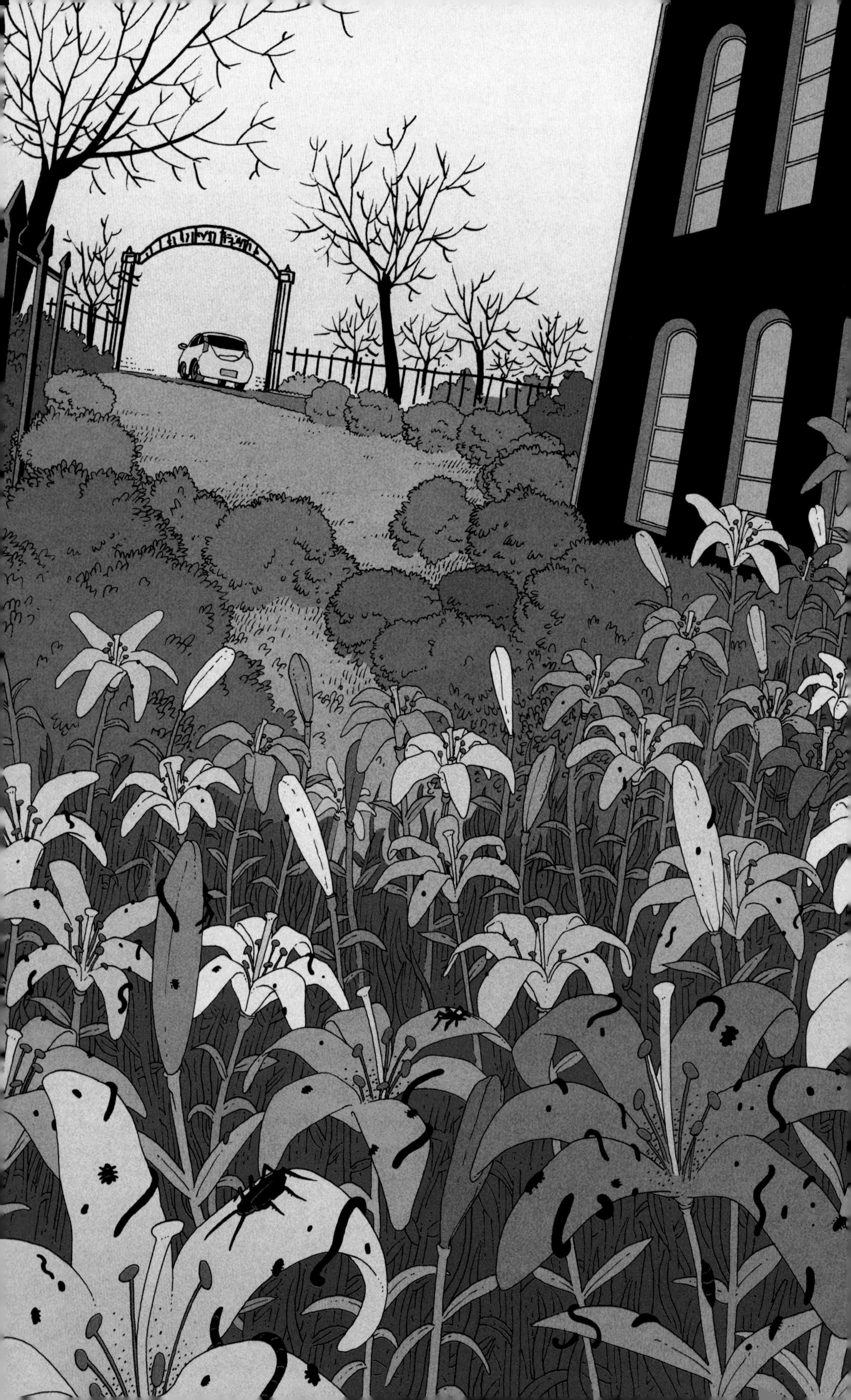

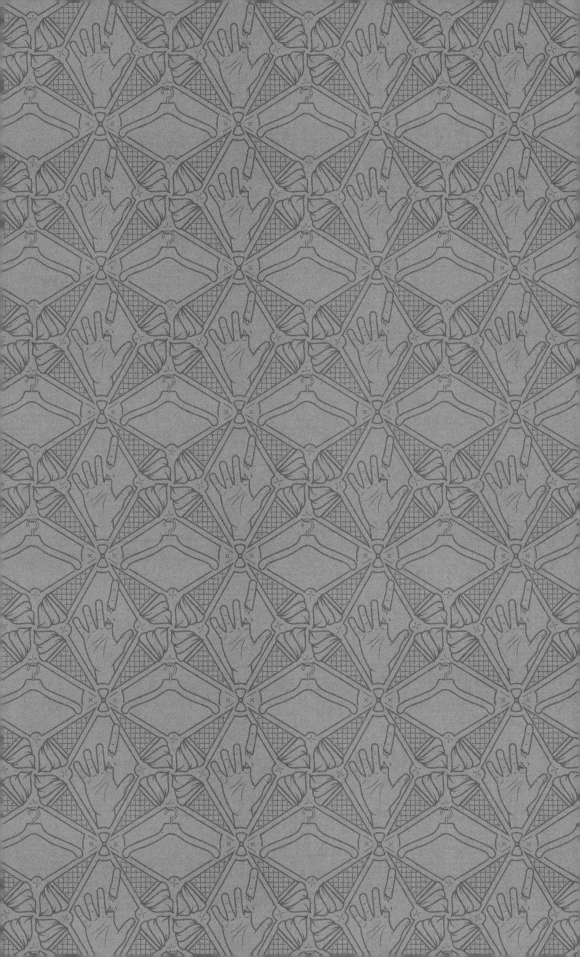

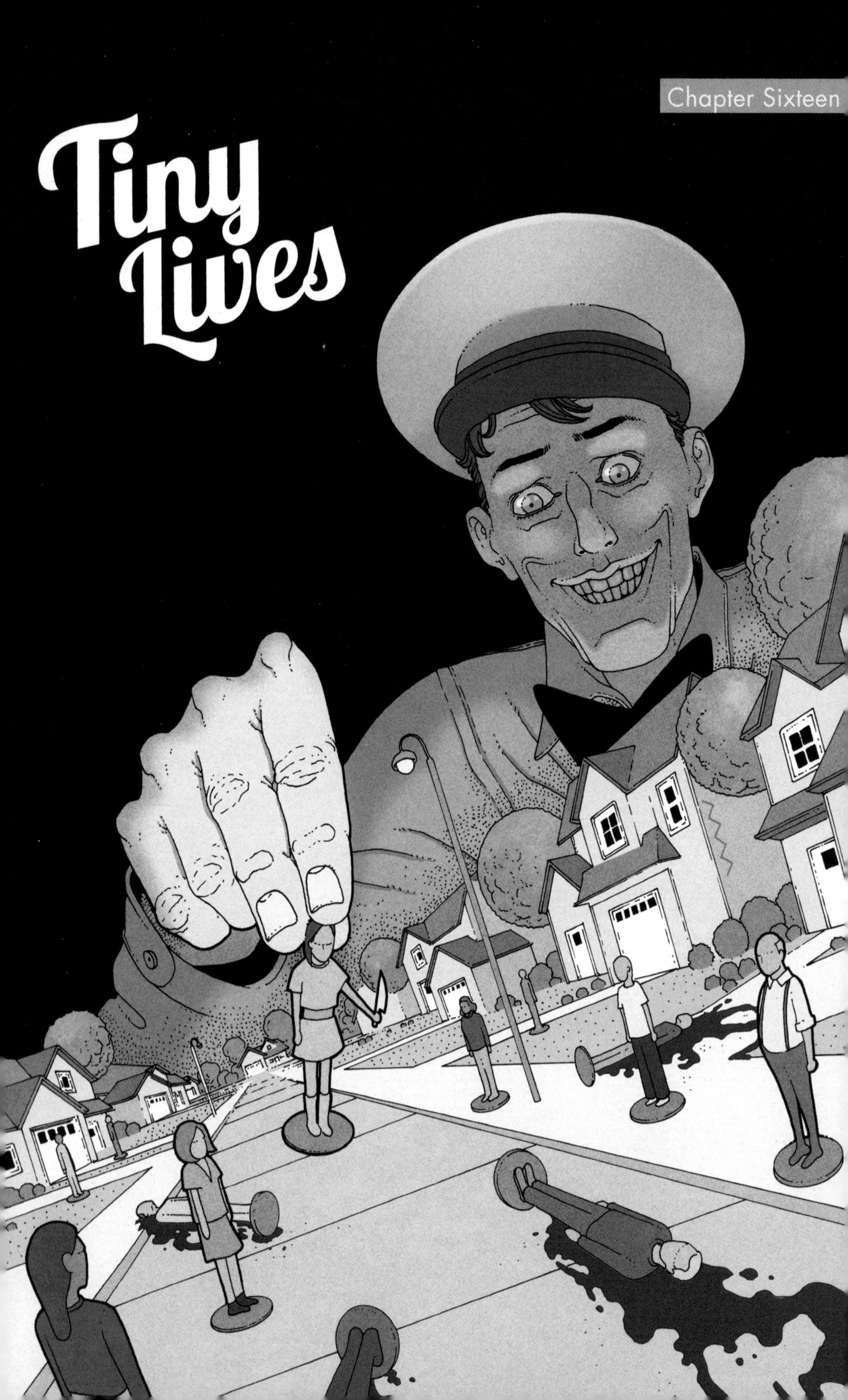
Chapter Sixteen
Tiny Lives

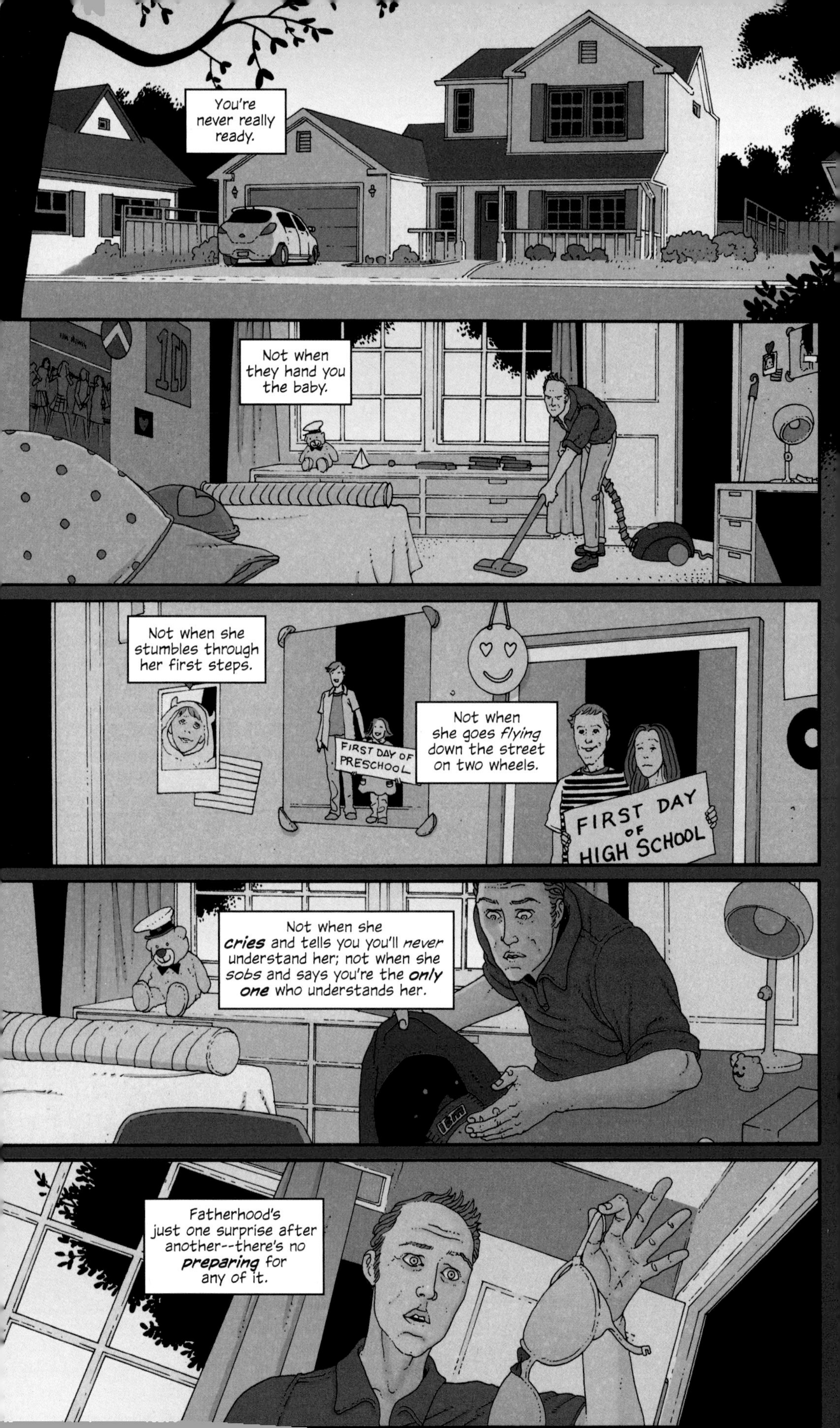
You're never really ready.
Not when they hand you the baby.
Not when she stumbles through her first steps.
FIRST DAY OF PRESCHOOL
Not when she goes *flying* down the street on two wheels.
FIRST DAY OF HIGH SCHOOL
Not when she ***cries*** and tells you you'll *never* understand her; not when she *sobs* and says you're the ***only one*** who understands her.
Fatherhood's just one surprise after another--there's no ***preparing*** for any of it.

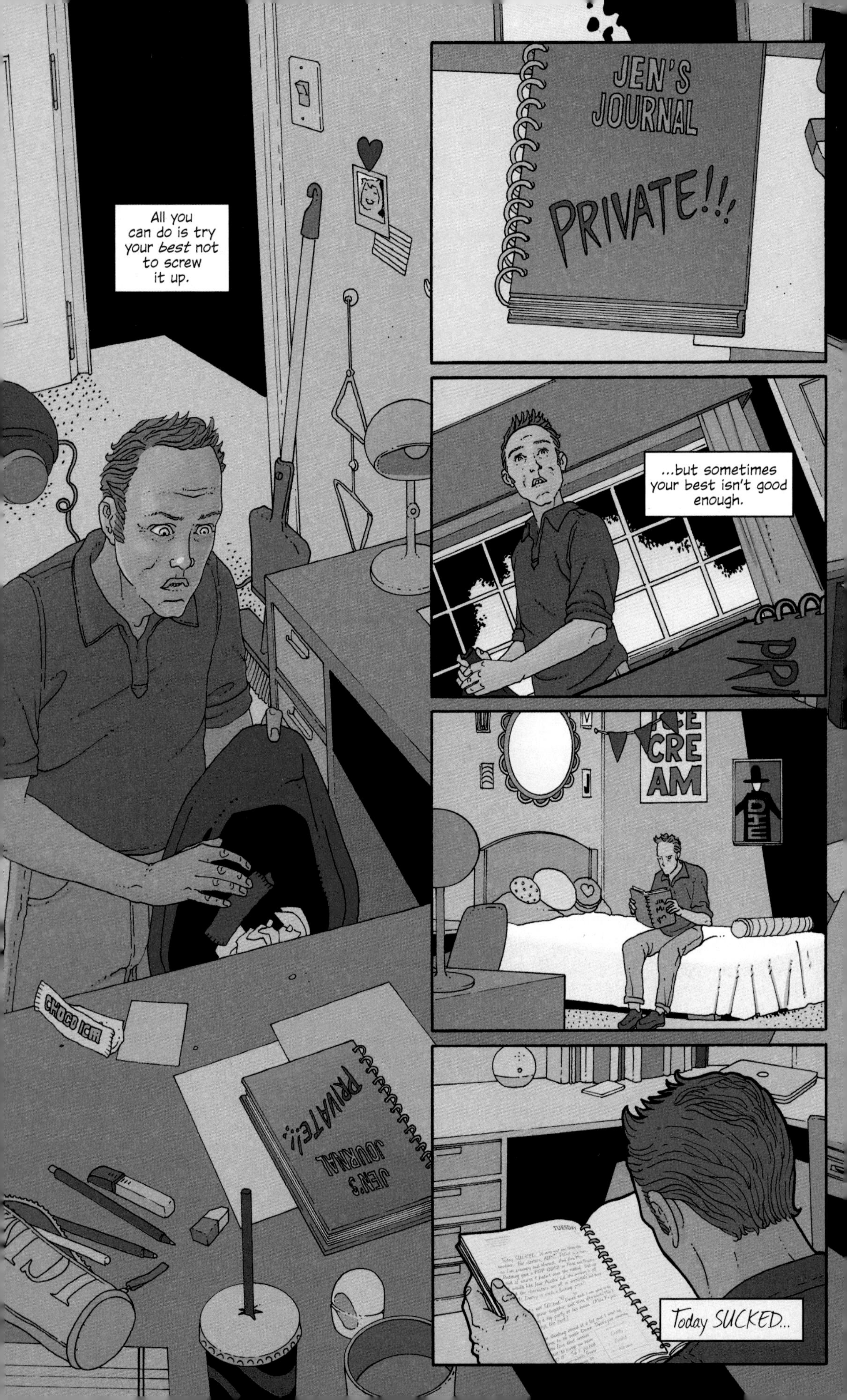
All you can do is try your *best* not to screw it up.
JEN'S JOURNAL
PRIVATE!!!
CHOCO ICE
JEN'S JOURNAL
PRIVATE!!!
...but sometimes your best isn't good enough.
Today SUCKED...

QUOTE OF THE DAY:
"Try to be a rainbow in someone's cloud."
—MAYA ANGELOU

TUESDAY

Nov
12

Today SUCKED. It was just one thing after another. For starters, AUNT FLO came to town, so I'm crampy and bloated. And then Mrs. Redding gave a POP QUIZ on Pride and Prejudice and of course I hadn't done the reading. Dad said I would like Jane Austen but the writing is stiff and the characters are all so unrelatable and dumb. (Mr. Darcy is such a fucking prick!)

But it's not SO bad. Derek and I are going to the football game together, and then afterwards Mike P. is having a big party at his house. (Mike P.'s parties are always the best.)

I've been thinking about it a lot and I want my first time to be with Derek. There's just something about his face that makes me want to jump on him and DO IT. So I picked up you-know-whats from the store... I wanna be ready when the time comes. Fingers crossed!

MOOD BOARD

1. Crabby
2. Excited
3. Nervous

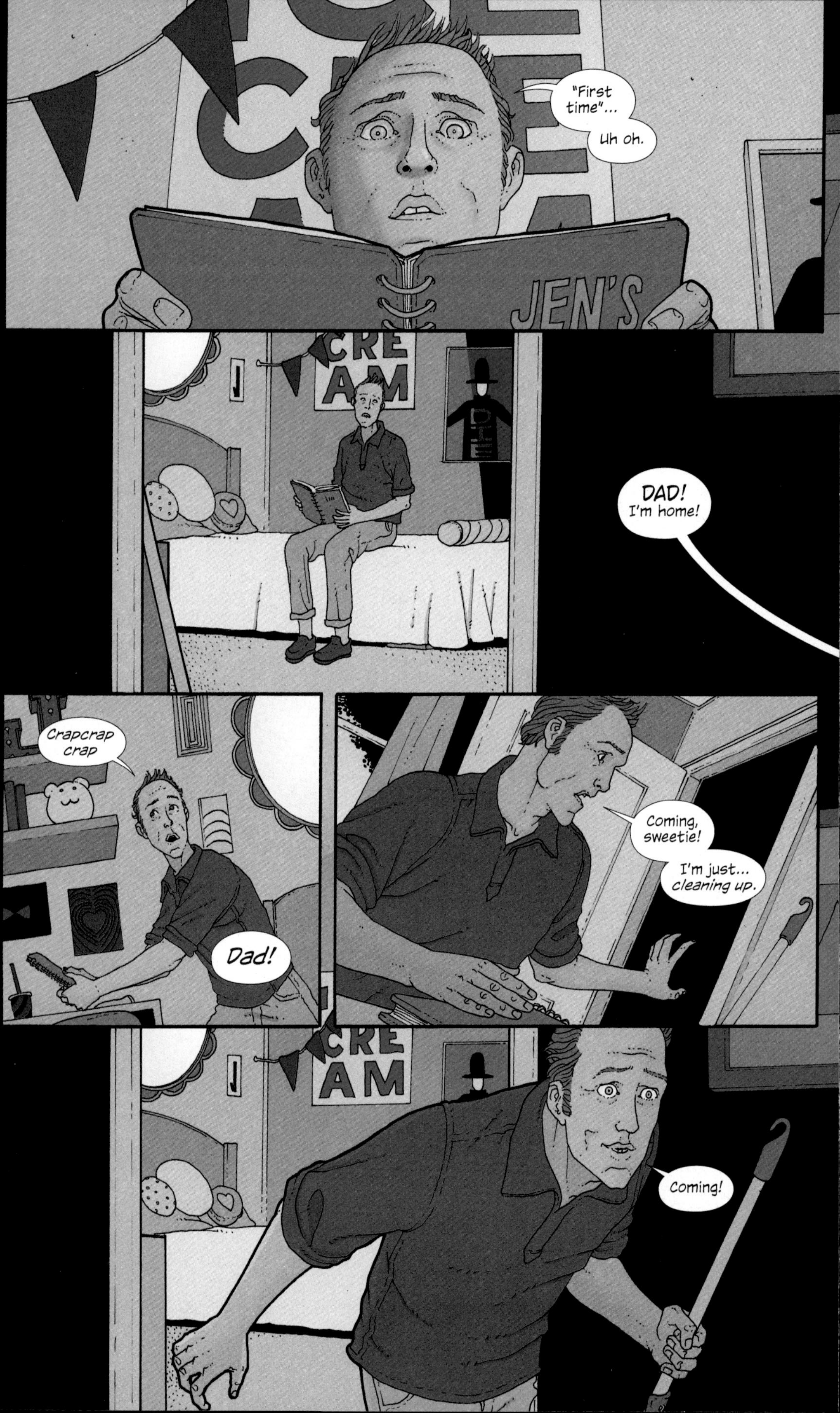
"First time"...
Uh oh.
JEN'S
CRE
AM
J
DIE
DAD! I'm home!
Crapcrap crap
Dad!
Coming, sweetie!
I'm just... cleaning up.
CRE
AM
J
Coming!

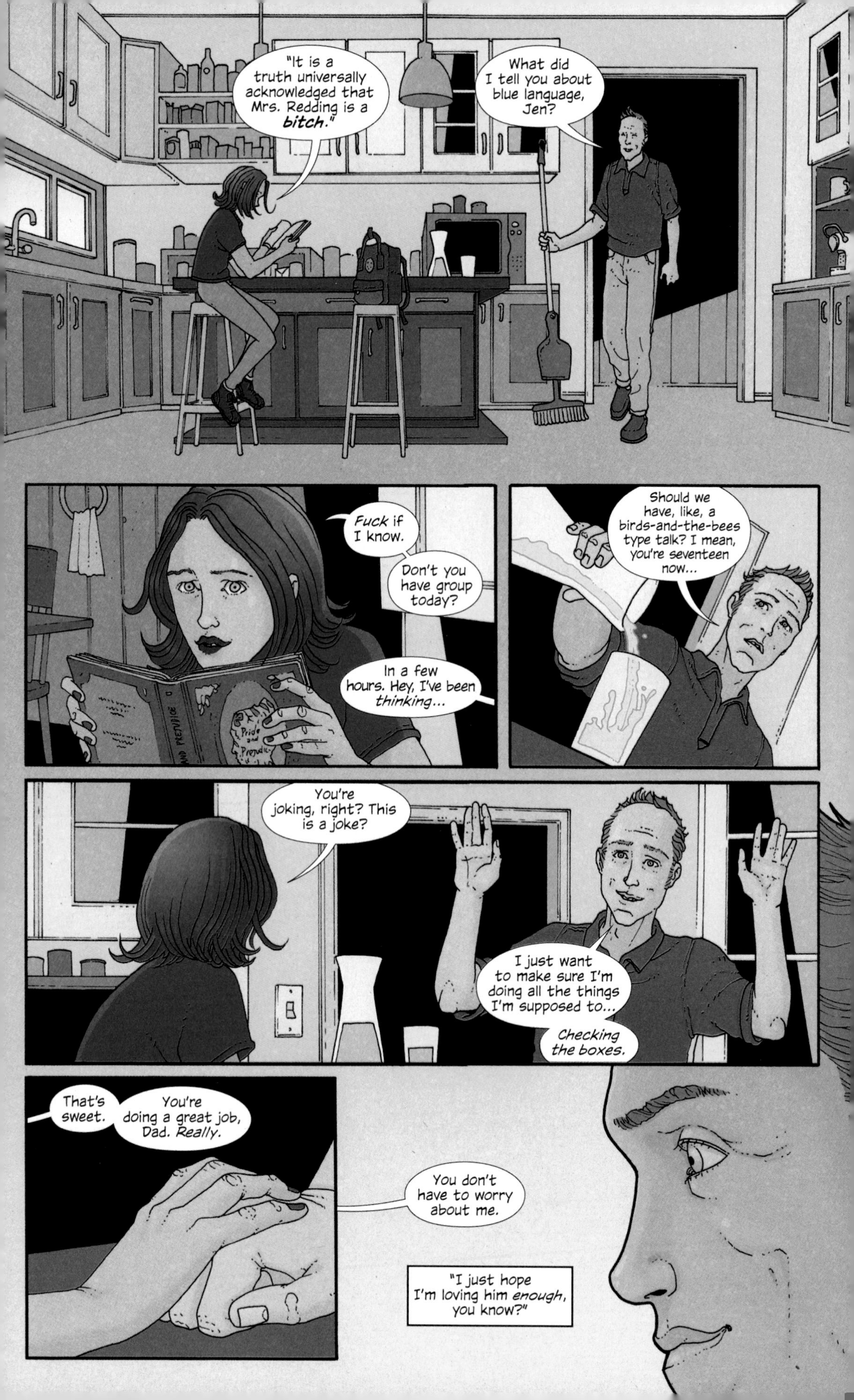
"It is a truth universally acknowledged that Mrs. Redding is a *bitch*."
What did I tell you about blue language, Jen?
Fuck if I know.
Don't you have group today?
In a few hours. Hey, I've been *thinking*...
Should we have, like, a birds-and-the-bees type talk? I mean, you're seventeen now...
You're joking, right? This is a joke?
I just want to make sure I'm doing all the things I'm supposed to...
Checking the boxes.
That's sweet.
You're doing a great job, Dad. *Really*.
You don't have to worry about me.
"I just hope I'm loving him *enough*, you know?"

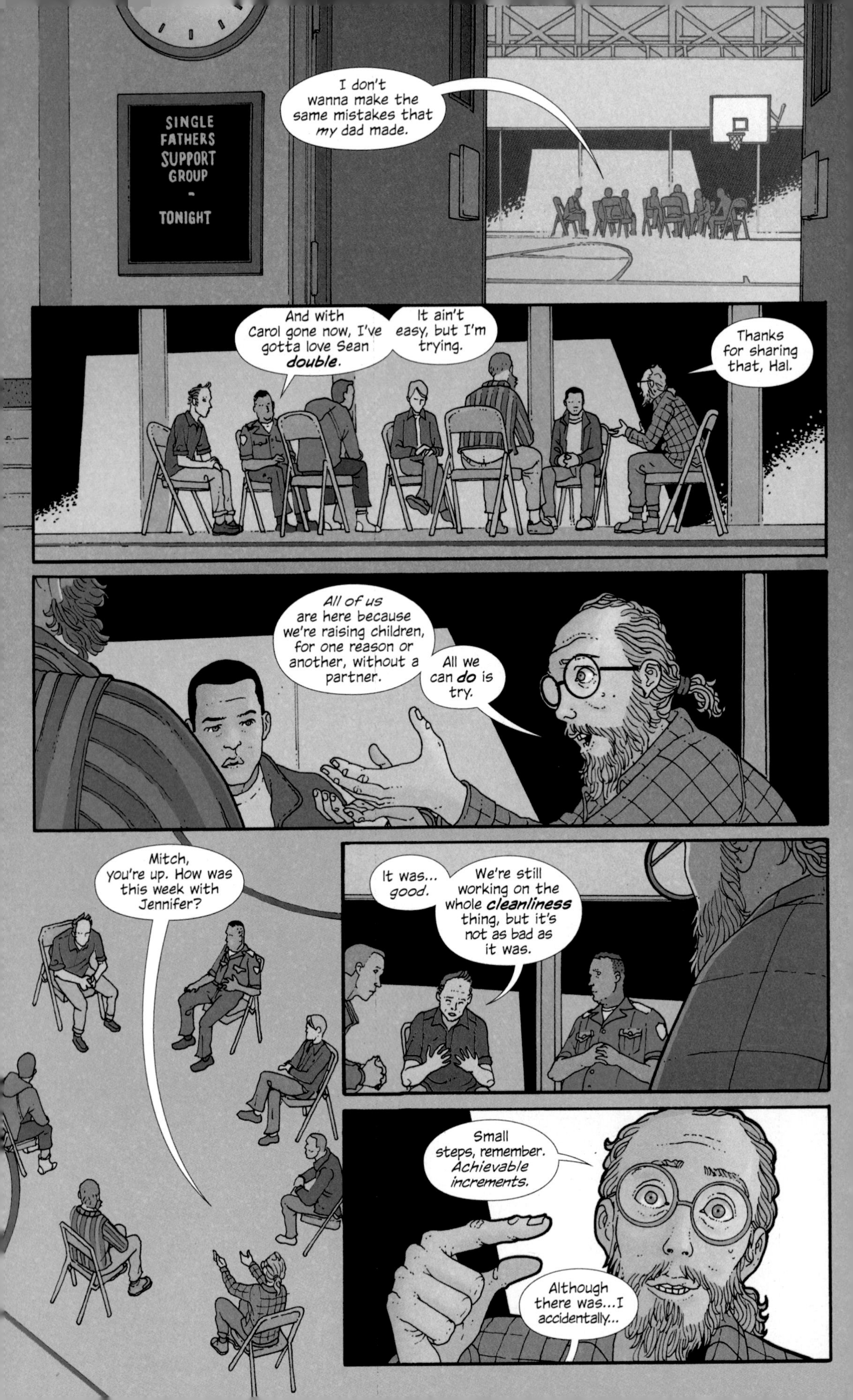
SINGLE FATHERS SUPPORT GROUP - TONIGHT
I don't wanna make the same mistakes that *my* dad made.
And with Carol gone now, I've gotta love Sean ***double***.
It ain't easy, but I'm trying.
Thanks for sharing that, Hal.
All of us are here because we're raising children, for one reason or another, without a partner.
All we can ***do*** is try.
Mitch, you're up. How was this week with Jennifer?
It was... *good.*
We're still working on the whole ***cleanliness*** thing, but it's not as bad as it was.
Small steps, remember. *Achievable increments.*
Although there was...I accidentally...

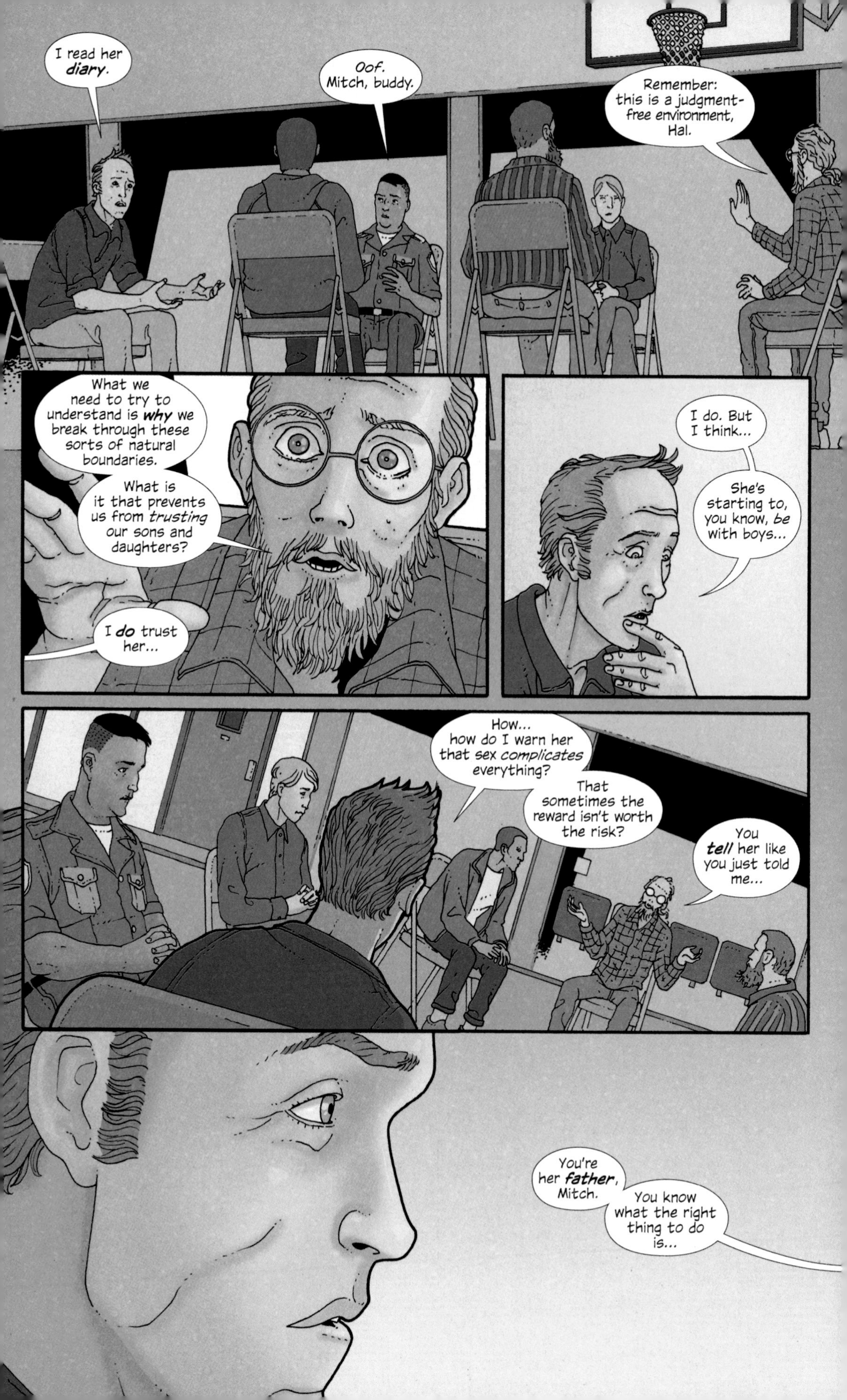
I read her *diary*.
Oof. Mitch, buddy.
Remember: this is a judgment-free environment, Hal.
What we need to try to understand is *why* we break through these sorts of natural boundaries.
What is it that prevents us from *trusting* our sons and daughters?
I *do* trust her...
I do. But I think...
She's starting to, you know, *be* with boys...
How... how do I warn her that sex *complicates* everything?
That sometimes the reward isn't worth the risk?
You *tell* her like you just told me...
You're her *father*, Mitch.
You know what the right thing to do is...

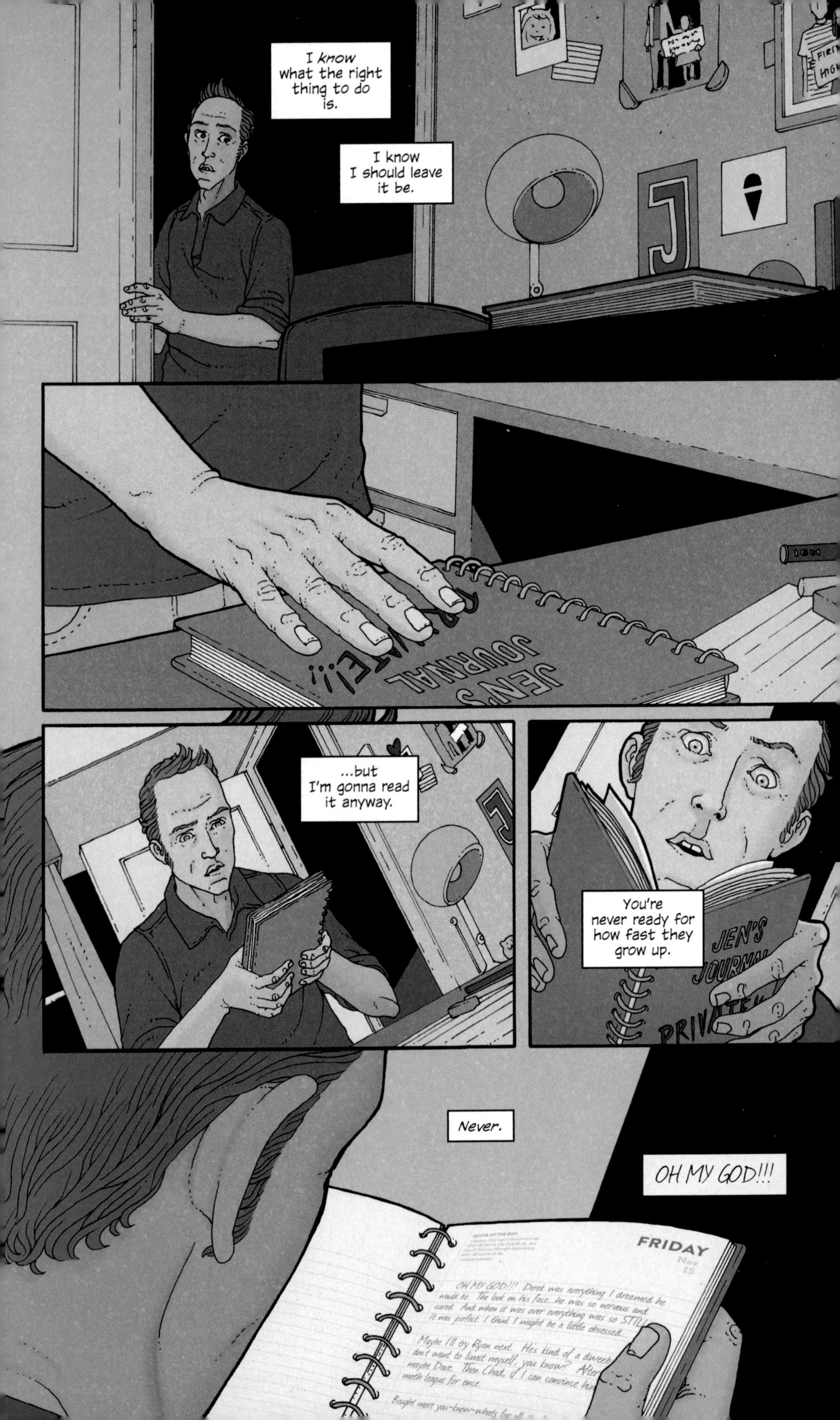
I *know* what the right thing to do is.
I know I should leave it be.
JEN'S JOURNAL
...but I'm gonna read it anyway.
You're never ready for how fast they grow up.
JEN'S JOURNAL
PRIVATE
Never.
OH MY GOD!!!
FRIDAY
Nov 15
OH MY GOD!!! Derek was everything I dreamed he would be. The look on his face...he was so nervous and scared. And when it was over everything was so STIL
It was perfect. I think I might be a little obsessed...
Maybe I'll try Ryan next. He's kind of a dweeb
don't want to limit myself, you know? After
maybe Dave. Then Chad, if I can convince hi
math league for once.
Bought more you-know-whats for

QUOTE OF THE DAY:
"I believe that a girl should not do what she thinks she should do, but should find out through experience what she wants to do.
—AMELIA EARHART

FRIDAY
Nov
15

OH MY GOD!!! Derek was everything I dreamed he would be. The look on his face...he was so nervous and scared. And when it was over everything was so STILL. It was perfect. I think I might be a little obsessed...

Maybe I'll try Ryan next. He's kind of a dweeb, but I don't want to limit myself, you know? After Ryan, maybe Dave. Then Chad, if I can convince him to skip math league for once.

Bought more you-know-whats for all the fun I'm gonna have...

I dont think I've ever felt this free. It's like a small voice in my head keeps saying:

LIVE!

MOOD BOARD
1. Turned on
2. Happy
3. Addicted

My little girl...
It all happens so *quickly*.
Fast as fast can be!

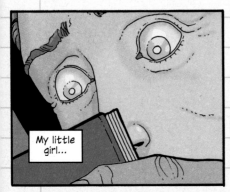

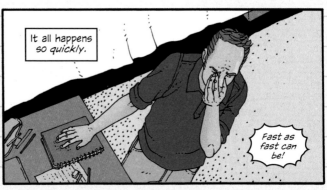

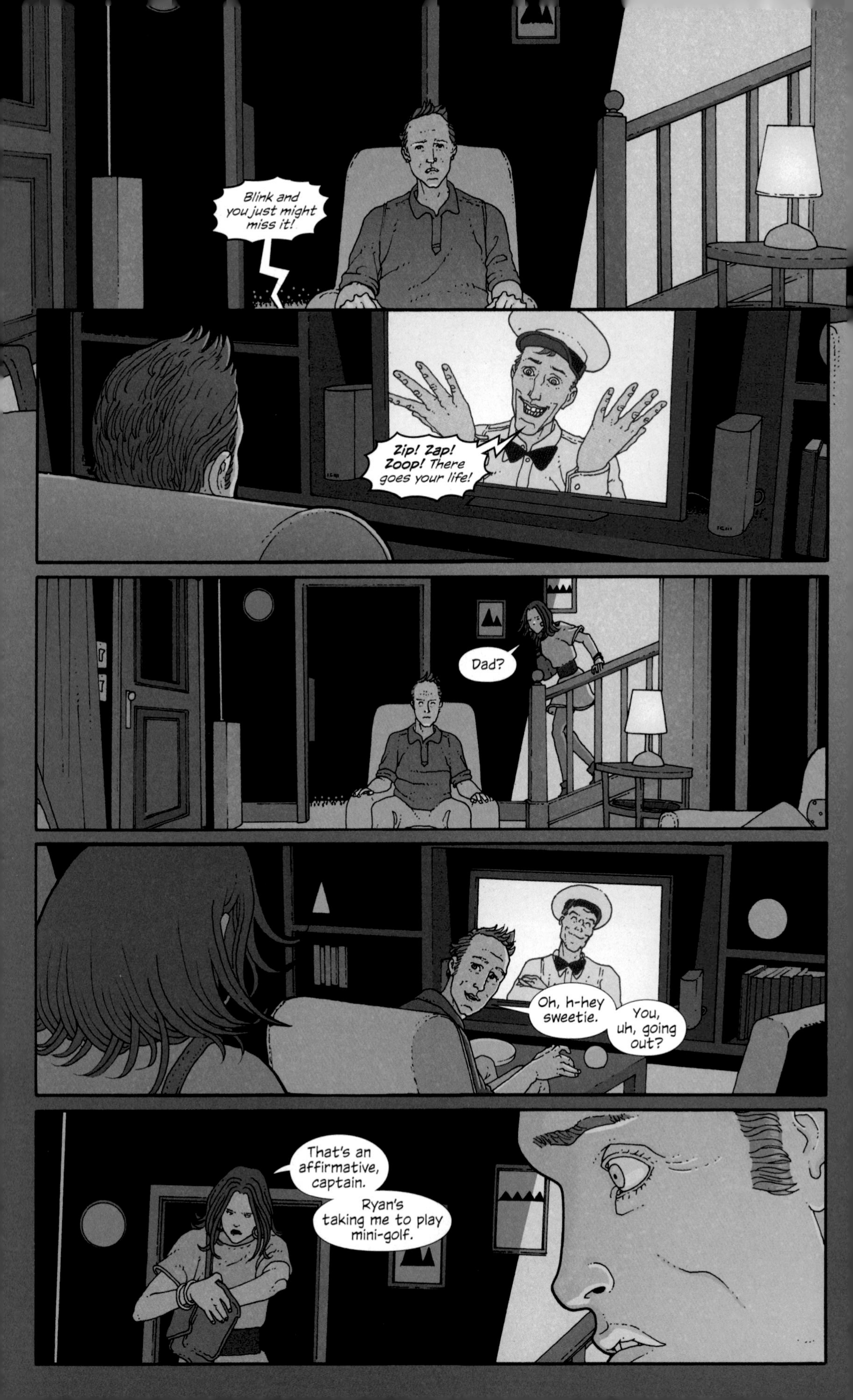
Blink and you just might miss it!
Zip! Zap! Zoop! There goes your life!
Dad?
Oh, h-hey sweetie.
You, uh, going out?
That's an affirmative, captain.
Ryan's taking me to play mini-golf.

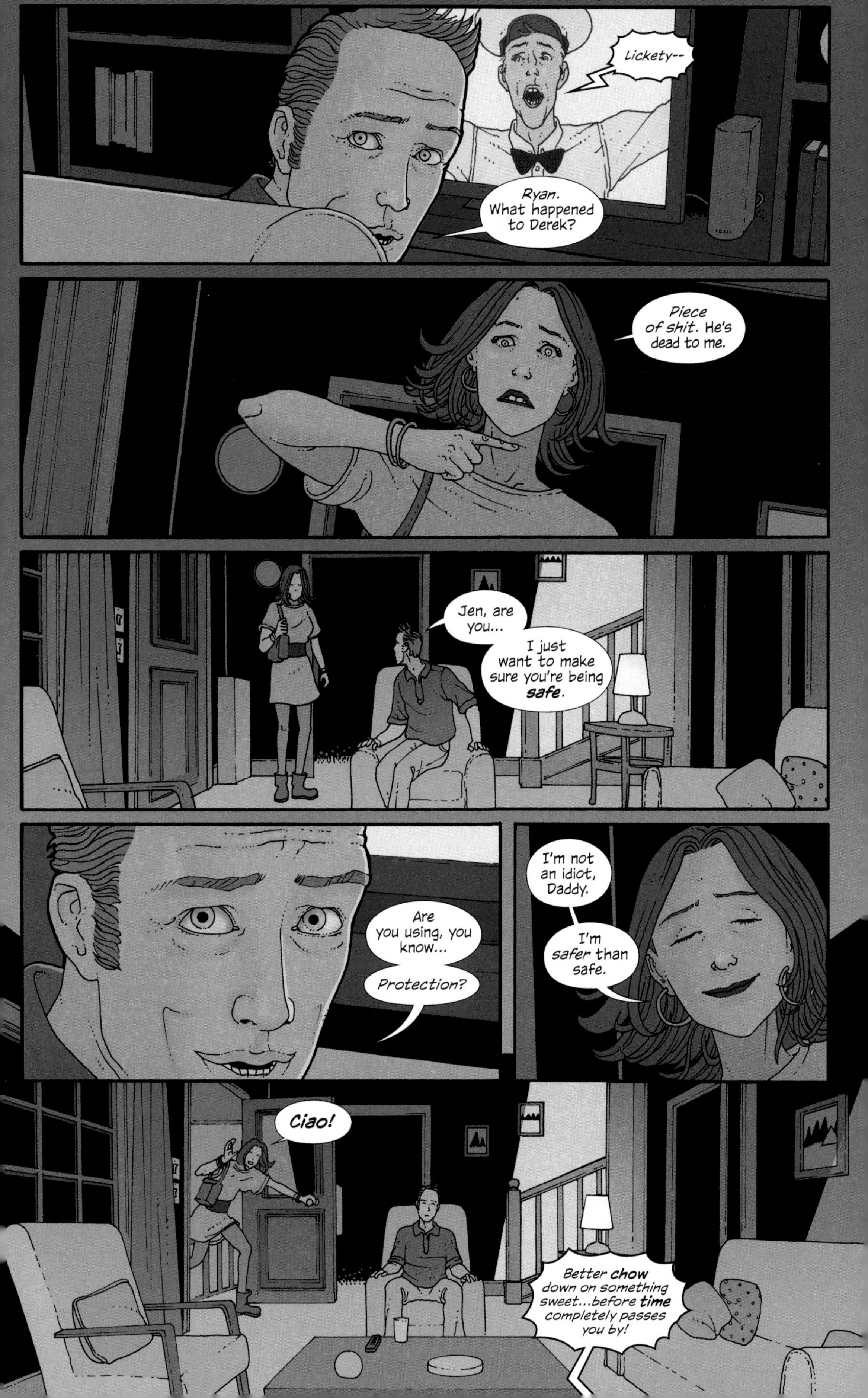
Lickety--
Ryan. What happened to Derek?
Piece of shit. He's dead to me.
Jen, are you...
I just want to make sure you're being **safe**.
Are you using, you know...
Protection?
I'm not an idiot, Daddy.
I'm *safer* than safe.
Ciao!
Better **chow** down on something sweet...before **time** completely passes you by!

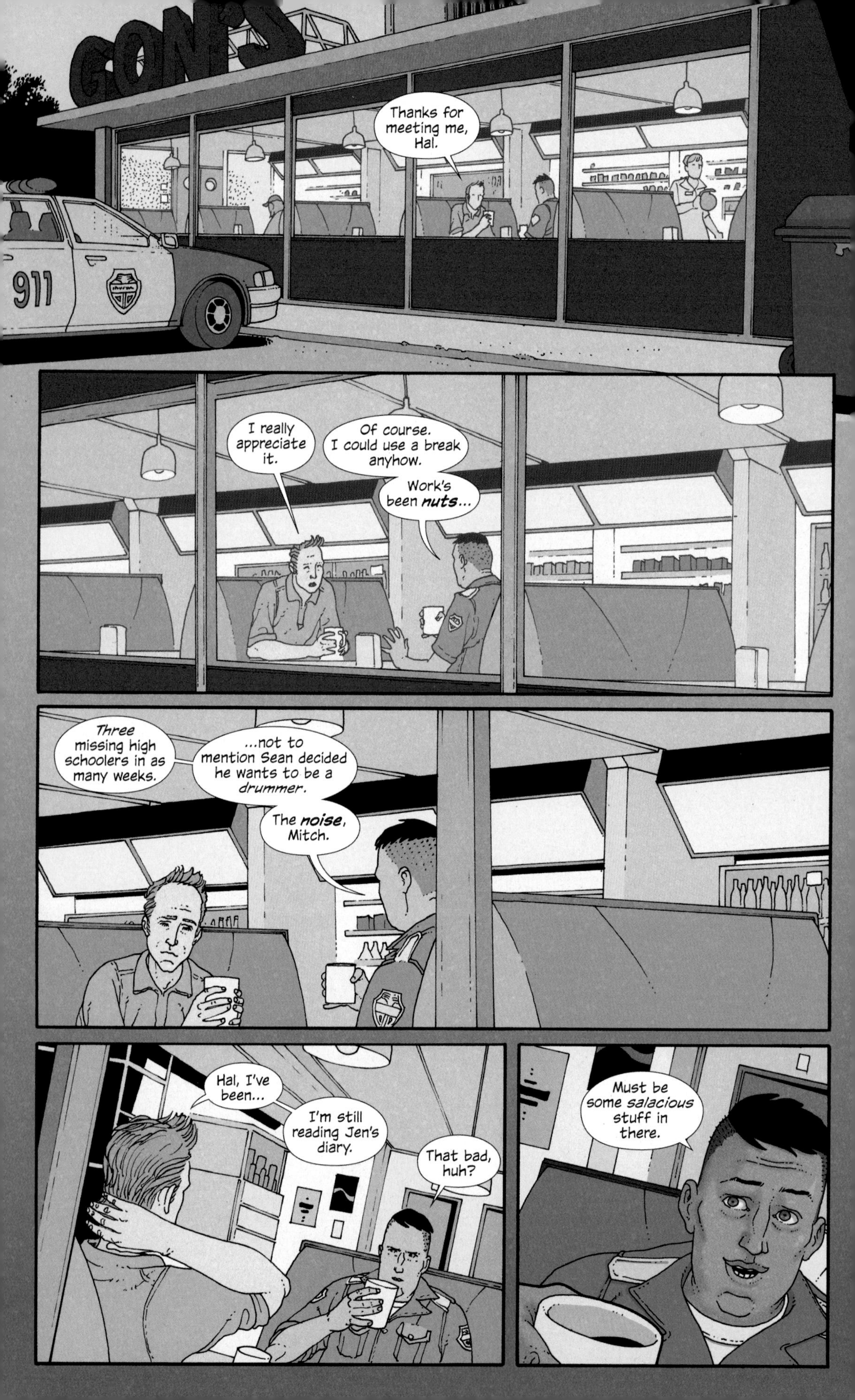
GON'S
Thanks for meeting me, Hal.
911
I really appreciate it.
Of course. I could use a break anyhow.
Work's been **nuts**...
Three missing high schoolers in as many weeks.
...not to mention Sean decided he wants to be a *drummer*.
The ***noise***, Mitch.
Hal, I've been...
I'm still reading Jen's diary.
That bad, huh?
Must be some *salacious* stuff in there.

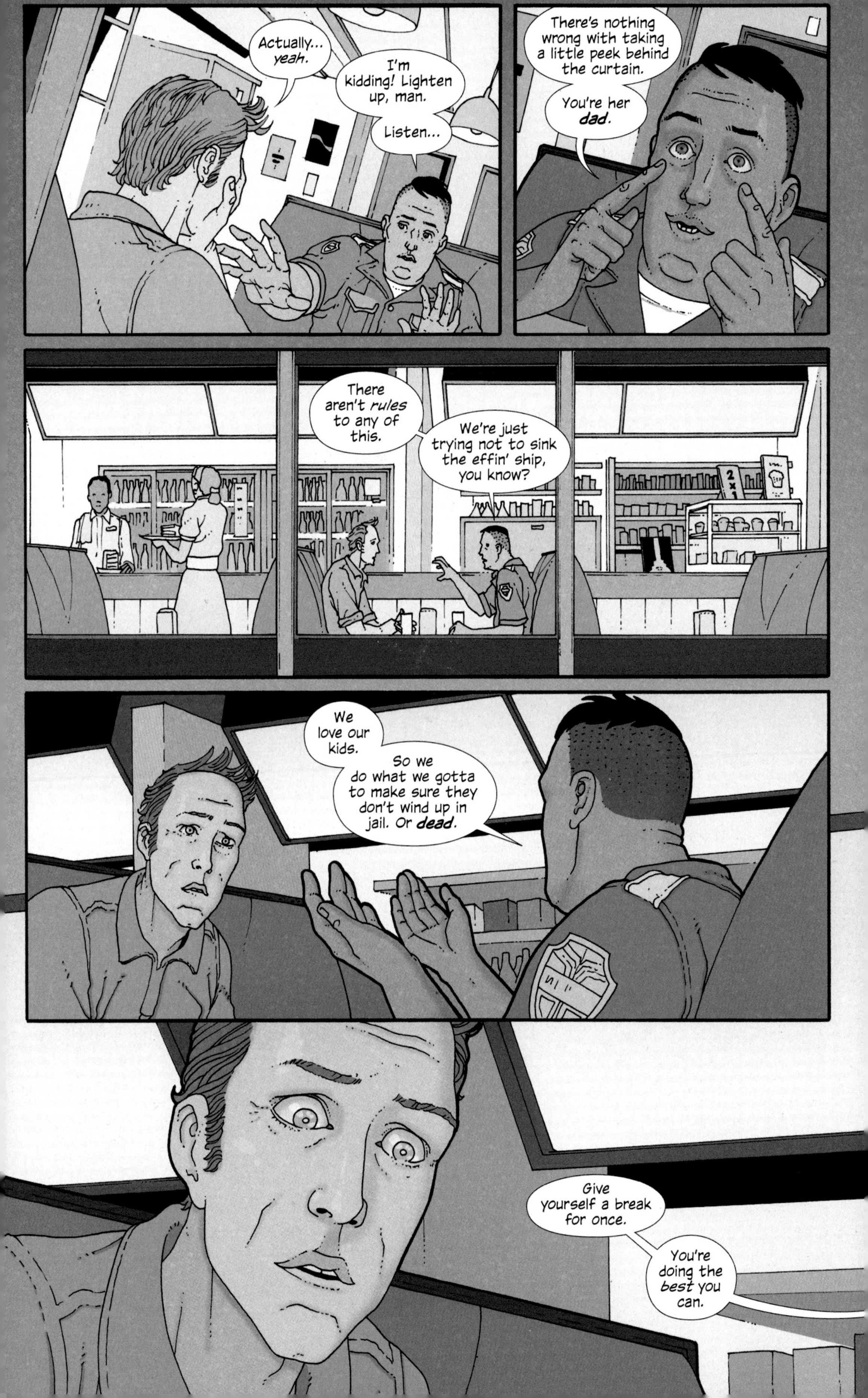
Actually... *yeah.*
I'm kidding! Lighten up, man.
Listen...
There's nothing wrong with taking a little peek behind the curtain.
You're her **dad**.
There aren't *rules* to any of this.
We're just trying not to sink the effin' ship, you know?
We love our kids.
So we do what we gotta to make sure they don't wind up in jail. Or **dead**.
Give yourself a break for once.
You're doing the *best* you can.

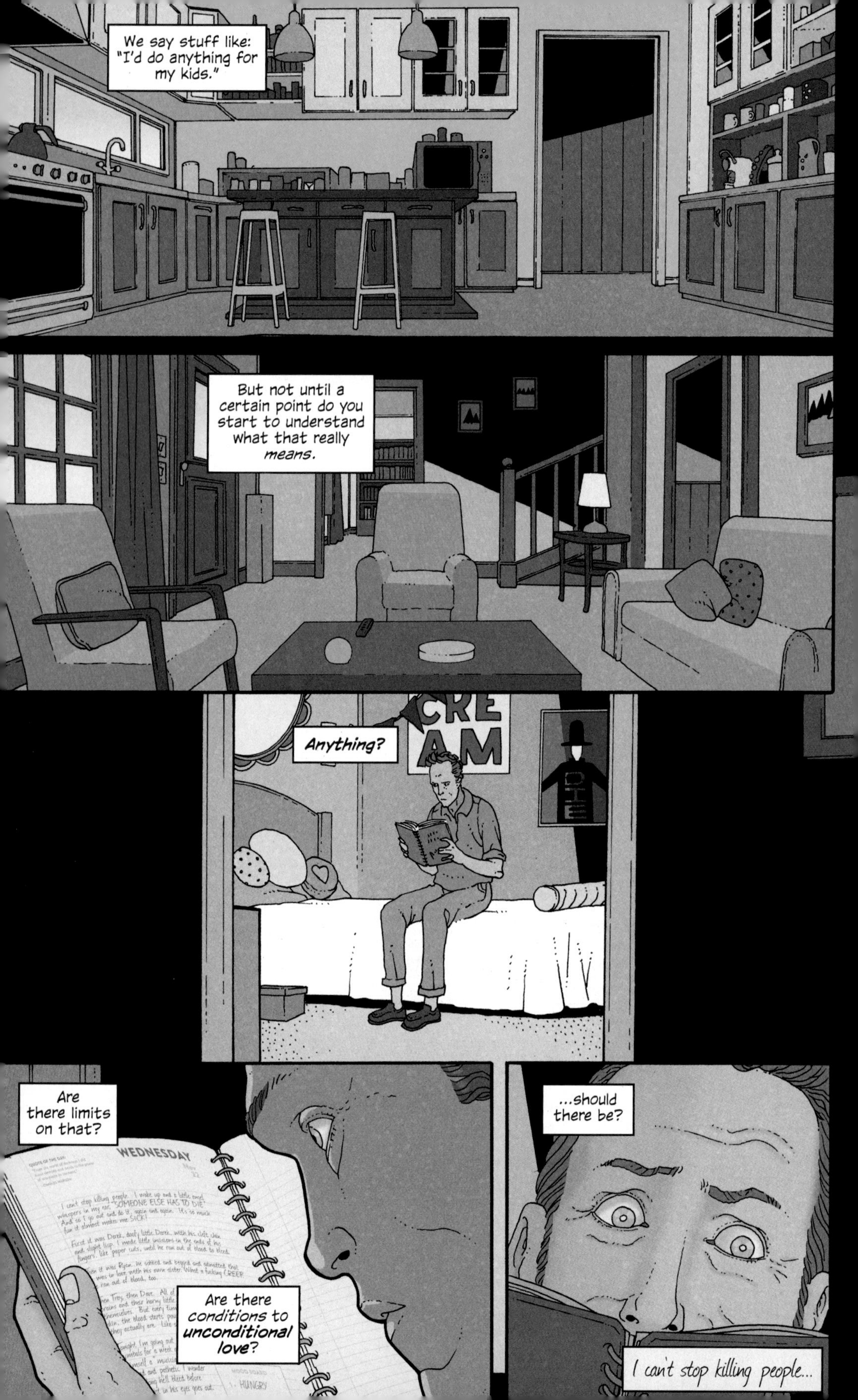
We say stuff like: "I'd do anything for my kids."
But not until a certain point do you start to understand what that really *means.*
Anything?
Are there limits on that?
WEDNESDAY
Are there *conditions* to ***unconditional*** *love?*
...should there be?
I can't stop killing people...

QUOTE OF THE DAY:
"From the world of darkness I did loose demons and devils in the power of scorpions to torment."
—CHARLES MANSON

WEDNESDAY
Nov
22

I can't stop killing people. I wake up and a little angel whispers in my ear, "SOMEONE ELSE HAS TO DIE." And so I go out and do it, again and again. It's so much fun it almost makes me SICK!

First it was Derek, doofy little Derek, with his cleft chin and slight lisp. I made little incisions in the ends of his fingers, like paper cuts, until he ran out of blood to bleed.

Then it was Ryan...he sobbed and begged and admitted he was in love with his own sister. What a fucking CREEP. He ran out of blood, too.

Then Troy, then Dave. All of these losers with their dumb brains and their horny little dicks. They're all so SURE of themselves. But every time the blade goes through their skin, the blood starts pouring out...and I can see how small they actually are. Like slimy little BUGS under my shoes.

Tonight I'm going out with Sean. Dude bangs on some cymbals for a week and considers himself a "musician." It's so sad and pathetic. I wonder how long he'll bleed before the light in his eyes goes out.

That's all for now.

I AM YOUNG AND THE WORLD IS BEAUTIFUL

MOOD BOARD
1. HUNGRY
2. FOR
3. BLOOD

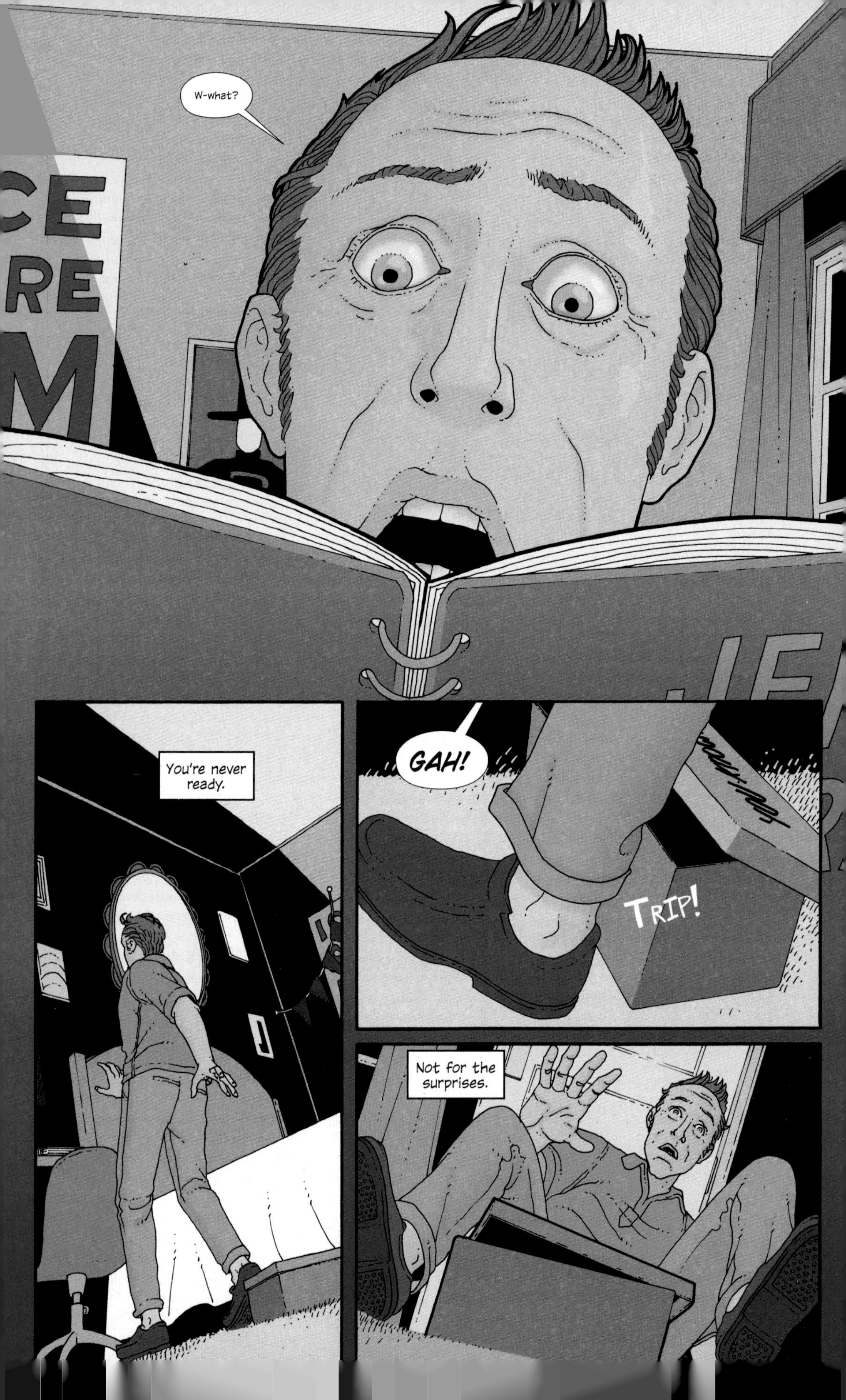
W-what?
You're never ready.
GAH!
TRIP!
Not for the surprises.

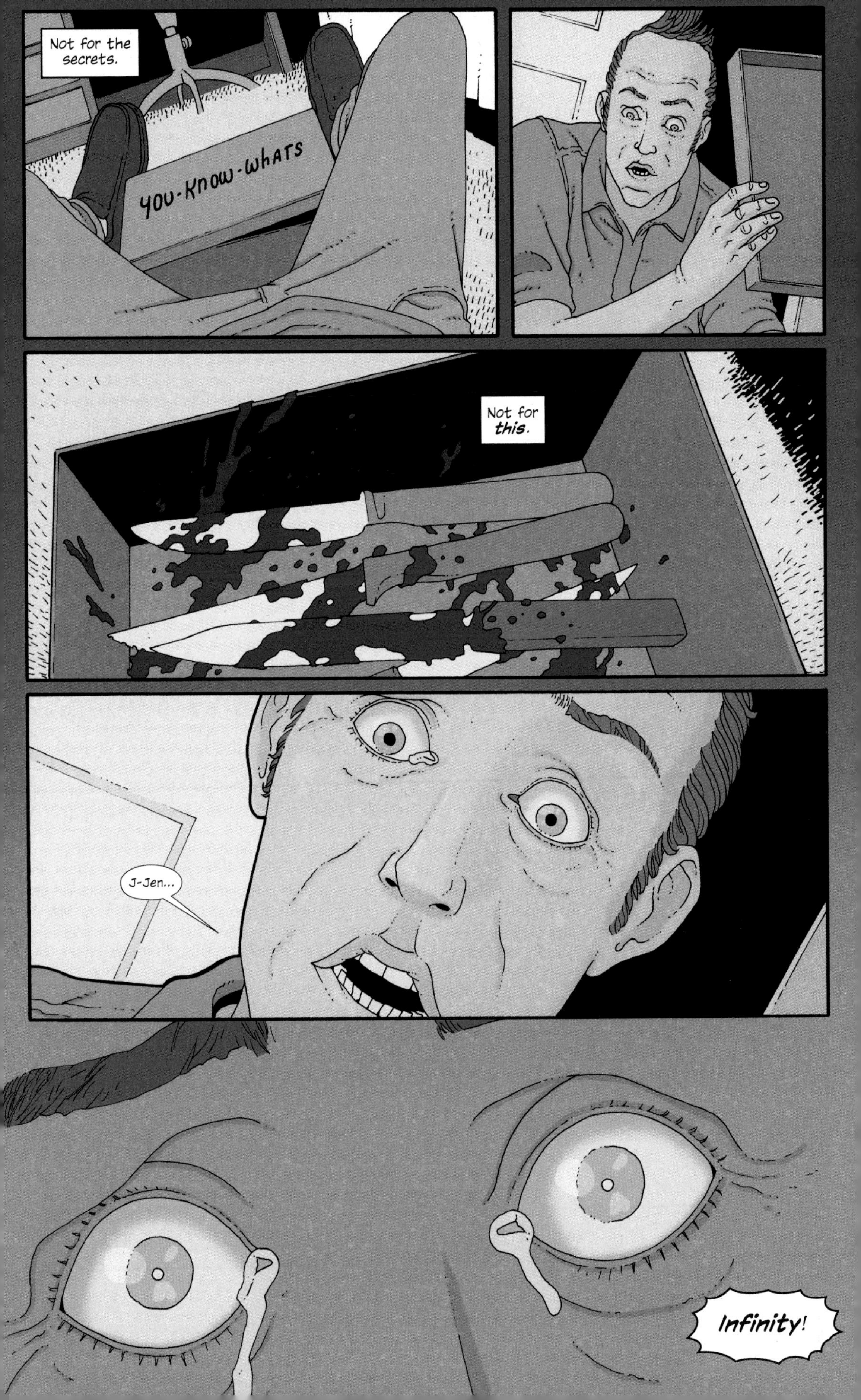
Not for the secrets.
YOU-KNOW-WHATS
Not for this.
J-Jen...
Infinity!

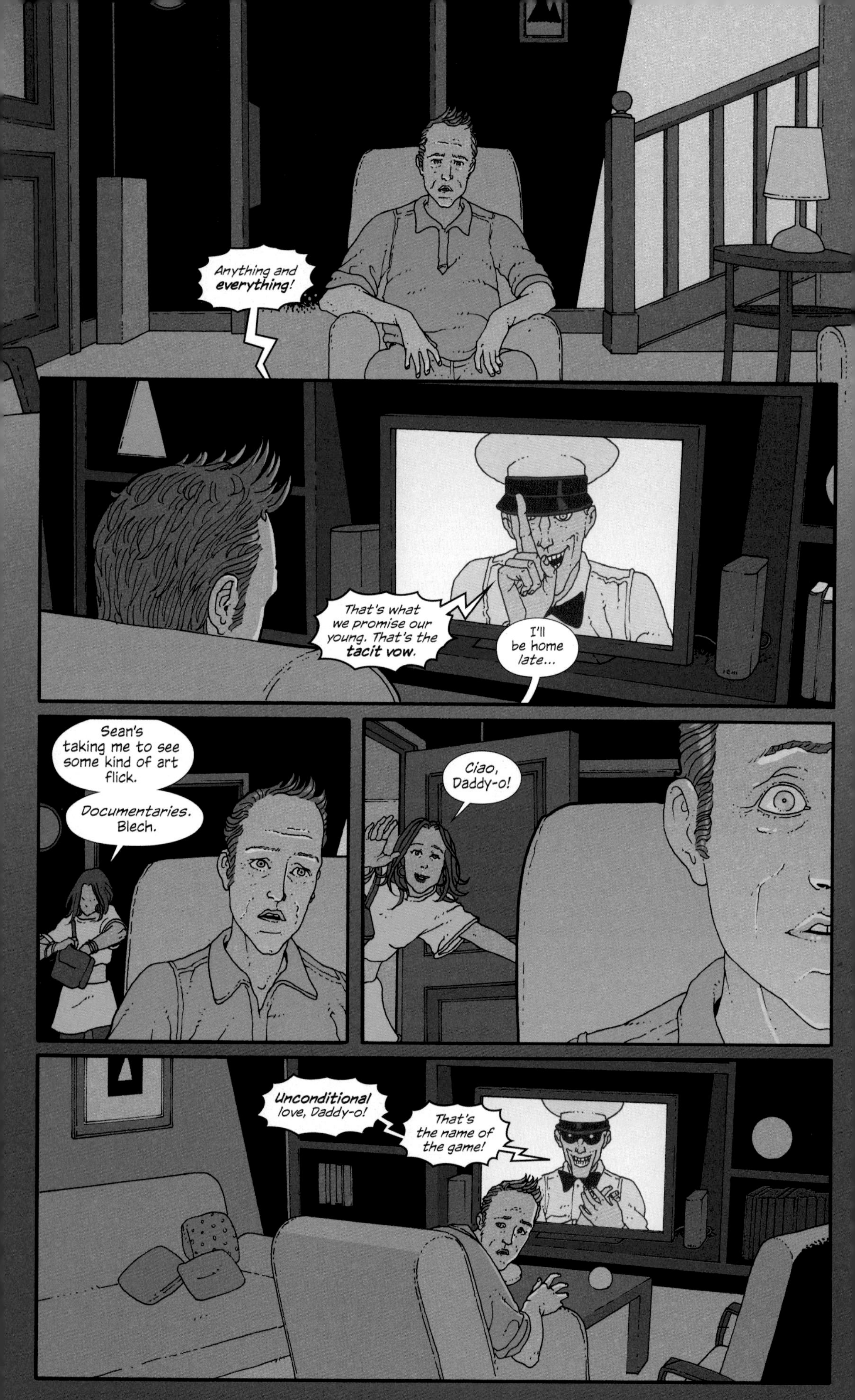
Anything and everything!
That's what we promise our young. That's the tacit vow.
I'll be home late...
Sean's taking me to see some kind of art flick.
Documentaries. Blech.
Ciao, Daddy-o!
Unconditional love, Daddy-o!
That's the name of the game!

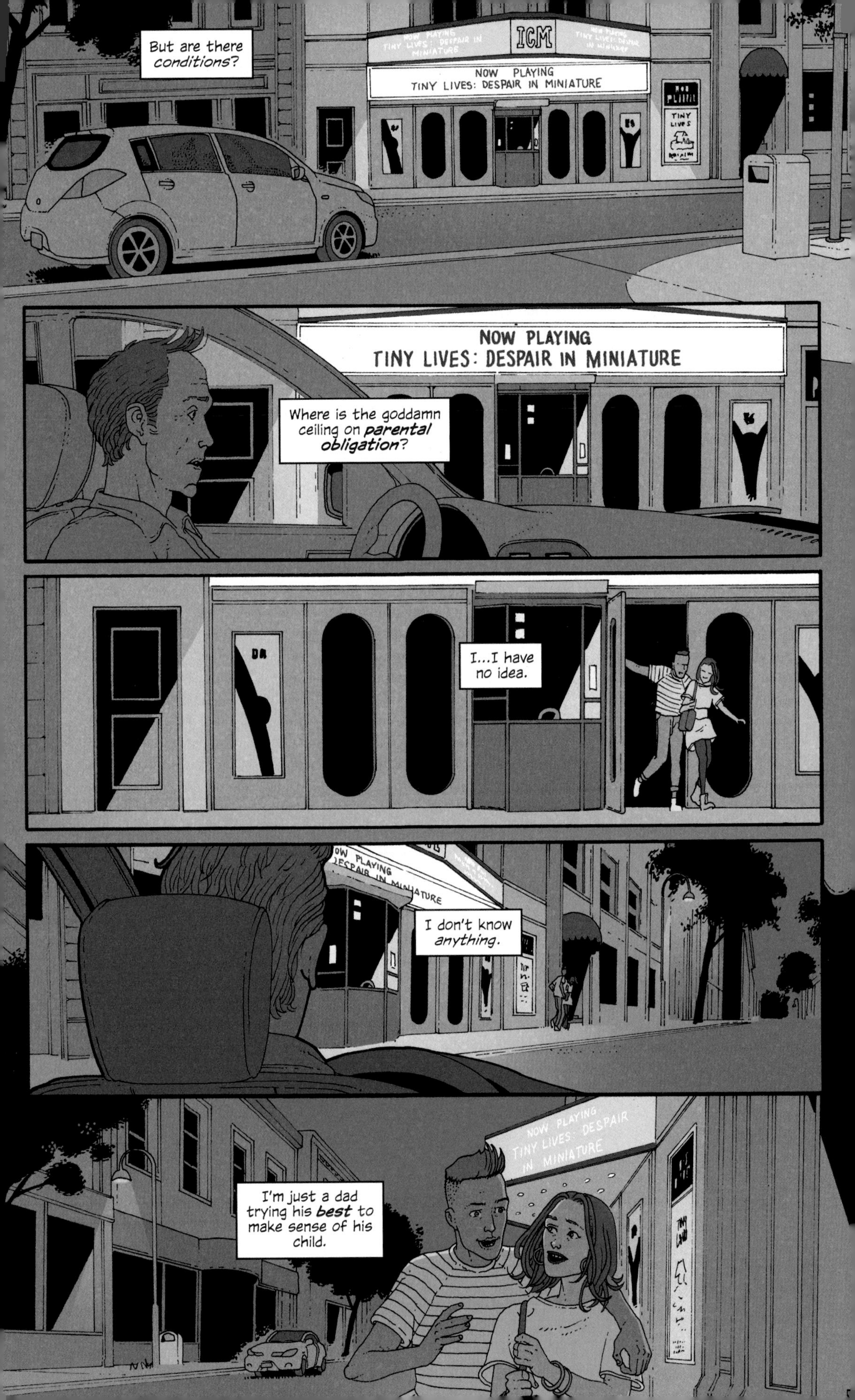

But are there *conditions*?
ICM
NOW PLAYING
TINY LIVES: DESPAIR IN MINIATURE
NOW PLAYING
TINY LIVES: DESPAIR IN MINIATURE
Where is the goddamn ceiling on ***parental obligation***?
I...I have no idea.
I don't know *anything*.
NOW PLAYING
TINY LIVES: DESPAIR IN MINIATURE
I'm just a dad trying his ***best*** to make sense of his child.

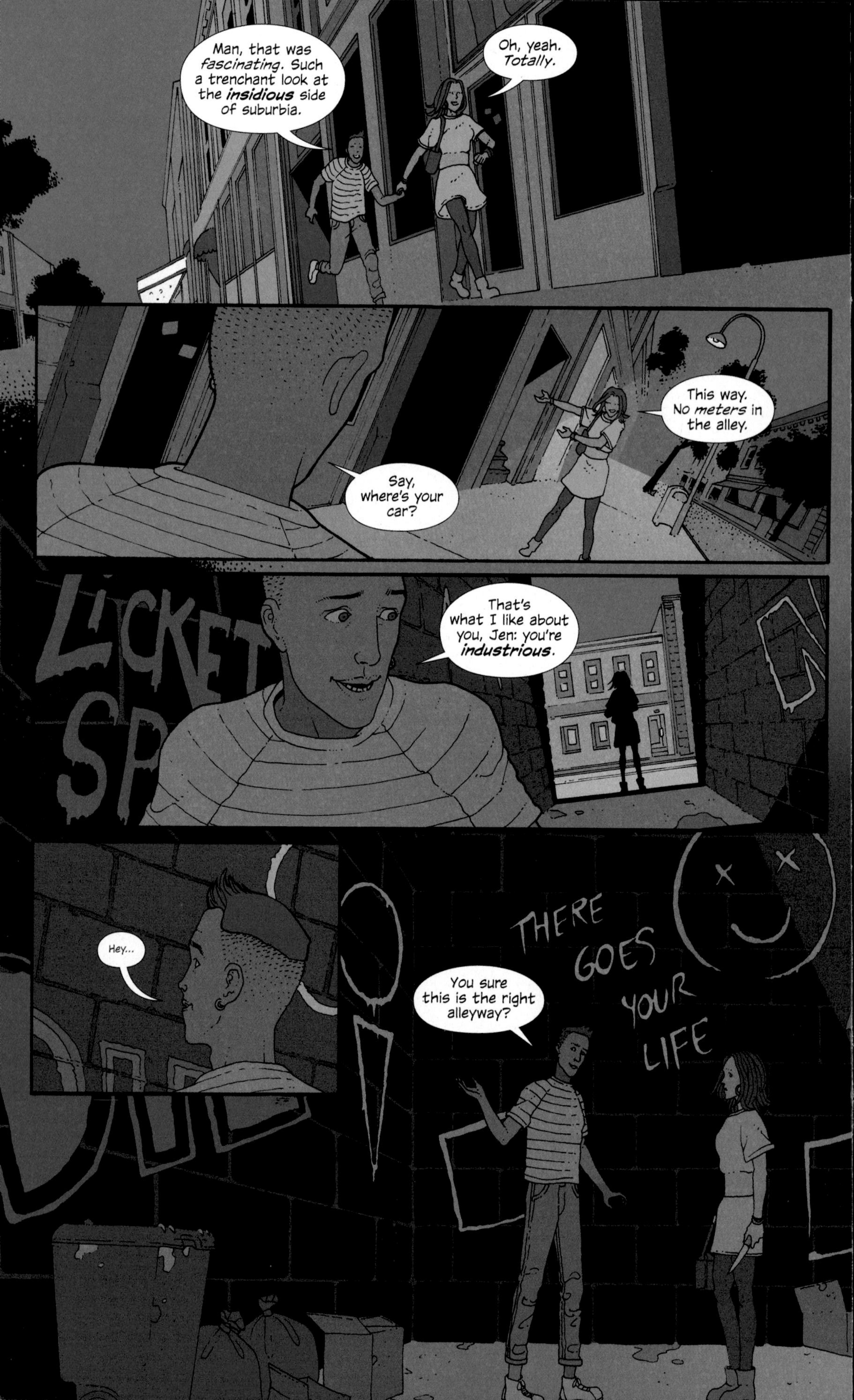
Man, that was *fascinating*. Such a trenchant look at the ***insidious*** side of suburbia.
Oh, yeah. *Totally.*
Say, where's your car?
This way. No *meters* in the alley.
That's what I like about you, Jen: you're ***industrious***.
Hey...
THERE GOES YOUR LIFE
You sure this is the right alleyway?

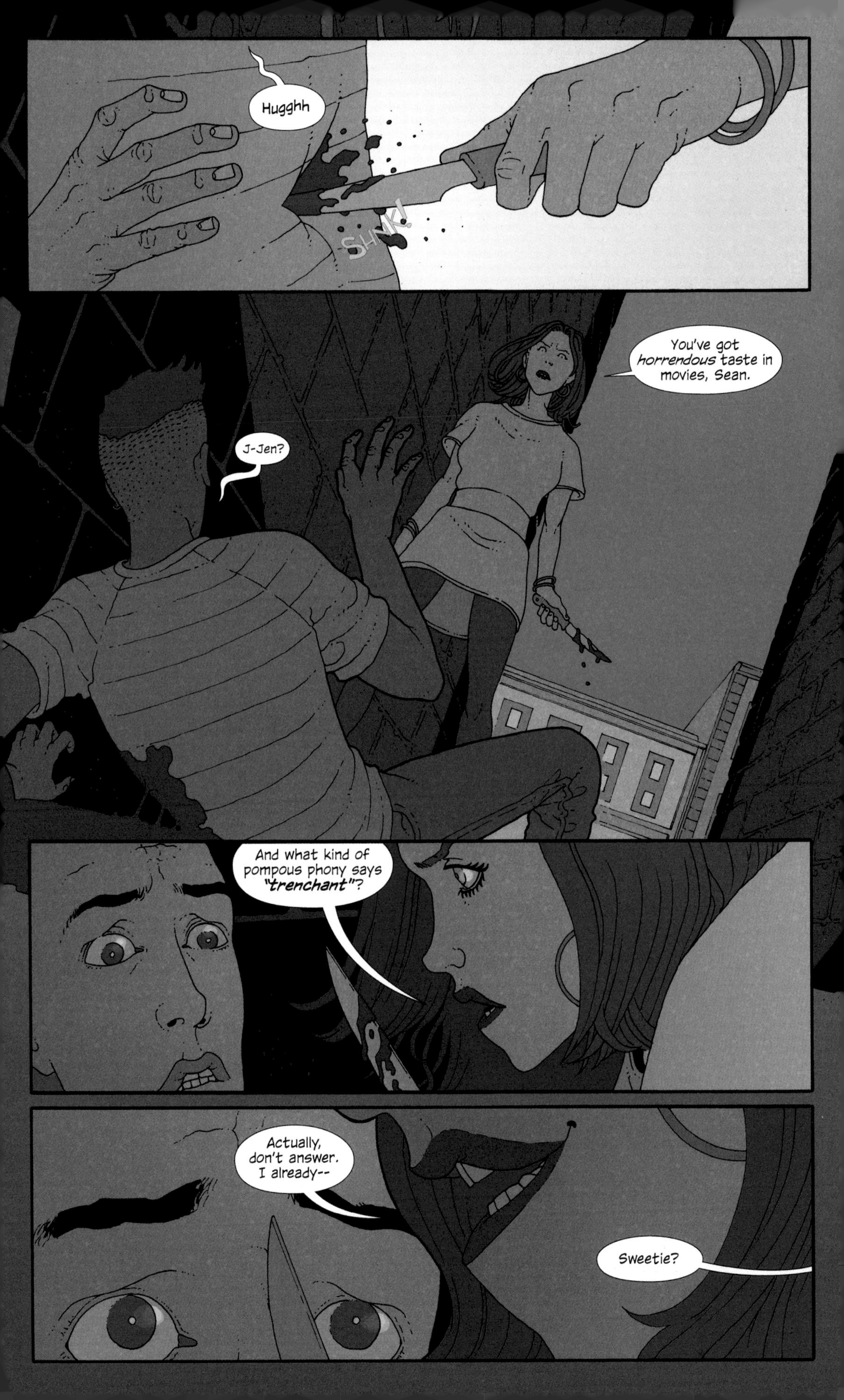
Hugghh
SHNK!
You've got *horrendous* taste in movies, Sean.
J-Jen?
And what kind of pompous phony says ***"trenchant"***?
Actually, don't answer. I already--
Sweetie?

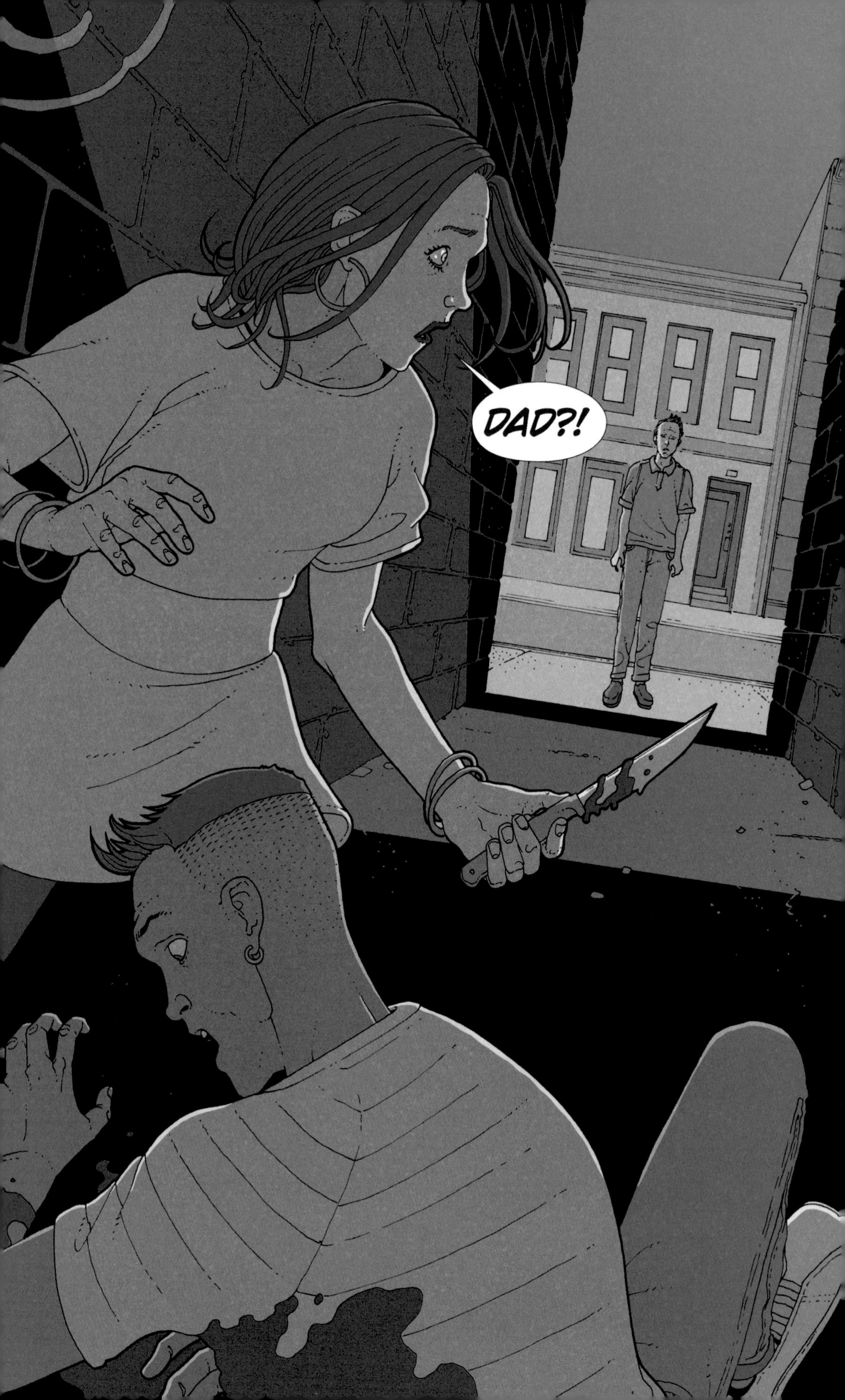
DAD?!

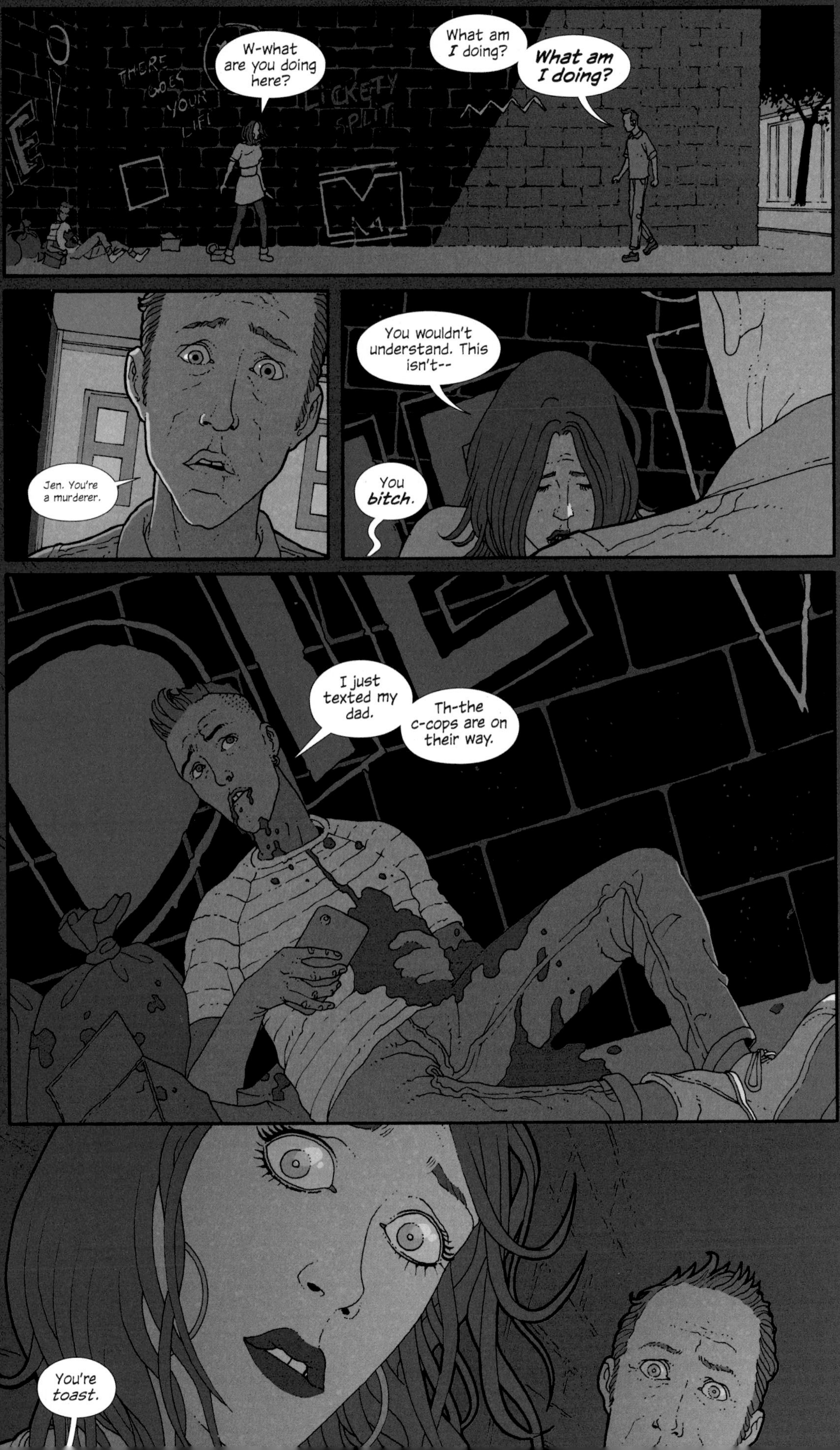
THERE GOES YOUR LIFE
LICKETY SPLIT
W-what are you doing here?
What am I doing?
What am I doing?
Jen. You're a murderer.
You wouldn't understand. This isn't--
You bitch.
I just texted my dad.
Th-the c-cops are on their way.
You're toast.

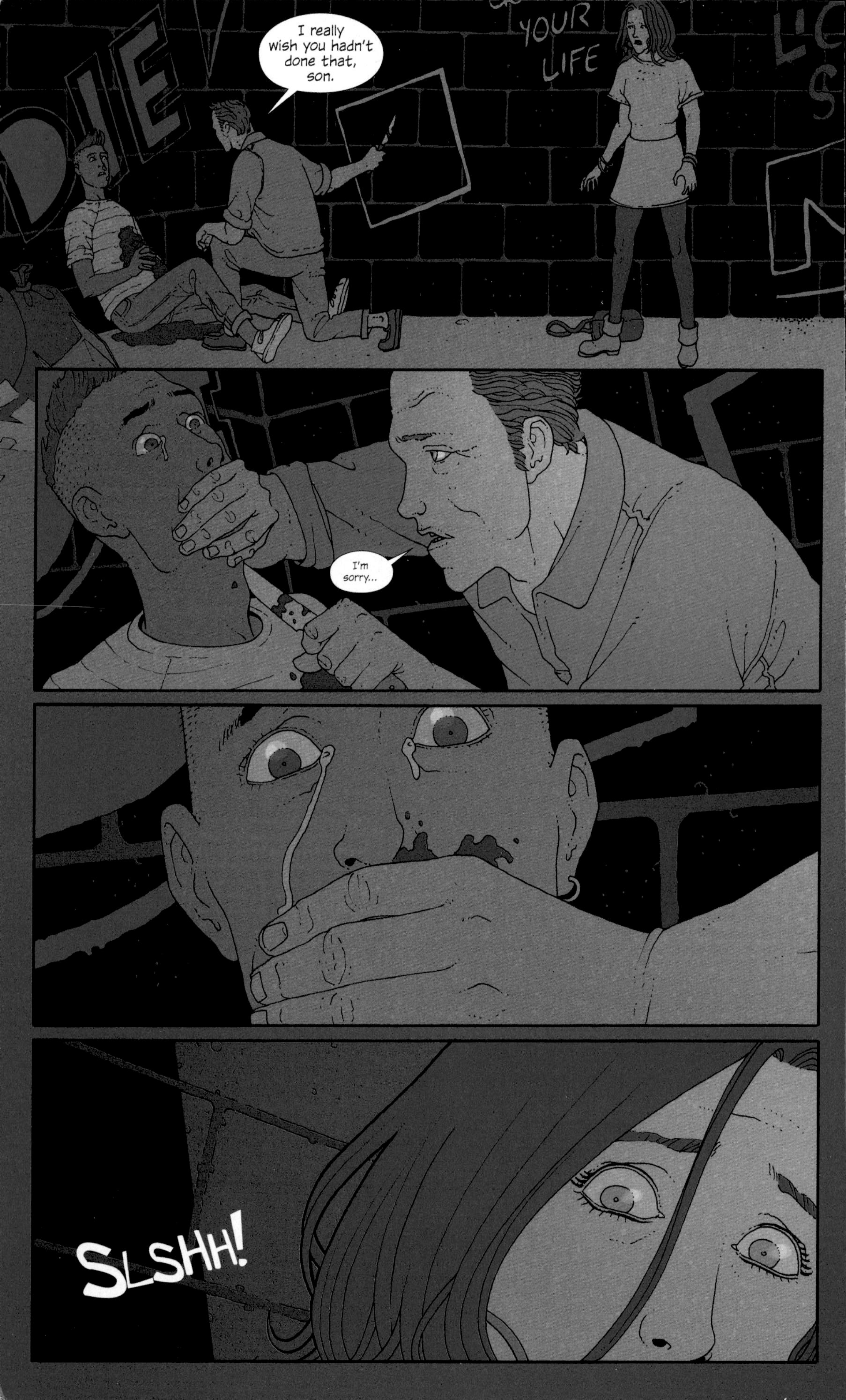
YOUR LIFE
I really wish you hadn't done that, son.
I'm sorry...
SLSHH!

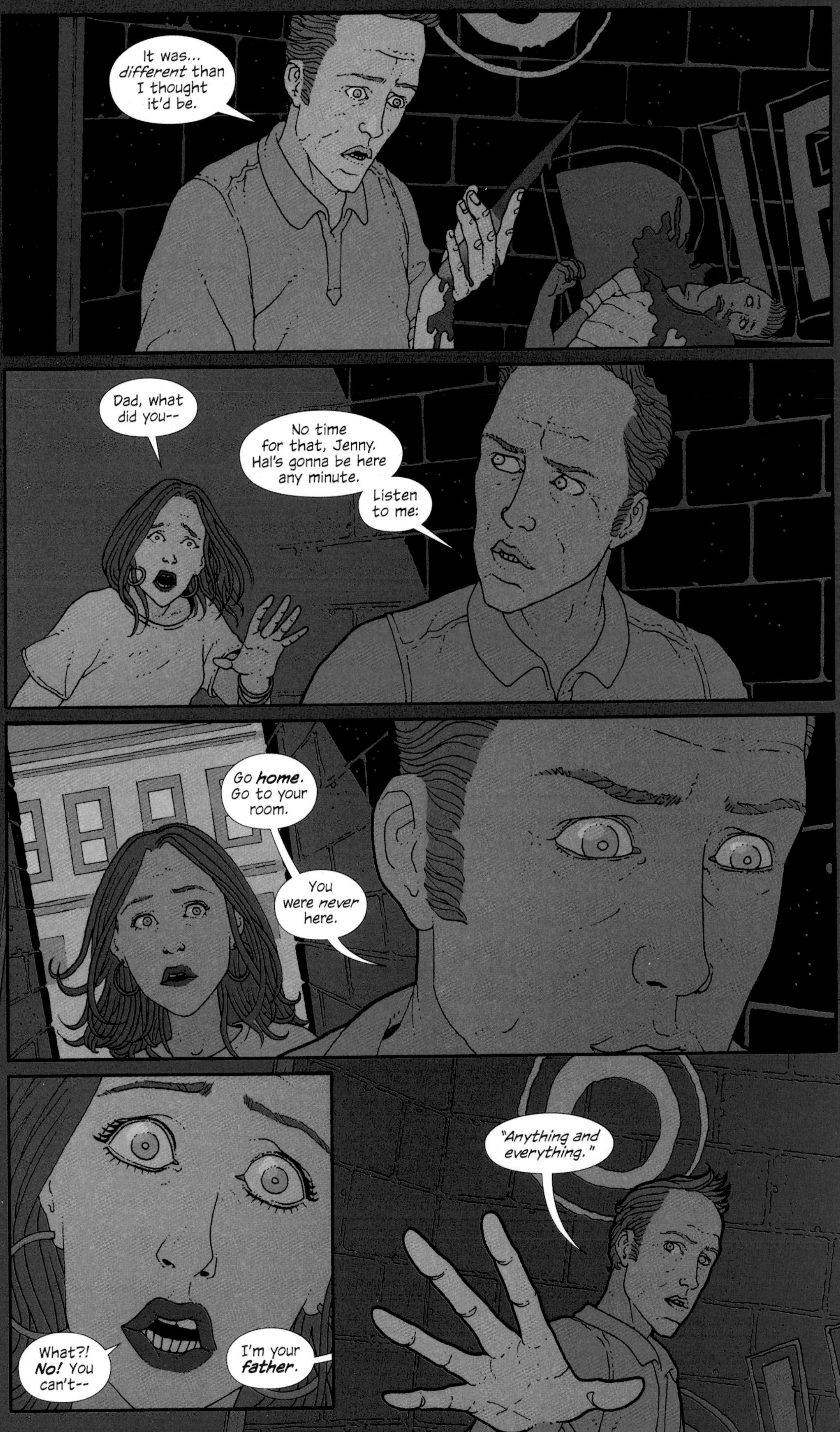
It was... *different* than I thought it'd be.
Dad, what did you--
No time for that, Jenny. Hal's gonna be here any minute.
Listen to me:
Go **home**. Go to your room.
You were *never* here.
What?! ***No!*** You can't--
I'm your ***father***.
"Anything and everything."

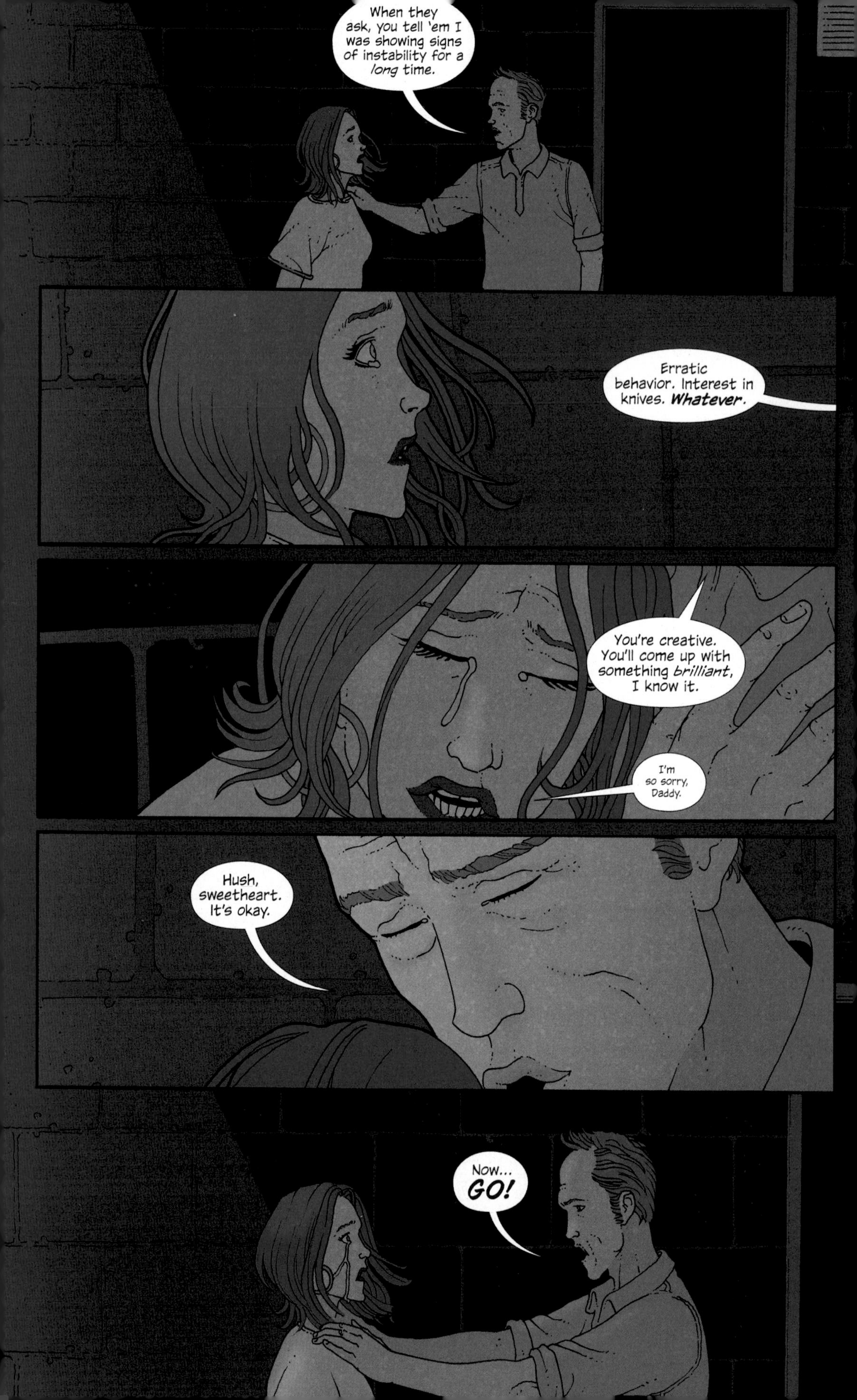
When they ask, you tell 'em I was showing signs of instability for a *long* time.
Erratic behavior. Interest in knives. ***Whatever.***
You're creative. You'll come up with something *brilliant*, I know it.
I'm so sorry, Daddy.
Hush, sweetheart. It's okay.
Now... **GO!**

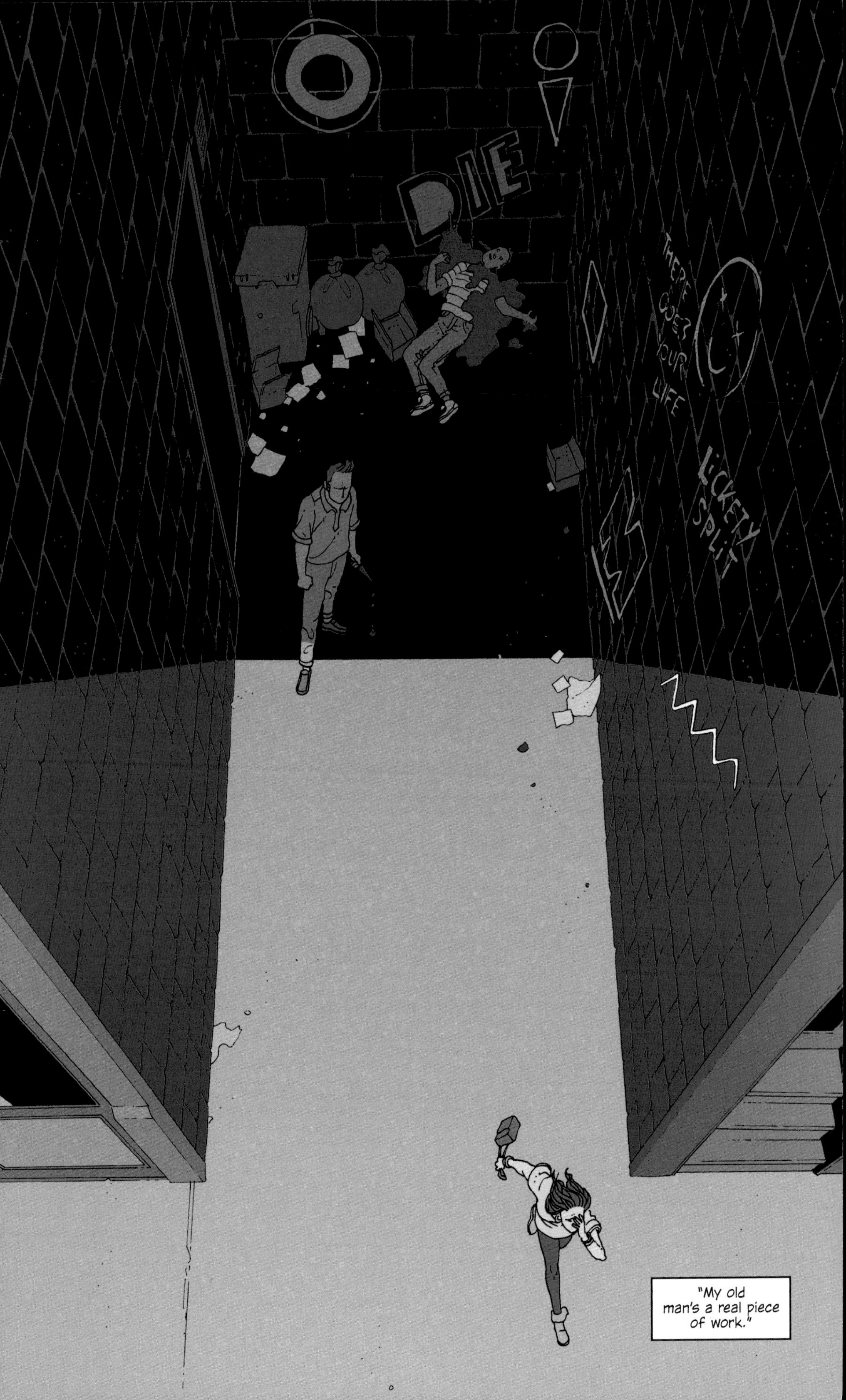
DIE
THERE GOES YOUR LIFE
LICKETY SPLIT
"My old man's a real piece of work."

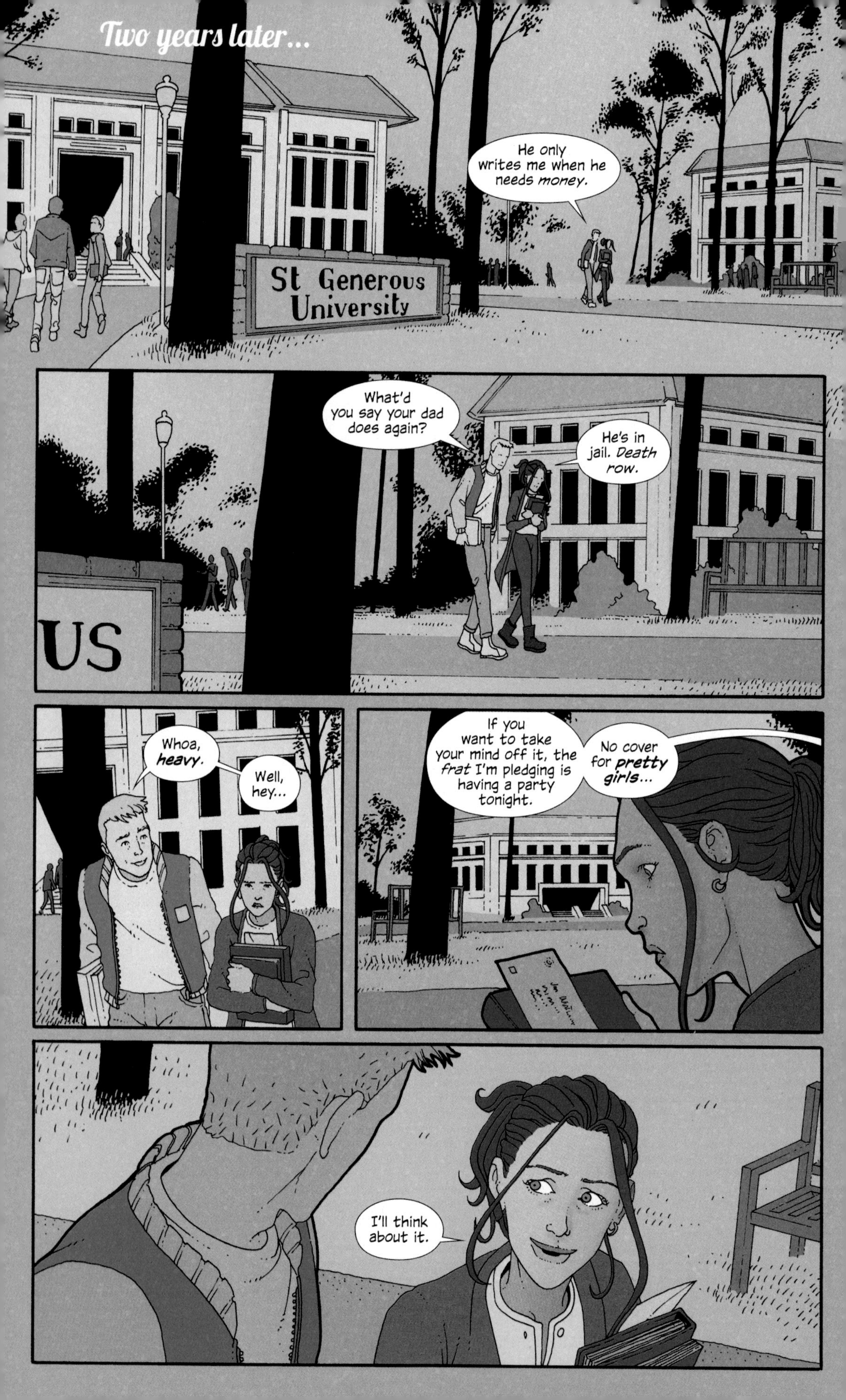
Two years later...
St Generous University
He only writes me when he needs *money*.
What'd you say your dad does again?
He's in jail. *Death* row.
US
Whoa, **heavy**.
Well, hey...
If you want to take your mind off it, the *frat* I'm pledging is having a party tonight.
No cover for ***pretty girls***...
I'll think about it.

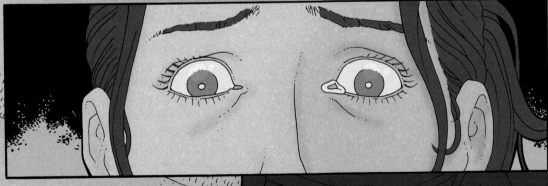

Only a few more days until they fry me alive.

MAILED FROM
A STATE
CORRECTIONAL
INSTITUTION

Only a few more days until they fry me alive. "Execution by electrocution." It's got a kind of funny poetry to it.

Jenny, I want to tell you something important before I walk down that corridor to get my brain zapped off for good.

I got life all wrong. I was so small, shrank things down to my size. I couldn't see how BIG it all is, how absolutely planetary: first you're a kid, then you somehow manage to RAISE a kid. Then your kid eclipses you. You lose yourself, but in the process you gain something better: INFINITY.

Anything and everything. It's a tacit vow, but it feels good to say aloud.

I know exactly what's gonna happen when they electrify me in that chair. I can see it clear as a movie in my mind's eye: my body sizzling, smoke rising off my skin. And then my SOUL will float out of my mouth and up through the ceiling, beyond this stone prison and into the open air, exceeding the atmosphere, out past the stars, rushing at light-speed into that final place where it's blacker than black, where all things good and evil meet at a single point and merge into one indistinguishable idea.

It might be the end of the road for me, but remember: you've got infinity. You can fold the world to your will like it's nothing but a glob of silly putty. Stretch it, knead it. It's endless. Make it the exact shape you want.

Whatever shape that is, it's already perfect. It's pre-approved. You are young, and life is beautiful.

I'm ready now.

Love, Dad

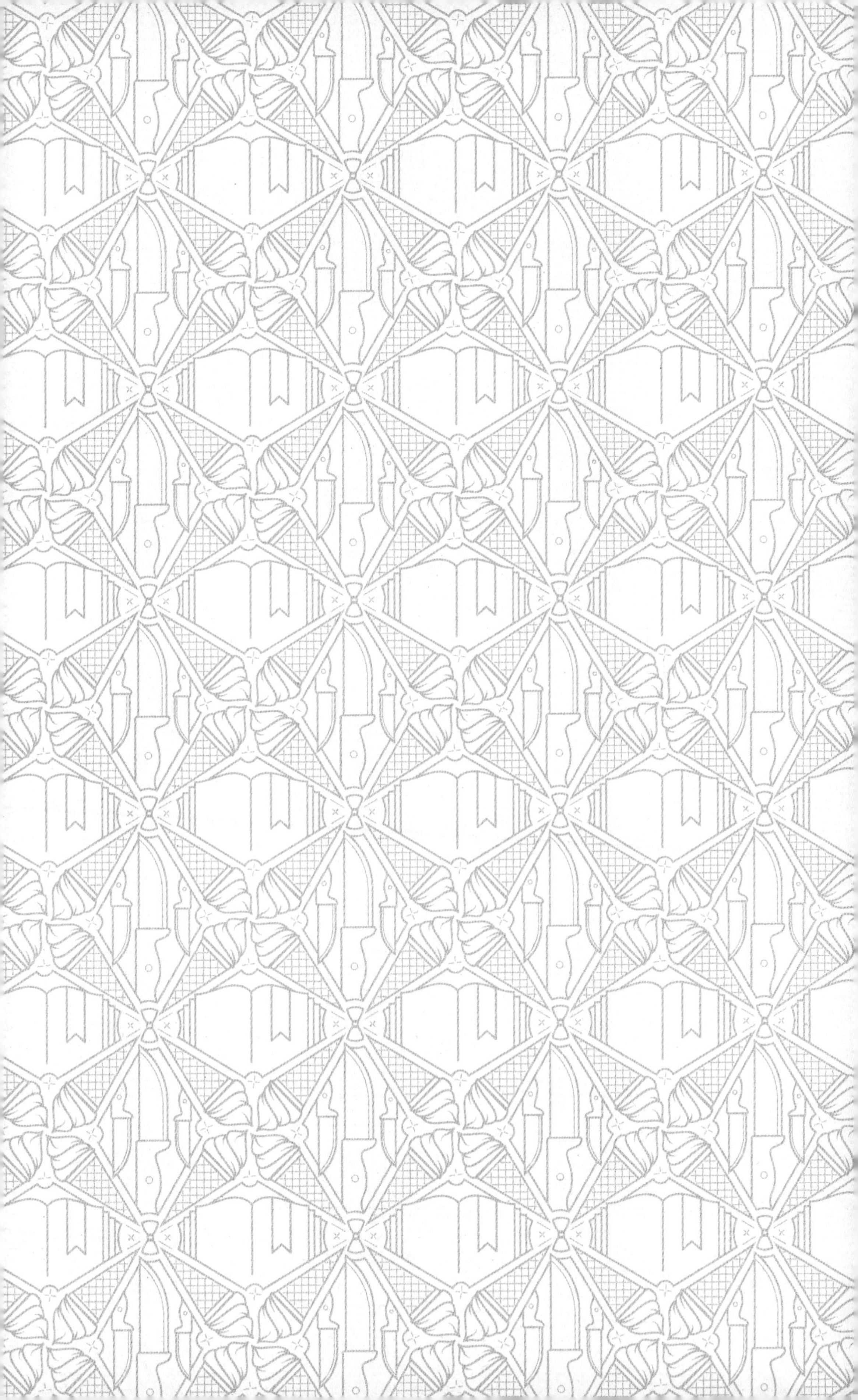

EXTRA SCOOPS

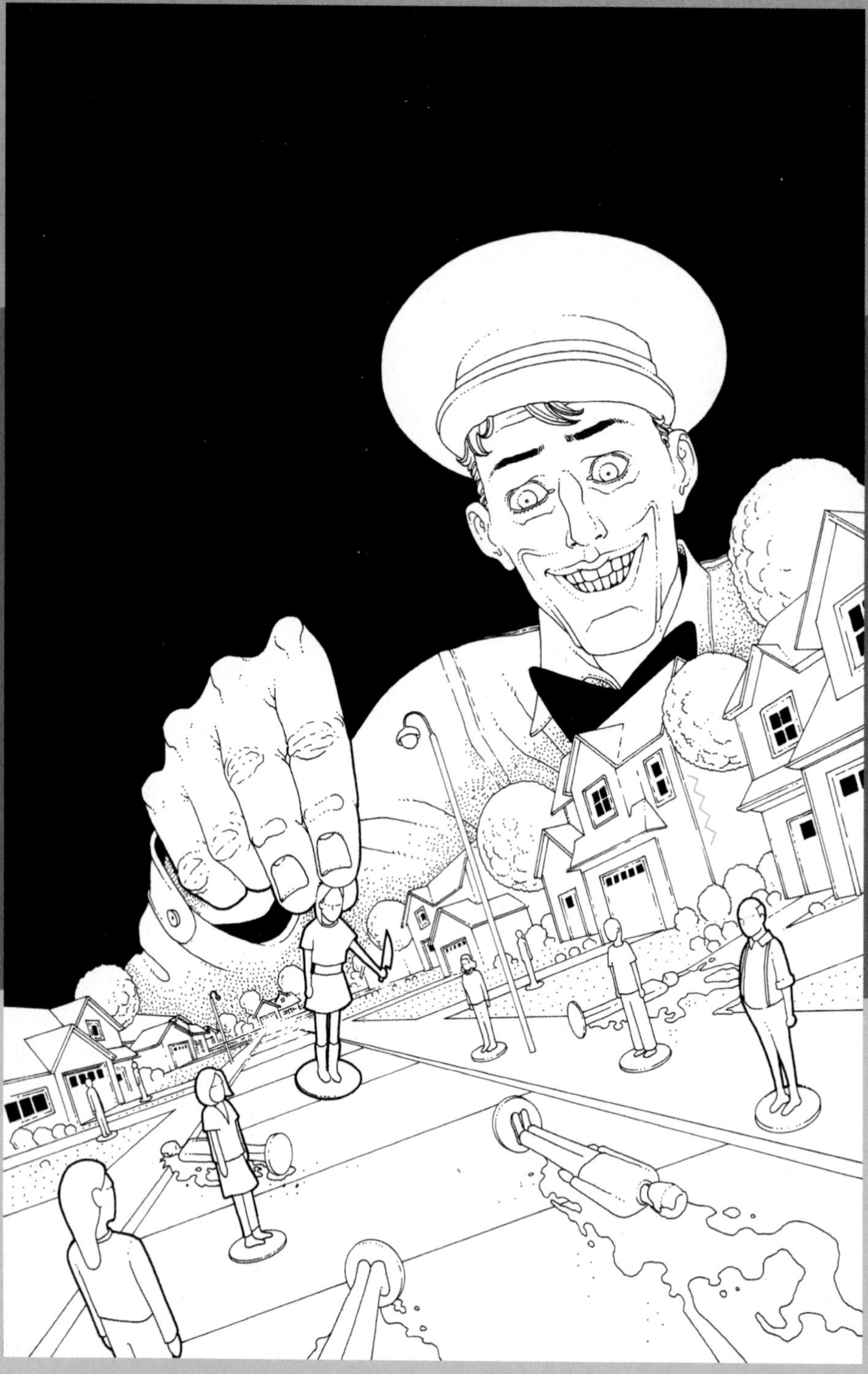

What follows are variant covers, sketches, and miscellany from the fourth volume of **ICE CREAM MAN**.

Thistles must be cut down before they flower...

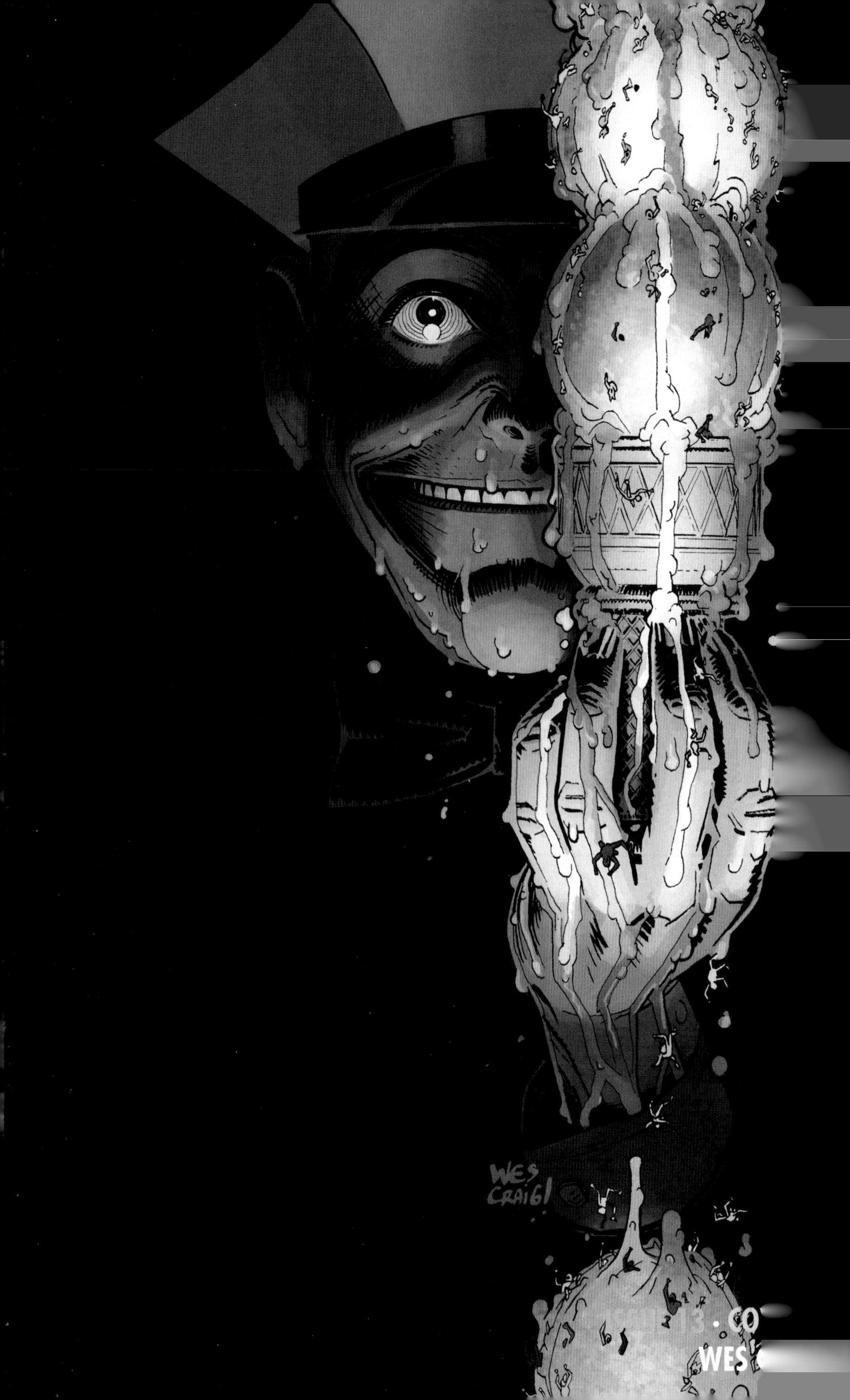
WES CRAIG
ISSUE 13 • CO
WES

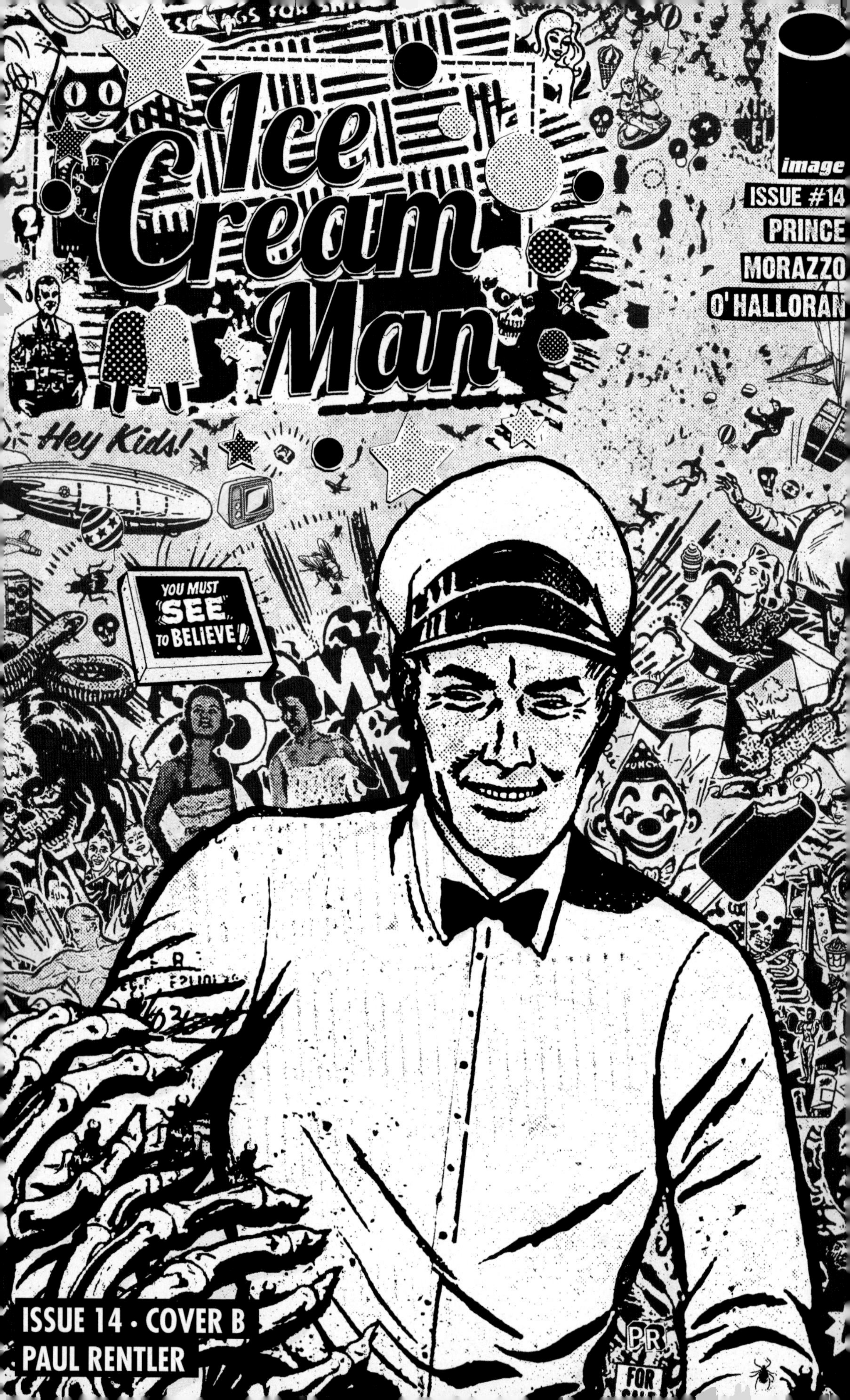
Ice Cream Man
image
ISSUE #14
PRINCE
MORAZZO
O'HALLORAN
Hey Kids!
YOU MUST SEE TO BELIEVE!
ISSUE 14 • COVER B
PAUL RENTLER

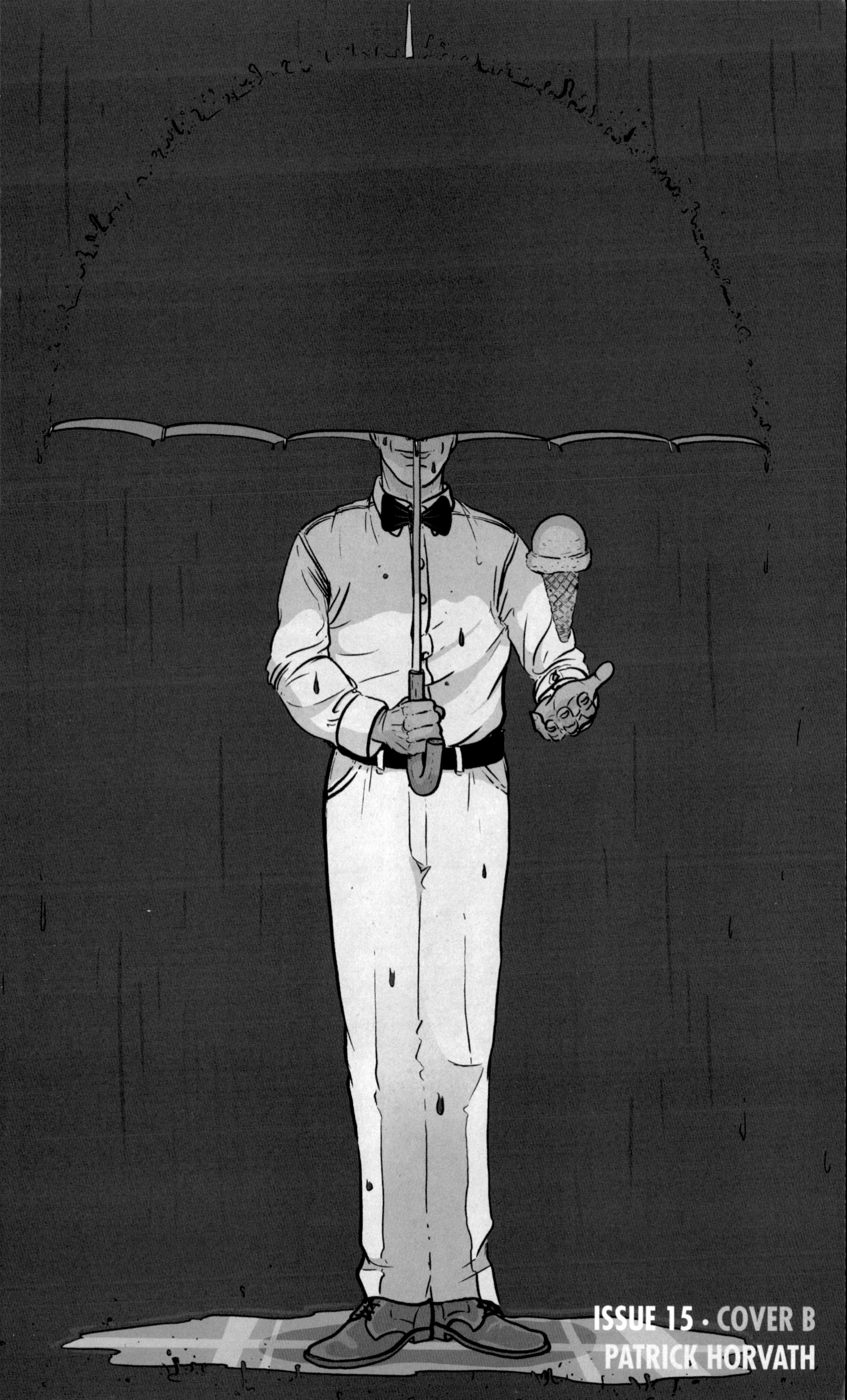

ISSUE 15 · COVER B
PATRICK HORVATH

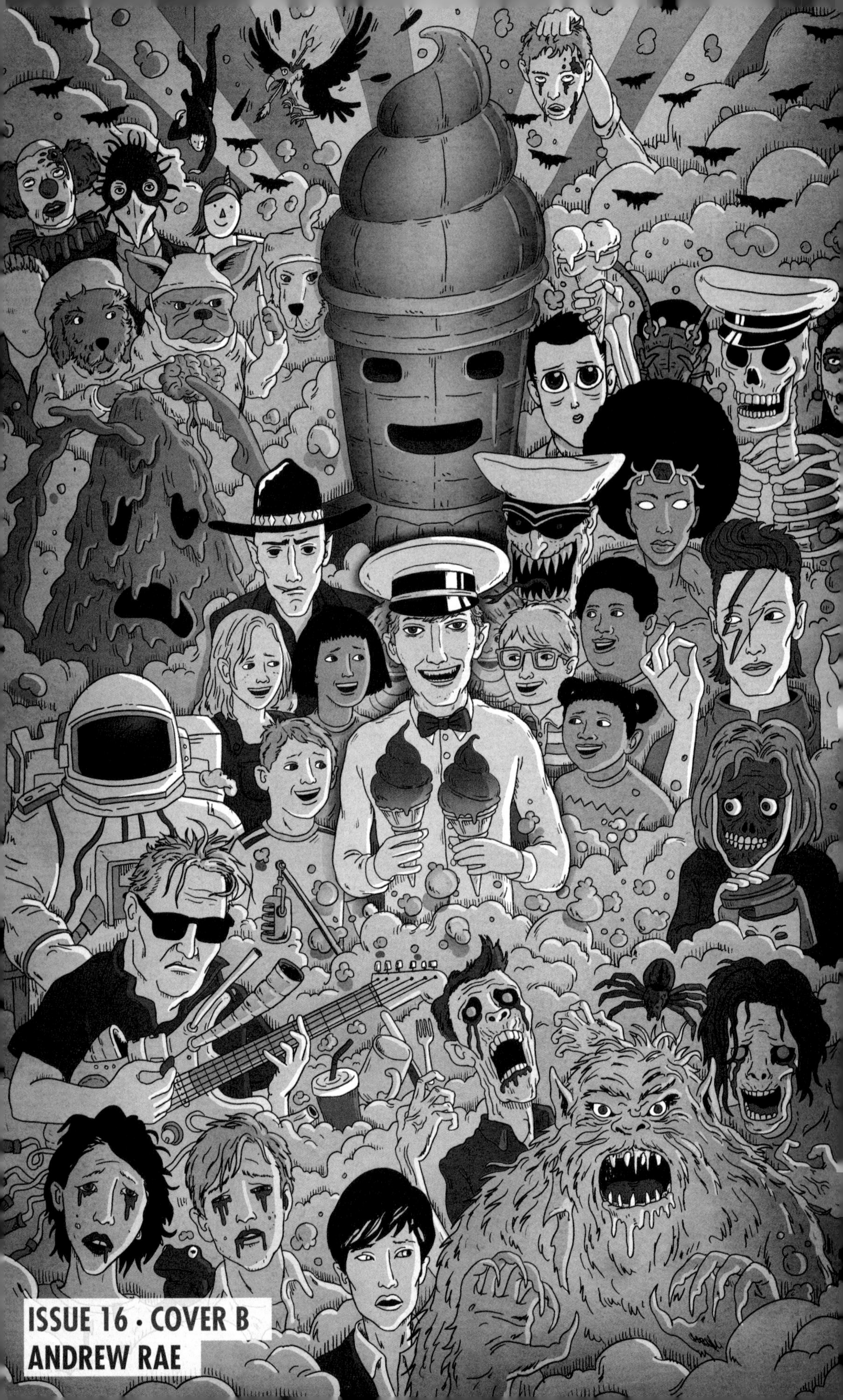

ISSUE 16 · COVER B
ANDREW RAE

FROZEN PHYSIOGNOMY

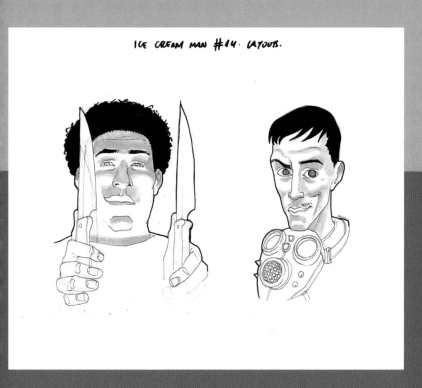

ICE CREAM MAN #14. LAYOUTS.

ICE CREAM MAN #14. LAYOUTS.

EARL.

RITA.

As ever, Martín's character sketches brim with stark life; they possess the power to spin any given chapter in an unplanned direction. Above, two menacing contractors and their suburban marks: puzzle-obsessed Earl and his lonely wife, Rita.

FULL MUGS

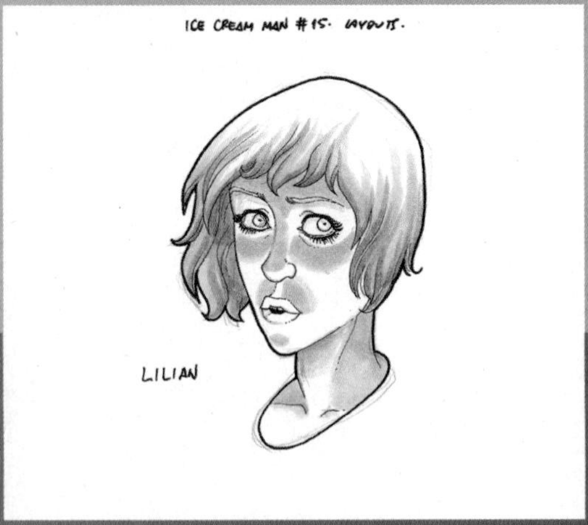
ICE CREAM MAN #15. LAYOUTS.
LILIAN

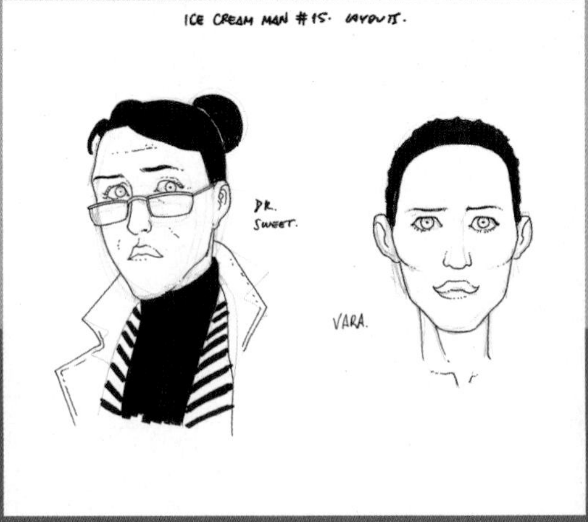
ICE CREAM MAN #15. LAYOUTS.
DR. SWEET.
VARA.

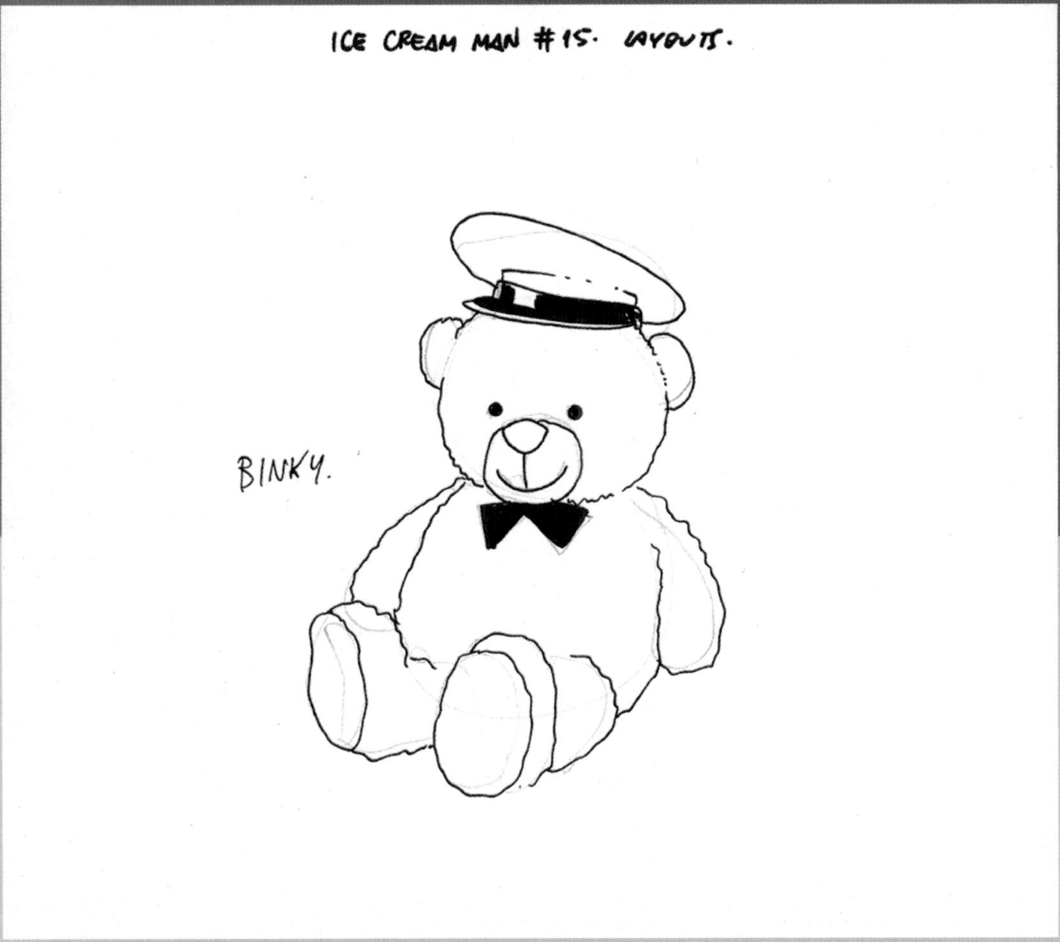
ICE CREAM MAN #15. LAYOUTS.
BINKY.

In the *Ice Cream Man* multiverse, **Binky** is the Plush Popsicle Purveyor of Earth 15, where he partakes in such acts of adorable menace as forcing Ruxpins, Paddingtons, and Poohs to reckon with their midlife ennui.

SOBER REFLECTIONS

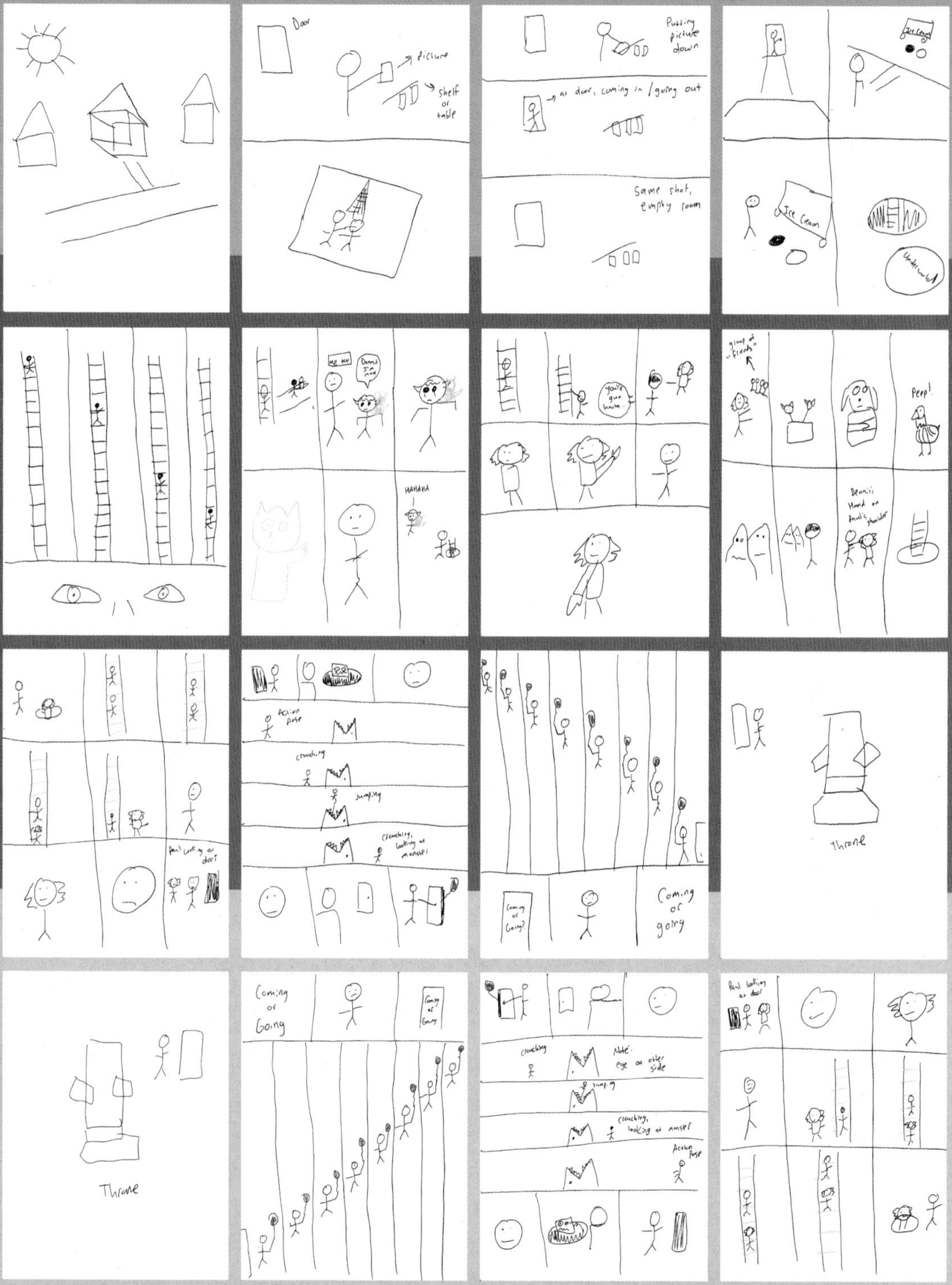
Door
picture
shelf or table
Putting picture down
at door, coming in / going out
Same shot, empty room
Ice Cream
Ice Cream
HAHAHA
group of "friends"
Peep!
Dennis's Hand on Paul's shoulder
Paul looking at door
Action pose
crouching
jumping
crouching, looking at monster
Coming or Going?
Coming or going
Throne
Throne
Coming or Going
Coming or Going
crouching
Note: eye on other side
jumping
crouching, looking at monster
Action pose
Paul looking at door

"Palindromes" unfortunately required the author to "draw" the entire issue alongside the standard script. Bless Martín and Chris for countenancing such a sorry display.

LIVE EVIL

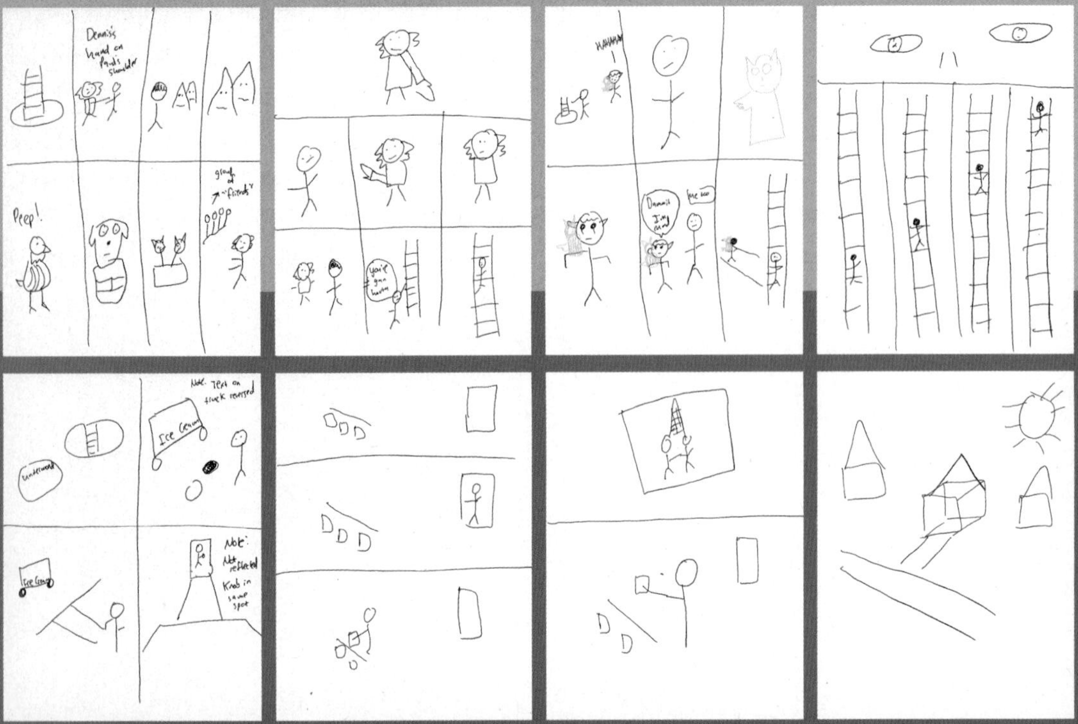
Peep!
Ice Cream

DAMMIT, I'M MAD
MR. OWL ATE MY METAL WORM
TOO HOT TO HOOT
HAHAHAH
DENNIS SINNED
GODDAM MAD DOG
SENILE FELINES
WAS IT A RAT I SAW?
WAS IT A BAT I SAW?
GODDAM MAD DOG
DOG, AS A DEVIL DEIFIED,
LIVED AS A GOD
BIRD RIB
PEEP
DUMB MUD
1234321
NEVER ODD OR EVEN

And here's a handy list of every linguistic palindrome featured in the chapter. Sadly, I couldn't find a way to include *Go hang a salami, I'm a lasagna hog!*

—WMP, October 2019